ANTHILL

ALSO BY EDWARD O. WILSON

The Theory of Island Biogeography, with Robert H. MacArthur (1967)

A Primer of Population Biology, with William H. Bossert (1971)

The Insect Societies (1971)

Sociobiology: The New Synthesis (1975)

On Human Nature (1978)

Caste and Ecology in the Social Insects, with George F. Oster (1978)

Genes, Mind, and Culture, with Charles J. Lumsden (1981)

Promethean Fire, with Charles J. Lumsden (1983)

Biophilia (1984)

The Ants, with Bert Hölldobler (1990)

Success and Dominance in Ecosystems: The Case of the Social Insects (1990)

The Diversity of Life (1992)

Journey to the Ants, with Bert Hölldobler (1994)

Naturalist (1994)

In Search of Nature (1996)

Consilience: The Unity of Knowledge (1998)

Biological Diversity: The Oldest Human Heritage (1999)

The Future of Life (2002)

Pheidole in the New World (2003)

From So Simple a Beginning: The Four Great Books of Charles Darwin (2005)

Nature Revealed: Selected Writings, 1949–2006 (2006)

The Creation: An Appeal to Save Life on Earth (2006)

The Superorganism: The Beauty, Elegance, and Strangeness of Insect Societies, with Bert Hölldobler (2009)

The Leafcutter Ants: Civilization by Instinct, with Bert Hölldobler (2010)

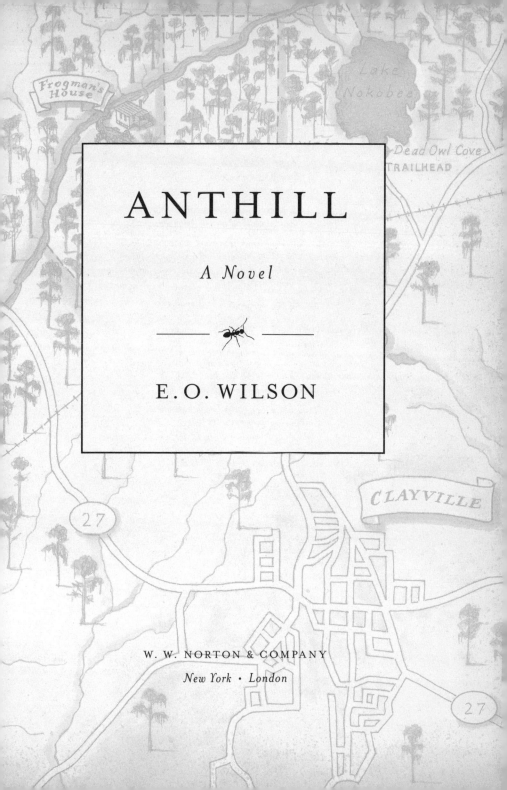

ANTHILL

A Novel

—— 🐜 ——

E. O. WILSON

W. W. NORTON & COMPANY

New York · London

"Nokobee County, Alabama" map by David Cain

For information about permission to reproduce
selections from this book,
write to Permissions, W. W. Norton & Company, Inc.,
500 Fifth Avenue, New York, NY 10110

For information about special discounts for bulk purchases,
please contact W. W. Norton Special Sales at
specialsales@wwnorton.com or 800-233-4830

Manufacturing by Courier Westford
Book design by Abbate Design
Production manager: Anna Oler

Library of Congress Cataloging-in-Publication Data

Wilson, Edward O.
Anthill : a novel / E.O. Wilson. — 1st ed.
p. cm.
ISBN 978-0-393-07119-1
1. Teenage boys—Fiction. 2. Naturalists—Fiction.
3. Nature conservation—Fiction. 4. Ants—Fiction.
5. Alabama—Fiction. I. Title.
PS3623.I5788A57 2010
813'.6—dc22

2009052140

W. W. Norton & Company, Inc.
500 Fifth Avenue, New York, N.Y. 10110
www.wwnorton.com

W. W. Norton & Company Ltd.
Castle House, 75/76 Wells Street, London W1T 3QT

2 3 4 5 6 7 8 9 0

For M. C. Davis and Sam Shine,

benefactors of America's natural heritage,

from tall tree to humble ant.

• • •

Anthill [ME *ante hil*, fr. *ante* + hil hill] **1**: a hill thrown up by ants or by termites in digging their nests **2**: a community congested with busy people unceasingly on the move <the human ~ — H. G. Wells>

— *Webster's Third New International Dictionary*

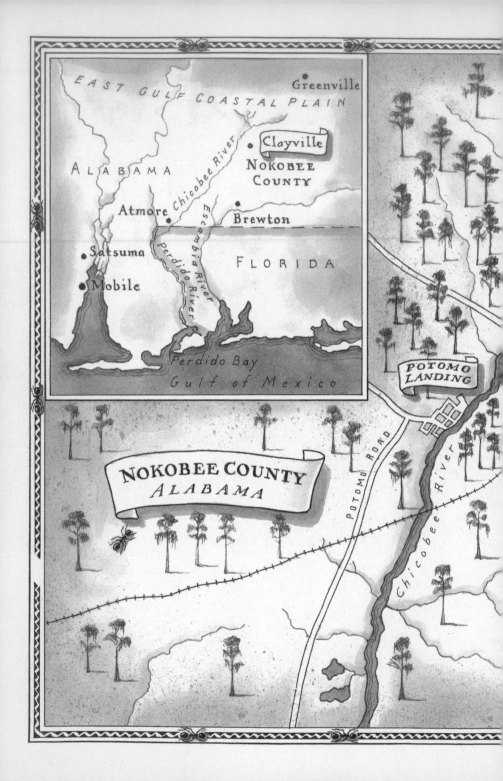

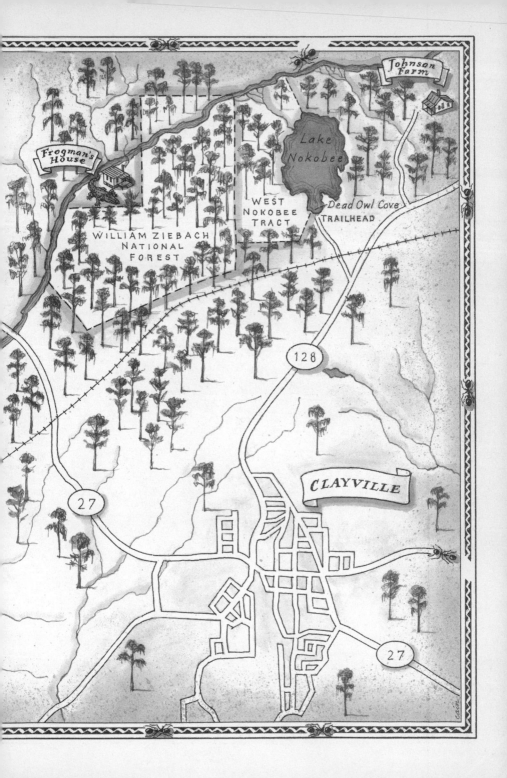

ANTHILL

· PROLOGUE ·

THIS IS A STORY about three parallel worlds, which nevertheless exist in the same space and time. They rise together, they fall, they rise again, but in cycles so different in magnitude that each is virtually invisible to the others.

The smallest are the ants, who build civilizations in the dirt. Their histories are epics that unfold on picnic grounds. Their colonies, like those of humans, are in perpetual conflict. War is a genetic imperative of most. The colonies grow and struggle and sometimes they triumph over their neighbors. Then they die, always.

Human societies are the second world. There are of course vast differences between ants and men. But in fundamental ways their cycles are similar. There is something genetic about this convergence. Because of it, ants are a metaphor for us, and we for them. Homer might have written equally of ants and men, *Zeus has given us the fate of winding down our lives in painful wars, from youth until we perish, each of us.*

Thousands of times greater in space and time is the third of our worlds, the biosphere, the totality of all life, plastered like a membrane over all of earth. The biosphere has its own epic cycles. Humanity, one of the countless species forming the biosphere, can perturb it, but we cannot leave it or destroy it without perishing ourselves. The cycles of the other species can be destroyed, and the biosphere corrupted. But for each careless step we take, our species will ultimately pay an unwelcome price—always.

I

———— 🐜 ————

FROGMAN

· 1 ·

TWO WEEKS BEFORE Labor Day, Raphael Semmes Cody sat with his cousin Junior in Roxie's Ice Cream Palace. Both were scooping out almond crunch ice cream covered with butterscotch syrup and sprinkled with chopped walnuts. Outside, heavy air grown humid from passage over the Gulf of Mexico and torrid from radiant heat off the Florida Panhandle had come to rest upon the little town of Clayville. The Alabama sky, mercilessly clear, offered no promise of an afternoon shower. Customers entering the Palace plucked at shirts and blouses stuck with sweat to their bodies.

"My Lord, it is *hot* out there," said a linen-clad businessman with a sigh as he pushed through the door.

A farmer sitting on a stool laughed. "Yeah, hotter'n a bucket of red ants."

Junior didn't care. He said to Raphael, "I got a great idea. Let's go see if we can find the Chicobee Serpent." He meant Alabama's equivalent of the Loch Ness Monster. Over the past century, hundreds of local people claimed to have seen something very big, snakelike, and definitely mysterious lurking in the deeper water of the nearby Chicobee River.

"Naw, that's crazy," Raff—as he was usually called—replied. "That's just a story people made up. There isn't any such thing as a Chicobee Serpent."

Junior had anticipated that response. "Yeah, there is. Lots of people have seen it. You just gotta drift down the river real quiet-like, don't use no outboard motor or anythin'. Make your boat look like a floatin' log, or somethin' like that, you know."

"Oh, yeah, if a lot of people have seen it," Raff said, "why haven't they taken any pictures?"

"Maybe they didn't have any cameras with them. They were just out fishin'. I tell you what, we'll take a camera. I got one. If we take a picture, you bet we'll be famous."

"What's it supposed to look like?" Raff asked.

"It's a lot like a real big snake. It curls around a lot. Nobody's seen the head, just parts of the body."

Raff shook his head. "I don't think so. My parents—"

"Oh, come on, don't be chicken." Junior flapped his arms and made clucking noises. "What we got to lose? It'd be a lot of fun. We'll stop along the way and visit Frogman. Maybe he'll show us Old Ben. Wouldn't you like to see the biggest alligator in the world?"

Raff shook his head again, this time harder. "Now I *know* you're crazy. Frogman'll kill us if we go on his property. They say he murdered some people up in Lownes County and got away with it. I hear if you get too close to his landing, even when you're just fishing around there, he'll come out and yell and tell you he's going to kill you."

"Aw, come on," Junior replied. "Old Frogman makes a lot of noise, but he wouldn't hurt a fly. It'd be real interestin' if we could visit him. Somethin' to tell people about. Maybe he'll let us take a picture of Old Ben. It would really be somethin' to show *that* around."

"Oh, yeah? I hear people disappear on the Chicobee and their bodies are never found."

"You think Frogman did that? No way. If they suspected him even just a smidgen, he'd be down at the Clayville Police Station and they'd be diggin' up his property to look for dead bodies."

"All right, then who *did* do it?"

"How should I know? Maybe the Chicobee Serpent. Maybe they just fell overboard and drowned. Their bodies got carried on down to the Gulf. Or maybe they wasn't really any people at all they couldn't account for. Maybe all that's just a story."

"I heard Frogman's a pervert," Raff came back. "He does things to little boys, you know."

"Like doing what?"

"You know, does weird things to them."

"Jesus, Raff, you really stink." Sixteen-year-old Junior, Raff's senior by a full year, decided to take a more mature approach to his cousin. He put on an indignant expression and shook his head slowly, as though surprised at such ignorance. "Maybe you heard somethin' like that somewhere, but if that was true, don't you think he'd be sittin' up there in Monroeville Prison right now?"

Raff kept silent, and Junior went on. "Don't be a yellow-belly. We'll take off first thing in the morning, get to the river through the Johnson Farm. I know where we can borrow a boat on the floodbank down there. Then we'll float on downstream a few miles, and pull over at the Potomo Landing. Be home by supper, no sweat."

"My parents would kill me if they found out. They already think you're going to get me into trouble. They don't like me to go out with you anywhere."

"Tell 'em that you and I goin' to spend a day at Lake Nokobee. Say we're goin' to go fish for bream. They won't give it a second thought."

TWO DAYS LATER Junior picked Raff up at eight in the morning. The two boys, after giving earnest assurances and promises to Raff's mother, rode their bikes northeast out of Clayville on Alabama 128 and onto a small county spur. There was almost no traffic; only two vehicles passed them going the other way, both loaded with croaker sacks of green tomatoes. The boys arrived at a forest-lined stream on the edge of the Johnson Farm, then hid their bicycles behind a dense clump of shrubs and weeds just off the road overpass. They climbed down to the edge of the stream, took off their shoes, rolled their pants up to their knees, and waded into the clear, smooth-running water. They enjoyed the feel of the sand between their toes and the scattered smooth pebbles of the bottom against the soles of their feet.

As they headed downstream, in the direction of the Chicobee, they saw small fish dart for protection into clumps of eelgrass and the hollows of the overhanging bank. A mud turtle, green-streaked with algae, remained still on the bottom as they walked past. A ribbon snake dropped into the water from an overhanging branch and swam swiftly out of sight. A red-shouldered hawk took off from overhead, screeching loudly. They looked up and spotted its nest, almost hidden from sight in the canopy.

"It's past the nesting season," Raff said.

Farther down, the water quieted and deepened into a pool to above their knees. The boys climbed up onto the bank, put their shoes back on, and walked along the overgrown trace of a trail. Whenever the trail petered out, they pushed their way through the thick understory along the watercourse as best they could.

After a mile or so the stream broadened and grew shallow again. It was partly diverted to one side by a thicket of cattails surrounding a small pond. The woods changed into widely spaced water oak, cypress, and trees of other kinds that dominate the coastal floodplain forest. The boys walked on carefully, heading diagonally away from the increasingly muddy bottom of the stream.

"Watch out for quicksand," Junior warned.

Raff fell in behind him, thinking that if they stumbled into something of the sort, Junior would be the first to sink. They proceeded in tandem like that, pressing on toward the river, hopping over little pools and easing their way around slick muckbeds.

Finally the Chicobee itself came into sight. The river's surface shimmered a silvery blue-green in the midmorning sunlight. As far as they could see up and down, it was walled in by the tops of floodplain tree canopies that rolled down like green waves to touch its surface.

Its current was smooth and slow. Its speed, which could be judged by the downstream travel of fragments of dead tree limbs, was like that of someone walking at a leisurely pace.

At this point the riverbank rose slightly to one side of the creek outflow. They could see from the thicker and different woods that the bluff was just high enough to escape all but the most intense floodwaters following heavy rain upstream. On the side facing the riverfront it dropped steeply, its face free of foliage and colored pale yellow by its sandy clay. On each side the bluff sloped more gradually, giving way to a mud bank that gently led to the water's edge.

A half dozen rowboats, unpainted and about ten feet in length, rested on the bank. Lashed to small sweet-bay trunks growing higher on the rise, their arrangement was clear: when the river flooded, which was often on coastal rivers like the Chicobee, the little boats would float up and move about, but were unlikely to break free and be carried downstream by any but the most powerful floodwaters.

Junior strode to one of the boats and began to untie the rope holding it. Raff followed closely. Looking inside the boat, he saw a cross-plank seat and, leaning against it, two oars.

"Who does this belong to?" Raff asked.

"I got no idea." Junior was beginning to work loose the knot on the mooring rope.

Raff laid a hand on Junior's arm. "Hey, wait a minute! We're not just going to steal a boat. We could get into big trouble."

"Relax, will ya?" Junior replied. "Who said we're stealin' it? We're just goin' to borrow it. We'll take it all the way down to the Potomo Landing and leave it there. Who owns it'll just pick it up there. Ever'body knows if you borrow a boat from here you leave it at the Potomo Landing."

Raff didn't believe Junior for one second. He knew his cousin well enough to figure Junior was just plain stealing. He also wondered how anybody could row upstream in a river as strong as the Chicobee, but then he saw that in addition to the oarlocks there was a mount on the stern of the boat that could hold an outboard motor. But they didn't have an outboard motor. How would he and Junior return the boat?

But in the end it didn't matter. Raff was swept up in the excitement of the moment. The shining river flowed deep a few feet away, and the Chicobee Serpent might be close by. Raff figured if they were caught with the boat, he could say Junior told him it was okay. He was obviously younger than Junior and so could avoid the blame and let Junior do the explaining.

Junior finished untying the line, and the boat came free. The two boys pushed and pulled it off the mud bank and into shallow water. Then they climbed over one side and began their journey. Picking up the oars and pointing the boat downstream, they worked it to stay close to the wooded river edge. They saw no one else on the river and heard no powerboats coming toward them, either up or down.

"On an average day you might see two or three fishermen," Junior said. "My dad brought me'n my sister along here once, and he said that's how it's always been."

"That's really strange," Raff replied. "It's so beautiful along here, and I bet the fishin's good."

"Yeah," Junior concurred. "But it's real hard to get onto this part of the river through all that mud, and it's really terrible when the water's up. People like to go into the river farther down. Most just skip the Chicobee, like to drive farther south to the Escambia. Lot more landings down there too."

Raff studied the riverine forest as far as he could see into it, and it looked like wilderness. They passed a fisherman's shack. Its single tiny room rested over the water on poles, and it looked deserted. Farther down, they came upon a rope dangling from the overhanging branch of an enormous swamp tupelo.

"Kids use that to swing out an' drop in the water," Junior said.

"But how do they get here? I don't see any trail or road."

"Must be a road come close by. Either that or they come down here by boat."

Cooter and slider turtles the size of a man's two hands sunned themselves on logs and low-hanging tree branches. They all slid into the murky water of the river when the boat got within fifty feet or so.

"They ain't any good for eatin'," Junior said. "Anyway, you'd never catch one if you tried."

The boys passed a water snake swimming toward shore. A great blue heron stood rigidly in shallow water at the edge of a sandbar, waiting for a passing fish. Two ducks passed overhead, going down the river arrow-straight in tight formation, driven by pounding wings. A turkey vulture and broad-winged hawk spiraled upward on a draft of warmer air, at such a distance and height they were little more than silhouettes.

Two smaller hawklike birds with long forked tails sailed over the canopy on the opposite shore.

"Those have got to be swallowtail kites," Raff said. "I never saw one of those before." He added helpfully, "They eat snakes up in the trees."

Their eyes lifted often to scan the sky and trees, but they stayed on the unspoken lookout for the Chicobee Serpent. Neither saw anything that could qualify as even a hint of it, but neither really expected the serpent to reveal itself in broad daylight on calm water. They kept hoping, just the same.

And then, like a door flung back, the forest opened. They came to a sandy landing on which rested a small boat similar to their own. A dirt path, cleared of grass and leaves, led about a hundred feet to a small box-shaped house with a slanted galvanized metal roof. The dwelling was well kept. Although unpainted, it appeared solid, with no sign of decay. Several planks on one side were much lighter in color and probably newly installed. Three steps led to a narrow porch at the front entrance. There was a window to the side of the door that faced the river, partly covered by a shade with a drawstring, but no curtain.

When their boat scraped bottom, the boys piled out and together pulled it partway onto the landing.

When they turned around, there stood Frogman, scarcely ten feet away. He must have spotted them and started out the door while they were pulling the boat up.

Frogman was an inch or two over six feet, narrow in face and body, about forty years old, weathered enough to look ten years older. His face was deeply tanned and creased at the eyes and corners of his mouth. He wore old-fashioned blue overalls with a front tool pocket and suspenders, a beige shirt buttoned at the cuffs, and a bill cap labeled FLOMATON LUMBER. He wore a short, neatly trimmed beard, and he had long hair tied behind in a ponytail. He was barefoot.

And in his right hand was a pump-action shotgun, which he held steady and pointed at the two boys.

He was not smiling.

"What in *hell* do *you* want?" he shouted. He pronounced it *hey-yell*.

Junior Cody, used to confrontations with his elders, lied smoothly. "Sir, we're Boy Scouts on a special trip we were told to take, and we thought we'd stop by just to pay our respects."

Frogman stood still, expressionless, and adjusted his shotgun slightly. Then he jerked the barrel in the direction of the river. The interview was over.

Raff had an inspiration. "Sir," he said, "you sure have a beautiful place here. They're such big trees, and there are all kinds of birds and butterflies. We saw them while we were passing by."

Frogman stood unmoving for half a minute, then answered loudly, "Damn straight, and any sons of bitches come around here and mess up my property, I'll kill 'em."

He fell silent again, the shotgun held steady, still pointed at the boys.

This too was an obvious dismissal, but Junior tried yet again. "We have to get movin' along right away, but could we maybe just see Old Ben first? People say he's the biggest gator in the world, like maybe twelve feet."

"Fourteen," Frogman shot back, lowering the shotgun a bit and speaking now in a normal voice.

Junior had broken through. Alligator pride was the key.

"Fourteen feet," Frogman continued. "They used to be gators bigger'n that around here, but they all got shot out. You ain't gonna see Old Ben, though. He comes out only at night. And he stays 'round here close to me. I watch over him, feed him catfish and frogs after I take they legs off."

Frogman, it was widely known, used a headlamp to gig bullfrogs on the river at night, then took the legs the next morning to the nearest gas station and one-stop store at Potomo Landing. He walked overland, never took his boat, made enough off the sales to buy sundries. He rarely spoke, the store owners reported, and he never stayed more than a few minutes. Each time the owners and any customers were happy to see him leave.

Frogman fell silent once again.

Time to go, for sure. But as Junior started to leave, he turned around and pressed his luck again.

"We know we got to leave right away, sir, but could you tell us—have you ever seen the Chicobee Serpent?"

Frogman continued to stare at the boys, but Raff sensed that something had almost imperceptibly changed. Frogman passed his tongue once quickly over his lips as though preparing to speak. He worked his mouth around a little bit, and finally said, "Maybe I have. Maybe I haven't."

He paused for a moment more, then unleashed a veritable oration. "I've seen somethin' big out there, always when it's gittin' dark, and heard some things too. It ain't a gator, for sure. It ain't no sturgeon either, come jumping out of the water big as a man. It might be a big old bull shark, come upriver out of the Gulf somewhere, long as a new-cut log, but I don't think so. That kinda shark don't break the surface, they come at you underwater."

Raff knew, if Junior didn't, that bull sharks are among the few species in the world that travel up rivers, and are also among the few that sometimes attack humans.

Frogman looked past the boys and seemed to be talking to himself. "But I seen somethin'. I heard somethin'."

Junior and Raff were riveted. They waited for Frogman to continue, but he was done. His mouth tightened, his eyes squinted, and the ogre of the Chicobee returned.

"Now you get the hell off my land, and if ever I see either one of you little bastards come here again I'll make you the sorriest you ever been your whole life."

They walked backward to the landing, kowtowing, heads nodding, murmuring, "Yessir, yessir." They quickly pushed the boat free, climbed in, and pushed off.

At the Potomo Landing, they worked the boat up onto the mud shore, walked up the grassy bank, and sat down next to the bridge abutment in the shade of a giant live oak. Raff opened his knapsack and pulled out a lunch his mother had prepared for the two: peanut butter and strawberry jam in white-bread sandwiches, apples, and Hershey's chocolate bars with almonds.

Raff and Junior then walked past the little convenience store and gas pump on down the one-lane blacktop Potomo Road until, twenty minutes later, they reached the crossing of the old Thomasville Railroad. They proceeded south along the track, sometimes hopping from one wooden tie to the next, sometimes navigating through the dense weeds growing on the embankment. When they came to State 27 they followed it southeast into Clayville. Along the way they agreed to hike the next day to the Johnson Farm to retrieve their bicycles. Then they exchanged solemn oaths never to tell their parents about their adventure, for fear of being grounded.

Exhausted by the long walk home but exhilarated, they arrived at Raff's house in time for supper, and Junior went on his way. At the kitchen table, over baked chicken, fried okra, and cornbread, his mother asked Raff how his day had been at the Nokobee tract.

"It was okay," Raff said. "I just wish Junior was more interested in natural history, though. And he's scared of snakes."

In the days following, Raff and Junior described the Chic-obee adventure in detail to their friends, each puffing up his own heroic contribution. Accounts of a stolen skiff, as opposed to a borrowed skiff, were reserved for only two or three of their closest confidants.

II

THE CITIZEN
OF NOKOBEE

2

I N ALL MY years at Florida State University I never met a
student more devoted to nature than Raphael Semmes
Cody. When he arrived there as an eighteen-year-old
freshman, he was already a practiced naturalist. In spite of our
generational difference in age, we became fast friends. I had
known Raff, as he was usually called, almost all his life. We met
at the unspoiled environment of Lake Nokobee, located in central South Alabama close to the border of the Florida Panhandle. It was a world few knew existed and fewer still could speak
of with any understanding, a world that we shared and loved. I
was the scientist and historian of this place, Raff the boy who in
a sense grew up there. His intimacy with Nokobee provided the
moral compass that was to guide his remarkable life. I was his
mentor, yet in many ways he knew Nokobee far better than I or
anyone else, and he cherished it the more.

My name is Frederick Norville. I am a professor of ecology at Florida State University, though now emeritus. For thirty
summers my wife, Alicia, and I traveled up from Tallahassee
to Nokobee for relaxation and research. My scientific interest
in the place was not the lake itself but the old-growth tract of
longleaf pine savanna that stretched from its shore over a mile

westward to the edge of the William Ziebach National Forest. Nokobee was a private reserve, one of the few in pristine condition remaining on the Gulf of Mexico coastal plain.

It was there we met Ainesley Cody and his wife, Marcia, who came up from nearby Clayville with their little son Raphael for weekend picnics. Whenever my work and weather allowed, we sat together on folding chairs around a card table and shared sandwiches, potato chips, and MoonPies, and sipped cold beer. In time we came to know one another like family.

It was on these occasions that Raphael, while little more than a toddler, developed a fascination for the wildlife of Nokobee. Without playmates and deprived of television and the other encumbrances—one could more sagely say freed from them—he turned to the mysteries of Nokobee's natural environment. His parents allowed him to explore freely and to bring me whatever creatures he could capture to find out what they were. They warned him to stay strictly away from the water and from snakes. That covered almost all the risks a child might take.

Among the treasures Raphael collected were several kinds of salamanders, boldly striped, spotted, or banded; chorus frogs, whose mating calls sounded like a fingernail scraped along the teeth of a comb; metallic-blue damselflies that bobbed through the air at the sunlit water's edge like flying gems on a string; and giant lubber grasshoppers that could be tamed to sit on your hand.

Once Raphael entered grammar school, he began to venture farther along the Nokobee Trail, and fearlessly. He brought me spiders of various kinds, small and harmless, plucked from their webs and transported in his cupped hands. Once he returned with a Nephila silk spider nearly the size of his hand, partly wrapped in the web from which it had been seized, its legs waving and fangs gnashing. He held the monster by its long abdomen between thumb and finger—aware that he should not allow the fangs to touch his skin, the same instinct that keeps the hand away from the mouth of a snarling dog. I didn't tell his parents about the incident. Perhaps that was wrong, but I was afraid they would cancel his expeditions altogether. Instead, I showed him how to scoop spiders and centipedes into glass jars without touching them at all.

I thoroughly enjoyed teaching Raphael. He was a good kid, and he grew quickly in knowledge and enthusiasm. I cannot say, however, that he was a born naturalist. Perhaps no one really ever is. I know I wasn't. But of one thing I am certain: whatever predisposition he had to become a naturalist was richly nurtured by the wild environment of the Lake Nokobee tract. All children have a bug period, unless they are frightened or otherwise discouraged by adults. I exited my bug period to become a botanist. Raphael never left. He stayed and simply widened his attention to become an all-around naturalist, with an interest in plants and animals both, in insects and invertebrates especially, and in Nokobee as a whole.

Because Alicia and I had no children of our own, Raff became a surrogate son to us. To our delight his parents encouraged him to call us Uncle Fred and Aunt Alicia, a gesture of exceptional friendship and trust in this part of the country. From one summer to the next, with each period between when I was away teaching at Florida State University, I watched his mind opening like the flowering of a plant seen in a time-lapse movie.

From the beginning I also sensed a strangeness in Raphael. He had a calmness of temperament unusual for a boy. He combined it with the ability to focus intently on a single subject for long stretches of time.

Raphael came to regard the Nokobee tract as a part of his home, and his personal space. By the time of his graduation from high school, he had become an amateur expert on scores of species in the local fauna and flora. He achieved a remarkable store of experience for someone his age. I thought that he would surely become a scientist, perhaps a great one.

But Raphael Semmes Cody, as it turned out, was to set upon a very different course. You may say it is impossible to predict the outcome of any person's life, including even one's own. Yet it seems to me that Raphael was bound for a life of achievement at a high level, if not in science then in some other field, but either way connected to the environment. I believe that, had I more logically pieced together all I learned of the influences acting upon him, I might have guessed correctly what he was to become, and why he ended up that way. I admit that this is probably just a conceit of hindsight. In any case, what really happened is important at several levels, and I think well worth the telling.

3

ONE DAY, WHEN Raphael Semmes Cody was in college and we were on more nearly equal footing, he told me a story he called "The Great Turkey Shoot." Raff treated it as a mildly amusing anecdote, good enough for after-dinner conversation. Yet it had a bittersweet tone, and I could tell its effect on him ran deep. He returned to it occasionally thereafter and added bits and pieces. In time, it became clear to me that the episode was the opening of a week in his childhood that was to shape his relationship with his mother and father and, from that, affect the outcome of his entire life. A lot he told me, but I have filled in a few gaps—confidently, because I knew Raff so well.

It began on an early Sunday morning, when Ainesley, accompanied by Raphael and his cousin Lee Jr., drove his cherry-red pickup truck out of Clayville north into Jepson County. The boys, Raphael and Lee Cody, Jr.—Scooter and Junior, to their close relatives—were ten and eleven, respectively. Junior was a husky boy on the cusp of puberty. He talked excitedly during the trip about the adventure ahead, peppering Ainesley with questions about turkey hunting. Raphael Cody, in contrast, was a wisp of a child, short for his age, and skinny. Fearful of what might await him, he kept quiet.

A boy's first hunting trip was and remains a rite of passage in rural and small-town communities in these parts. No one can say when the practice began. It probably dates to the Stone Age. The emotions expressed are too instinctive and powerfully expressed, too tightly linked to the bonding of adult males, to be anything else. There are whoops of joy when the kill is made, slaps on the back of the shooter, punches to the arm, photographs made of the hunter's band with guns and the slain animal, cutting off and presentation of a body part as trophy to the shooter, and, finally, capering and telling hunters' war stories around the campfire that night. I know folks don't talk this way anymore, but it's how we think. Real men hunt, real men find the prey, and real men pull the trigger. Girlie and disabled men stay behind in camp and cook the meat.

Soon after crossing the county line that morning, Ainesley turned the truck off State Highway 128 onto a weed-grown dirt road. Not on most ordinary road maps, it ran in a wavy line through three miles of pine-oak scrubland. Scattered on either side were scores of abandoned tenant farms. Most of the occupants had left nearly half a century before for better jobs opened by shipbuilding and other such changes in Southern cities during World War II. Black and white the same, they had escaped at last their exhausting indentured labor in the indifferent fields.

Given opportunity elsewhere, these emigrants broke the debasing chains of farmland rental. They left without regret, having owned neither the land nor even the houses in which they lived. Now the roofs of the houses were crumbling and falling in, and their porches sagged to the ground. The weedy seedlings that took root in the abandoned yards had grown to sizable trees. The last remnants of old cars jettisoned in the front yards had been carted off for scrap metal. Outhouses and chicken coops in the rear no longer manufactured blowflies and dung beetles.

"Good country for deer and turkey," Ainesley said.

The land they entered was accessed by a tracery of overgrown logging roads and unused foot trails. Few of these led to any discernible destination, often instead petering out in shallow, rain-scoured gullies. The wild turkeys and white-tailed deer native to the land had been overhunted to relative scarcity, but enough were still about and free enough for the taking to make the odds for a one-day hunt favorable.

A mile down the bumpy road, Ainesley slowed the truck and turned it onto a nearly invisible logging track. He inched it along for fifty yards before stopping. Then he opened the door on his side and climbed out. Hawked, spit, and hitched up his pants.

"Looks good," he said to the boys. "We'll get something today. But we got a lot of work to do. Now get your asses moving."

He let the boys out the other side, and, directing his gaze up the logging path, he intoned the venerable adage of the outdoorsman.

"Don't see anything yet, but they're there. The woods are empty only if you're a lousy hunter."

"I got to pee," said Junior.

"Me too," said Raphael.

Ainesley nodded assent. He lit a cigarette and leaned against a fender of his truck, waiting as the boys walked a few yards into

the bush to relieve themselves. When they returned, Ainesley tossed the still-burning cigarette to the side of the trail and
walked to the rear of the truck. He untied a tarpaulin there and
pulled out a break-action, breech-loading shotgun. It looked
old enough to be a family heirloom.

"Now, you guys, the first thing you've got to learn is how to
handle your weapon safely."

Raphael only half heard. He was watching Ainesley's cigarette. When the dead oak leaves around it mercifully failed to
catch fire, he turned his attention back to his father.

"First, we break the barrel like this and check it out. Come
over here and see how clean and oiled I got everything after the
last time I used it."

To Raff, who held back, he said, "Son, what the hell's the
matter with you? Git over here with Junior and take a look."

The boys bent forward and peeked down through the
breech. Raff glanced back and forth over the trigger casing, trying to figure out where the bullets were.

"Okay, next we load."

Ainesley reached into a pocket of his yellow waterproofed
hunter's jacket and pulled out two cylindrical shells of number 5
lead shot. He pointed them up in the air for the boys to see and
fed them into the barrel heads. He intoned, "Then we close the
barrels," and clicked them shut. He aimed the gun away from
the boys and turned it slowly to the right in a semicircle, as he
would leading a turkey passing in front.

"Allrightee! We're set to fire. It's as easy as that. One, two,
three, bang, dead turkey."

Raff didn't think it would be that easy, and with each passing
moment he was getting more anxious about the whole thing.

Ainesley cradled the gun under his right arm, with the barrels pointed downward and slightly in front of his feet. He started down the trail, and without looking back continued his lecture to the boys. They double-timed to catch up.

"Always carry a shotgun like I'm doin' it now. That way if you stumble and fall, or you're accidentally bumped by somebody, you don't shoot him or blow your own damn fool head off."

He paused, then added, "Remember this too, and it's *real* important. Watch every step you take."

The party proceeded several hundred yards down the path, which soon became hemmed in by dense second-growth pine and oak. After a while they came to a shallow wash partly covered by wire grass and dotted with rotting pine stumps. Two bobwhite quail exploded out from behind one of the stumps and flew away through the trees on the opposite side.

"You don't see much of them anymore," Ainesley said. "Ever since they started protecting coyotes and chicken hawks and other vermin such as that, a bobwhite's most likely to get gobbled up before it even gets out of the nest."

Crows could be faintly heard calling from treetops a mile away. High above them a turkey vulture circled, its wings rigid and unmoving, the terminal feathers curved upward. The air in the clearing was still and dry. The heat of the sun bounced back up from the patches of hard bare soil, and the air around them was still and uncomfortably hot.

Ainesley turned to Junior and handed him the shotgun sideways, so the boy could take it with his hands held well apart.

"That's good, that's the way, so you won't slip and drop it. Next, you shoot it."

Junior gave him a puzzled look. "What do I do?"

"Don't be nervous. Just take it slow. Hold the barrel in your left hand here, and your right goes behind the trigger guard there. Now, very carefully raise it and point it straight ahead. Pull in the butt tight against your right shoulder. That way, when you fire, the gun will push you but it won't break your shoulder. You're right-handed, aren't you? There, you're ready."

Junior was left-handed. But he didn't want to complicate an already delicate situation by quibbling. He had never held a gun in his life. His own father did not hunt, and kept the single weapon he owned, an old .38 police revolver, under lock and key with the bullets hidden in his desk drawer. Junior handled the shotgun as best he could, but gingerly, as if it were a dead snake.

"Now, very gently," Ainesley said, "put your right index finger 'round the trigger. Don't pull it yet! Hold the gun steady. Now let's point it at that old pine stump over there." Junior closed his eyes. He tightened his lips and his breath came fast and shallow.

Ainesley laid a hand gently on Junior's left shoulder and continued the lesson.

"Now, before you shoot, let me warn you, it's going to be loud and it's going to buck your shoulder. But don't worry, it's not going to hurt you. Don't let it scare you. You aren't the turkey. Whatever you do, *don't drop that gun.*"

Raff was thankful his father had started with the other boy. The shotgun seemed almost as big as he was. Maybe Ainesley would settle for the one demonstration with Junior, so they could all just move on. He figured that if they found a turkey, Ainesley himself would do the shooting. Then Raff wouldn't have to do anything at all except watch. For the time being, as far as he was concerned, he was going to be invisible. He discreetly backpedaled to a small pine tree nearby and stood partly behind it.

Ainesley put his arms around Junior's shoulder and gripped the gun himself so it wouldn't kick out of the youngster's hands when it was fired.

"Okay, now, slow and easy, boy, squeeze the trigger."

The blast roared through the silent forest. Pieces of bark flew off the stump and landed around the near side of the base.

Junior held still for a moment, stunned. Then he abruptly threw his arms out to give the gun back. The barrels were pointed at Ainesley, who gently turned them away.

Taking the gun, Ainesley walked back to Raff, who was stepping from the tree onto the trail.

"Okay, your turn, Scooter."

Raff froze, speechless. His apprehension had been building all morning, and now it turned into paralysis. He had no words with which to protest. Instead, terrible images crowded his mind. *Violence, handling big dangerous machines you can't understand, killing animals as big as the family dog. Blood all over the place, smashed heads. No sir, no sir, please, no sir.* He turned his gaze away from his father's face.

"Come on, son," Ainesley snapped. "Don't be a sissy, boy. It's not going to hurt you. You've got to do this sometime. Now's the time. You'll feel a lot better. Look at your cousin there. He did real good. You can shoot a gun just like he did. All you gotta do is pull the trigger. Come on, show us you can be a little man."

Raphael stayed rigid, scrunched like a trapped animal, hoping all this would somehow just go away. Junior was silent too, but relaxed in posture, with arms folded proudly across his chest. He'd come close to refusing the gun himself. Now he was basking in his uncle's approval. Junior Cody, not his cousin Raphael Cody, was the little man of the day.

Ainesley stiffened at the refusal. He closed his lips tightly together, as he did whenever he was angry, and worked them up and down over clenched teeth. He turned away from Raff without another word and walked on down the trail. The boys hurriedly fell in behind him, like a pair of ducklings chasing after their mother.

The hunters pressed on for another half mile, through mostly scrub slash pine and wire grass. Finally, they came to a meadow, fringed on the far side by a stand of denser woodland.

"Turkey country," said Ainesley cheerfully. He sat on a stump, broke the shotgun, lit another cigarette, and started talking again.

"When you're hunting, you've got to be *quiet*. Otherwise your turkey or your deer is going to hear you coming a mile away. It'll scoot off and you'll never even know it was there. You gotta listen for your target, you gotta *stalk* it, and you gotta shoot straight. Sometimes that's got to be from a good distance. You got one shot, win or lose. There's a lot of hunters that set up blinds, and they just sit back and drink beer and whisper to each other, waiting for something or other to walk by. Maybe they make a gobble call with one of those little hickey things, to bring the turkey closer in, if that's what they're after. Hell, that's not real hunting! It's just sitting around on your ass and waiting! It's only real hunting if you go out and find the animal, not the other way around. The best I ever did that way was two birds in one day. Big cocks, with beards hanging off their chests."

Ainesley rose, flicked the cigarette without looking onto

another pile of dry leaves, and led the hunting party onward. Raff didn't watch the smoking ember this time. If that catches fire, he thought, maybe we can put it out on our way back. I'll help out and that'll make me look good to Dad and Junior.

They continued on for another half mile, Ainesley peering this way and that, with no game in sight. Feeling bored, Raff began to watch for little animals along the trail, ones more the size he preferred, the kind he knew so well at Nokobee. He spotted a tiny scarab beetle, bright green and copper in color, rolling a sphere of dung across the trail. A wondrous jewel that came from nowhere, it was bound for a place Raff could not imagine. Ainesley and Junior didn't see it, and Junior came close to stepping on it.

Raff was startled next to see a coachwhip. The elegant tawny and black-headed snake, easily four feet long, was moving through a swath of ankle-high grass well ahead and to the side of the trail. Its head was raised the way coachwhips do while they're hunting mice and other prey. As the hunters drew closer, the snake pulled in its head and disappeared. The others had missed it entirely, and Raff was glad. He said nothing, because Ainesley might have stopped and blown it away with the shotgun.

The trio continued on for another half mile, Ainesley leading and looking this way and that. Still there was no game in sight. Ainesley abruptly sat down on a fallen pine trunk that lay along the trail. Raff was alarmed to see that he had started to breathe heavily.

"I think we ought to head on back," Ainesley said, more to himself than to the boys. "I don't feel too good today, and there aren't nearly as many turkeys around here anyway as there used to be. Just too many goddamn hunters coming in from outside, excuse my French. They're clearing the game out. Maybe the state ought to raise young turkeys and turn 'em loose in the woods here, the way they stock trout and some of the other kinds of fish in the lakes. Might finally do some good with my tax money."

With that, Ainesley headed back toward the trailhead, at a noticeably slower pace than when he had started out. Raff walked closely behind, relaxed now, aimlessly scuffing pine cones off the trail, thinking, Dad didn't do too well today either. Maybe he won't be too mad at me after all.

At the pickup Ainesley ordered the boys to relieve themselves one more time so that they wouldn't have to ask later. Then he put away the shotgun and dragged on a last cigarette while he waited. They all climbed into the cab, with Raff squeezed in the middle, and began the hour-long drive down two-laned Alabama 128 to Clayville.

Halfway there, Ainesley announced that they were going to stop at a farm and get a guinea hen. He pulled over to the owner's neat, recently painted house. It had a cornfield to its immediate left, chickens in the yard, two torpid basset hounds on the porch, and a large sign in front on the edge of the road that proclaimed JESUS SAVES.

"We're gonna pick up our dinner here," Ainesley said. He climbed down out of the cab and walked across the yard. At the porch he stepped around the dogs, one of whom raised itself and uttered a single *Wuff!*, then lay down again. Ainesley knocked on the door. A voice called out for him to come on in, and he pushed open the door and entered.

In ten minutes or so Ainesley came out again with a heavyset man, about sixty or so—hard to tell. He was dressed in shorts, ankle-high shoes, and a T-shirt decorated with a faded palm-tree logo and the word ARUBA.

Ainesley walked to the rear of the truck while the man waited, pulled open the tarpaulin again, and this time took out a bolt-action, single-shot .22 rifle.

"Come along," he said to Raff and Junior, "I'm going to show you how to get your own food."

Following the owner, they passed a toolshed and the abandoned shell of a truck, then a tiny plot of land surrounded by a low white picket fence. Inside the fence was a gravestone bearing the single word BELOVED.

Pointing with his thumb, the owner said, "That's where I bury my dogs."

Soon the group came to an outdoor pen enclosed by a wire fence. The owner said it was two acres, but it seemed much smaller. Thirty yards inside the fence they saw a flock of a dozen guinea fowl resting in the shade of an oak tree. The owner wagged an index finger in that direction. "These here is the only guinea birds you're gonna find all the way down to Mobile."

Ainesley pulled the bolt of the rifle back and down, chambered a slim cartridge, and hooked the bolt back into position. He flicked off the safety.

"Now, what you remember when shooting small game like this is always go for the head. You do that and you get a sure kill, and you don't mess up the body. We've got to clean the bird when we get home and I don't want to have to dig a bullet out of the best eatin' part."

The flock, disturbed by the approach of the humans, began to stir. Ainesley sighted on a cock in its midst.

Raphael clenched his whole body, gritted his teeth, and

tightened his fists. He half closed his eyes. He'd never seen a warm-blooded animal bigger than a mouse killed, and certainly nothing executed with a gun.

The shot made a popping sound, surprisingly quieter than the shotgun. The bird's head kicked back, and the rest of its body simply collapsed onto the ground. The owner went into the enclosure, scattering the flock as he approached. He scooped up the slain bird in a newspaper and handed the package to Ainesley.

As they drove the rest of the way past farms and pine plantations to the little town of Clayville, Ainesley was in better spirits. He took a shot of Jack Daniel's from a small paper-bag-covered bottle lying above the dashboard, cleared his throat, and continued his lecture on the hunter's life. "You saw how I took that bird down. The big thing down in this part of the country is marksmanship. In the early days most people had to get some of their food from the woods, and they couldn't afford to waste any ammunition doing it, either. That's why the Confederates—and there were Codys in action during that war, believe me—they were able to pick off so many of the Union infantry at places like Shiloh and Antietam. Our boys have always been the best shots. They've always been the best soldiers in America too."

Later, he continued his lecture on Southern marksmanship. "Right around here, they used to hold shooting matches every year. For example, one contest was 'snuffing the candle.' You had to clip the wick at fifty yards and put the flame out. But— and this is important—it was just the tip of the wick you were supposed to cut, so the flame would go out but then it came back on again.

"My dad told me about another contest they called 'bark the

squirrel.' Shooting squirrels was a big thing in those days. Some of the country people around here still make squirrel stew, with okra and tomatoes and stuff, and I'll tell you, when done right it is real tasty."

Chuckling, he added, "If you like squirrel meat, that is." He took another sip from the bottle and wiped his mouth with the back of a sleeve.

"Anyway, you didn't want to tear up the squirrel any more'n you had to, so you tried to bark the squirrel. So here's how it was done. You let the squirrel run up the tree and stop to look back at you the way they always do, then you move real slow until you're looking at it from the side. Then you fire, but you don't hit the squirrel, you hit the bark just under it. If you do that just right, a piece of the bark flies up and stuns the squirrel. And you got your meal."

By the time they got Junior home and made it on to their own small house in Clayville, it was growing dark. Clouds from the Gulf of Mexico gathered and closed gently over them, hastening the night. With a slight breeze whispering its approach, a warm soft rain began to fall.

4

FTER SUPPER, RAPHAEL LAY in bed, worrying. He stared sightlessly at the screen of his twelve-inch color television set, last year's Christmas present from his Uncle Cyrus. Two rooms away Ainesley and Marcia were talking loudly. He could not make out the words, but he knew from the volume and tone that it was an argument. From past experience he was certain that this one was about himself.

During the meal of fried calf's liver, turnip greens, and biscuits, he had averted his gaze from the two adults and uttered not a word. It was not easy being an only child. After the dishes were washed and dried, his father departed for the Delchamps Supermarket in Clayville for groceries. As soon as Ainesley left, Marcia took Raff aside and gently worked out of him the main events of the day. As he described the firing of the shotgun and conquest of the guinea fowl, her narrow, pleasant face turned increasingly grim.

Now his parents were squared off, as they had been many times before, on the issue of how their son should be raised. They were coming at each other from different positions Raff could sense but not understand. It ran a lot deeper, he knew, than just a turkey hunt. The ten-year-old's loyalty was divided by the conflict. That was bad, because the fissure appeared to be insoluble, and he did not know to whom his loyalty was owed.

Raff worried that Ainesley and Marcia might separate, leaving him without a father or a mother, one or the other. Maybe he would have to live with a relative or some stranger. He knew kids at school in that fix. They seemed mostly okay, but in his case, he thought, it would strip away his own security and upset his life completely. He fell asleep trying to puzzle this dilemma.

Toward dawn, as Raphael slept, the rain slackened off. By the time he was roused for breakfast, the wind had picked up and a slight chill was in the humid air. The blond weatherwoman on Mobile Television Channel 5 said with a clipped midwestern accent that the Alabama and Mississippi coasts would be cloudy, but with no more rain. Still, Marcia made Raphael put on a slicker, which he hated, and a rain hat, which he hated even more. They made him look like a sissy, he thought. His father thought the same, an opinion he had let recklessly slip to Marcia more than once.

Raff rode his bicycle down Charleston Street to the first light and then left three blocks to the Martin Luther King, Jr., Grammar School. Once, many years ago, it had been the Robert E. Lee School. Through the day he couldn't think about anything much in class. Geometry, English, and American history churned on past him like the talk of strangers in a shopping mall. During lunch and recess he stayed away from his best friends. He kept thinking about Ainesley, worried about the wrath to come. He feared the angry spells, the way his father occasionally raised his hand as though to hit him, although he never really had. He felt ashamed that he had refused simply to hold the gun with his father's help and pull the trigger. He felt guilty that he told his mother about the incident.

He thought, Am I a sissy? Even though I get in fights with other boys and don't run away? He felt even worse for letting his father down, because he knew Ainesley thought of him as a special and very precious boy, and maybe a *little man* too, after everything was said and done. Once he had heard Ainesley refer to him in conversation with some neighborhood friends: "I wouldn't take a million dollars for this one or give you a dime for another."

When he arrived home from school that midafternoon, he was surprised to find his father waiting for him. Ainesley had returned home early from the hardware store and was sitting on the porch in the rocking chair, cigarette in hand.

"Git in the car," Ainesley said, "I want to talk to you."

They drove into Clayville, down streets lined with live oak and trimmed hedges, past the Nokobee County Courthouse and on to Roxie's Ice Cream Palace. The latter social center, like the Cody home, was virtually downtown—no surprise, because if you kept on driving you'd come out the other side of Clayville in under five minutes. Inside Roxie's, they squeezed into a booth and Ainesley told Raff to order his favorite dish. It was, they both knew, a butterscotch sundae with chopped walnuts.

As Raff started to eat, Ainesley said to him, "Son, I'm sorry I pushed you so hard yesterday. You're pretty young to be firing guns anyway, and I don't think you'd have a lot of fun at your age killin' a turkey anyhow. It don't count that Junior was willin' to fire the gun and you wasn't. He's older and he's a lot bigger than you, and to tell the truth, compared to you he's dumber than a stump."

Managing a mouthful of ice cream, Raphael nodded and thought, Yeah, that's the truth. Junior was held back last year and was still only in the fourth grade. He'd have to endure another year of disciplinarian torture in Mrs. Maddon's class. Middle-aged, steely eyed behind glasses, her graying hair worn in a bun, she was both strict and given to quick anger. Out of earshot the students called her the Mad Ox.

"What I was trying to do," Ainesley continued, "was not start you huntin' game animals, exactly. You might not like it very much even when you're older. I don't know. I was just try-ing to show you things that when you grow up you gonna need to know to be a real man, not the kind of girlie man you see all over the place nowadays."

He paused to let that sink in, and—Raff could feel it coming—lit a cigarette. There was more talk coming from Ainesley, he was sure. No matter. Fear and remorse were slid-ing off him. He had been forgiven. For the first time he looked directly into his father's face—tanned, lines around his mouth, with blue eyes that now had a sad look.

Ainesley took a deep draw into his lungs and turned his head to blow the smoke to the side. He flicked a crumb of tobacco off his lip with a middle finger and continued, "You probably don't know what I'm talkin' about, so I'm gonna add a little bit more for you to think about. And maybe some more later, whenever we get together, so you'll understand about how I feel."

How *he* feels? Raff thought. He was beginning to get anxious again.

"You know I don't have the education your mother and Uncle Cyrus have. You'll be gittin' one like that yourself, for sure, and I feel real good about that. But I want you to grow up

(Sorry about the stains)

to be like me in one important way. When you're on your own, I want you to stand up straight and tall and be the kind of man everybody respects no matter how much money they have, or how many fancy titles they have, or whatever.

"Now, what does that mean? It means honor. It means you keep your promises, you pay your debts, you meet your responsibilities, you do the best you can, even though sometimes things get tough. And you don't talk about it, you keep it inside of you. People meet you and work with you, they don't need to have your word on it. They know they can count on you—all the time, and not just when *you* feel like it. You understand that?"

Raff said, "Yes sir," and put another spoonful into his mouth, savoring the butterscotch.

"But being a man is more than that," Ainesley continued. "It's bein' a gentleman. Our people have a code that people may laugh at who live in big houses and take vacations in Italy and places such as that. I certainly wouldn't talk about any of it with your Uncle Cyrus, who incidentally I respect a great deal. But it means everything in the world *I* live in. You might say that code is raw, you might say it's too simple, but it sure stays right there on the surface of things, and it suits me. It's this. Never lie or cheat. Never ever hit a woman. Never hit a smaller man, if you can keep from doing it, Raff. Never hit anyone first, but *never back down* when you know you're in the right."

He paused, took a sip of coffee, stubbed out his half-burned cigarette, and lit another. Raff was wondering how a man of his father's diminutive size would make out if ever he were hit by anyone, especially a big man. His father stood under five feet eight inches tall and weighed only 130 pounds, "soaking wet," as he liked to say.

In time Raff was to learn that this question was moot. Ainesley carried a long jackknife in his pocket that he compulsively sharpened with a small rectangular whetstone. He kept a .22 pistol in the glove compartment of his pickup, "my equalizer," he called it. He could also produce an illegal blackjack suddenly, like a magician, from a hidden place Raff was never able to discover. If Ainesley on any occasion actually defended himself, Raff was never in future years to hear of it.

Raff took another large scoop of ice cream from the bottom of the goblet, afraid his father's pause meant he was getting ready to leave. But Ainesley picked up again.

"Here's another thing," he said. "Show decent respect to other people. There's something a gentleman down here does they don't do in other parts. You go up to another man, he's working in a filling station, and you ask him, 'Excuse me, but can you tell me where some street or other is located?' And he'll say, 'Yessir, I can.' He does *not* say, 'Yes, sir, I can.' He does not say, '*Yes sir!*' He's not your servant. He says, 'Yessir, I do,' or 'Nosir, I don't know myself.' That means he's polite but he's your equal, and you show it too, you talk back to him the same way. Now, you're specially, extra polite to people who deserve it. That's why your mom and I have you say sir and ma'am to grownups, and why we do the same ourselves to old folks."

Ainesley lit yet a third cigarette, and fell silent again and flicked his hand as though to say, *Well, there you are*, as though his outpouring had gone a bit far and he was afraid Raphael might respect him the less for it. He searched his pocket for a few coins and put them on the table for a tip, stubbed out the cigarette, and got up to leave. Then, holding on to the rear of his chair and looking out the restaurant window toward the parking lot, to really nothing in particular except maybe a rainbow oil streak under the closest truck, he spoke softly, this time with a touch of bitterness.

"Here is what I want to pass on to you, Scooter. They can take away your money, they can take away your freedom, they can laugh at you behind your back, but if you're a man the way I'm trying to tell you to be, not some kind of a girlie man that snivels all over the place and backs off from trouble, they can't take that away from you, and that's why I'm going to keep after you even if once in a while I seem to ride you a little hard."

Raff believed him, totally. He remembered that when he was smaller and scraped his knee and started to cry, Ainesley said, "Stop that, be a little man."

He could just barely recall another occasion—he was perhaps three years old, and sleeping next to his father on some otherwise forgotten occasion—when he woke up during the night and asked to go to the bathroom, and Ainesley said, "Hold it in, wait till morning, like a little man."

5

T HE FOLLOWING SUNDAY it was Marcia's turn. She let Raff sleep late, then noisily opened the door and walked into his room. Singing to herself, she raised the shade of the single window and let sunlight flood his bed. She paused there, leaning forward to peer at the bird feeder placed in the crepe myrtle tree next to the window. Sure enough, the resident squirrel sat on the feeder platform, while birds perched in the surrounding branches waiting for the monster to leave. On rare occasions, when it was not raining and Raff was not at school or outdoors, he sat on a chair and watched the birds come and go—mostly house sparrows, blue jays, and cardinals, but also the occasional common grackle. Ainesley had offered to shoot the squirrel and give the birds more feeder time, but Marcia indignantly forbade him to so much as threaten the family rodent.

Marcia shook the bed and pulled Raff's thin wool blanket partly off his huddled body.

"Time to get up, Scooter. We're going to church, then we're going down to Mobile to have supper with the family."

Church meant the main Methodist church in downtown Clayville. Marcia and all the relatives on her side were Episcopalian, but the closest services held in that denomination were in Brewton, half an hour's drive away. Visits were made there only on special Sundays. Ainesley was a lapsed Southern Baptist and a sometime private atheist who thought poorly of Baptist pastors. But he dutifully took Marcia and Raff to church every Sunday that he wasn't at his store taking inventory. Usually he dropped them off and picked them up after service. Occasionally, however, he put on a coat and tie and sat next to them, enjoying the sonorous comfort of the organ and good hymns, but fretting through the scripture readings and homilies that seemed planned to go on into Monday. The worst part was that he couldn't smoke or take a sip of anything, sitting there in the midst of two hundred or so righteous Alabamians.

Family to Marcia meant her own Semmes family. Her full name was Marcia Semmes Cody. Her son bore the grand name Raphael Semmes Cody. Marcia had made the decision to name him after the Confederate Admiral Raphael Semmes, whose warship the *Alabama* had savaged Union shipping up and down the Atlantic Seaboard before being sunk by a bigger Union gunship while on a provisioning trip off the coast of England.

Semmes was a big name in these parts. To the north of Mobile was the little town of Semmes; and near Bienville Square in downtown Mobile stood the old Admiral Semmes Hotel and a heroic statue of the man himself. There was even an Admiral Semmes Drive, in the better part of the city, as expected. There were the Semmeses of Mobile and the Semmeses of America, spread out with their collateral lines and spousal surnames like the branches of some great oak tree far and wide across the Republic. Their distinguished heritage extended back in multiple lines for three centuries, almost as long as that of America itself.

There were Codys too, of course, distributed widely across South Alabama and over into Mississippi and the Florida Panhandle and beyond, with one branch of the family having recently colonized Australia. They were successful and Southern Baptist and upright for the most part. One was a doctor living just across the Mississippi state line in Pascagoula, but most of the current generation were solid working class—truck drivers, nurses, real estate salesmen. By Marcia's lights they were below the Semmeses, and there was nothing among them that should give pride to her or Raphael. That is, no admirals, generals, governors, senators, or golf champions. No inherited wealth, second home, or memberships in the right charitable foundations, and no invitations to gubernatorial inaugurations.

Although she never spoke of it quite so bluntly around him, Ainesley knew the way Marcia felt. He sensed that she sometimes regretted the rash decision she had made, as a headstrong young woman, to marry him. It was the unspoken tension that haunted their marriage, but he would love her and Raff without reservation no matter what her social origins or how she expressed them. He didn't care about his own relatives very much anyway, one way or the other. He was, for all his foibles and lack of education, a self contained man. He was intelligent, and passionate at times, and there was of course his code, which no one who knew him well would wish to dispute within his hearing. Without knowing who Epictetus was, or much about the ancient Greeks in general, Ainesley was an authentic philosophical stoic. As he had explained to Raphael, he really lived by the code he had internalized; he dwelled content within it. Marcia understood this solid core of his character, and it meant a lot to her.

This day, however, Marcia's mind was on Mobile and her

parents and the home in which she grew up. She prepared to reinvest herself with the grandeur of the Semmeses.

Ainesley stood by the front door. He had cleaned the cab of the pickup and filled the gas tank, and he was beginning to fidget.

Marcia shouted at her son, "Please come on! We haven't got all day!" A chronically high-strung woman, she was especially keyed up this morning as they waited for Raff. She fidgeted around in the kitchen and living room, lining up objects that seemed even slightly out of place, glancing at herself in the hall mirror, adjusting her hair.

After the church service, which seemed agonizingly long to all three of them, the Codys dodged through the crowd of lingering parishioners and hurried home. They scarfed a light lunch sitting at the kitchen table. There was no Sunday dinner this day; they would all be dining sumptuously at her parents' home in the evening. Without changing from their best clothes, they hurried out to the pickup and headed south on the hour-long drive to Mobile.

They did not, however, go directly to the Semmes family home on the Azalea Trail.

"We're going first to drop by and see your Aunt Jessica," Marcia said to Raff.

"Oh, dear God!" murmured Ainesley. No way I'm going in there, he thought. I'm going to sit in the shade somewhere and smoke, and kill a soldier or two. He'd thoughtfully iced some bottles of beer—soldiers—and stored them under the truck tarpaulin the night before, just in case.

On Marcia's command, they pulled off at Satsuma, an exurban settlement just north of Mobile. After several turns they came on to Savannah Street, in the old section. Halfway down the first block, in a neighborhood adorned exquisitely with mature live oaks and magnolias, Ainesley brought the pickup to a halt in front of a run-down little house set well back from the line of other properties. The structure had a single floor, a slightly sagging front porch with a swing and two rocking chairs, and a roof in critical condition. Weeds fought crabgrass for possession of the spacious lawn. Lovely unpruned azaleas and crepe myrtles added to the overall aura of decaying gentility.

"This place must have looked great a hundred years ago," quipped Ainesley.

Then he announced his escape strategy: "I'll stay here in the truck until I see you go in. Then I'll be back to pick you up in two hours. Tell her I've got business." He looked straight ahead to avoid back talk, and waited for them to get out.

Almost as soon as Marcia knocked on the front door it was opened—and there stood Aunt Jessica, snow-haired, gap-toothed, and encased in an ankle-length flowered smock. She must have seen them through the front window as they approached. Of course she would be there and waiting for anyone who cared to come by. She was known never to leave the house.

"Good Lord have mercy on my soul, look who's here! Y'all come right on in!"

Aunt Jessica was a few years north of ninety. Born just before the turn of the century, she had lived all her life in the Savannah Street house, and even when young had never traveled farther away than the Mobile watering holes of Fairhope to the east and Biloxi to the west. Her grandmother had been a young woman living in Navy Cove at the time of the War Between the States, close enough to Fort Morgan to hear the thunder of artillery and watch Farragut's fleet break through into Mobile Bay. An enemy cannonball overshot the fort and landed in the family's backyard.

After the war, her grandfather had bought a little farm on what was then called the Old Savannah Road. In recalling the occupation, her grandmother allowed to Jessica, "The Yankees never did any harm to us." On one occasion, a trooper was reprimanded for stealing a chicken from the backyard, and his immediate superior apologized to the family. "They were mostly nice boys," she said. "They just wanted to get home themselves." The war had nevertheless devastated the economy, and land was cheap. Sections could be bought along the beach of the Fort Morgan Peninsula, over across the mouth of Mobile Bay, for ten dollars an acre.

Aunt Jessica herself had met and talked to many Confederate veterans when she was a teenager. They were old men by then, and it was customary to address them all as "Cap'n" in the Gulf seacoast manner of respect. She lived through the Great Depression, when much of rural Alabama was still an impoverished developing country, and Mobile little more than a backwater town compared to Savannah and New Orleans. She had witnessed the great immigration during World War II of tenant farmers, black and white, who poured into the city to help build the shipyard and Brookley Field.

Jessica and her family believed that "our people" were superior to all others, as demanded—not just encouraged—by the culture of her youth. Even the poor white tenant farmers who came from upstate were dismissed as "white trash" and "peapickers," with their "towheaded kids." Towheaded meant blond, and it was a strange inversion that the trait should so contemptuously identify that part of the lower class mostly descended from Scotch-Irish pioneers of America.

Black people were given a measure of respect, at least in Jessica's day. They were called Negroes in polite communication, and racial purity within white families of any class who believed it to exist was protected fanatically. The one-drop doctrine was obeyed without exception: one black ancestor made you a Negro. White working-class people were so afraid in particular of losing their perceived birthright of racial superiority that to be called a "nigger lover" was a fighting insult.

Jessica, like most girls of her tribe, had little education in the ways of the world beyond Mobile. She seldom read newspapers or books. Television had not invaded her home, even now. But she was an encyclopedia of local lore and a great storyteller in the congenial Southern tradition. She seldom stopped talking when she got hold of you, and she could render spellbound any who cared even the least for Southern culture in an authentic form.

Jessica was not, as it turned out, Marcia's aunt. That title was traditionally bestowed on any woman, white or black, who was a close and beloved friend. Nonetheless, Jessica was at least a Semmes, and certainly Marcia's distant cousin at some unknown degree of remove. Marcia had been introduced to her when a little child by her father, and she grew up recognizing her as the official genealogist of the Mobile Semmes clan.

As Jessica walked with Marcia and Raff into the parlor, a pale woman of about seventy stood, without salutation. This was Sissy, who had lived with Jessica for longer than anyone could exactly remember. No one was even sure of her surname, although some believed it was Dupree or something close to that. Among the Semmes cognoscenti it was also rumored that Sissy was descended from the first French settlers of Old Mobile. Others guessed, more reasonably, that she came as a young woman with a dissolute sharecropper family, and at some point Jessica hired her and then took her in. None of the Semmes women ever spoke about it in Jessica's presence. It was an old Southern custom to keep improvident elderly relatives and family friends in the house, if such was large enough.

Jessica had no children of her own, so there was no one obligated to inquire into that or any of her other business. If Jessica had money—there had to be some—or a will, no one knew. She never in anyone's memory had given a gift of any value, nor asked for help of any kind.

Sissy was dispatched to bring lemonade and crackers. Marcia and Raff followed Jessica into the parlor, and were struck by the telltale scent of neglected old age, a mix of unwashed flesh and decayed upholstery with just a hint of urine. If this fazed Marcia, her composed features gave no sign. As the two women seated themselves, she gently nudged Raff and commanded, "Give your Aunt Jessica a kiss."

The ten-year-old was well practiced in this drill. He walked over and delivered a peck on Jessica's forehead, sidewise to avoid the hairy mole on her nose.

Jessica smiled. "Thank you, Mr. Raphael." Raff gave the expected response, "Yes, ma'am," and sat in a chair under the parlor window. A cat appeared from behind a pot of plastic ferns and rubbed against his legs, then sat back and stared up at him in hungry supplication.

Marcia drew her chair close to Jessica's, and the two fell

quickly into soft, animated conversation. Jessica seemed to have memorized the genealogy of the Semmeses and all their collateral lines back into the seventeenth century. In particular, her archival knowledge of the Mobile Semmeses was total. The two women browsed through episodes about the local family and their antecedents, sharing pleasure in every detail, hopping from topic to topic. Raff was able to catch only fragments.

"Your cousin Tommy on your Aunt Sara's side . . . No, no, I'm sure of it, she's buried with little Mary Jo right there on the west edge of Magnolia Cemetery . . . Oh, I know, those were such dreadful days, there was such suffering . . . Well, believe it or not, I actually met him once, I must have been only five or six . . . No, I don't know what happened to them after they moved to Texas, that was such a long time ago . . . A captain? Oh, no, he couldn't have been a captain although I know Cousin Rosalee claims he was, because, think, he was only eighteen when he went in . . . Oh, my, yes, divorced not once but would you believe it *twice* . . . Arrested you say, maybe, but he was back in Mobile the very next morning . . . A Southern *Baptist*, now? Lord God have mercy on us all . . ."

Marcia was enraptured, as befitted an acolyte and the family historian-designate.

Raff tried to listen and learn something about his ancestry on the Semmes side, as Marcia had instructed him to do, but he couldn't hear enough or follow even a single story. He preferred to read comics; he was neither the genealogist nor the mathematician required for such a celebration of the deceased multitude. He closed off his mind and began to fidget. Reached for the cat, crossed and recrossed his legs, squirmed in his chair a lot. Then he let his eyes wander. There in a dim light next to the hallway entrance was an oil painting of the Confederate warship *Alabama* and next to it a faded photograph of the admiral who had commanded it, Raphael Semmes himself. And all around the room, frame almost touching frame, there were photographs of people, singly or in groups, many hand-tinted. Judging from the style of clothes, the pictures were about a century old, dating mostly to the late 1800s and turn of the century. Interspersed were also a few yellowed newspaper clippings, and above one a framed brace of military medals. Nearby hung a gold-trimmed certificate from the Mobile Daughters of the Confederacy. In its center was the battle flag, its red faded to pink. None of the pictures was labeled.

After the better part of an hour, Sissy returned with the lemonade and a plate of soda crackers. "Scooter," said Marcia, "why don't you take your drink and go with Sissy to see the chickens?"

His face brightening with relief, Raff sprang from his chair. He stepped around the cat, which had drifted off into a ball of sleep, and followed Sissy down the hall. They proceeded through a kitchen filled with jelly glasses and cracked enamel cookware, and on out to the backyard. The yard was a small fenced-in enclosure lined by crooked catalpa trees, a broad-leafed species that seemed to thrive best in bare urban yards. Its packed dirt floor was spattered with chicken droppings and shed feathers. Along one side of the yard was a coop with a cast-iron roof and sides made of chicken wire. The interior, crowded with roosts and nest boxes, was a bedlam of hens making chicken noises. The smell of ammonia was overpowering. A rooster and several hens were running loose outside. They scattered as Sissy stepped in their direction and shooed them away with waving arms.

Walking the length of the coop, Sissy began to laugh, pointing to one thing or another, saying, "Look there! Look there!" over and over. Otherwise, she was a lady of few words. Raff tried but could not make out anything special in the places she indicated. When they reached the end of the coop and circled back, Sissy's commands continued and her laughter grew louder. Raff was getting rattled, and started to move past her on his return to the house. Sissy stopped laughing and came to a halt, as if to hold him back. Then she abruptly turned around and chased one of the loose hens down the length of the small yard. She cornered it at the angle of the rear wooden fence, gathered it struggling and squawking in her arms. She grabbed its lower legs with both hands and turned it upside down and held it that way, with its wings flapping and its head hanging down, for Raff to see. Then she walked over to a low wooden table next to the farthest coop, freed one hand, and picked up a small axe lying there. Turning to face Raff, holding up the chicken and axe, she uttered her last word of the day.

"Dinner."

Raff was shocked and frightened by what was about to happen. Then he quickly pulled himself together. He was determined not to witness the execution of another large bird, the second in just a week, and this time in an unimaginably grisly manner. So he said loudly, "Thank you, Miss Sissy, that was fun," then walked to the back door of the house and stepped inside. Behind him, the rooster crowed. Sissy stood stock-still and watched him go.

Ainesley returned at the appointed time, and to the minute, afraid that Marcia might call him in to say hello to Jessica. After prolonged goodbyes, with thankfully no kisses asked this time of Raphael, he and Marcia climbed into the cab of the pickup and the family continued on their journey toward the center of Mobile. Marcia was silent, not easily jarred out of the pleasant interlude with Aunt Jessica. As they passed out of Satsuma, Ainesley turned to Raff with crinkled eyes and an ironic smile.

"Hey, Scooter, did you have a good time?"

Marcia scowled, watching her son from the corner of her eye. Raff hesitated. His best diplomatic response was needed to solve this little crisis.

"It was all right, I guess."

Marcia countered, "How was Sissy and her chickens?"

Raff looked straight ahead. He wanted off the hook, fast.

"Okay, I guess. She's a little strange, though."

"Insane, you mean," Ainesley said.

Like a spring-loaded trap Marcia snapped back with the correct upper-class response: "Ainesley, I told you before not to be prejudiced against anyone just because they're different from you."

6

T
HE SEMMESES' ANCESTRAL home was set on a full acre in the heart of old Mobile and situated on the Azalea Trail just off Old Shell Road. It was an authentic antebellum mansion, with a spiral staircase leading to the family living quarters on the second floor. It even had a name of its own, Marybelle, after the first owner's wife, who died during a yellow fever epidemic in the 1840s. The builder was Richard Stoughton, a furniture manufacturer who had come down from Providence with his family and set up a thriving business. Mobile was in its boom period then, having emerged as the key and virtually only transit port for the rich cotton and tobacco production of the Mobile Basin. In less than forty years it had grown from a ten-block village with mud roads to a small city.

When the Alabama legislature voted Alabama out of the Union in 1861, Stoughton knew that war was inevitable. He hurriedly transferred his funds to a New York bank, illegally as it turned out under Confederacy law. He put Marybelle and his extensive upriver property in the hands of a caretaker, and sailed with his family back to Providence. Despite the carnage afterward that laid waste to so many great mansions of the South, Marybelle remained intact during the war. Mobile was blockaded by the warships of the Union fleet, but otherwise out of the range of battle until it was occupied by infantry following the Battle of Mobile Bay. With the blockade throttling the supply of arms and other imports, little threat remained to Union forces on the move farther north, and Mobile was spared the ruinous fate of Atlanta and Savannah. The little city was not pillaged and burned like these other Confederate strongholds. Its citizens were able to lead more or less normal lives, albeit impoverished and closely watched for the short remainder of the war. Marybelle was heavily looted but remained structurally intact, and in fact was given extra protection as a Union battalion headquarters into the early years of the Reconstruction. Some family friends spoke of it jokingly as "Yankees' Rest" or, less kindly, "Bluebelly Haven."

Mr. Stoughton died in 1867, before he could return to Mobile. His heirs, comfortably settled in Providence, had no wish to leave. The prospects in their old home, they believed, were grim. And truly, in every aspect of life a darkness had fallen upon the South. Although the Confederate states were again part of the Union, in fact they were treated as occupied territories. Their industrial base, never large before the war, had been turned to rubble. Cotton, tobacco, and timber, the main economic base, were picking up, but at a slow and erratic pace. No one could gauge what kind of adjustment the newly freed slaves would make, where they would go, what labor they would accept. Their former white masters chafed under the punitive laws of the Reconstruction, their hopes laced with a sullen resentment at the radical change forced upon them. They prepared for an era of racial and civil strife.

Back in Providence, the Stoughtons could see that this was

not a good time for defected Southerners to come home. With good reason they feared they might receive a hostile reception from the faithful who had stayed and suffered.

The family still held on to Marybelle and a scattering of cropland properties to the north of the city—of that they made sure in the restored federal district court. But Marybelle was now a liability. It generated no income while remaining at high risk from vandalism.

The Stoughtons decided to cut their losses and get out of the South altogether. They put up Marybelle for sale. It was quickly picked up by Thomas Semmes, an Alabama investor who had built a fortune before and during the war. He had sensibly traded most of his profits for waterfront properties in and around Mobile. The value of the land grew rapidly with the revival of the city as the major port east of New Orleans.

On this day, his fortunate descendants who currently occupied Marybelle were gathered, like aristocrats of old, at the porte cochere to greet the Codys of Clayville. Standing in front were Marcia's brother, Cyrus Semmes, and his wife, Anne.

"Well, isn't this wonderful, you all look so *good!*" exclaimed Anne, hugging Marcia. Cyrus and Ainesley shook hands, like businessmen.

"Yes, it's just so *nice* to be here!" responded Marcia.

Cyrus turned to his nephew Raphael with special attention. He shook the youngster's hand, then stooped and gave him a hug.

"Hey, guy, you're looking good, looking real good. We're all so proud of you, including Granddog."

Granddog was what Raphael as a toddler had called his grandfather when they'd first met.

The warmth of Cyrus's greeting was understandable. Standing before him was the sole male of the next generation in his immediate branch of the Semmes family. Cyrus's older daughter, Charlotte, now a sophomore at Emory University, scandalized her parents by refusing to join the Junior League. She vowed to join the Peace Corps after her graduation—and never thereafter return to live in "dull, dull old Mobile." Her sister, Virginia, a high school junior, was entirely different. A strikingly pretty blonde but something of an airhead whose principal interest was boys and whose idea of high culture was Nancy Drew books and rock concerts, she was considerably less promising academically than Charlotte.

They all walked into the splendor of Marybelle. Once again Ainesley, and now even Marcia, was struck not so much by its size as by its interior furnishings, which had been variously supplemented and refined during nearly 150 years of loving care. There was an authentic grandeur of family oil portraits along the main hall and staircase walls. The floor was the original West Indian mahogany. The banister of the staircase, a masterpiece of carved ebony, had been featured twice in *Southern Living*. The silverware they were about to use was a nineteenth-century Semmes heirloom.

The group proceeded directly to the long table of the dining room. Dinner had been prepared by a chef and her assistant from a catering service founded by one of those Junior League women on whom marriage had not looked kindly. The meal was now briskly served by the two Semmes house staff. The appetizer was crab gumbo made in the ineffably seasoned Mobile style, followed by a salad and main course of venison, quail eggs, and snap peas. California wines, including a Napa Valley merlot recently recommended to Cyrus by a business associate, were served to the grown-ups. Dr Pepper went to Raff and Virginia. Dessert was pecan pie à la mode.

The conversation cut back and forth obliquely across the table, so that all listened when any one person was speaking. Pleasantries quickly gave way to family news, then gossip, and finally stories of recent travel and amusing gaffes. Cyrus, a University of Alabama graduate, brought up the better-than-average record achieved this year by the Crimson Tide. If Alabama could defeat its archrival Auburn University in the upcoming classic match, it would have a clear shot at the Southeastern Conference championship. Football was one of Cyrus's passions, and he occasionally traveled up to Tuscaloosa with other alumni from Mobile for an important home game.

"If Coach Harrison loses the Auburn game, he's out of a job," Cyrus joked. "If he wins, we'll put him up for governor of Alabama."

Ainesley then managed to spring a conversation-stopper.

"I bet you didn't know, but one of my cousins, Bobby Cody, they usually call him Bubba, don't you know, is a left tackle on the Auburn team. He's had a great season and they say he might make All-American this year."

Grandfather Jonathan got up to leave at this point, annoyed at the Auburn reference and visibly tired, a result of his second heart attack four months earlier.

"I hope y'all will excuse me. It's been a long day, but then every day's been a long day for me lately. Marcia, Ainesley, and Scooter, we sure hope to see y'all again soon."

Virginia took the occasion to excuse herself also, to go to her room to study for a geometry exam, she said, but in truth to watch a bachelor reality show. Being properly brought up, she kissed her Aunt Marcia on the cheek, and then addressed Ainesley by carefully coached protocol. "Mr. Cody, sir, we're all so happy to see you and Scooter here. We want to see all of you again soon, y'hear?"

The Semmeses and Codys soon thereafter rose themselves and proceeded to the library for coffee, regular or decaffeinated, with or without chicory, and hot chocolate for Raphael. A variety of pecan candies, made at Cyrus's pecan grove out near Wilmer on the Mississippi line, were spread on a tray. Raphael took a generous handful, slipped some in his pocket for future survival purposes, and peeled off on his own to see if he could find any books on jungle adventure. He hit on a copy of William Beebe's *High Jungle* and scrunched up on an upholstered chair to read.

The three women—Anne, Marcia, and Charlotte—pulled their chairs close together to continue family talk. Marcia was primed for this gathering. The junior expert on Semmes lore, she was eager to share stories harvested from her mentor Aunt Jessica that afternoon.

This left Cyrus and Ainesley to square off. Given their different backgrounds and the continued anxiety of the Mobile Semmeses over the future of Marcia and Raff, there was an inevitable tension between the two men. But it went well enough. They needed no prompting, nor any reminder given by word or expression. They knew by instinct that they should seek common ground away from any topics or language associated with a privileged social class. The talk went from deer hunting, which was good this season and how bow hunting was making a revival, to red snapper fishing off Dauphin Island, not so good lately, on to the troubles between Vietnamese and local shrimpers in the Gulf waters out of Pascagoula. Ainesley had thorough knowledge of these subjects, and he handled them well, adding that he thought they were letting too many of those Asian people into the country.

By evening's end an easy peace had settled over Marybelle. Talk in the library quieted to murmurs and soft laughter, and the telling of family stories. Ainesley admitted to himself that Cyrus was a "fine man," which within families in this region meant solid, a man of probity and success. Cyrus, for his part, thought Ainesley was responsible and hardworking, enough anyway to be sufferable, and he wanted the best for him. And not least, and thereby, the best for his own blood in the Cody household.

Ainesley's judgment was not misplaced. Cyrus Semmes at forty-two had led what most would call an exemplary life. Ten years older than his sister, Marcia, he had assumed very early the traditional persona of eldest son. Ainesley was impressed that this evening Cyrus had sat at the head of the dinner table, with his ailing father to the side.

Cyrus was not physically imposing. Scarcely an inch taller than the jockey-sized Ainesley, he was naturally stocky and starting to go to flab, which strained the waist buttons of his monogrammed shirts. Nor was he handsome in the conventional sense. He had thin lips that tended to tighten when he was lost in thought, slightly hooded eyes, and thin dark hair that had made a significant retreat from his forehead. He was a habitual pencil chewer and chin scratcher. He seldom laughed. Usually he just chuckled, and then only briefly, with a slight nodding of the head. Cyrus's smile was never brilliant; it was usually bestowed as a greeting or as a reward, and then only fleetingly. He was nevertheless a polished conversationalist, which meant that he listened a lot. He focused on others with a mild and friendly repose and he listened. That relaxed people. But on the other hand his memory for detail was frightening. He could summarize a two-hour business meeting in a few paragraphs, as though reading from a script. He spoke in complete sentences, in the manner of people who do not like to be interrupted.

While at the University of Alabama, Cyrus had gone through the full course of the Reserve Officers' Training Corps, starting in the fall of 1967. After graduation, he had served three years in the army as an infantry second lieutenant, then first lieutenant, for a full term in Vietnam. He seldom spoke about this period of his life, but on Veterans Day and the Fourth of July he wore on his lapel the tricolored ribbon of a bronze star. He never regretted the Vietnam War, only the way it had been waged and lost.

Returning home after Vietnam, Cyrus entered the Law School of the University of Alabama. Afterward he joined his father's brokerage firm. He soon began a round of cautious dating, and within a year met Anne, an attractive, dignified young woman of good pedigree—the Baldwin family of Mobile and Montgomery, whose patriarchs included a Governor Baldwin in the 1890s and a full-bird Colonel Baldwin in the First World War.

Cyrus and Anne were married within six months of meeting. The event had been the lead item in the *Mobile News Register* society page. After Jonathan's first heart attack, Cyrus took over the firm as acting president. Within a year he had made his mark by launching Semmes Gulf Associates, a consulting and

investment firm, on a program of expansion across the southern tier of states from Florida to Louisiana. The eighties were
a decade of rapid economic growth in the South, and Semmes
Gulf Associates rode up with it.

As an upcoming young conservative Republican and
churchgoing Episcopalian, and not least as a decorated war veteran, Cyrus Semmes was occasionally spoken of as a possible
future governor of Alabama. He was flattered by this talk, but he
had no such aspiration. Semmes Gulf Associates had his complete attention.

As the evening wore on, the conversation slowed, infiltrated
by pauses and murmured responses with affirmative head-
nodding. Cyrus knew how to end it. He glanced at his watch,
then again a minute later, turning his wrist slightly each time.

Whereupon Ainesley rose and said, "We gotta go. I gotta be
at the store first thing in the morning, and I expect Cyrus has to
be off and running too."

"Well, yes," Marcia replied. "We hate to leave, but I just
never want Scooter to be late to school."

"Yeah, it's a long ride on a Sunday night," Ainesley added.
"You got heavy traffic almost halfway to Clayville."

On the way back Marcia noticed that Ainesley's driving was
erratic. At dinner multiple glasses of Napa Valley's best and a
snifter of Cointreau had been added to the three Millers that
had comforted him during the stopover at Aunt Jessica's. Several times Ainesley let the truck drift over the center line, then
abruptly jerked the wheel to bring it back.

Then bitterness invaded her emotions. It settled in like pol-
luted air. Each visit to Mobile, she knew, just reinforced the
understanding of her sorry circumstance. Here she was, Marcia

Semmes of Marybelle, taken away by a drunk from her birthright of status and economic security, to a four-room bungalow in a dreary small town. This would most likely be her life forever. In one catastrophic move, through her marriage, she had traded all the advantages she owned to enter a meaner world of few options.

It was not in Marcia's nature either to fight her way out of a corner or search for a life of fuller meaning by adapting to changed surroundings. Yet, though she was a passive woman not given to invention and struggle, there was one hope left to her, one grip on her past that remained to her. There was little Raphael, squeezed next to her in the cab of the pickup truck, a Semmes by blood and the incorruptible survivor of her true identity. As her gaze lifted again to the stream of oncoming headlights, she summoned a silent prayer, that her son would somehow retrieve her birthright.

7

W HAT AINESLEY SAW WHEN he first encountered
Marcia over a decade previously at the FloraBama
Restaurant was a pretty twenty-one-year-old, small,
almost tiny in stature, with the blue eyes of her father, and still
blessed with a teenage trimness. Her smile was quick and welcoming, albeit only for those who approached her first. By nature she
was relatively shy, the more so due to her sheltered upbringing.

Marcia had spent two years at Hartfield Academy, an elite
finishing school at Hattiesburg a short car trip from Mobile
across the Mississippi line. Well taught there, she had impec-
cable manners, and her knowledge of dinner arrangements
and protocol was almost professionally thorough. She fitted the
mold of her region and class. The Old Rich are more polite than
others around them. Southerners are more polite than those of
other regions. Therefore Southern Old Rich are the most gracious people in America. And egregiously proud—it has often
been remarked that Southern gentlemen and would-be gentlemen are both the best mannered and most heavily armed.

At the time she met Ainesley, Marcia was a junior at Spring
Hill College, a small Catholic liberal arts college of good reputation. The campus was within convenient walking distance of

Marybelle, with much of the route lined by live oaks and the photogenic gardens of sufficient quality to regularly make the Home and Garden section of the Sunday *News Register*.

Her social life at Spring Hill had thus far been almost entirely with other girls who themselves had not yet settled on boyfriends. Disciplined and compliant by both nature and training, she was a dutiful student, earning mostly A's and B's. Only moderately talented in art and music, she possessed a compensatory intellectual passion for American history. Her parents, Jonathan and Elizabeth, were more than a little pleased to see that from an early age she was fascinated by stories of the extended Semmes family, of Mobile, and of the South, in that order. While still in her teens, she had spent three afternoons interviewing Aunt Jessica for a research paper on Semmes antebellum genealogy.

When she came of age in the mid-1970s, America's great social revolution had already spread across the South. It had reached Mobile, and engaged the full attention of the faculty and students of Spring Hill—short of bra-burning and cafeteria sit-ins. Women were increasingly seen as capable of gaining professional and economic parity with men. Neither Marcia nor her parents, however, particularly wanted her to enter the venues now opened by this change. She was raised to be a Southern lady. Her vision of an appropriate life was to be Old South: white women of the middle and upper classes the customary rulers of the home, and men the providers.

The preferred professional venues of the best families were law, medicine, and the military, with esteem graded in each according to rank, income, or both. And all the better if a successful older son later took over management of the family estate. Business was acceptable, especially if conducted as a member of the family firm. A political career was also acceptable if taken to a sufficiently high level. Congressman, senator, or governor were excellent. Mayoralty okay, if of a decent-sized city, preferably also accompanied by membership in the Cosmopolitan Club or an equivalent elite group.

Marcia's expectations for her own eventual place were lofty. At least it never occurred to her that she might someday descend to the warrens of the proletariat. She had witnessed herself some of the great changes that were still sweeping across the South. Studying history, she knew how so much of the region had emerged from poverty, finally to join modern America only during the Second World War.

Marcia was wholly aware of the changes occurring immediately around her. She had watched the gobbling up of the highways out of town by strip malls, so that the suburbs of Mobile turned into warm-weather replicas of those around, say, Pittsburgh and Indianapolis. The rural South had been further transformed by the conquest of disease. One seldom heard anymore of hookworm, pellagra, or dysentery, the former scourges of poor country folk.

Marcia's parents could remember WHITE ONLY signs on drinking fountains. They could tell her when fast-food restaurants began to replace "cafes," and when strip malls pushed out five-and-ten downtown stores. When their own parents were young, they saw highways crowded on Saturday mornings with the mule-drawn wagons of sharecroppers, white and black, on their way to market. Now there were cars and trucks driven by employees with paychecks and credit cards in search of the best affordable satellite dish.

The voters of Alabama, currently among the most conservative states politically, had flipped in only one generation from populist Roosevelt Democrat to hard-right Republican. Marcia was used to seeing bumper stickers that advised GOD, GUTS, AND GUNS MADE AMERICA, LETS KEEP ALL THREE. On one side of the rear bumper, that is. A sticker on the other side might read SO MANY PEDESTRIANS, SO LITTLE TIME or DON'T LIKE MY DRIVING? CALL 1-800-EAT-SHIT.

But that fierceness was softening too. New homes in the best parts of Mobile and across the bay in the arts-and-literature pockets of Fairhope were as likely to be occupied by a Stanford-trained neurosurgeon or an architect from Chicago as by a scion of old wealth. They were coming in, and joined by their equals born in South Alabama. All were welcomed. They were the spearpoint of the New South.

Yet hereditary privilege and its aura persisted. In Marcia and her parents and many others of their class, a residue of antebellum glory still lingered. It could be summarized by the Three Graces of Southern Nobility. First, there was Old Family and Money; next, Gracious Living, including spacious houses surrounded by sumptuous gardens that displayed large showy flowers, and indoors featuring antique furniture passed down, not bought; and finally, the gray wool of the Confederacy. For this last, forebears were better remembered if they had been officers. If that was fortunately the case, portraits would hang in the library or along the center hallway. A general was a treasure for the ages, and lower-ranked officers were certainly acceptable,

while enlisted men were best left as add-ons during postpran-
dial conversation.

Marcia Semmes was a modern young woman but her roots
were in an antebellum ghost town. People there, if they accepted
you socially, delighted in telling you their family history. More
than the members of any other American subculture, they
wanted to discourse on their "people"—their forebears, back
more than three generations, back to participation in each war
in turn, back, if their phylogeny could be so documented, to the
English-speaking pioneers who had settled the land. And they
wanted to show you their homes, if those homes were sufficiently
large and grand, and the better if built not by themselves but a
long time ago, by their people.

Marcia's branch of the Mobile Semmeses was descended
from a cousin of the Confederate "Sea Wolf," Admiral Raphael
Semmes. Although direct descendants of the great man were
also present in her generation, and her own line was only collateral, she was later to say to Raff more than once, "Remember, son, you are what your people are." And, "You need all of
the help you can get in this life, and down here a great name
means a lot." She never admitted to herself the possibility that
Raff might eventually settle elsewhere in the world, like some
ordinary person looking for a job up north, or that the trea-
sured memory of the great man for whom he was named might
someday be reverently folded and put away for good in some safe
and remembered place along with the stars and bars of the Confederate battle flag.

· 8 ·

THE FLORABAMA RESTAURANT was a famous establishment located on the coast precisely at the line between Florida and Alabama. Out back lay a sugar-white beach and shallow turquoise water that stretched unbroken from Perdido Bay on the east all the way west to Fort Morgan at the entrance to Mobile Bay. It was already famous in the 1970s as a center of Redneck Chic, where families could eat piled-up shrimp off paper plates, and men could drink American beer directly from longneck bottles. Young lawyers and stockbrokers squeezed in at the bar among truck drivers and oystermen— among real people, in other words, the ones who actually produce and fix things for a living.

On a Saturday afternoon Marcia came to the FloraBama with a group of other Spring Hill College coeds. One of the real people present when Marcia arrived was Ainesley Cody of West Pirate Beach, Alabama, a graduate of Fairhope Senior High School and an expert automobile mechanic and part-time persimmon and strawberry picker. He was seated at a table next to the bar with four of his friends, sipping beer and rating young women as they came through the entrance. They were assigning scores from zero to ten for overall attractiveness, and planned to confer a crudely made imitation gold medal to the first one given a unanimous vote of ten. After an hour and a half without a winner, the impatient judges were arguing over whether the requisite score should be lowered to nine.

When Marcia walked in, Ainesley was startled, then riveted by the look of her. First was her petite size, matching his own. She was even smaller than Ainesley. This was an increasing rarity in the well-fed South. Most young women were his size or bigger, and they had *big feet*. Marcia's were much smaller. Her clothing size, he was to learn later, was petite small. Then, in the two-second survey hard-wired in males, he saw in sequence: nice shape, lovely face, well-groomed hair, neat clothes, graceful walk. Summary: a really great-looking young woman. Moreover, she was talking with animation, flashing an orthodontically corrected perfect smile.

"Do you see that, the one on the left?" he said to his scruffy companions. "Check it out. A perfect ten, you gotta vote ten. This one I'm gonna personally meet."

With that, he stood up and walked across the floor to the girls, who were settling at their table. Ignoring the others, straightening his shoulders, he looked into Marcia's eyes and assumed the winsome grin he had practiced so often in front of a mirror.

"Excuse me, miss. My name's Ainesley Cody and I live close to here and I come in a lot and I've just got to say, and the other fellows over there agree with me, that you are the prettiest girl that ever walked into this place. You are just terrific!"

Marcia glanced nervously left and right, then back to Ainesley with a surprised *You mean me?* expression. The other girls giggled. Several, all larger than Marcia, were thinking they were just as pretty.

Ainesley, the talented fast-talker, abruptly shifted gears. A sadness came into his face, and he continued in a calmer voice, shaking his head slowly, in mock remorse.

"Well, I guess I just made a fool of myself. Believe me, I've never just walked up to someone like this before. I hope you'll forgive me, and I apologize to you, ma'am, and to you all."

Marcia stayed stock-still. The girl to her right elbowed her in the side, laughing, then turned to Ainesley and said, "Do you mean *me*?"

Without answering, he walked back across the floor to rejoin his buddies and stood with them, making gestures and facial expressions meant to look both serious and concerned. He cautioned the others not to laugh or raise their voices. He knew Marcia and her companions would be looking his way in eager conversation of their own. He kept them in view furtively, with sidewise glances.

Later, as the girls were heading for the door, none carrying the gold medal, Ainesley eased up to Marcia, making a pleading gesture with his hands up, palms forward, and fingers spread.

"Excuse me," he said, then hesitated. He knew what he wanted to say, but in an un-Ainesley lapse was beginning to feel confused. The would-be ladies' man and casual seducer felt a pang of sincerity.

"Could I say something?"

Marcia halted politely. Two of her friends stayed with her as he finally put the words together.

"Listen, I'm sorry if I seemed rude when I came up to you.

But you do look like such a terrific person. I'd appreciate if I could just talk to you sometime, maybe get a cup of coffee, like they say in the movies. That's all." He turned his head down a bit to imply modesty, then added, "May I at least give you my name and number? And maybe could you give me yours? Just to give me a chance to talk a couple of minutes on the phone someday, that's all. And then I'm gone. I promise."

Ainesley nervously handed her a pencil and two scraps of paper torn from the table mat. One had his name and telephone number written on it, and one was for her to write hers. Marcia was flustered. This was not in her finishing-school playbook. Trying not to be rude, she took the slips of paper and said, "Thank you. Excuse me, I have to go." And walked quickly to the waiting van.

She thought, Ms. Rhodes at Hartfield would have given me an A for that. Or maybe not. Did I just make a mistake?

Ainesley caught up with one of the girls who had stayed with her, and commanded, "Quick, what's her name? Please, I'm a good guy. I just gotta know."

"Marcia Semmes."

With that innocent betrayal, Marcia Semmes's fate was sealed.

A few days later, with a telephone directory of Mobile and Pensacola, in which few Semmeses were listed, Ainesley quickly tracked Marcia down.

"Is Marcia there?" he asked on the telephone.

"No, she's at the college today," Elizabeth Semmes responded.

"Spring Hill College, I guess."

"Yes. You can reach her there. Who shall I say called?"

"A friend. I'll call her there. Thanks a lot."

Knowing he wouldn't be given her number at the school, Ainesley simply waited until the first holiday weekend and called her at home again. This time she was the one who answered.

"Yes?"

"Hi, is this Marcia Semmes?"

"Yes. Who are you?"

"I'm Ainesley Cody. We met at the FloraBama a month ago. I sort of hoped you might remember. I'm a senior at the University of West Florida, over in Pensacola," he lied. "I hope you'll forgive me, but I didn't want to bother you. After I saw you, I just wanted to talk to you, you know, maybe for a couple of minutes." He strained to sound casual. "So here I am. I won't come around or bother you or anything."

Marcia was intrigued. After all, he sounded like a nice guy, who was really, truly interested in her. She said, "Oh, no, no, that's all right. A couple of minutes is okay with me."

Two weekends later, after several telephone calls, each longer and warmer than the last, the ersatz senior of the University of West Florida showed up at the Semmes home for a first date. He was driving a new 1976 Chevrolet, on which he'd made a down payment the day before. He wore his best clothes. His hair was freshly cut and brushed. In his pocket were two tickets to a bull-riding competition in nearby Chickasaw.

Ainesley was startled by the magnificence of Marybelle, its colonnades, its spacious lawn and circular drive. When he got out of the car and searched for the street number, unaware that great houses do not as a rule display their street numbers, he found instead a bronze plaque installed by the Alabama Historical Society identifying Marybelle as a state historical site.

While Ainesley waited anxiously in the main hall for Marcia to come down the spiral staircase, her father Jonathan stepped out of the library to speak to him.

"Isn't bull-riding a rough kind of sport to take a young lady?"

Ainesley was prepared for this.

"Well, sir, I see your point, sir. It's been my experience, though, that young ladies among my friends sometimes get tired of going to concerts and stuff like that, and it's a nice change of pace for them. You can learn a lot from bull-riding."

Jonathan was worried by this response. He opened his mouth to probe some more, then let it pass. He had documents to review, and an important meeting with a committee of state senators in Montgomery the next afternoon.

Marcia joined them at that point. She was dressed in a vaguely cowgirl outfit of jeans, kerchief, and low boots.

"Oh, Daddy, I'm so excited! Have you ever been to a real rodeo before?"

"Yessir," Ainesley said. "Nothing less than the real thing."

What attracted Marcia to Ainesley was his vitality and self-confidence. Despite his bantam size, he seemed strong, able to address her father as one adult to another. That evening and later, he implied dark deals in his past he wished not to discuss. He told stories, all with a kernel of truth even if they had happened to someone else. All were richly embroidered. To Marcia, Ainesley was a man above the callow youths of her acquaintance, with a deep and significant history relative to her own meager experience. The highway was in his eyes, the airways, the sea lanes. He had destinations, he had plans, and he had connections implied but still undisclosed to Marcia. She tried to imagine, as he intended, how it would feel to be at his side during these adventures.

This persona of Ainesley was not deliberately false. It was an accretion of stories and poses, at the center of which lived undisturbed his personal sacred code. This much was unalterable: he would always meet his obligations, if at all possible, and he would never tell a lie that could hurt his family or friends. He would never assault another except in self-defense, and in conflict he would never bend to anyone if he knew he was right.

If all else came apart in Ainesley's life, the code would remain. It was the definition of his manhood and the safety net of his sanity.

What Marcia could not understand about Ainesley, nor could her parents, was that he was a commonly encountered denizen in the particular stratum of the world he inhabited, and that he was working his way through a biography appropriate to it. He would in good time settle down, but not to the end that he imagined and wished the Semmeses of Mobile to believe. Ainesley was endowed with powerful self-respect, but he lived one day at a time, and sought the pleasures awaiting him in each one. He was not a man to put off rewarding himself. Since his teenage years he had been a heavy smoker, although he could still cut back, as he now did in the presence of Marcia and her parents. He thought sipping hard liquor and holding it well to be a masculine virtue. He had occasional weekend binges, but none Marcia was allowed to see.

True to his culture, Ainesley was a gun lover. His father and paternal grandfather had gathered collections of firearms as large as the law and household space allowed. In his parents' home at West Pirate Beach hung a photograph of his grandfather with two brothers standing behind a fallen black bear, cradling their rifles in folded arms. The slain animal had been one of the last of the endangered Florida subspecies seen in Escambia County.

From early boyhood Ainesley enjoyed, along with excursions to hunt and fish, trips with his father to an abandoned farm in Jepson County to try out items from the family armory. On those occasions he was allowed to fire an old army-issue Colt .45 and a rifle used by a distant cousin during the Spanish-American War. Ainesley, then and afterward, was awed by the spectacle of objects bursting into pieces at the pull of a trigger.

Ainesley was a patriot. As a boy, he had a fantasy of wiping out pillboxes with a machine gun and grenades and marching in a victory parade down Government Street with a chest full of medals. During the Vietnam War he tried as a seventeen-year-old to join the Marine Corps, but was turned away for reasons he preferred thereafter to keep to himself.

Finally, Ainesley was a racist. But he had a way of squaring that with his code. He was a separatist, he said. He had a formula to recite when in polite company: "I got nothing against colored people; I just want to be with my own kind." Otherwise, he stayed muted and ambivalent on the subject—except when drinking in bars and on fishing trips with like-minded white male citizens.

Ainesley did, at least, have a boast-worthy pedigree. He and his close relatives claimed that there had been a Cody in every American war since the Revolution, and that might well have been true. Several of his forebears were Hodgeses, one of the clans that settled Blakeley and the fertile land of what was later to become Baldwin County across the bay from Mobile, when that city was still a mud village. Another ancestor, John Tom Cody, along with his brother Lee, were among the Mobile hotheads who joined the Alabama Artillery as soon as they heard news of the attack on Fort Sumter. Buck privates to the end, they helped lay the "hornets' nest" of concentrated cannon fire that drove back the Union forces at Shiloh. Lee was captured at Murfreesboro, but John Tom fought on despite an injured right leg. He was captured at the last battle of the Civil War, fought the day after Robert E. Lee's surrender at Appomattox and before the news reached the gathering battalions. The battle site was providentially Fort Blakeley, in South Alabama, so that John Tom had only to shoulder his rifle and other belongings and walk home in a single day. Settled back in Mobile, he married and fathered a large family.

Ainesley and Marcia's courtship proceeded uneasily under the noses of the elder Semmeses. Her parents were as beguiled as Marcia by Ainesley's charm and unfailing good manners. He returned her home on time, every time. He told her parents he was a junior executive in his father's business, and a sometime student at the University of West Florida.

Their surveillance of Ainesley was cursory. They saw the image he projected, not the real young man remaining hidden. They asked the mandatory questions, and were satisfied with the answers they got and the easy assumptions they made.

"Who are his people? The Baldwin County Codys? That's a good family," Jonathan Semmes said to Elizabeth.

He was thinking of the Codys of relatively posh Fairhope, not the Codys who inhabited West Pirate Beach on Perdido Bay a short distance away.

To the Semmeses, Ainesley relentlessly displayed what he himself considered to be his three most genuine and impressive qualities. He believed in himself, in what he said, and he was passionate about it all. Truth was whatever Ainesley thought for the moment to be factually true—that is, true for sure or mostly true, or at least very possibly true. His cocky self-confidence cut through the exaggerated good manners and foggy urbanities of Marcia's own class. Ainesley focused his energies on Marcia solely as a desirable woman. He was sexually passionate but never forced himself on her. He showed no desire to use her or her family to climb the social ladder, and, while polite to her parents, was otherwise indifferent to them. He just didn't care about anything but her, and that endeared him still more to Marcia Semmes.

Jonathan Semmes saw Ainesley's intentions the same way. He thought the young man rough cut but "up and coming." Marcia's mother Elizabeth alone remained suspicious. She called him a "zircon in the rough."

No matter. Marcia fell in love with this earnest man.

Marcia's parents learned of the depth of her feelings too late. They were uneasy about the match, but not enough to be openly hostile to so intense a romantic attachment. In any case, most of their ambitions were invested in their son, Cyrus, ten years older than Marcia, and already a vice president of the family firm. They hoped—in fact, they expected—that Marcia herself would soon end the affair and regain her freedom to meet other young men, this time of her own class.

They were therefore stunned when she announced upon returning from an evening date that she and Ainesley were engaged to be married. She found them in Jonathan's study and held up her left hand to display a diamond ring just given her by Ainesley.

"We've decided to have the wedding as soon as possible," she said.

She paused to examine their faces, her face screwed tight in anxiety. She was torn in loyalty between the two forces she was pitting in opposition.

Jonathan stood up, his mouth curling down, and started to speak. "Are you—"

Marcia interrupted quickly, "Oh, no, no. Nothing like that, Daddy. I'm not pregnant or anything like that. It's just that we love each other and want to start our life together."

She forgot to bring her left hand down, and left the ring posed in the air like a flag.

Elizabeth grabbed the arm of a chair to sit down. Jonathan tried to speak again. "Let me get this straight—"

But Marcia interrupted. "We want to keep it simple, nothing too fancy. I hope I haven't upset you too much. I'm real tired right now. Can we talk about this tomorrow?"

The necessary act had been performed, and now she could escape. She lowered her hand and busied herself with something in her handbag, then turned and rushed upstairs to her room.

Jonathan picked up the nearest telephone and summoned Cyrus, who with his wife, Anne, and their little daughters lived in the west apartment of Marybelle.

"Cy, we've got a family emergency. I need you over here in the library right away."

Cyrus arrived three minutes later, wrapped in his favorite green Chinese bathrobe, and sat. Jonathan explained what had just happened.

"The son of a bitch didn't say a thing to you, did he?" Cyrus said. "Of course he wouldn't ask permission."

"I want you to take charge of this problem, Cy. First thing in the morning, I want you to hire a private detective. You might try that outfit over on Oak Street, I think it is. Jim Holden's their attorney and they've got a solid reputation. I want a report about this guy and his family, and I want to know everything about all his people, and I want it yesterday. I think they all live over in Baldwin County, but dammit, to tell you the truth, I'm not even sure about that."

One of the rich elite of Mobile had issued a command. At the end of the day one week later, Cyrus laid a seventy-page report on Jonathan's desk.

It was not as bad as Jonathan and an increasingly distraught Elizabeth had feared. At least the Codys of West Pirate Beach were respectable. Ainesley's father, George Cody, was a certified public accountant who worked contracts along the Emerald Coast as far east as Fort Walton Beach. He had been divorced ten years. His ex-wife had remarried and now lived in Jacksonville. George had a girlfriend, a pleasant, fortyish divorcée who waited tables at a Gulf Shores restaurant and had a son of her own. Ainesley had two older brothers, both married and working in construction jobs, mostly on the Florida Panhandle. All three of the Cody brothers were solid citizens, paid their taxes, stayed out of trouble. One of Ainesley's brothers had been charged with criminal assault following a bar fight, but the charge was dropped. Ainesley was the wild card of the bunch. He'd been in some scrapes involving property damage and petty theft as a teenager, but now, at twenty-five, still had no felony record. He was known as something of a confidence man. But as far as the investigation could uncover he had not parlayed his talents into any potentially criminal scam. Basically, he was just a "bullshit artist" who liked to brag on himself to impress girls and his male companions. Otherwise Ainesley seemed passable. No wives, no girlfriends abandoned in pregnancy. He was generally regarded by the redneck circle around him as "real smart." He loved cars, was especially knowledgeable about auto parts. He'd changed jobs a lot, but not enough to be of concern, and was judged to be reliable when on a job. He had graduated from high school but showed no interest in going further.

"Well," Jonathan said to Cyrus, "let's think worst-case scenario here. Maybe if we send some breaks Cody's way, he might work out at least reasonably okay. At least it seems he won't be a disgrace to the family. I don't think! But before we go any further, let me first try to get Marcia to hold off awhile, say six months, before the wedding. You know, have a decent engagement period for the family's sake. Maybe, if she's got time to think a little more, she'll change her mind."

But Marcia would have none of it. When Jonathan suggested the delay, "for decency's sake," she gave the response he both feared and expected.

"No, Daddy. We love each other. We've got our life together all planned. We're not going to wait. Did you and Mom wait?"

Jonathan was forced to admit they hadn't. In any case, he'd already chosen not to alienate his daughter. He had decided to accept Marcia's decision and make the best of it. After all, it wasn't as though he'd been grooming Marcia or her husband, whoever that would turn out to be, to take over the business.

Upon arriving at the Loding Building an hour after the meeting with Marcia, he called Cyrus back into his office.

"Cy, we've got another crisis on our hands here. Marcie is not going to delay the wedding, and I can't force her to. She wants the wedding as soon as possible. Since your mother has to make the arrangements, we can delay the whole thing a little while, but I doubt if it can be more than two months."

"So what's the crisis?" Cyrus asked.

"Cy, surely you are joking to ask me that. I will not have my daughter living in some squalid little apartment in West Pirate Beach, and with a part-time automobile mechanic, for God's sake!"

"Well, what can we do about it?" Cyrus was still puzzled. "At least he's not some other race, or worse."

"I want you, and whatever staff around here you need, to drop what you're doing—just pass it on to someone else on the staff, if necessary—and find Cody a better job. Set him up in a little auto-repair business of his own, if that's absolutely necessary, and I want you to find an affordable small house close by that business we might buy for them, and I want the job and the house to be not too far from here, right in Mobile or a suburb close by. Do you think you can do that?"

He was standing up as he said this, and pressing the buzzer on his desk to summon his secretary.

"Yessir," Cyrus said. "I think we might manage that. I'll get started on it right away."

"Eileen," Jonathan said to the gray-haired woman entering the office, "I want you to go with Cyrus for a while and help him get started on the job I just gave him. This is top priority, and top privacy too, you understand?"

Eight days later Ainesley Cody sat in the chair across from Jonathan Semmes's desk. He had not yet graduated in status enough to cross the room and be seated with Jonathan on the sofa next to the fireplace.

"Ainesley," Jonathan began, "thank you so much for coming by." Then he paused for an answer.

"Yessir, thank you, Mr. Semmes, I appreciate it."

"First of all, I asked you to come here today to welcome you into our family."

"Yessir, thank you. I consider it a kind of an honor to be a member of the Semmes family."

"Ainesley, I believe you can understand I want the best for my daughter. Any father would. And for you too, of course."

Ainesley nodded vigorously. "Yessir." He smoothed his hair and straightened his tie.

Jonathan continued, "They tell me you're an expert on automobiles and into parts and things like that."

Ainesley continued nodding. He licked his lips nervously. "Yessir, I think I'm pretty good. I've had a lot of practice."

Jonathan smiled and nodded back. "Well, here's what we're going to do. Our company owns a nice hardware and auto parts store in Clayville, and they need an assistant manager. The pay will be pretty good, at least not bad for a young couple, and it's a steady job, with a real future. I've been speaking with Jesse Nichols, the manager, and he'd be glad to take you on. When you start up, you could get on-the-job training in marketing and such, so you'd be in a position to run a little business for starters, if everything works out."

Ainesley started to raise his hand. "Yessir, but—"

"Now, here's another thing. Jesse Nichols is close to retirement age. The job as manager will be open in a year or two, and you'd be the logical person to fill it. You might even find yourself in a position to purchase the business, given time, and maybe down the line you might want to expand some."

"Mr. Semmes—" His hand dropped back down.

"Now, here's one more thing. Elizabeth and I have been thinking about the right kind of wedding present for Marcie, and we've decided to do the following. We've found a real nice little starter house in Clayville that would be ideal for you and Marcie. Just blocks from the store. Nothing fancy, you know, but real nice. We've put down a binder fee on it, and if the job part looks okay to you, we're going to buy it for her and help give you both a really decent start in your marriage."

Jonathan Semmes paused. Ainesley remained quiet now, rendered speechless by all the largesse. New possibilities began to flow through his fertile imagination. The good life had just come within his grasp. Money, status, prestige among the other Codys and his friends.

Jonathan smiled brightly and lifted his hands, as though pleasantly surprised by his own offer. It was his favorite way of closing a deal.

"Well, what do you say? Is that okay with you? I know it will be with Marcie." In fact, he hadn't spoken to Marcie. He wanted Ainesley on his side first.

Ainesley was not a man to pass by an open door of opportunity, which in his life was rare and usually quickly closed.

"Why, that would be wonderful, Mr. Semmes. And I know Marcie will love it too."

The wedding was two months later, in St. Paul's Episcopal Church. Marcie wore an ankle-length white gown designed for her by the family's usual couturier, Thompson's on Dauphin Street. Ainesley looked sharp in rental black tie and shiny patent leather shoes. Jonathan gave his daughter away, and the elder of Ainesley's two brothers served as best man. Five of Marcie's closest friends, two from the neighborhood and three from Spring Hill College, were the bridesmaids. A surprising number of Ainesley's cousins, friends, and their families, a total of over thirty, made their appearance. An even larger number of friends of the immediate Semmes and Baldwin families, together with neighbors and friends, also showed up.

All from both sides shook hands and complimented the young couple. Elizabeth Semmes was in mild shock, deepened by one bourbon too many taken as an anesthetic after breakfast. She smiled nonetheless, and accepted congratulations. True to her upbringing, she did not break down or leave the assembly at any time. And she cried only during the ceremony, quietly, into a lace-edged handkerchief, socially correct to the end.

9

WHEN THE COUPLE returned from their honeymoon, it was to their newly purchased bungalow in
Clayville. Two ladies from the Semmes Gulf Associates staff had thoughtfully furnished it with new kitchen
appliances and basic pieces of furniture, leaving most of the
remainder to Marcia's taste. The refrigerator and cupboards
of the little house were filled with groceries. An inexpensive set
of cooking utensils, dishes, and flatware were laid out, with the
expectation that these would be replaced by Marcia. A bright
floral arrangement sat upon the kitchen table. A working telephone under the name of "Cody, Ainesley" had been placed
upon a shelf above the kitchen sink.

As they left for Sanibel Island and their honeymoon, Elizabeth had quietly handed Marcia a small leather handbag with
her name engraved on it. A checkbook showing a balance of
forty-two thousand dollars was discreetly tucked inside.

For his part, Jonathan had slipped Ainesley an envelope of
thick white linen paper embossed in gold with Jonathan's name
and the return address of Marybelle.

"This is a personal gift for you from the family," he said.
Inside was a note handwritten in precise Palmer script.

Dear Ainesley,

Welcome to our family. We debated for a while over the best wedding gift to give you personally, and finally decided the nicest would be something that aids you in your new position and family life. (We discussed this secretly with Marcie!) So if you would pick out a new pickup truck that you consider best, Elizabeth and I are looking forward very much to purchasing it for you.

Sincerely,

Jonathan Semmes

The Monday following their return from the wedding, Marcia happily set out writing to-do notes to herself and calling friends. Ainesley departed for his new job at the Clayville Hardware and Auto Parts Store. He arrived at eight A.M. on the dot, walked in, and warmly shook hands with Jesse Nichols. They sat down and chatted for a while. Then Nichols took Ainesley on a guided tour of the premises and its well-stocked shelves. They were interrupted every few minutes or so by customers. Ainesley, already familiar with most of the products, cheerfully assisted with the sales.

He noticed that there appeared to be no other employees. But just before noon a heavyset woman of about fifty came in and was introduced to Ainesley as Dolores. She proceeded to the coffeemaker, drew a cup, no sugar or cream, and settled down by the cash register. By this time Ainesley could see that the store was a nickel-and-dime operation. No matter, he thought, it's a living. In a year or two I'll be in charge, and we'll see what happens then. I'll bet I can make some serious money out of this place.

Three weeks later, Jesse Nichols telephoned Jonathan Semmes and said, "He's doing just fine, Mr. Semmes. He shows up on time, he works hard, and he seems to enjoy the job. It's certainly taken a lot of pressure off me."

Then he added, laughing, "It gives me time to go to the bathroom once in a while."

Jonathan relayed this good news to Cyrus. "Well, keep your fingers crossed, Cy. He's got serious limitations, of course, but I think eventually we might be able to move him someplace or other into middle management. And thank God Almighty, Marcie's safe. Elizabeth says she's deliriously happy."

But if Jonathan and Cyrus thought Ainesley could be remodeled into a small-bore Semmes, they were wrong.

In the years immediately following the wedding he stayed close to his young wife, but after the birth of Raphael, he began to return to the delectations of his bachelor days. Further education and financial security were not high on his list. Partying with old friends once a week were among the pleasures that meant the good life to Ainesley Cody. So were occasional one-night stands with women picked up at bars, hunting anything legal that moves, and trash fishing, where the angler drops a baited hook in and is satisfied with whatever bites. In his mind, a job was a part of life you tried to do well and something you had to do to meet obligations, but nothing you lived for. Honest compliance to a boss's orders was in his code of honor. Striving to attain his personal potential was not.

By his early forties, Ainesley's daily cigarette consumption had risen to two packs a day. That went well with three beers fortified by a frequent pint of Jack Daniel's. The index and middle fingers of his right hand were stained yellow with cigarette tar. With the addition of low-stakes poker and an aversion to unnecessary physical activity, Ainesley had grown a sizable paunch. His chances of reaching old age were growing dimmer by the year. His manner had become more abrupt and irritable. He had picked up chronic bronchitis, frequent coughing, and a shortness of breath that should have sent him to a doctor. But Ainesley disliked hospitals and didn't trust doctors. When Marcia raised the issue of his mortality he declared, "I'll go when the Good Lord calls me."

10

EETING THE CODYS each summer at Lake Nokobee, catching fragments of their conversation, I
could see that Ainesley and Marcia had reached a
point when they were barely able to hold their morganatic marriage together. Their struggle for Raff's loyalty had turned him
into a nervous, unhappy child. By the age of twelve he no longer trusted the alcoholic bravado of his father. He could not
help but contrast the relative penury of life in Clayville with the
privilege and security of the family at Marybelle. His mother's
obsession with the Semmeses' tribal glory clashed unpleasantly
with knowledge of the Semmes privileges that were denied him.
He came to reject his mother's fantasy, and made the most of
plebeian reality. The genealogy of the Semmeses held no more
interest for him than the succession of the British royalty.

Above all, Raff dreaded the possibility that his parents
might divorce. Several of his classmates at the Martin Luther
King, Jr., Grammar School had divorced parents. They seemed
all right in how they behaved, but he knew from kids' talk that
they were confused and conflicted, and often upset. Two sets of
parents were commonplace, with tangles of half-siblings and
siblings-in-law living here, living there, sometimes arguing in

other rooms and in other towns, behind closed doors. It was a nightmare that could happen. Raff just hoped Ainesley and Marcia would at least stay together, even if they fought a lot, just to avoid a catastrophe for himself.

It is natural, I understand looking back, for a child under sustained and close domestic stress to search for other venues. Some invent fantasy places of escape and survival, dream worlds in faraway places—treetops with Tarzan and Jane, a magical world at the center of the earth, a camouflaged shelter next to a pure bubbling stream in an enchanted forest. At a certain age, usually between eight and twelve, children often construct simulations of their dreams in the form of treehouses and lean-tos and teepees made of cut saplings and rope.

During pleasure drives with his parents on Sundays down the meandering byways around Clayville, Raff often had glimpses of the floodplain woodlands that lined the creeks and rivers in this coastal region. He peered as deeply as he could into their junglelike interiors. They were the Amazon and Congo of which he read, writ small. He imagined walking along one of the clear, gentle streams to a place far away, completely wild and never seen by any others, where he could live awhile.

In time, Raff recognized that he already had such a refuge. Ten minutes' drive from the Codys' home, down a side road north off Alabama State 128, was Lake Nokobee. The southern perimeter of the lake was often visited by townspeople and fishermen for recreation. Raff's parents had been taking him there on weekend picnics since he was a baby. Along the western lakeshore was a strip of nearly pristine hardwood brush. Inland from these peripheral woods stretched a large tract of longleaf pine savanna dotted with dense hardwood copses. Most people within fifty miles knew of this inland portion of the Nokobee tract but believed it to be private and off-limits. In any case, it was in their eyes little more than unhealthy piney woods and impenetrable thickets, the haunt of bugs and snakes. They believed that insects, poisonous snakes, and thorny bushes that tear your clothes were dominant elements. Beyond Nokobee lay the much larger William Ziebach National Forest. Because it was even more remote, approachable only by a single logging road on the northwest, it received even fewer visitors than the Nokobee tract.

This domain was all that Raphael Semmes Cody needed to satisfy his dreams. At the age of twelve he began to explore the Nokobee tract on his own. He went whenever he could find half a day free. He said nothing to his parents, who thought his excursions were with friends to the Clayville town center or high school recreation field.

Raphael Semmes entered the Nokobee world as a child, playfully and joyfully, without fear. He had no adult hand to restrain him. The towering longleaf pines and the wild native flora beneath them became as familiar to him as the shrubbery and gardens of Clayville. One or two snakes were always there to be caught on any given day, examined closely, and released. Raff found insects, spiders, and other arthropods of endless variety and put many in jars for temporary captivity. In spring and summer, bird nests could always be found, and a few were low enough to be monitored for eggs and nestlings. Hawks and other large birds high overhead came reliably in sight, to be watched as they drifted to unknown destinations. Herons and egrets of a half dozen species speared frogs and fish in the lake shallows. Rattlesnakes, cottonmouth moccasins, and black widow spiders provided excitement, but were to be avoided—at least, no more than poked with a long stick.

Raff dared say nothing of his adventures to Ainesley and Marcia, who if he did would learn he had lied earlier about his whereabouts and ground him. But he could confide in me, his honorary uncle. After all, he and I were doing the same thing. The difference is that I was constrained to research projects well defined in advance, in order to find and document enough new original material to publish in scientific journals. I was locked into the cycle of the professional scientist: seeking grant money to discover enough to earn more research grants. I would have liked to return to childhood and be a true explorer like Raphael. Little of what we found was truly new to science, but it was novel to him, and he was in a constant state of exhilaration.

"I want to do a complete map of the Nokobee tract," he said. "And maybe go on into the Ziebach Forest and make a list of all the kinds of plants and animals in there too. Maybe I can find new species and take photographs of snakes."

I realized that my easy acquiescence in our earlier encounters had trapped me. I couldn't break my promise to Raff by telling his parents; he wouldn't ever trust me again if I did. But I could not allow a twelve-year-old boy to go wandering secretly and alone into a wilderness like the Nokobee tract and Ziebach National Forest. So after struggling inwardly with the dilemma for a moment, I finessed my response.

"I won't tell your mom and dad, but I want a couple of promises from you in return. I don't think you realize how easily you could get lost in those places. If you had an accident you could lie out there injured or even dead for days before anybody found you. I want you to promise you'll never go beyond the trailhead and those places y'all have your picnics. And I want you to tell your dad and mom every time you go, and exactly where you'll be, and the exact time you'll come home. Now, do . . . you . . . promise me?"

"Okay," Raff said.

His prompt response startled me. I thought, He's been waiting for a grown-up to approve his plans and bring some order into his secret life.

"Raff, now let me give you some more advice on all this. Go slow. You're still very young. There are probably new species out there, all right. But take everything one step at a time. Learn the fauna and flora as you go. And above all, be real careful in everything you do. Stay away from poisonous snakes and out of the water. Take someone with you if you can, maybe your cousin Junior or some friend at school. Nokobee is a wonderful place. I just want you to stay alive to enjoy it. I want you to promise me this much."

"Yessir. Okay."

The response this time was a bit too pat. I only half believed him. But I had done what I could, and I let it go.

11

LAKE NOKOBEE WAS at that time one of the least developed bodies of water on the Gulf of Mexico coastal plain. Middling in size at twelve hundred acres, remote in location, it was surrounded by privately owned land still protected from suburban creep and several lakeside cottages on the eastern shore. Its waters, fed by small tributary streams and breakout seepage of groundwater, were unpolluted and clear. In sunlight it was possible to catch glimpses of gar and spiny softshell turtles as they glided past schools of bream hidden in submerged stands of eelgrass. Five medium-sized alligators, their territories well spaced out along Lake Nokobee's shores, sunned themselves on the banks. Because their kind had learned well from centuries of persecution, even just the distant approach of a human was enough to send them crashing into the water and out of sight. At night following heavy rains, congo eels, a kind of giant aquatic salamander, prowled through the overflow waters in search of crayfish. Six kinds of water snakes, including the poisonous cottonmouth moccasin, hunted through the shoreline vegetation and shallows for frogs and small fish. Lake Nokobee was an unspoiled aquatic ecosystem, unchanged from what it might have been at this spot five thousand years before.

At the northern tip of Lake Nokobee a narrow creek flowed out through a thicket of broadleaf cattails and primrosewillow. The unnamed stream traveled onward in the shade of a dozen species of scrub hardwood along its banks and the interlacing canopies of hardwood trees higher above. Its waters meandered thence north to join the Chicobee River, a tributary of the Perdido River, whose broad strong waters then flowed straight south to define the Alabama-Florida border all the way to Perdido Bay.

The shoreline of Lake Nokobee bulged outward into a dozen small inlets. Each was lined with aquatic grasses and sedges and thin strips of hardwood thickets. The largest, located at the lake's southern edge, was Dead Owl Cove—or Dead Owl Slough, as some old-timers still called it. The name of the cove, which, granted, is peculiar even by Southern standards, was widely believed to be just a mapmaker's whimsy—or just as likely an early cartographic misprint of Dale Arle, or even Dale Errol. There had been both Arles and Errols in nearby Jepson County, Alabama, since before what often was still elliptically called The War. Dale Arle (or Errol) himself was a somewhat shadowy figure, who in the late 1700s explored northward by skiff from the Gulf Coast along the floodplain forest of the Blackwater River, running down east of the Escambia and parallel to it. According to oral tradition—any possible written documents were destroyed in the Jepson County Courthouse fire of 1883—he camped for a while at the southern edge of Lake Nokobee. No one knows why he went there, if he really did, or what he hoped to find.

Dead Owl Cove—too late to call it anything else now—was at the end of a dirt road that led out of cornfields into one of the last remaining tracts of old-growth longleaf pine.

One of the most prominent forms of wildlife at the cove, if I may stretch that loose zoological term a bit, was a kind of ant species whose colonies built conspicuous mound nests along the banks of the lake. The species was and remains widespread but very locally distributed across the Gulf Coastal Plain. It could be found associated with longleaf pine in sites all around Lake Nokobee, with the highest concentration at Dead Owl Cove. The lakeside soil, a well-aerated mix of sand, clay, and humus, was ideal for native plant and insect life. The exposure of the nests to the sun's warmth in its open spaces gave the ants an early start in the season and each morning on warm, dry days.

These anthills are special to the history I have chosen to record. They were to play a principal role in the life of Raphael Semmes Cody, and, even more remarkably, in the ultimate survival or destruction of the Nokobee environment itself.

The relative openness of the Dead Owl Cove shore was not due to frequent human activity. It was both ancient and natural. The tract around the cove was a tongue of the much larger stretch of longleaf pine habitat that stretched west from the lake all the way into the William Ziebach National Forest. The grassy high pine woodland was more savanna than forest, with scattered pines of varying girth, the older ones with flat tops and the youngest forming clusters on the landscape. The space between the pines was filled with bunches of wire grass and a veritable garden of ground plants—croton, bluestem, dogfennel, three-awn, beargrass, Florida dogwood, and many more, all bestowed delightful names by English-speaking settlers. Pond pine, myrtle-leaved holly, titi, tall gallberry, and pond cypress clumped together to form occasional low-bottomed, seasonally flooded hardwood islands called domes. Sparse it may seem on casual examination, the longleaf pine savanna is nevertheless biologically one of the richest botanical environments of North America. As many as 150 kinds of plants, almost all located in the ground-level cover, can be found in a single hectare. Many of these species are endemic to this habitat. That is, they are found in no other place on earth.

The Nokobee tract harbored in full array the signature animal species of the longleaf pine savanna. There were the bobwhite quail, beloved of hunters with retrievers and shotguns. Their numbers were declining, ironically not from overkill but by the assault of increasing numbers of coyotes and other predators that flourish around human populations. Also on the list were spadefoot toads, nocturnal cat-eyed ambushers of ground-dwelling insects. They gathered in rain pools to breed during a short season, summoning one another with wailing calls that sounded like a chorus of the damned. Gopher tortoises dug long burrows that were miniature ecosystems all on their own, and were the preferred home of indigo snakes, gopher frogs, and strange creatures such as a kind of ant that feeds on the eggs of subterranean spiders.

Among the inhabitants of the Nokobee tract were species that were rare, even endangered. The most famous was the red-cockaded woodpecker, which built its nests within cavities high in large longleaf pines. The most impressive in size and appearance, aside from the occasional bear that might wander through, was the heavily muscled indigo snake, its length reaching seven feet, its body blackish gunmetal blue. The indigos emerged from the tortoise burrows and consumed a variety of prey that included smaller members of their own species. At the opposite extreme among the reptiles in size and appearance was the mole skink, a subterranean lizard with vestigial legs, reaching a maximum length of six inches, and resembling an armored earthworm. So secretive was the species that it was almost never seen except by expert naturalists.

To this distinctive part of the longleaf pine fauna can be added three kinds of ants: the spider-egg eater of the tortoise burrows; a species that lived in pine trunks and canopy and served as a major source of food for the red-cockaded woodpeckers; and finally, the mound-building ants, whose colonies lived on the shores of Lake Nokobee.

The exquisitely beautiful and biologically rich pine flatland at Lake Nokobee was only a tiny remnant of what was once the dominant habitat of the Gulf of Mexico coastal region. For thousands of years it covered sixty percent of the plain from the Carolinas to Texas. Its rolling expanse was interrupted only by hardwood forest strongholds, principally the tributary ravines of rivers, streams, steepheads cut deep in sand by outbreaks of groundwater, and the cypress-dominated floodplains of the principal watercourses. There were also the countless domes growing in and around moist depressions that filled with rainwater in the winter and dried out by late spring. Stumpholes, the last decaying remnants of fallen pines, were homes to a small fauna all of their own.

For Indian tribes the longleaf pine savanna was a source of life. They could hunt the buffalo and white-tailed deer that teemed within it. For the first Spanish explorers it was a highway through the Florida Panhandle along which they thrust their way with horse and armor into unknown lands north and west. In the eighteenth and early nineteenth centuries the flatland yielded much of its space to the early English and American farmers. Then, following the Civil War and on through the next half century, the magnificent tree species that formed its centerpiece and helped sustain its integrity was almost all cut down. Longleaf pine has the misfortune of being both easily harvested and ranked with redwood, cypress, and white pine as one of the finest of North American timber species. Great fortunes were made by land and mill owners from its destruction. The timber barons enriched investors in both the Southern and the Northern cities. They built plantation-style mansions and helped lift the South from its deep poverty. When they were done, however, they left behind a wasteland of stumps overgrown by weedy stands of slash and loblolly pine, among which grew up an often impenetrable hardwood brush. Such was the secondary growth that surrounded the pristine longleaf pine area at Dead Owl Cove and most of the eastern perimeter of Lake Nokobee. But to the west of the lake on the Nokobee tract and into the Ziebach National Forest for almost two miles, the longleaf pine grassland remained close to its original state.

Odd as it may seem, fire was and remains the friend of the ancient longleaf savanna. Without human interference, lightning strikes set off fires at frequent intervals, which then spread slowly through the surface detritus. The richly diverse natural ground vegetation not only survived the low-intensity burnoffs, it needed them every several years to sustain growth and a dominant presence. This was the phenomenon that I and Alicia, my wife—and an experienced ecologist herself—studied for so many years on the Nokobee tract. We were able to confirm with detailed records that when natural fires are suppressed, the invading trees and shrubs set seed and start to overgrow the original flatland ground vegetation. Within a decade, the dense scrub takes over, dominated by slash and loblolly pine, water and laurel oak, sweetgum, and a host of other shrub and small tree species. The new woodland builds up a thick litter of fallen leaves and tree branches. Much of the layer is suspended high enough off the ground to be well aerated and easily dried out. It becomes superb tinder, so that when a fire is started it can flare into a wildfire, raging outward, clawing up to the canopies of the smaller trees, and leaping roads and streams to bring biological destruction to a vast area.

The longleaf pine savanna, renewed almost continuously by lightning-sparked ground fires, has existed as an ecosystem for thousands, possibly millions of years. Its stability and equitable conditions have allowed the evolution of an abundance of ground flora and animals closely adapted to it. Once the cycle of ground fires and regrowth is broken, however, it is lost and cannot be easily restored. It is fragile, and the last of it might easily be wiped away.

· 12 ·

THE BONDING OF Raphael Semmes Cody to the Nokobee tract began when as a small child he came to Dead
Owl Cove with his parents for their weekend picnics.
There at the water's edge Ainesley and Marcia would sit and talk,
smoke cigarettes, and occasionally fish for bream and large-
mouth bass. Little Raff was turned loose to wander about on his
own. His mother let him go, but each time with the same sen-
sible command.

"Stay in sight. And you come right back when you're called,
you hear? Keep away from the water and don't go in the bushes.
Watch out for snakes! Come running if you see a snake!"

Raff, as best he could without getting caught, disobeyed all
of these injunctions, as he later admitted to me and Alicia. He
undertook what small children do when stripped of mechani-
cal toys and playmates and placed in a natural environment.
They explore. They become hunter-gatherers. If they are fearless, and Raff was innocently fearless, they discover a multitude
of creatures of kinds they have never seen in a zoo or picture
book or on television, and for which there is no name. Each
kind of plant and animal, because of the immediacy and its nov-

elty and strangeness, is for a small child an entity of boundless possibility.

Raff began a rich self-education in natural history by happenstance at Nokobee. While still little more than a toddler, he spotted a velvet ant running swiftly in a straight line over dead leaves at the woodland edge. The insect was the size of a hornet and wore a thick red and yellow coat of hair. Unknown to him, it was not an ant. It was a wingless parasitic wasp, a female searching for beetle grubs to serve as hosts for its own larvae. Raff dashed to this prize, bent over, and grabbed it with his hand. And was instantly shocked by the velvet ant's quarter-inch-long stinger. He dropped the wasp, which continued on its way as though nothing had happened. His stung hand felt on fire. He sat down and cried from the pain—but softly, so he could not be heard. When he rejoined his parents an hour later, the hand still throbbed, but he said nothing. He knew that if he did tell the story, his parents would make him stay put with them on future visits.

The velvet ant taught Raff an elemental principle of natural history: don't mess with colorful creatures who show no fear of you. On a later occasion, the Cody family terrier learned the same lesson from a self-confident skunk that passed through their yard clad in a loudly striped pelage of black and white. These rabbit-sized animals snuffle along the ground in daylight, searching for food in grass and fallen leaves. They move very calmly for a wild animal, as though oblivious to enemies. If a dog tries to seize one, the skunk doesn't stab it with sharp canine teeth, nor does it rip the dog's skin with razorlike claws. Instead it lifts its long tail and sprays the dog with a musky mercaptan from its anal glands. The stench lasts for days. Some dog owners say it can be removed by washing the dog's fur with tomato juice.

I don't know. Never owned a dog, and I always stayed a good distance from skunks.

One summer day when he was a little older, as both families sat in a circle of chairs for lunch, Raff asked me an interesting question about the velvet ant.

"Uncle Fred, if pretty colors tell you an insect has a sting and you should stay away, why don't butterflies have a sting?"

It was a strain to come up quickly with an answer for that one.

"Butterflies can fly away when you get too close," was the best I could manage. "Velvet ants can't fly; all they can do is sting you and teach you a lesson. Birds can catch butterflies, but then they learn the lesson a different way. Some kinds of butterflies taste terrible, they're even poisonous, so the birds learn which ones to stay away from. Some of the prettiest butterflies you see flying around here at Dead Owl Cove are like that."

Later in the summer of the velvet ant, Raff was startled when a red-shouldered hawk flew low over his head carrying a dead field mouse in the talons of one foot. The next week he came upon a water snake swallowing a frog. The lesson he learned was that animals die in nature, and some die in order for others to live.

Raff discovered that when he turned over small rotting logs, he was rewarded with the sight of hundreds of insects and other tiny creatures that hide there. When exposed, some froze in place. Others leapt away or ran off to hide in the surrounding leaf litter. Woodlice, the little crustaceans often called pill bugs, and millipedes, also known as thousand-leggers, rolled themselves into armored spheres. Centipedes, or hundred-leggers, as they are often called, slithered to safety like miniature snakes, halting at the first object that covered their bodies. None of the tiny animals attacked Raff; all were afraid of him.

Raff never succumbed to the "icky factor," by turning away from anything, even the slime-dripping slugs. On the contrary, he never tired of grubbing under logs and other debris like this, over and over. Every excursion yielded something new. He learned that most animals in nature are very small and live underground. He put spiders in jars and watched them spin webs. The most common denizens of the subterranean byways, he noticed, are ants, which come in several sizes and colors. He put some in a jar of soil and watched them dig tunnels.

Nature works, Raphael learned, because it has order, and from order, it has beauty. Little birds sing in the morning. Cicadas shrill in the afternoon, and katydids rasp at night. Crickets come forth at twilight to chirp in the grass. And lantern flies write dots and dashes with their on-and-off luminescent abdomens through the black air of evening, flashing brighter than the stars in a moonless sky. Each creature, Raff came to understand, has a clock. Every passing hour retires some of the players and brings forth others.

In one important sense, Raff's learning process was ordinary. It was also primeval. For two hundred thousand years or more of their prehistory, human beings had to learn a great deal the way Raff did in order to survive. Stone Age parents could speak of what they knew, but they could not leave an enduring written record. Their mathematical prowess was limited to counting, perhaps to "one, two, many"—if that far. Travel beyond the tribal boundary rarely occurred and was undertaken at great risk. Geographic knowledge stopped at a river's edge, a mountain ridge, or strip of gallery forest. Beyond lived people who spoke and dressed differently. They were deceivers, the locals could tell you, and poisoners, and cannibals. They were ruled by demon-gods.

Such ignorance did not extend, however, to the living world. The tribe had to have near-encyclopedic knowledge of all of the important plants and animals within their home range in order to survive. To keep everything straight, hundreds, even thousands of species had to be given names. If an ordinary person could not master all that knowledge, elders and shamans could be called on to serve as the tribe's walking archives.

Although spirits and mythic histories were imputed to many of the plant and animal species, practical information about them remained exact. It was regularly retested by experience. A single fragment of misinformation could result in disaster. Every child knew answers to the kinds of questions never asked a modern child. Where do camouflaged vipers wait for prey? Which of the many kinds of mushrooms are edible, and which are deadly? Where can you find the deep-growing tubers that carry us through in times of drought? And where do you dig for water? Such was the proto-science acquired by children through talk and imitation, and picked up still more by cautious individual exploration on their own.

That was the quality of Raff's Nokobee self-education, which his parents mistook for frivolous child's play. It was enjoyable, and thereby true to the way the brain is constructed. It was ordained by genes to which modern classrooms and textbooks are ill-fitted.

Raff's learning was kinesthetic, by which is meant it employed action that engaged all the senses, and it was channeled by instinct. As Uncle Fred Norville, his mentor, I could

ask him, *What is the best way to learn a frog?* And say, *Not by reading.
Not by seeing a picture or even by holding one in your hand. To learn a frog
in a full and lasting manner, you must find one where it lives in nature, watch
it, listen to it if it is calling. Study its habitat, Raff, take note of where it has
chosen to sit, stalk it, capture it, put it in a jar, and keep it a little while. Study
it there, release it next to the edge of the water where you found it, watch it kick
away and submerge out of sight. The concept of frog will be with you forever if
you follow this kind of education. You can pick up additional information from
science and literature and myth, and all those things you have at school, but you
will be wiser for being rooted in the full reality of frog. You will care about frog
too, like nobody else.*

It was predictable that Raphael Semmes Cody should seek
the company of those who saw the world as he did, and for which
I offered him encouragement. On the earliest possible date, his
twelfth birthday, he joined the Boy Scouts of America.

Both parents were pleased with the decision, and I added
affirmation.

"It'll teach you how to get along with other people," Ainesley
said to Raff. "You spend too much time by yourself. You'll learn
how to do some grown-up things. Come graduation from high
school, it'll help you get into West Point or someplace like that,
in case you thought about going into the military."

Marcia wasn't keen on the military aspect, but otherwise was
happy to see this sign of ambition in her son, and the status it
might give him early on.

As a former Boy Scout myself, who stayed into my late teens
and achieved the rank of Eagle Scout, I could not have been
more pleased.

"You've got to understand," I said to Ainesley and Marcia
when we met again at Nokobee, "this organization was made for

Raff. You know he's a boy who just loves the outdoors, and he's already learned an amazing amount of natural history for a kid his age. He'll fit right in, and I may be wrong, but I'll bet he's going to do wonderfully well."

I can't say I score very high on predicting human behavior, but this time I turned out to be right. The Boy Scouts of America don't run a boot camp, which would have repelled Raphael Semmes Cody. They don't sit you down for scheduled tests, which boys naturally detest. They don't discriminate or try to classify you by intelligence, or talent, or anything but your own personal effort. Effort and achievement move you through the ranks, and at your own speed. From Tenderfoot (nobody wants to stay a Tenderfoot) to Second Class (nobody likes the sound of that either), then First Class, Star, Life, and finally to Eagle Scout. Tests are self-paced. If you fail at first, no problem. Work at it some more with one of the scout leaders, and try again.

Raff was able to move quickly upward by himself or in small groups, reporting his progress in each rank to the scoutmaster. The merit badges, forming the main steps to the advanced ranks, rewarded achievement in a manner suited to the orderly development of the adolescent mind. To Raff's delight they included the outdoor activities for which his talents and passions were best suited. Swimming, lifesaving, hiking, campcraft, pioneering, first aid, zoology, botany, and entomology, each was mastered and its badge added to the growing rows on his uniform's sash.

The Boy Scouts did something else that was important as well. They legitimized the life for which Raff had been unconsciously preparing himself. They bestowed a spiritual and a social blessing upon the wildness of Lake Nokobee.

13

RAPHAEL SEMMES CODY was a citizen, I said to his parents one summer day, if any member of the human race can be called that, of the Lake Nokobee wildland. He came to know it better than the neighborhood of his home five miles away, better than the classrooms and playing fields of the schools he attended. He loved this tract of land as though it were his own, and he knew deep in some seldom-visited part of his reflective mind that if he ever failed in the venues of ordinary life, he could return to the solace of his life membership in the Nokobee wildland.

As Raff matured, inevitably he became a naturalist explorer, and a scientist. He came to know when the wild azaleas bloomed; which flowers were favored by the dogface sulphur, Gulf fritillary, and other butterflies; which salamanders came to the vernal pools, and when. He knew the habits of the strange creatures hiding in the deep sandy burrows of tortoises. He was privy to secrets of the toad-eating hognose snakes, which are dead ringers for poisonous pit vipers but in reality as harmless for people as a stick of dead wood. Red-tailed skinks and all other lizards were harmless too, he found. You'd never touch one anyway, because they ran from you like the wind to their retreats in piles of fallen tree limbs. Up in the longleaf pine canopies red-cockaded woodpeckers feasted mostly on ants nesting there in the millions. The minnows that schooled in the shallows of the lake had a name and a place in the food chain two links down from the five alligators that patrolled the shores.

Bachman's warblers once nested in swampy canebrakes of the South but were now extinct. The last one had been seen in 1965. Or so it was said. But perhaps they were not completely gone. Raff believed that maybe they weren't really. Maybe a lucky naturalist like him could be rewarded for long hours at Noko-bee by the insectlike buzzing of their song and the glimpse of a survivor.

Ivorybills, the largest of America's woodpeckers, were supposed to be extinct too. But who could say for sure? Uncon-firmed sightings had been reported in the Choctawhatchee floodplain forest east of Nokobee. Maybe, Raff said to me, he might be the one to recognize the distinct call, like a toy flute, *peet! peet!* deep in the outflow woodland of Lake Noko-bee, then hear the loud double-hammer strike of a beak as the bird peeled the bark back and uncoiled its long tongue to seize a beetle grub lying hidden. Then he would look up through the foliage to see a pair working their way among the dead hard-wood trees standing there, their long white beaks working as organic drills, their flashing white feathers on the upper wing surfaces plain to see, like the field guides said. Then he would understand why they were sometimes called the Lord God bird. "Lord God, what is that?" settlers were reported to say when they first saw one.

Raff would tell you if you asked him that the woods at Noko-bee were safer than any city street. Yet they were far from being any kind of a real-life Disney World. Nothing was posed in those woods. Nothing present was crafted by human hands. Habitats like this one had existed across the South for many thousands of years before any human being set foot on the continent of North America. No human hand or mind could begin to duplicate even a small part of such a place.

On Raff's thirteenth birthday Ainesley presented him with a Model 1938 Red Ryder lever-action air rifle. It would change Raff's relationship to the Nokobee fauna. The rifle had a capacity of 650 BBs—small rounded metal pellets, powered by air pressure built by working the lever and fired one at a time. From the instant he held it, Raff was enchanted by the very idea of a personal weapon. It was not like his father's cannon-sized shotgun that had so frightened him three years earlier. The Red Ryder was his size, and it belonged to *him*, Raphael Semmes Cody. He felt a primordial surge of unfamiliar emotion. The gun was power, not earned, not promised, but instantaneously passed from one hand to another.

When Marcia first saw the Red Ryder, Raff was clutching it against his body at port arms, savoring its weight and balance. She clapped her hands to the sides of her head and shouted, "Ainesley, what in *God's* name have you done?"

Raff turned away to remove the offending weapon from her inspection.

"You promised. You *promised* me! Do you want to get him killed? Or kill somebody else?"

Ainesley shook his head as in disbelief, while holding up his hands with palms turned up to placate his wife.

"Nonono," he said. "You don't understand. This isn't a real gun. It can't hurt anybody. It don't shoot nothing but little BBs at targets. Even if it hits somebody, it can't do nothing but raise a little welt."

Marcia came right back, "He could blind someone!"

"No, no, that won't happen. Look here, you can hurt somebody with almost anything. Even a screwdriver. Even a pencil, for God's sake. All Raff has to do is to be a little bit careful. It's time he learned at least something about guns. It's time he took a little responsibility about things like that."

Raff was easing out of the room, thinking about where to hide his treasure in case this dispute turned out badly.

"I've told you a thousand times if I've told you once," Marcia came again at Ainesley, "I don't want him growing up like some kind of a savage. I want Raff to have a better life, and while I'm at it, when he gets older I want him to live in a better, safer place than we have around here."

"You mean you want to live with your goddamn fancy family in Mobile. My own people aren't good enough for you."

Then Ainesley caught himself. They couldn't afford to blow up with Raff in hearing range, and him the subject of the fight.

"I know how you feel," he said, "and I'm not going to take any offense. But let me ask you, use some common sense. We live here and not down there in Mobile, and Clayville's where I make our living."

Marcia tightened her mouth, struggling for equanimity and the right response.

Ainesley, seeing her pause, pressed the initiative. "Look here, half the boys in Clayville Scooter's age own a BB gun like this one. If we was living in downtown Mobile that's one thing, but we live here in Clayville, and Scooter's got a right to grow up in a normal way like other boys."

Ainesley and Marcia went on like this for a while, cooling off slowly. Raff was by that time in his room out of earshot, examining the Red Ryder, sensing he was going to keep it, thinking about the meaning of it all. *Soldier in the army, Sergeant—no, make that Captain—Raphael Cody. A sniper, picking off charging enemy soldiers, machine guns rattling to the side. A hunter, having closed to within the killing range of a ten-point buck, hunter friends admiring him, watching as he took very . . . careful . . . aim. A man with power, a hero.*

After a half hour more of debate, flare-ups, pauses, and back-and-forth, his parents reached a compromise and called him out. Raff could keep the gun if he used it only to shoot at targets set up on the backyard fence, with his father supervising.

Right after dinner Raff was out in the backyard with his Red Ryder. Ainesley showed him the simple procedure of firing an air gun. Pour the BBs into the chamber, pump the lever, aim, shoot, pump the lever, aim, shoot. Continue for up to 650 times before reloading.

Raff took quickly to this routine. The vestigial shame of the shotgun incident during the turkey hunt faded completely as his father guided him. The last residue of his earlier fear was also soon gone. He found deep pleasure in simply pulling a trigger, then seeing a physical impact far away. It was a kind of control he had never experienced. It was precise, and far better than slingshotting a stone.

He kept going the next day, this time without Ainesley and whenever Marcia was busying herself at some task away from the back door. His aim improved steadily. Raff, it turned out, was a born marksman. He thought himself one of those keen-eyed Southerners of olden times described to him by Ainesley.

Raphael's imagination soon led him from Red Ryder in the backyard to Red Ryder at Nokobee. He could be a *real* hunter! Maybe without actually killing anything, just stunning them and letting them recover. There were lots of small animals at Nokobee that were so elusive and fast it was next to impossible to catch one with your hands. Five-lined skinks and six-lined race runners, the sprinters among lizards, were so alert that almost as soon as you saw them they were gone—vanished into a wood-pile or tangle of scrub. Green anole lizards were mostly seen perched on tree trunks. Like squirrels, they were able to scoot to the other side and up above you before you got close enough to grab them. Water snakes were poised to race into the lake shallows by the time you came within ten feet, and you almost never saw them again.

The escape strategies were hereditary. For millions of years their ancestors had been stalked by predators a great deal faster than Raff. Few of these experts in surveillance and escape had ever been caught by unaided human effort. Now maybe Raff could catch them at will and hold them in his hands for close study.

Raff told his mother he wanted to take his Red Ryder into Clayville Center to show to his friends. He offered to let her hold on to his ammunition, the BBs, as a guarantee. He didn't mention the spare cylinder he carried in his pocket.

When she gave her reluctant permission, Raff placed the gun across the handlebars of his bicycle and rode out of the driveway. He turned in the direction of Atmore Street and the town center, in case Marcia was watching from the window. He proceeded on to the first street corner, then out of sight of the house, cut ninety degrees at the next corner, rode one street over, and continued on toward Nokobee. After twenty-five minutes' hard cycling he arrived at the trailhead.

As usual at this time of day, there was no one else at Dead Owl Cove. Raff walked onto the trail around the west side of the lake and off it, into the forest. He held his head up, staring this way and that. He gripped the air rifle in both hands, ready to pump and fire. He entered the hunter's trance, scanning now back and forth, up and down, his senses open for any sign of an animal that might be a suitable target. A giant sulphur butterfly—hard to catch even with a net—flashed across the trail in front of him and alighted on a flowering bush. It was big and showy, but he paid it no attention. Close by, a murder of crows began quarreling. Their loud clamor meant nothing to the searching rifleman.

A skink started up and raced a short distance down the trail before halting. A target! Raff froze. He raised the rifle slowly and carefully. But the little lizard, watching his movements intently, sprinted into the undergrowth and disappeared.

Farther along the trail, Raff spotted a green anole lizard resting on the trunk of a small pine. It was a large male, pumping its scarlet dewlap up and down, the instinctive response to a male encroaching its territory. At fifteen feet it was a perfect target. Raff turned around so his back was to the target and his arm movements could not be seen. He pumped the lever of the gun, turned back slowly, aimed at the lizard just behind its front legs, and fired. The lizard flipped off and fell to the ground. Raff ran over and laid it in his open hand. He examined it closely, pulled the red dewlap out, and let it fold back.

There was a small tear in the skin just back of the left shoulder, with the skin pinched upward. The pellet had evidently struck at an angle and bounced away. Raff was unsure whether the lizard was dead or just stunned. He placed it gently on the ground and moved on in search of his next trophy. No candidate was found, and after an hour Raff returned home.

Over the next several excursions, Raff stayed most of each day, stunning or killing dozens of lizards, small snakes, and one tree frog that he knocked off a pine branch too high to reach by hand. He looked up the victims in a set of field guides he kept at home. When finally he was tired of this level of wildlife slaughter, he turned to sparrows and other small birds. In this endeavor he was consistently unsuccessful. The targets were usually constantly in motion. They kept too far away, and at the distances he could approach, thick feathers shielded their bodies too well for the pellets to have much effect.

Raff intensified his effort to kill or at least capture a bird. Finally, he found an ideal target. It was a tiny golden yellow bird perched on a low branch in a swampy portion of the lakeside scrub. It stood stock-still, calling in a continuous monotone, *Sweet, sweet, sweet* . . . Raff raised the rifle into firing position, stock to his shoulder, and walked in slow motion toward the bird. When he had closed within fifteen feet, he took careful aim at its head, remembering his father's advice when bringing down the guinea hen several years previously. Always shoot for the head. Raff squeezed the trigger. There was a slight pop, and the bird leaned to the side and fell to the ground.

Raff walked over and picked up his trophy. Lying in his open hand, the bird looked up at him with expressionless eyes.

It struggled but could not get up. Its left wing hung low, obviously broken. He had struck the bird's shoulder. Its legs quivered slightly, seemingly paralyzed.

Raff was faced with an unpleasant dilemma. If he took the bird home and tried to nurse it back to health, his parents would see it and know he'd been lying about the rifle. If he just left it on the ground, it would suffer before it died, maybe taking a long time. There was only one solution: kill it, put it out of its misery.

Raff lay the bird down and fished out a National Park Service notebook from his hip pocket. He made a rough sketch of the bird and wrote down the color: deep yellow with blue-gray wings. Then he brought the muzzle of the air gun to within six inches of the eye of the bird and pulled the trigger. He glanced down and saw that its head was thrown back. Its body was still. Without touching it he turned abruptly and walked away, mounted his bicycle, and rode home.

Back in his room, Raff thumbed through his field guide and found a perfect match for the fallen bird: *male prothonotary warbler*. He had brought down a prothonotary warbler, and while it was looking at him, while it was singing. Raphael Semmes Cody, big-time hunter, had bagged a prothonotary warbler.

By supper that evening, the excitement of stalking and shooting a bird had died completely. It was replaced with shame. Struggling with that emotion, he had a revelation. With his little gun he had taken power over Nokobee. It had been so easy. Now, suppose, he thought, he had a better weapon, say a .22 rifle; he knew boys only a little older than himself who did. With it he could kill birds easily, shoot anything at all he wished out of the trees. He could roam the woodland back and forth until he hunted down almost all the birds and everything else that moved. Any person could do that, any boy could kill part or the whole of it.

Then it came to Raff with sickening clarity that Nokobee was not at all the edge of an infinite nature he envisioned as a younger child. It was just a tract of land that could be walked from one end to the other in an hour. The Nokobee he loved was a fragile entity, and today he had thoughtlessly disturbed its grace and beauty.

14

A S MUCH AS RAFF loved the creatures of Nokobee, none of his fellow citizens there loved him back. All of the birds, lizards, and mammals were frightened by even his most cautious approach. They either moved along to keep their distance or else they tensed, ready to run or fly to safety in a split second. Except for an occasional snake or turtle rendered torpid by a winter chill, or a frog hiding among waterweeds, he found it almost impossible to stalk and touch an animal of any kind. Surely they would be pleased to see this giant intruder fall down dead. And if he did perish at Nokobee, a dozen kinds of scavengers would come to fight over his body, rendering it down to the last fragments of flesh and skin, until only the skeleton was left, and that too would in time be strewn about by scavengers and covered in humus by rivulets of the unfeeling rain.

Nokobee was nevertheless perfectly safe for people. Well, *almost* perfectly safe. You could walk the length and breadth of the tract for days or weeks, step anywhere, come close to any object that caught your eye, and suffer no ill consequence. Statistically, however, if you came back enough times and stayed cumulatively long enough, and if you were consistently careless to boot, then in a flash, and likely for some mundane reason, Nokobee could cripple or kill you.

One day, when he was fifteen years old, a few weeks after his trip with Junior Cody down the Chicobee, Raphael Semmes Cody learned this harsh lesson of cumulative probability. While taking one of his frequent hikes around the lake, he saw an unusual animal submerged in shallow water a foot from the shore. It appeared to be a medium-sized frog with a dark cross-shaped pattern on its back. This was the kind of discovery Raff was primed to make. Totally focused, he stepped close and slowly extended a hand to seize what now was certainly an animal of an unfamiliar kind. At the last moment he was surprised to see a large cottonmouth moccasin less than a foot from the frog. The snake, coiled in a clump of sedges, was evidently stalking the same animal.

In an eye blink there it was, all very familiar in form but in a new context, terrifying, seen from this close monstrous in size, the body woven through the aquatic stems of the sedges, the tawny bands of its species spaced along its blackish brown flanks, the coarse keeled scales of its upper surface fitted together like armor, and dry, not slimy or wet. The triangular head was swollen behind by the poison-filled oral glands, the mouth fixed in a mirthless smile. In another eye blink the snake lunged, its head coming like a spearpoint on the uncoiling neck and straight and fast as though a stone thrown by a hand. The maw opened wide, its lining dead white as shaded snow. The fangs unfolded and unsheathed, transforming the whole of the snake into a perfect predator, an instrument of death. In reflex Raff started to pull back but could move his hand no more than an inch or two when the snake struck.

Its fangs did not hit Raff directly. They passed through the top of one of the rolled cuffs of his shirt, spurting venom on the cloth instead of into flesh. Then they became entangled in the cloth as the moccasin tried to pull them out. In an instant the snake gnashed its jaws a second time, and Raff jerked his arm all the way back, causing the tips of both of the fangs to scratch the skin on his wrist as the cottonmouth pulled free.

There followed a splash and a swirl of water, and both the snake and frog were gone, each in a different direction. Raff fell back, squirming away from the lake edge with a frantic push of arms and legs. The enormity of what had happened, spanning less than five seconds, was stamped crystalline-clear in his mind, and it would remain so forever. He felt the rush of adrenaline, and his mind dissolved into a confused jumble. He'd been bitten by a deadly snake! Not a full strike, but the venom-laden fangs had broken the skin. He had no idea what was to follow. He might faint before he could make it out of Nokobee and find help. He might die. He got up and started to walk back to the trailhead. Don't run, he remembered, that would speed up the heart and circulate venom through his body faster. What about getting the venom out? He stopped and sucked on the scratches for a few seconds. He had a knife, and he thought maybe he could cut into the scratches and suck the blood from around them. Then he remembered reading that this old method doesn't work very well. It could even push the venom more deeply into the bloodstream.

The bite of a big poisonous snake is, next to drowning,

the most feared natural cause of death in the wildlands of the
Gulf Coastal Plain, although, that said, very few people actually die from it. Raff often considered the possibility of such
an attack. His fantasy usually featured a diamondback rattlesnake coiled and camouflaged among dead leaves, poised
to strike before you knew it was there. But he didn't think it
would ever happen to him.

He stared at the two inch-long scratches on his wrist with
all the detachment he could muster, as he walked slowly and
carefully back to the trailhead. Every minute or so he held his
arm up to look for signs of swelling. He waited for numbness
to creep into his hand and arm and next into his body, slowly
paralyzing and strangling him. But nothing happened. Maybe,
he thought, the cottonmouth had failed to inject venom into his
bloodstream. Finally he reached the trailhead, and lifted up his
bicycle. His heart still pounded and his hands trembled, but
he suffered no faintness or nausea, or any other symptom. He
rehearsed the event in his mind as he rode on into Clayville. He
had mostly calmed down by the time he reached home. He did
not tell his parents about the incident, then or ever.

Raff folded the moccasin encounter into his lifelong experience in the Nokobee. In time it became part of the whole. As
this and the many other memories piled one upon the other, his
devotion to the tract became stronger, but also more realistic.
From his passion for Nokobee's wildness, he drew his version
of the land ethic. Where farmers love the land for what it yields
to their labor, and hunters love it for the animals they kill and
take away, Raff came to love Nokobee for its own sake. It became
to him another way to look at the world, different than what he

heard at school and from his parents. He constructed a broader context in which he drew a picture of humanity, and of himself. The image was at first vague, but it grew thereafter steadily in clarity. In time he understood that nature was not something outside the human world. The reverse is true. Nature is the real world, and humanity exists on islands within it.

III

THE LAUNCH

· 15 ·

ONE DAY DURING the summer when Raff was preparing to enter his senior year in high school, Cyrus Semmes called his sister on the telephone.

"Marcie," he said, "Anne and I were wondering if you folks might join us for dinner sometime soon. I've got some important family business I want to discuss with you and Ainesley."

"Well, sure, Cy. We'd love to come anytime, you know that. We always look forward to coming home and seeing you and the family. What kind of business are we talking about?"

"I'll tell you when you get down here. Can you manage this Sunday?"

"Ainesley has some kind of fishing trip planned for the morning, I think, but sure, you bet, we'll be there. Will the usual time be okay?"

"Yes. And be sure to bring Scooter with you. Can you do that for certain?"

As she hung up, her mind was racing. Scooter, for sure. Cy wants to talk about Scooter. Cy's in good health, we're not going to discuss a will here. The girls are gone, and there's space, but he won't be inviting us to live at Marybelle. He doesn't want

Ainesley anywhere closer than Clayville, and he isn't going to offer him some kind of a better job. So it must be Scooter.

Marcia thought some more about the current status of the Mobile Semmes family, and what Cyrus might be thinking. Their father, Jonathan, had passed away five years before. As a World War II veteran, Jonathan had been laid to rest with honors in the military section of Magnolia Cemetery, beneath a simple gravestone designating his branch of the service and date of death. This monument meant more to the Semmeses than any mausoleum with stone angels and Byronic epitaphs. There were rifle-fire salutes and a presentation to Elizabeth of the American flag ritually folded after it was taken off his casket.

At dinner this evening, Cyrus soon focused his attention on Raff, causing Marcia to think, I guessed right. It's Scooter. Her excitement grew throughout the meal.

Her guess was further confirmed when Cyrus looked up from his okra and Cajun jambalaya, turned to the teenager, and said, "Scooter, you're almost grown up now. I'm very proud of you, son. Have you given any thought to what you want to do with the rest of your life?"

Raff's response was immediate. His plans had already been explained to Marcia and Ainesley during the previous year.

"What I want to do, if I can go to college, is be a park ranger, or maybe a naturalist, or maybe a teacher somewhere. Something that would let me work outdoors a lot, you know. I think I'm pretty good at that kind of thing."

Marcia had planned otherwise. She had decided to pressure her son onto a more ambitious course. It would be for his own good, she reasoned. It was his birthright. He would likely outgrow his boyhood preoccupations and aim for an adult existence more appropriate to his social class. Raff's achievements in the Boy Scouts had pleased her no end, and she had praised every step in rank he had earned. The strong entrepreneurial spirit he displayed in that organization, she believed, presaged Raff's entry into one of the professions that count in the world of the Mobile Semmeses. This time, however, in order to keep the evening's harmony undisturbed, she chose to remain silent.

Ainesley felt no such restraint.

"Marcia and I have different feelings about this, Cyrus. I told Scooter a dozen times if I told him once that there's nothing wrong with wanting to stay outdoors. I'd sure do the same myself if I didn't have to spend my life in a lousy hardware store or some such thing. But you can't make any real money that way. If I was Raff I'd try for a job in a big business operation somewhere and work my way up. I think he could find something real good in Mobile, maybe, if you helped get him started, Cyrus."

Marcia tried to head Ainesley off with a frown and slight head-shaking, but he was not to be stopped. Raff was his son too.

"Another thing that's been on my mind a lot is the military. A man can find a good life there. You won't be rich, but you get real security, like Harry and Virginia over there at Eglin Air Force Base. Course, if Scooter went that way, he ought to be darn sure he gets into Officer Training School."

Everyone seated there knew there was no way the Codys could manage much more than keeping the pickup truck and small box house they owned in Clayville. They might help out with college a little, maybe even take out a mortgage on the house. They were hoping that Raff might win a scholarship in a college somewhere. Maybe he could help by getting a job on the side or in the summer. Or get a loan. With these possibilities in mind, they had assured Raff that one way or the other he'd be okay. As far as they were concerned, he was going to go to college.

After listening to Ainesley, Cyrus said, smiling, "Let's have some coffee and, if you'd like, some dessert, maybe a little of the new liqueur I like. Scooter, I want you to go in the library and wait a little while. I have something I need to talk over privately with your mom and dad. I think we're going to have some of that pecan pie you like so much. I'll send in a piece and some cocoa while you wait."

Raff got up, ambled out the double doors of the dining room, and proceeded down the hall. He paused to examine the oil painting of his great-grandfather Joshua Semmes, resplendent in a formal World War I army uniform, the silver oak leaves of a lieutenant colonel glinting on its shoulder tabs. Raff went on into the library, flicked on the light switches, and perched on the horsehair sofa next to the fireplace. In a few minutes Ellie, the family cook, brought in a tray bearing cocoa and pecan pie. After his dessert, Raff stood up and started exploring the library. His eye fell on a row of old *National Geographic* magazines, and he pulled out five at random. Returning to the sofa, he began to flip through the pages. Bhutan, Asia's hidden kingdom. Romania's royal art treasures. Metallic-blue Morpho butterflies, flying jewels of the tropics. Louis Pasteur and the secret world of bacteria. The amazing wildlife of the Brazilian Pantanal. Throughout, marvelous blazing pictures of wild animals in their natural habitat. Wildlife photography, he thought, now, that's something I'd like to do. There were plenty of good subjects right there at Nokobee. And not far from Nokobee the three-hundred-square-mile swamp of the Mobile-Tensaw Delta sheltered bear and deer. It was, people said, an almost impenetrable jungle.

After about another hour Cyrus returned with Marcia and Ainesley. They drew up chairs in front of Raff. He began to feel nervous. Had they learned something about his forbidden trips to Nokobee and the Chicobee? Was this going to be an interrogation about his lies and criminal activity?

"We've been talking about you, Scooter, and your future," Cyrus said. "We're just wondering. Looking beyond college, have you ever given any thought to the possibility of law school? You know, like I went to at the University of Alabama?"

Raff felt relieved. He wasn't about to be arraigned and prosecuted after all.

"I never thought about it," he said. "I don't think I want to be a lawyer or anything like that."

"Well, now, let's look at this a little bit," Cyrus continued. "What you probably don't realize is that with a law degree you don't have to be a lawyer if you don't want to. You can use what you learn at law school to do a lot of other things. You can get a high-paying job in business. You can even go into government. You can get a commission in the military. Your dad is right about that one, Raff. And you'd be some form of adviser or legal administrator, and never have to go into combat if there's a war."

Ainesley was nodding his head and started to speak. "I've been saying to you, son—"

Cyrus stopped him by raising his hand. Then he smiled and waggled his finger.

"And here's something else you might like right away. You can work in an environmental organization, doing work on things like parks and wildlife. In other words, you'd have all kinds of options with a law degree. I know you'd do real well and be very happy."

"I really hadn't thought about it that way," Raff said. "I guess . . ."

Cyrus, the practiced negotiator, moved in quickly. "All right, then, I'm going to make you an offer. You're going to have to agree it's a really good offer, but it's got a condition. Here it is: if you'll promise to go to law school after you graduate from college, I'll pay all your expenses through any decent college you can get into and then I'll pay for the law school on top of that."

Raff sat for a moment, stunned. Then he pushed his hands down to sit up as straight as he could, causing two of the *National Geographic* magazines lying next to him to slide off and crash to the floor. He bent over to pick them up, but thought better of it and sat back, looking in wonderment at his wise and powerful Uncle Cyrus sitting right there smiling at him. He turned to glance at Ainesley and Marcia. They were smiling too, and slowly nodding their heads. *Take the offer, son*, they were signaling. *Take the offer.*

Cyrus put on a slightly disappointed expression and said, "Well, I don't expect you to make up your mind right now if you don't want to. It is a really big decision, I know. Why don't you take a little time, maybe even go on home, and let me know when you're good and ready?"

Raff stayed put. He was immobile for another minute, licking his lips, looking down at the floor, his mind churning. He didn't want to let the moment get away from him. He'd had fantasies about something like this. There had been a rumor around Clayville that Lake Nokobee and the Nokobee tract might go on the market and be turned into a housing project. In his daydreams about that he was a hero of the environment. He was the governor of Alabama who declares the land to be Nokobee State Park. He was a rich man who buys the whole property and decrees that it be kept pristine forever. He was president of The Nature Conservancy who leads a successful crusade to save the property.

Now he saw that something approaching one of these dreams might just become a reality.

So he looked up and blurted out, "I don't need any time, Uncle Cyrus. I'm really grateful, and I'm gonna pay you back too. I'll work in the summer and maybe I'll be able to get some kind of part-time job while I'm at school."

Cyrus shook his head, his smile warm now. "I don't think you understood me, Scooter. I didn't say I'll arrange a loan. I didn't say anything about your paying me back. I said I was making you an *offer*. You don't have to pay me back one cent, *any*time. I wouldn't let you anyway, because I want you to give your whole attention to your studies and your career later on. I want you to become the fine man I know you're capable of being, and I want you to bring credit to our family."

With that, he stood up, stretched his shoulders and back. "It's late. Why don't you go on home with your mom and dad, and we'll all talk about this again soon? But let me say, I'm really pleased with your decision." Cyrus had no intention of giving Raff wiggle room. The matter was settled.

On the ride back to Clayville, Ainesley said to Raff, "Good thing you took that right away, Scooter, before he changed his mind."

Marcia said gently, "Now, Ainesley, you just shut up. This is the best thing that ever happened to Scooter, and to you and me too, to be truthful about it."

Marcia was barely able to suppress her emotions. She was almost hysterically happy. The past hour had been one of enormous personal significance. She recognized that this was about more than just Raff's education. Cyrus had opened the door and invited Raff—and her too, by extension—to rejoin the Mobile Semmeses. They were going to stay in the class of their birth.

A little farther down the night road, the pickup truck ran over a large rattlesnake.

Ainesley exclaimed, "Damn, did you see that big ol' snake I ran over?" Ainesley was in euphoria too. Got his son in college, killed a rattlesnake, all in one evening.

Less than ten minutes later, the pickup, weaving slightly, hit a stray dog, flinging its body into the weeds along the roadside ditch.

"Hot damn!" Ainesley exclaimed. "I do think tonight we are goin' to break the Alabama record for roadkill."

Ainesley was drunk. He'd been a mite too pleased with the exotic taste of the Château Gruaud-Larose served at Marybelle, and Cyrus's offer had raised him one notch higher to giddiness.

But Raff paid scarce attention to rattlesnake, dog, or his parents' remarks. His gaze was fixed on the road ahead brought up by the truck's high beams cutting through the night. His mind had lifted and traveled on down that blacktop path. He was bound elsewhere now, far away.

· 16 ·

NOKOBEE COUNTY REGIONAL High School, located on the western edge of Clayville, had some good, dedicated teachers when Raphael Semmes Cody was there, but it was not among the premier public schools, even of the southern border counties of Alabama. But even with the relatively light demands placed on him at Nokobee Regional, Raff had not been a distinguished student. His grades had drifted around a B average, with occasional A's and C's. He could have done much better, he knew, but he had little interest in conventional schoolwork. His mind dwelled instead in the educational venues of Nokobee and the Boy Scouts of America. Unfortunately, neither was accustomed to writing letters of recommendation to institutions of higher learning. Therefore, he supposed, Duke, Emory, and Vanderbilt, the South's equivalent of the Ivy League, were out for him. So were the two dozen or so top-ranked liberal arts colleges sprinkled across the South.

These options were a matter of no great importance to the seventeen-year-old. Even with his uncle's money behind him, he never gave high rank and prestige serious thought. He had only one school in mind: Florida State University, where I taught. From our summers of conversations at Nokobee, Raff already knew a great deal about FSU. It was nationally ranked among public universities—not at the top, but high enough, and rising. But what mattered more to Raff was that the FSU campus was only several hours' drive from Clayville and nearby Lake Nokobee. And it was literally only minutes from the longleaf pine forest and hardwood enclaves of the Apalachicola National Forest. He saw Apalachicola as the Nokobee tract writ large, hence a great living library to him.

A month after the meeting with his Uncle Cyrus, Raff applied for admission to Florida State University. As much as a high school senior could, he put all his cards on the table, and then some. In his mind privately, it was FSU or nothing, at least nothing this first year. To the standard application forms he added his experience in natural history and the informal training in ecology he'd received from me at Nokobee. He expressed his hopes for a career in law and the environment.

> *I am especially interested in herpetology* [he wrote in the introduction of his essay]. *In a forest near my home in Clay-ville, I have been able to capture and identify 14 species of snakes.*

His expertise in big animals established, he continued with his love of entomology, and his breadth of interest in ecology and conservation.

> *I have been especially interested in a very abundant kind of mound-building ant at Lake Nokobee and, because I go there often, have watched and taken notes on these ants for the last six years. Profes-*

sor Norville from Florida State, who has helped me a great deal in this subject, tells me these ants are unusual and may even be a new species.

Ants are very important in the environment, I have read. If you weigh all the insects, ants make up two-thirds. They weigh four times as much as all the birds, mammals, reptiles, and amphibians put together.

I am very interested in the longleaf pine savanna and its conservation . . . I plan to go to law school and hope to have a career working for the environment.

Finally, Raff wrote a personal letter appealing to me. It was composed in a relatively formal style, suitable for scrutiny by an admissions committee.

Dear Dr. Norville,

As you well know, I am now a senior at Nokobee County Regional High School. I've continued my involvement in the Boy Scouts, as an Eagle Scout and the Junior Assistant Scoutmaster of Troop 10 here in Nokobee County. I have spent most of my life studying Lake Nokobee and the longleaf pine savanna around it, and hope to do more research on them. During the last year since your visit, my favorite insects have become the ants that build large mounds in the savanna, and I believe I have discovered the secrets of their life cycle. I hope to continue research on them while in college.

I have applied to come to Florida State University next year to study ecology and entomology. I'm very grateful for the help you've given me. It would be great to work with you. If you could help me be admitted, I would surely appreciate it.

> Yours sincerely,
> Raphael Semmes Cody

Innocently penned, perhaps, but probably a little less than innocently, and if so, then to defensible purpose. Raff had used the right words, written in the right tone. Only later did I learn, and should not have been surprised, that the essay and letter had been edited by Louise Simmons, his English teacher at Nokobee County Regional High School, an M.S. from FSU's School of Education and a fierce advocate of correct grammar and sentence structure.

I could do no other than acquiesce, of course, and with enthusiasm. I wrote on my own to the admissions committee to suggest that they should ignore his grades at the high school. *Raphael Semmes Cody,* I testified, *admittedly has participated in no team sport, or sport of any kind. He plays no musical instrument. He has never been more than two hundred miles from Clayville, Alabama. But then, one recalls, Henry David Thoreau was similarly limited. Like Thoreau, young Cody walks to a different drummer's beat. As his Eagle Scout record shows, he is ambitious and hardworking in a unique way, with goals of his own choosing. I predict that among the ten thousand students admitted this year to FSU, he will someday be one of the alumni of whom this university will be most proud.*

The result of all this overkill was that in the following February Raff was thrilled to receive the fat letter of early admission to the university. It further informed Raff that he was invited to join the Florida State University Honors Program, designed to provide gifted students with opportunities for creative work.

For their part, Marcia and Ainesley were delighted that their son would stay close to home. Only Uncle Cyrus protested: "Why not the University of Alabama, my own alma mater?" But he was quickly mollified. FSU was altogether okay, and what counted anyway was Raff's planned admission to law school down the line. Cyrus was satisfied that he had brought at least one worthy male heir into the Mobile Semmeses.

In the second week of September Ainesley and Marcia accompanied Raff to Tallahassee in the latest version of Ainesley's red pickup, and helped Raff pick his way through the crowd of students to his assigned dormitory room. Raff pledged to come home regularly. If they could believe anything he promised, they could believe that. They had Nokobee on their side as a powerful attraction.

Alicia and I joined the three Codys for dinner at a small roadside restaurant, the kind often called a cafe, in Sopchoppy, just outside of Tallahassee. We shared in the all-you-can-eat offering of fried mullet, turnip greens, and the small balls of cornmeal and chopped onions called hushpuppies. All chose sweet-tea, or else failed to decline it, forgetting that in the real South you are served unsweetened tea only if you request it. Ainesley chastely avoided beer or worse. As darkness fell, we watched through the window as Mexican free-tailed bats swooped in and out of the lighted parking area. They cut swaths through the gathering insect hordes, mercifully including mosquitoes among their prey. In this atmosphere of complete Southern authenticity, I promised Raff's parents to help him and let them know if he was having any special trouble at the university.

When Raff arrived at Florida State, he found it still surrounded by an abundance of natural open space. That was the case even though the campus had grown to become a small city in itself, with forty thousand students, twenty-five hundred faculty members, and thousands more of supporting staff. From our conversations at Nokobee, he knew he could drive away from the center of FSU in any direction, and within half an hour find extensive natural habitats of all kinds that grace the Florida Panhandle. There were longleaf pine mesic flatwoods, longleaf pine and turkey oak flats, turkey oak sandhills, and hardwood-covered steephead ravines to the north. Traveling west, you encountered the series of floodplain forests that border the Gulf-bound coastal rivers. To the south awaited some of the best-preserved coastal wetlands in the southern United States. Immediately adjacent to the FSU campus was the magnificent Apalachicola National Forest itself, containing most of the principal habitats of the central coastal plain.

During his first two weeks at FSU, Raff was swept along by receptions, orientation tours, and introductory class meetings. As quickly as he could manage, however, he made an appointment to see me.

Exactly to the minute of the assigned appointment there came a soft rap on my office door. The Raphael Semmes Cody who entered was different from the one I had known. He walked stiffly and erect, rather like a soldier reporting for duty. His handshake was sweaty. This was not the easygoing kid I knew at Nokobee. He was responding, it was clear, to my professional persona in an intimidating new environment.

As he stood there, it was "Yessir" to this and "Yessir" to that after almost every sentence I uttered. That needed correcting. So I hugged him, showed him to a chair, and pulled mine over to face him.

"Welcome to Florida State, Raff," I said in as warm a tone as I could summon. "I'm so glad you're here. I couldn't be happier to see you."

I peppered him with questions about his family and first impressions of FSU, in order to bring him out and put him further at ease. And I congratulated him on his admission to the Honors Program.

"Oh," I added, "I hope you'll find time to join us at some of the special lectures and symposia scheduled this year. It doesn't matter that you're just a freshman. You'll be real welcome. Of course, I mean if you can find time, Raff."

I studied him closely as we talked. Small in stature, about Ainesley's height, perhaps five-nine, but slightly heavier than his father—at a guess 140 pounds. Because I'd read a biography of his namesake, I knew he was, coincidentally, about the same size as the original Admiral Semmes. His face was thin, more Marcia than Ainesley. His hair, groomed in his Sunday best, was newly trimmed, brushed, and parted, a condition almost never seen at Nokobee. It was light brown in color, almost blond, perhaps enhanced through exposure to the sun of the Florida summer.

He was dressed in what I took to be his best clothes: dark lightweight wool pants, mauve cotton sports shirt, and a newly pressed linen jacket. The latter I was never to see again. On its lapel—and I liked him for wearing it—was a small silver Eagle Scout pin. He wore off-white shoes and thick white cotton socks. Except perhaps for the jacket and lapel pin, he would go unnoticed, I thought, in the mob of students flowing continuously along the university mall outside. For that matter, given his youthful appearance, he would fit in any high school hall in Florida.

Within half an hour, yielding to my efforts, Raff began to relax. "Dr. Norville" changed back to the honorary "Uncle Fred" of Nokobee. Because I had in mind most of what he knew about natural history, our relationship soon turned from one of professor and student to that of senior and junior colleagues.

The tribal bonds of naturalists, you should know, are woven out of war stories from past field trips. No war stories, no bonds. A good starting point on the Gulf Coastal Plain is the impressive variety of poisonous snakes. Everyone talks about poisonous snakes, and it seems that all who grew up in the rural South have personal stories to tell. For naturalists in particular, such accounts make ideal war stories, and, more importantly, *scientific* war stories. As Raff already knew, I'd survived two diamondback rattler strikes, and nearly died from the second one. My scary experience considerably outpointed his near-miss with a cottonmouth moccasin.

"Let me tell you, Raff," I said, smiling, "if you've got to get bitten by a rattlesnake, pick something other than a diamondback. I'd make it a pygmy rattlesnake. That's the smallest species there is, you know. The worse you'll get is maybe a swollen arm or leg for a week. But let's keep this serious. I'd say the best advice I could give you or anybody else is just don't mess with poisonous snakes, period. If you *have* to handle one for some reason or other, and even if you're pretty sure it's not poisonous, always use a snake stick and a bag."

"I just try not even to get near the poisonous kinds," Raff said.

I didn't believe that, figuring he was a lot like me when I was his age, but I didn't say so.

"Fine," I responded. "And it's always a good idea when you're in the field to have someone with you. Oh, and be sure you're aware of the nearest hospital that has a supply of antivenins."

There was a pause as a supersized lawn mower with a workman in the seat passed beneath the open window of my office. The smell of cut grass drifted in. While we waited I thought, Well, there they are together, the twin symbols of our middle-class culture: noise and lawns, they're eating up what little is left of the natural world.

Our conversation began to taper off. I looked at my watch. Raff, however, was reluctant to go.

"It isn't just snakes," he said. "There are a huge number of kinds of frogs and salamanders at Nokobee. I thought I might check to see if there are any special kinds that live in pitcher-plant bogs. We have some at Nokobee, but I just never got around to checking them out."

"Well, yes, that would be interesting, all right. If you get the chance why don't you look down into the water inside the pitchers and see if you can find any tadpoles living there? There might be some tree frogs breeding there. That would be a terrific thing if you found it."

A young woman student, smiling brightly and loaded with an armful of books, had arrived at the door for my next appointment. Twenty pounds overweight, eyeglasses, wearing artificially weathered jeans and a loose T-shirt, no bra—in short, a coed of liberated America. I stood up to let her in. Raff also stood up, but continued talking as we walked across the office.

"Another thing I want to see is the torreyas at the Apalachi-cola Bluffs. That's the only place they grow in the wild, and I understand they're dying off."

"Yes, yes," I said, feeling a bit impatient. "It's because of a fungus. Same sort of thing that wiped out the American chestnut."

Torreyas—or "stinking cedars," from the odor of their wood—are conifers left behind in the Deep South when the continental glaciers retreated ten thousand years ago. Most, but not all, cold-tolerant plants retreated with them. The torreyas decided to stay behind.

"There are a few they've got growing in a nursery outside Clayville." Raff was still talking as I admitted and shook hands with the new student. "They make nice ornamental trees, and the cultivated ones don't have the fungus."

"Sure," I said. "Okay, okay. We take field trips out of here to the Apalachicola Bluffs from time to time. Why don't you come with me and some of the other students on the next one? I'll see you around."

Finally, Raff relinquished and walked away. This kid, I thought, has come to the right place.

· 17 ·

BECAUSE HE'D COME to Florida State University, I was Raphael Semmes Cody's ready-made first college mentor. He acquired his second mentor when he audited the beginning undergraduate course in entomology. William Abbott Needham was a world authority on beetles. That was no mean accomplishment, because four hundred thousand kinds are known to science, and possibly twice that number remain undiscovered. He was also the leading authority on the boll weevil, ravager of the South's cotton fields in the early 1900s. Because of his passion for the subject and scholarly reputation, he was surrounded by a cadre of dedicated graduate students. He was addressed as Professor Needham to his face, and Uncle Bill behind his back. He didn't mind the latter at all.

Bill Needham, in his late forties at the time, had the lean hawklike looks one expects to find in a veteran field biologist but almost never actually does. He spoke in a low, carefully modulated voice, and enjoyed pronouncing scientific names in the exact original Greek or Latin. His imperturbably calm, measured manner hid a passion within.

When outdoors, Needham always wore a porkpie hat made to his specifications. The top was a mesh that allowed air in to cool his head. Under the brim was a neatly folded mosquito net that could be dropped at the pull of a string to protect his face and neck from the bloodsuckers. Needham was, he explained, allergic to mosquito bites. He carried a bright orange book bag that held, in addition to notes and manuscript pages, bottles for insect specimens, and a tightly folded butterfly net, another of his inventions. The net could be taken out in an instant and opened like an umbrella. Anywhere Needham spotted a flying insect that interested him, even in a crowd of people, he pulled out the "Needham net" to ensnare the specimen for close inspection.

Needham was a genuine eccentric, by which I mean his peculiarities were not affectations but simply a way of enjoying the world as he saw it. Every place, including the busiest parts of downtown Tallahassee and the campus of Florida State University, was to him a habitat teeming with insects. He knew the names and habits of most of what he saw and he was alert to any newcomer that crossed his path. He was often assisted by his third wife, a former graduate student who—by necessity, and at last, after the first two had departed—shared his entomological obsession.

This genial scientist and Southern gentleman was adored by the students closest to him. Most college teachers merely take pride in their subject and are eager to convey it, then go home for dinner and unrelated diversions. Needham was consumed by his work. His acolytes could not help but be drawn into the world he occupied around the clock. They learned to see human artifacts as but a matrix within which insects lived in countless numbers, pursuing their missions in mysterious ways. Few students ever entered his world completely, and then only for a few semesters. But for the rest of their lives all would retain at least a basic knowledge of entomology and remember the spirit of the scholar who had taught it. He was an ornament to his profession, a Gold Medalist of the Entomological Society of America and named the 1994 Teacher of the Year by the Association of Southeastern Universities.

Each Wednesday at four in the afternoon Needham opened up his office to all in order to preside over a freewheeling seminar popularly known as the Bug Bash. He served hot tea poured into Styrofoam cups along with supermarket cookies shaken out of cardboard containers. The conversation typically began with some current event in the news or major report in the latest weekly issue of *Nature* or *Science*. Then it skipped about erratically, not avoiding more sensational topics of university and national politics. Invariably and soon, however, it drifted back to the vast and arcane world of entomology. Needham always started and often led the conversation, but he preferred to listen. He liked to say it was an important part of his own education.

He would prod the Bashers in his response, not always politely. "You got a reference for that?" Or, "That sounds like some kind of an answer to me. So what's the question?" Or, "I've got a dryinid wasp here. Anybody ever seen a dryinid? I bet you all will think it's some kind of an ant when you see it." Then he would shake the dryinid out of a glass tube onto the table in front of him, and all would watch as the little wasp scurried across the surface and jumped off the edge.

He was also kindly. He liked to draw timid students out. "Hey, George, didn't you get one of those blind cave beetles last summer up in Cave Springs? I think it's a species of *Pseudanoph-thalmus*. It was amazing to see one alive. You still got any in your terrarium, and can we look at it?"

As a student in the Honors Program, Raff was allowed to take entomology while only a second-semester freshman. He also insinuated himself into the Wednesday afternoon Bug Bashers, simply by showing up and sitting on a chair at the edge of the group. Soon he was asking questions, and he was able to offer a few frissons of entomology from his life at Nokobee. He had a stock of bug war stories to tell: an outbreak of giant rhinoceros beetles, winged dogfights among cardinal butterflies, the arrival of a honeybee swarm at an abandoned woodpecker nest.

Raff had enough such anecdotes to hold his own with the older students. But his ace was an account of the anthills of Dead Owl Cove. He'd mapped all the nests he could find, as part of the requirements for the Boy Scout merit badge in insect life. He had taken notes as well on the denizens of two of the anthills. He'd also recorded prey that their foraging workers brought home. Finally, he'd had the good luck to witness a late summer wedding flight in which winged queens and males flew up from the scattered anthills simultaneously and mated in midair.

Needham was especially drawn to the ants, as I had been.

"I'm pretty sure I've seen that species in other parts of the longleaf savanna," he said. "It might be a new species. Hills like that are pretty rare in this part of the country, but as I recall it, where you do find them they're densely crowded. My guess is that each hill is a nest for a separate colony, but I'm not sure about that at all."

Raff responded eagerly. "I think they're separate. I've seen workers from different nests fighting a couple of times."

"Hey. Why don't we go over to Nokobee some Saturday soon and take a look?" Needham said. "We could get a few of the guys together and make an expedition of it."

Two Saturdays later the expedition to Nokobee was launched. Raff was home that weekend. He'd given Needham instructions and a hand-drawn map to get to the lake.

Early that morning Ainesley drove him to the Nokobee trailhead so he could be waiting for the others when they came in from Tallahassee. As soon as Needham and six of the Bug Bash students arrived, Raff led them on a tour of the anthills around Dead Owl Cove. They then took a walk along the west shore of the lake, looking for more of the nests. Several were found, but none as densely grouped as the population at Dead Owl Cove. All of the students carried nets, and dropped ants and other kinds of insects in killing jars and vials of alcohol for later study.

On the way out Raff lingered with Needham at the anthills, observing a bit more of whatever activity could be seen on their surfaces. Then all drove back together to Tallahassee and the Florida State University campus. Needham asked Raff to sit next to him during the return trip.

"I've got a suggestion that you shouldn't feel obligated to take if you're not interested. I'm sure this species of ant has never been studied before. If you were to start a complete study and add that to the notes you already have, it seems to me it might make a very good honors thesis. You could do it pretty conveniently because you live so close."

Raff nodded enthusiastically. "Yessir," he said.

"I know your senior year is still a long way off," Needham continued, "but believe me, you can never have too much time to do a good honors thesis. You might even be able to publish a paper in one of the entomology journals. I'd be glad to advise you if you give it a try. But of course that's just a suggestion. There are a hundred things you might want to do more, at Nokobee, or around here, or anywhere. But does that sound at all interesting to you?"

Raff said, "Yessir, you bet it does, it really does. I think I'd like to keep working on the anthills."

When they met later in his office, Needham pressed his earlier suggestion. "This is an interesting species. We're really just beginning to study ants properly. And don't let anybody tell you they aren't important. Keep in mind that ants not only rule the insect world, but societies like the ones at Nokobee are the most complicated on earth next to humans."

In effect, Needham had said to Raff, like a prince of old to an explorer, *Go out and search. Everything you find will be important. Record it. Then come back here and report it, to me, and to all.*

Needham knew what he was doing. He understood that nothing propels the postadolescent mind more powerfully than to be told by someone in authority, *You do this well, you like doing it, it is interesting and important. So I hereby commission you to take charge. Pursue this as far as you are able. Make it your special mission.*

Such was the spirit, Needham knew, that has driven much of the history of biology. Carl Linnaeus, the great eighteenth-century Swedish botanist and founder of biological classification, profited by it. He instructed his best students—his "Apostles," he called them—to be his eyes and hands as they visited foreign lands. And so seventeen gifted young men went forth variously to the Levant, Japan, South America, and the North American colonies, to be the first to collect the plants, to study them, and to bring specimens back to Europe for further research by all generations into the future.

When Charles Darwin was twenty-two years old, he was told, in effect, *Charles, we know you love natural history. There's a job open, as naturalist on HMS* Beagle. *You can have it. We want you to travel on this ship to South America and learn all you can about the geology, plants, animals, and people. Then come back and tell us what you found.* In the following five years the great naturalist deduced the geological origin of atolls, he collected countless new species of plants and animals, and not least, and to the immense benefit to science, he invented the theory of evolution by natural selection.

Raff's parents knew nothing of this principle of apprentice-ship when he told them he would be studying ants at Nokobee. Indeed, Marcia was baffled by his choice of subject.

"I don't understand it, Scooter. I know it's for your educa-tion, and I'm very happy that Fred Norville and Dr. Needham have taken you under their wings. But what good are ants? Wouldn't it be better to take some subject connected to medi-cine, or maybe agriculture?"

"There are a whole bunch of reasons, Mom. I want to do real research out at Nokobee. I know the place real well—you know that. I've been watching those ants at Dead Owl Cove. Uncle Fred said he wanted you and Dad to know that the research is going to be important. Ants may be small, people laugh at them and all, but you know, they're a huge part of the environment. They're the most social animals in the world. Anybody who knows anything knows we learn a lot about social behavior in people by studying things like that."

"Well, now," Marcia said, "I guess the professors know what they're talking about. If they don't, who does? And it's just wonderful that you're going to be able to do your study right here at home."

Ainesley didn't much care what Raff did. What mattered to him was that his son was a college student and had a real future ahead of him.

"Hell, Scooter, I don't know what this is all about, but I'll even go out to Nokobee and help you if you want me to, whenever I get a little time off from the store. I'll bring along a shovel."

Soon after Raff began the actual studies, his new friends at the Bug Bash began calling them the Anthill Chronicles. Bill Needham's engagement in the project increased with time, as he lent his own expertise and insights to the events unfolding in the population at Dead Owl Cove. Month by month, whenever Raff brought in new observations, Needham helped him piece them together with whatever was known of the social behavior of other kinds of ants.

· 18 ·

THREE YEARS PASSED as Raff commuted between Clayville and Tallahassee. When he turned in his senior thesis, two months before graduation, the Anthill Chronicles had matured into an epic of miniature civilizations. The foibles of ants, Raff learned, are those of men, written in a simpler grammar. Compared with those of humans, the anthill cycles are short in duration, instinct-driven, and hence truly ordained by fate. The ant societies proved different in most fundamental ways from those of humans—of course—yet also convergent to them in other, also important ways.

The half dozen committee members of the Department of Biological Science who reviewed the thesis judged it as one of the best they had ever seen—in conception, in originality, and in execution. Raff dedicated it to the two sponsors of the research.

For Professors William A. Needham and Frederick Norville,
whose generous help and dedication made this study possible.

Bill Needham and I both valued that simple acknowledgment as much as any we'd received in books and journals from our fellow professional scientists.

What Raff found deserved to be preserved, and I set out to do so, with Bill Needham's assistance, shortly after Raff's graduation. We omitted Raff's measurements and tables, and translated his sometimes stiff language into less technical form. The merit of this account, to follow, is that it describes what actually occurs in such anthills during their remorseless struggles and wars. It presents the story as near as possible to the way ants see such events themselves.

At another level, in my experience, nothing expresses better than the anthill epics the energy and dynamics of all life in the Nokobee tract, and for that matter other fragments of the living natural world left for us to observe.

At the very start of the study Raff had fixed his attention on the large colony at the Lake Nokobee trailhead. This was the first anthill encountered upon arrival at the lake, and the one on which he had taken the most notes in earlier years. Naming it the Trailhead Colony, Raff decided to make it the prototype for his thesis studies. He chose wisely to record its habits and social behavior as thoroughly as possible without digging it up or disturbing it in any other way. Needham suggested further that these observations would serve as a baseline for later studies, including those of other colonies scattered over Dead Owl Cove. A more nearly complete picture might then be drawn for the whole species.

Among Raff's earliest childhood memories was the Trailhead Colony as a dominant presence in the open space of the picnic area. On every warm rainless day, its foragers patrolled ten yards or more from the nest mound. And several times an hour, some of them returned to the nest entrance bearing various fresh prey, fragments of scavenged dead insects, nectar from plants, and the sugary excrement of sap-sucking insects.

When Raff began a more than casual study late in the previous year before coming to Florida State University, he noticed that the activity of the Trailhead Colony had declined sharply from the high intensity of its past. Many fewer foragers ventured out of the nest, and proportionately less food was coming in. When Raff went so far as to prod the mound surface with a trowel, only a small number of defenders rushed out to mount a defense. Something was wrong with the mighty Trailhead Colony.

"I think it's sick, and it's getting worse," he said at a Bug Bash, "and I have no idea why."

Bill Needham nodded. "Sounds like the queen has died on you. No queen, no eggs, no more larvae. The colony doesn't need as much food, so the workers are staying at home. Sort of like old folks at a retirement community."

"But why should the whole colony quit like that?" Raff said. "Are they having a memorial service or something?" That brought approving laughter from the Bashers, a rare tribute to a beginner like Raff.

"Well," Needham said, "you've got to understand what a powerful stimulus a queen is to all the workers. When she goes, they're less responsive. Something goes out of their spirit—so to speak."

Circling an index finger in the air, as he often did when he was about to introduce a new idea, Needham asked, "How long have you been watching that colony anyway?"

"Well, believe it or not," Raff replied, "since I was a little kid, I'd say ten years or so. It's hard to miss when you first get to the trailhead."

Needham reached for a volume on the shelf next to his desk, searched the index, opened to a page, and pointed to an entry. He said, "That's no surprise. In ants similar to your species, we have records of the mother queen living over twenty years."

"Twenty years? That's older than I am."

"Yep. I'll admit that's an amazing life-span for an insect," Needham said. "It's longer even than for the seventeen-year locust. But it does occur in the queens of a few kinds of ants. My guess is that it's a world record for insects. On the other hand, very few of the workers live more than two or three years. That's true even though they're all the queen's daughters, and all have her same heredity. Now, that's a real strange situation. Longer than that must seem like an eternity for them. They exist, you might say, in a mental world that's got no beginning or end. They have no concept of their mother queen dying. She's just always there. Even when it finally happens, even the retinue that takes care of the old girl doesn't realize at first that she's dead. I suggest you keep a close eye on that colony."

The death of the Queen was to have consequences critical to the fate of the Dead Owl Cove ants, across the five seasons their history was recorded by Raphael Semmes Cody. For that reason Needham and I chose to place this event at the opening of the Anthill Chronicles.

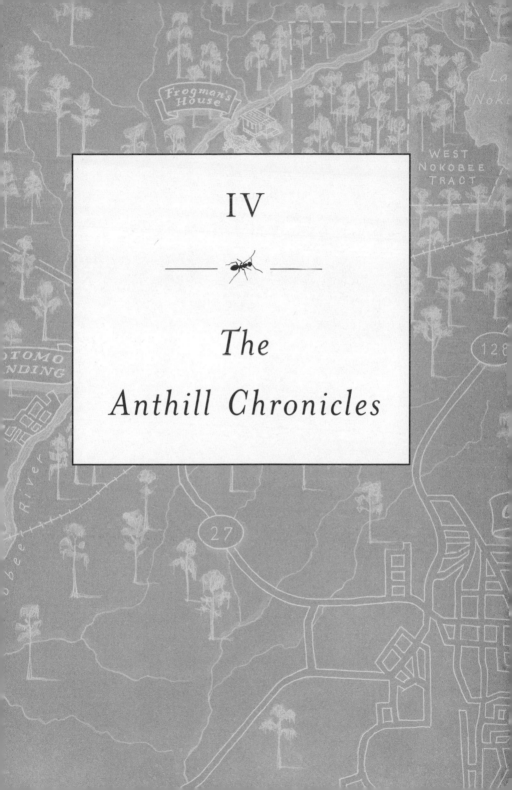

IV

The
Anthill Chronicles

· 19 ·

I T WAS TRUE. The Trailhead Queen was dead.

In the first days there had been no overt sign that her long life had ended. There was no fever, there were no spasms, no farewells. She simply sat on the floor of the royal chamber and quietly died. As in life, her body was prone and immobile, her legs and antennae relaxed. Her stillness by itself failed to give warning to her daughters that a catastrophe had occurred for all of them. She lay there in fact as though nothing had happened. She had become a perfect statue of herself.

The deception was the result of the way the bodies of insects decay after death. Where humans and other vertebrate animals have an internal skeleton surrounded by soft tissue that quickly rots away, insects are encased in an external skeleton. Their soft tissues shrivel inwardly into dry threads and lumps, but their exoskeleton around them remains, a knight's armor fully intact long after the knight is gone.

Hence the workers were at first unaware of this mother's death. Her quietude said nothing, and the odors of her life, still rising from her, signaled, *I remain among you.*

She smelled alive.

The deception was made easier because in life she had never

given orders or led them in activities of any kind—even though her brain was fully programmed to perform all of their tasks if she chose.

She was to all purposes a winged wasp who lived in a neutered wingless society. Yet the only initiatives she ever took were all in a burst at the beginning of her adult life—with approximately twenty years left to go—when she left the colony of her birth, abandoning along with it her mother and sisters. She mated then, once for all time—no more sex for her—and started a new colony of her own. Furiously, during a very short period of activity and alone, she performed almost all of the instinctive behaviors of a female of her species, and on top of that the same labor as sterile workers of a developed colony.

The hereditary programs were there, in the sense organs of the Trailhead Queen and in her nerve circuitry, all expressed in the required correct sequence of her actions. These programs faithfully repeated the routine followed by the ancestral wasps that evolved into the first social ants as they crawled among dinosaurs over a hundred million years ago.

Leaving the nest of her birth to start this process, she first spread her four membranous wings and flew into the air. There she joined a swarm of flying males and other virgin queens. One of the males was able to catch her. He clamped his legs around her body, and the couple spiraled down to the ground. On landing, he used large claspers at the rear end of his body to hold their genitalia together and complete the insemination. Within five minutes the act was finished, and the Queen shook the male loose. All of the sperm she received flowed up into a special bag-shaped organ in her abdomen to stay there until called on to fertilize more of her eggs. That might be years into the future. Each sperm was endowed with a potential life-span equal to her own.

In contrast, the father of all her children was programmed to die almost immediately after the mating. The only thing he had ever done was accept meals regurgitated to him like a nestling bird by his sisters, and wait, and wait some more, and finally take the one short flight from his home followed by five minutes of copulation.

The male had started his life as an egg laid by the Queen of the mother colony. The egg hatched into a grub-shaped larva, which was fed by the all-female nurses. Upon reaching full size, the larva metamorphosed into a pupa. This final immature stage was encased in a soft, waxy, temporary exoskeleton with the form of an adult and three body parts—head, thorax, and abdomen. A pair of antennae and three pairs of legs sprouted from the body. Inside, the masses of undifferentiated tissue, protected by the waxy outer skeleton, grew into his final internal organs.

When the transformation was complete, the outer layer was stripped away and eaten by the workers, and the adult male stepped out, complete with wings, large eyes, massive genitalia, rudimentary jaws, tiny brain, and the one big purpose programmed in his tiny brain followed by quick death.

In short, the male was no more than a guided missile loaded with sperm. His life's work would be a single ejaculation. Up to the climactic moment, he had been a parasite in his mother's colony, a layabout fed and groomed by his sisters. He performed no public service. After his world-defining five minutes, he was left with only one instruction that would be enforced if necessary by his sisters. *Don't come back here. Just die.*

He would not even try to return to the nest. He had no

chance at all of survival. A delicate creature, he was not provided with defenses. He had no way to find food, or feed himself if he stumbled across some. He had been issued a one-way ticket. He would die by dehydration, or crushed in the beak of a bird, or chopped into pieces by the jaws of an enemy ant, or, less quickly, pierced by the bloodsucking proboscis of an assassin bug.

To escape the same fate, the newly mated future Queen of the Trailhead Colony, full-brained and powerfully muscled, hurried to find shelter. She had to get back underground as quickly as possible after receiving her sperm load. First, however, she had to take a few minutes to shed her four wings. To do that she simply bent her middle legs forward, pressed them against the base of the wings, and snapped them off. This mutilation caused no injury to the rest of her body. It caused no pain. From the start the wings had been lifeless films and struts of chitin, joined to the body in a way that made them easy to break off painlessly and then discard.

The Queen was a parachutist that slipped her harness upon landing. Now she could move more quickly to avoid ants, spiders, and other predators hunting around her in the grassroots jungle. She was fortunate to come upon an open space between grass clumps, a small, ant-sized clearing at the Lake Nokobee trailhead. By luck she had found it an ideal site. If she could build a nest there, it would be her home for, perhaps, twenty years. She set out at once to dig a vertical tunnel in the sandy clay soil. Her movements were swift and precise, and within minutes she had deepened the shaft to more than her body length. It provided some degree of protection, but needed to be completed as quickly as possible. She had to hurry. Her life remained in constant danger; there was not a minute to lose.

At a predetermined depth, which she measured by the time it took her to climb up and down the shaft, the young Queen turned to the side at the bottom and began to excavate a wider space. She continued until she had fashioned a round chamber about three times wider than the vertical shaft. Her safety was now enhanced but far from ensured. Predators and marauding ants could still climb down the shaft to attack her. At least now the enemies would be confined to a narrow space by the walls of the shaft and forced to confront the young Queen's thrusting sting and snapping jaws head on before they could reach her vulnerable body.

With this much achieved, and as the shadows of the surrounding pines lengthened across the trailhead, she had beaten odds of about a hundred to one. For every hundred young queens leaving the mother nest in order to be mated and start a new colony, only one at the end of the day now sat in the bottom chamber of an incipient nest.

Yet in spite of this huge achievement, and no matter how securely she had constructed her home, the odds against final success were still stacked against her. The chance of progressing from being the architect of a nearly excavated nest to being the mother of a large, mature colony was also about one in a hundred. Thus the Trailhead Queen would be statistically the single one in ten thousand who flew from the mother nest and went on to finish the entire process. She alone would enjoy a long life in the deep royal chamber of a mound nest. Defended by an army of fierce daughters, she would be as safe as any insect in the whole world could expect to be.

Even with the excavation of the first chamber complete, the Trailhead Queen still had heavy work ahead. First, she laid a small cluster of eggs on the earthen floor. These tiny objects she was compelled to lick continuously. It was an urgent task, because to the peril from enemies above was now added the threat of bacteria and fungi teeming in the soil all around her. If the eggs were not regularly cleaned and coated with antibiotic saliva, they would be soon overgrown by an invading mold and consumed. And from a single bacterium in the soil excavated by the Queen, millions could proliferate on any ant tissue left unprotected.

Other young queens around the Trailhead Queen were digging in on their own. All failed: one by one predators killed them. No sister worked side by side with the Trailhead Queen, no worker had yet been born that could support her. Outside the sisterhood of the mother colony that produced her, nature remained a battleground in a pitiless and total war every minute of the day. Intruders winkled the survivors out of their little nests and ate them. Other risks were present inside the nests themselves: the eggs might not be properly inseminated, or the sperm might be genetically defective.

But the dice fell right time and time again for the future Queen of the Trailhead Colony. As tiny larvae hatched from her eggs, she fed them highly nutritious food secreted from a large gland that partly filled her head and emptied through her mouth. This baby food was manufactured from masses of fat stored in the rear segment of the Queen's body. It was also created by metabolism of her now-useless wing muscles.

From the reserves of her own body the young Queen reared a dozen workers. All were female. They were tiny and weak, barely able to perform the work necessary for the little colony to survive. By necessity they came into the world as midgets. If each were larger in size, fewer of them could have been raised. The number would have fallen below the level necessary to provide adequate labor for the survival of the newborn colony.

Some of these pioneers, guided entirely by instinct because no one existed to teach them, set out to forage for food. Others took care of the Queen and reared the next generation of workers to maturity. Still others devoted time to enlarging the nest. Failure to perform all these tasks with exactitude would mean death for the colony. The young Queen could help no more. On the contrary, she desperately needed help herself to continue living. Her expendable body tissues were depleted. They had almost all been fed to the larval daughters, and now she was starving. Her body was a shell of chitin containing only tissues necessary for her own life.

The first foragers venturing timidly away from the nest were able to bring back a few scraps of food. Their prizes included a fallen mosquito, a bit of shed caterpillar skin, and a newly hatched spiderling, which were enough to keep the colony alive and allow the Queen to regain some of her weight and strength.

Workers of the next generation, raised on food harvested from terrain outside the nest, were somewhat larger in physical size than the first generation, and stronger. They began to dig out many more tunnels to accommodate the growing population. As the colony and their habitation grew, the endangered home assumed the form of a labyrinth of chambers and connecting galleries. It became an enemy-proof fortress. A mound of excavated soil formed above it, reinforcing the roof and capturing the warmth of the sun.

As the months passed, the Queen, growing heavy with egg-filled ovaries, retreated ever deeper, distancing herself from the still-dangerous nest exterior. She had become an extreme specialist. She alone laid eggs, she alone was the growing tip of the burgeoning colony. The workers performed all the labor needed to raise her offspring, their sisters. They were the Queen's hands and feet and jaws, and increasingly they replaced her brain. They functioned together as a well-organized whole. They were altruistic toward one another, and they divided labor without regard to their own welfare. The Trailhead Colony came to resemble a large, diffuse organism. In a word, it became a superorganism.

By the time the colony reached its full mature size two years after the nuptial flight of the Queen, it contained over ten thousand workers. It was then able, in the following year, to rear virgin queens, and males, and from them to give birth to new colonies. By that time the Queen was producing eggs at the average rate of one every fifteen minutes. Heavy and torpid, she lay in the royal chamber at the bottom of the subterranean nest, five feet below the surface, a distance of four hundred ant lengths. By human scale the ant city was the equivalent of two hundred underground stories. The mound of excavated soil capping the nest added another fifty stories aboveground.

The Queen may not have been the leader of this miniature civilization, but she was the fountainhead of all its energies and growth. She was the key to its success or failure. The metronomic pumping out of fertilized eggs from her twenty ovaries was the heartbeat of the colony. That it should continue strong and true was the ultimate purpose of all the workers' labor. Their careful construction of the nest labyrinth, their readiness to risk life in daily searches for food abroad, their suicidal defense of the nest entrance, all their sacrifices were for her and for the creation of more altruistic workers like themselves.

One worker, or a thousand workers, could die and the colony would go on, repairing itself as needed. But the failure of the Queen, if not corrected, would be fatal.

Now after twenty more years that catastrophe had occurred. The death of the Queen was the greatest challenge the colony had faced since the days of its founding. Yet the workers could not take action until they learned for certain that the Queen was dead. They knew that something was not right, that something unnamed had settled upon them, but they did not yet realize the extent of her problem. The signs were not yet strong enough. So the Trailhead Colony thrummed on for a while longer with bustle and precision. Like a large ship at sea, it could not be easily turned from the shoals coming at it.

The reason for the continued momentum of the Trailhead Colony lay in the way ants communicate. Because they live most of their lives in underground darkness, they cannot speak to each other with sight or sound. Instead, they are forced to communicate with chemical signals. Human beings think in sound and vision. Ants, forced to be pheromonal, think only in taste and smell. No human can understand the chemical sensations that crowd the brain of a worker ant. We have no understanding of the entities she conceives, or the tones, the accounts, and the blends that course through her mind. While the Trailhead Colony may have been silent to unaided human perception, it was thunderous with pheromonal chatter among the ants.

The Trailhead Colony communicated using about a dozen chemical signals. The retinue of workers crowded around their dead mother were locked to her by several of these pheromones still oozing from her body. Translated into a human voice, they whispered a ghostly command: *Come here, gather around me, stay close to me.*

The attendants licked her body lasciviously with their pad-shaped tongues. They continued eagerly to clean her, picking up substances from her to pass on to others outside the retinue. The pheromones that triggered their intimate care spoke through taste and smell: *Wash me, eat the substances you clean from my body, share them with your sisters.*

The substances commanding the retinue were held in the forward chamber of the gut of each of the ants. They mingled there with liquid food. The ants smelled each other constantly by sweeps of their antennae, the "feelers" on their heads, the equivalent of the human nose. An ant that was well fed, with lots of food resting in her gut, said to a less well-fed nestmate, *Smell this, and if you are hungry, eat.* If the ant approached and was in fact hungry, she extended her tongue, and the donor ant rewarded her by regurgitating liquid directly into her mouth.

The exchanges among the sisters continued in this way. The combined intelligence of the colony listened to the flood of crosstalk among its members. They spoke in pheromones in all the messages they were programmed to send and receive. The colony exchanged information within itself in the same way the body of one ant, one human, or any other single organism exchanges information within itself by hormones. The superorganism pheromones suggested, begged, and commanded.

Outside the nest, not far from the Trailheader mound, a wood thrush flew by one day carrying a grasshopper to her own nest. Part of the crushed insect broke off and fell to the ground. In less than a minute a patrolling worker found it, triggering a chain of action of the kind followed countless times by Trail-headers before. She examined the grasshopper, tasted it briefly, and ran back to the nest entrance. On the way, she touched the tip of her abdomen to the ground, laying down a thin trail of chemicals. Entering the nest, she rushed up to each nestmate she passed, brushing her face close to theirs. The odor-sensitive antennae of the nestmates detected both the trail substance and the smell of grasshopper. The signals now proclaimed, *Food, food. I have found food, follow my trail!*

Soon a mob of ants ran out. They followed the trail, and gathered around the delicious haunch of grasshopper. Some of the first to arrive ran back to the nest, laying trails of their own, reinforcing the message, saying, *Come on, come on, we need help.*

The ants working on the grasshopper piece began to drag it toward the nest entrance. A catbird perched on the branch of a tree nearby saw the activity and swept down to investigate. She pecked at the grasshopper, scattering the ants and injuring several. The ants expelled a pheromone from a gland that opened at the base of their jaws. A chemical vapor spread fast. It shouted, *Danger! Emergency! Run! Run! Get out of here!*

And so the business of the Trailhead Colony was conducted by a vocabulary of odor and taste. Pheromones were emitted, occasionally reinforced by touch. Messages were created, some-times with a single chemical substance, sometimes with the same substance at different concentrations, and on occasion two or more in combination. Meanings were changed according to where the substances were delivered. The vocabulary grew. Different messages were delivered.

Here, let me lick and clean you.

Get to work, do what others are doing here.

This is my caste, and this is my condition.

Let us lay down territorial pheromones, announcing to rivals our dominion over this land.

We don't have enough soldiers; raise more in the nursery.

We have too many soldiers; raise fewer.

Who is leading the struggle to become our new Queen?

The members of the Trailhead Colony lived every second of their lives by instructions in the clouds and torrents of pheromones around them. Some signals such as the alarm pheromones spread and faded fast, drawing the attention of many nestmates as needed locally, but not holding on long enough to create panic throughout the colony. At the opposite extreme, some odors spread slowly and lasted a long time. Among them were the royal pheromones of the Trailhead Queen. Even as her body began to decay, the pheromones she had manufactured in life persisted in the minds and bodies of her colony.

The royal presence had been woven into the pheromone life of the Trailhead Colony a second way. Her secretions were blended with other substances to create an odor unique to the colony as a whole. The odorants were absorbed into the waxy cuticle that covered the body of every member of the colony. Each colony of ants had a personal bouquet that all its members shared and learned and to which they remained absolutely faithful. When two ants met, regardless of their origins, they both swept their antennae back and forth over the other. The movement was too swift for the unaided human eye to follow, but the brain of each ant almost instantly processed the information. If the two ants shared the same odor, the message was, *She belongs to my colony, no other.* The two then either continued on their way without pause, or paused to groom each other, or exchanged food. If, on the other hand, their odors differed even slightly, the message was, *Different colony, look out!* Like strange dogs meeting in the street, two ants of separate origin stopped to examine each other more carefully. They then either launched an attack or ran from each other.

No words, no signals of motion were used to establish an ant's tribal identity. None was needed. The Trailhead Colony was united simply and entirely by possession of the same smell. If that were to disappear, the superorganism would quickly dissolve into a mob of disoriented organisms. They would fight among themselves. Enemies would scatter them. Predators would close in for an easy meal.

The Trailhead Queen lay in state. It could not last forever. Eventually parts of her body were eaten and the rest carried away to the ant cemetery. For a week the pheromones licked off the remaining fragments continued to broadcast her existential message. Thereafter the chemicals gradually dissipated, and at last the message faded away.

A few chemical signs appeared early, but it was on the third day after she died that the Queen's pheromones began to be overlaid by the faint evidence of death. Her overall odor became ambiguous, and with it the posthumous messages she sent. Still, nothing mattered in the recognition of her corpse other than the odor of decay. Visual appearance and the cessation of movement meant nothing. The Queen could have lain on her back with her legs held rigidly up in the air. She could have turned any color: red, black, metallic gold, or any other hue or shade, it would not matter. Instead, the Queen had to *smell* dead in order to be classified as dead. And not from the blends of substances in corpses repellent to the human nose—not, for example, from the loathsome skatole and indole that distinguish human feces, nor the trimethylamine that rises dramatically from spoiled fish. Such chemicals, when encountered alone, would cause alarm in the ants and repel them. The same was true of other volatile toxic substances. Only oleic acid and its ester, which are decomposition products of fat, were effective messengers of death. They mean little or nothing to the human nose. But they mean *dead* to an ant. When encountered on the corpse of a nestmate, they caused the ants to pick it up and carry it away for disposal.

Within a week, the constant licking of the royal corpse in the Trailhead Colony started to break it into pieces. One by one the fragments, reeking of the oleic compounds, were carried out of the royal chamber. Unknowingly the ants bade farewell to their mother. No ceremony was performed. Instead the workers bearing the body parts wandered alone through the nest galleries in search of the Trailheader cemetery. This special place was not marked by ceremonial trappings. It had no special shape, nor did it contain any token of remembrance, even for a queen. It was merely a chamber at the periphery of the underground nest. The ants dumped all kinds of debris into it, including discarded cocoons shed by newly emerged adults, inedible parts of prey, and deceased colony members.

When the corpse carriers came close to the refuse chamber, they turned their burdens over to cemetery workers. These specialists were ants who constantly rearranged and added to the refuse piles. They stayed close to their work and were for the most part avoided by their nestmates.

In cemetery work and all other activities, the Trailhead Colony organized its labor by altruistic rules of labor specialization. Everything they did was restrained by some degree of self-sacrificial altruism. Above all, the workers had given up the chance to reproduce, at least so long as the Queen was alive and healthy. They accepted service in foraging, soldiering, and other dangerous occupations that increased their risk, often to the point of certain early death. The dominance of the Trailhead Colony over its individual member ants was total. The welfare of the superorganism was paramount, and a worker's life story was programmed to be subordinate to the superorganism's needs. If a worker died, the loss weakened the colony to some measurable but relatively inconsequential extent. The deficit could be quickly made up by rearing another worker in the nursery. If, on the other hand, a worker behaved in a selfish manner, consuming for a good part of its life more resources than it contributed, it weakened the colony far more than if it just had the decency to desert or die.

The decency of ants was, in disability, to leave and trouble no more. The self-sacrifices that led to the success of the Trailhead Colony were evident in every task performed by all of the worker force in all circumstances. The sick and injured received no care. In fact, they avoided such attention, moving on their own to the outermost nest chambers. The disabled were among the colony's most aggressive fighters. Dying workers often left the nest completely, thereby avoiding the spread of infectious diseases.

Older workers that stayed healthy but were approaching the end of their natural life-span also emigrated to the nest perimeter. From there they were prone to become foragers, leaving the nest to search for food, which exposed them to a much higher risk from enemies. When defending the nest, elders were among the most suicidally aggressive. They were obedient to a simple truth that separates our two species: where humans send their young men to war, ants send their old ladies.

The Queen had been the exclusive reproducer of the colony, the mother of the entirety of its inhabitants and the new colonies they were able to produce. All the sacrifices offered by the workers were made to protect her life and to enhance her fertility. Whether the Trailhead Colony would now live or die depended upon its ability to replace the mother Queen. That would require all their skill in retaining their strength until a new Queen was installed.

· 20 ·

A T THIS POINT the ancient colony seemed doomed. Grow or die was the iron law it must obey. Population growth, positive or negative, up or down, is of life-and-death importance to any ant colony. Constant population growth and ever-rising productivity in the nurseries are the superorganism's bottom line. Both social and personal life are geared to serve this central purpose. The reason is elementary: the larger the colony, the greater its net growth, and hence the more virgin queens and males it can contribute to the next generation of colonies. Genes that prescribe robust colony growth spread across the land and through the species as a whole; those that do not prescribe robust growth shrink before the expanding Darwinian winners, and disappear.

The Trailheader myrmidons themselves instinctively knew they were in trouble. In time the chemical signals had dropped to a hardly detectable level in the outermost reaches of the nest. The workers began to understand that their Queen was incompetent.

Still, the instinct machine could not be turned off. The pheromone messages continued. They flowed ant to ant, spreading the latest news, the gossip, the health and wealth of the commonweal. The worker castes performed as before, and foragers still left in the early morning to search for food in the surrounding terrain. But the Trailheader workers had begun to change in subtle ways. The throttle of the colony was easing, a little at a time.

The Queen's health had been declining weeks before her death. The clues were all around her. Her egg production had plummeted, then halted. There were fewer and fewer larvae to feed. More nurse workers were idled, and colony growth slowed. The number of foragers taking the field dropped.

Yet there was hope for the colony. Even when the Queen still lived, the thinning of her pheromones had caused subtle changes in the bodies of young soldiers headquartered in the nest. These largest members of the worker caste had massive heads filled with powerful muscles, which slammed their sharp-toothed jaws together like serrated wire cutters. They were the iron, the physical power, the instinctual viciousness of the colony. They usually served only to defend the nest from intruders. Sometimes they went out along the odor trails with the ordinary workers to guard large food sources against rival colonies. But they also had the ability to reproduce. Their capacious abdomens contained a half dozen ovaries that, when enlarged by further growth, could produce viable eggs. Amazons all, they could change from warriors to mothers.

As the Queen pheromone declined, the soldiers were alerted. The sensory cells in the outer segments of their antennae noted the change. The information was relayed along nerve cells to the soldiers' brains. Circuits within the brains transmitted instructions to endocrine glands located elsewhere in the head. The hormones released from these glands stimulated growth in the ovaries of the young soldiers. Lines of eggs then appeared inside the ovaries. They began as microscopically small masses near the outer tips of the ovaries. The eggs grew in size as they migrated downward toward the openings of the ovaries, reaching maximum size just before they were laid.

The soldiers with the potential to become the new queens of the Trailhead Colony and no longer inhibited by the mother Queen pheromone abandoned their regular duties. With their ovaries swelling with eggs, they moved deeper into the nest interior and closer to the dwindling piles of larvae and pupae. As the last shards of the old Queen's body were carried into the cemetery, several of her rival successors began to lay eggs. They were now soldier-queens, and the only hope the colony had to restart its own growth.

The ordinary workers around them accepted the new status of the soldier-queens. Their tolerance represented a profound shift in the behavior of the colony as a whole. If the mother Queen had remained alive and well, and she had continued to broadcast her special scent, the response to any usurper would have been swift and violent. The Trailhead Colony had previously obeyed a basic rule of antdom: to reproduce in the presence of a healthy queen is strictly forbidden. The odds against success of such an affront to authority are long. The gamble is dangerous, and only a very few make the attempt. When a usurper starts to lay her own eggs and place them among those of a healthy queen, or even when she just becomes capable of doing so, she is harassed by her nestmates. Her sisters refuse to regurgitate food to her. They climb and stand over her, pulling at her legs and antennae. They may use their stings to cripple or kill her, or else spray her with a poisonous secretion. And they eat any eggs she manages to lay. Only when the Queen dies is the taboo lifted—and then only for a few individuals.

When the taboo ended in the Trailheader nest, a second crisis arose. The candidate royals began to quarrel among themselves for control. They converged on the brood chambers and jostled for position there. They struggled to climb on top of their rivals. Winners in these encounters seized their opponents' legs and antennae and dragged them away from the brood chambers. Unlike the thousands of their ordinary nestmates, they recognized one another as individuals. In time a dominance hierarchy formed, similar to pecking orders among chickens and rank orders among wolves. The Trailheader female who emerged as the alpha contender, in other words was able to chase away all her rivals, won the reproductive role. Egg-laying and larval growth resumed in a reduced but orderly manner. The crisis had ended by combat.

If the Trailhead Colony could not understand the history of its own species, how much did it know of its current condition? How could it make the right decision for survival? In fact, the Trailhead Colony knew a great deal. Worker ants are far more than just automated specks running around on the ground. Even with a brain only a millionth as big as that of a human, an ant can learn a simple maze half as fast as a laboratory rat, and remember the directions to as many as five different destinations when she forages away from the nest. After exploring a new terrain, a worker can integrate all the seemingly haphazard twists and loops she made and, amazingly, return to the nest in a straight line. She can learn and recall the special odor of the colony to which she belongs. In some species, she can recognize her own personal smell in odor trails over the ground to which she has contributed her own pheromones.

The Trailhead Colony, when all the learning and thought of its workers came together, was very smart by insect standards. With the unifying power of its Queen taken away and its population growth plummeting, it needed to act with all its group intelligence to regain its balance.

When one of the soldier-queens dominated its rivals and became the new Queen, the recovery of the colony seemed to get under way. A stream of eggs were laid. Larvae began to fill the empty brood chambers. Their odor and hunger signals joined with the pheromones of the new Soldier-Queen and spread through the nest. The power was returning. The workers found new energies. More foragers took the field.

One of the ants that led the way in restoring order was an elite worker that had served in the Queen's entourage during the final days. About ten percent of the worker force deserved this status, which they kept all their lives. All achieved it by labor; none belonged to the soldier caste, which was specialized for combat and called into action only when the colony was threatened. The elites were nervous and vigorous in movement. They initiated more tasks. They worked harder and more persistently, and they usually stayed on the job until it was finished. Other colony members were stirred to join them at the tasks they began. They were not just statistically at the upper end of the activity curve. They were a distinct group all on their own, forming a bump on the high end of the curve, and important to even a temporary prolonging of the life of the colony.

This particular elite worker was typical of her class in initiative and energy. After leaving the dead Queen, she proceeded directly to the nest entrance in search of new duties. Food was low, and fewer ordinary workers, grown lethargic, were leaving in search of new supplies. The defense of the colony had been weakened by the thinning of the sentinel force spread around the nest perimeter. Sensing the negligence of its nestmates, the elite left on solitary patrols, circling first close to the nest, then farther and farther away.

The renewed activity, led by the elites, was short-lived, however. The colony was destined to die, doomed by a hereditary trait even more basic than the altruism of the workers and the pheromonal ties that bound them together. The trait is the following. The Trailheaders, along with all ants of all kinds that ever existed back to the birth of ants in the late Jurassic period, used a strange but elegant genetic method to fix the sex of an individual at birth. Fertilized eggs develop into females, which can become queens or workers, and unfertilized eggs develop into males, which can do nothing but inseminate females.

The Soldier-Queen had never mated. Her children all arose from unfertilized eggs and were therefore male drones, contributing nothing to the welfare of the colony. They had weak mandibles and small brains but huge eyes and genitalia. They were wondrously adapted for mating after flying, up in the air with virgin queens, but even if that occurred it would do nothing for the Trailhead Colony. Those created by the Soldier-Queen would not mate with her or other potential Soldier-Queens. They were programmed to mate during nuptial flights away from the nest.

No way out existed for the Trailheaders; the colony was in a terrible fix. The linchpin of its social existence was gone and could not be replaced. Like a player in a Greek tragedy, it had been undone by the unfolding of events prescribed by its own unalterable nature. The source of its early success had become its fatal flaw. The colony could for a while contribute, through its production of males, to the gene pool of the population of colonies all around Dead Owl Cove, and in that way tweak out one more bit of Darwinian profit. But it could do nothing more for its own physical existence. With each passing day it became more vulnerable as a superorganism.

As the Trailhead Colony struggled in this pitiless world, its territory and even its very flesh were coveted by others. It would not merely fade away, holding on until a final worker sat alone in the nest. On the contrary, the neighboring colonies were likely to learn of its decline, and when that happened there would be war. And when war came, there was only the slimmest chance that the queenless Trailhead Colony could win.

21

FOR A WHILE the Trailhead Colony, while stricken, still retained most of its military strength. Fifteen percent of its adult members were soldiers. They were contracted to be hoplites, or heavily armored infantry. Twice the size of an ordinary worker, a soldier's exoskeleton was literally heavy armor: thick, tough, and pitted in places like a shield for resilience and strength. A pair of spines projected backward from the midsection of the body to protect the waist. Spikes extended forward from the midsection to protect the neck, and the rear margin of the head was curved forward, turning that part of the surface into a helmet. When attacked, the hoplite soldier could pull in her legs and antennae and tighten up the segments of her body in order to turn her entire body surface into a shield.

The ordinary Trailheader workers, while built for labor, were also available for combat. Then they served as the equivalent of light infantry. Because their exoskeletons were much thinner than those of the hoplites, they were not inclined to stand fast in battle. Instead, they used the swiftness and agility of their supple bodies, running around their enemies, darting in and out, seizing any leg or antenna available, holding on to it, slowing the opponent enough for nestmates to close in and seize another body part. When the adversary was finally pinned and spread-eagled, others piled on to bite, sting, or spray it with poison. This swarm attack, in which a crowd of fighters rush a formidable opponent simultaneously, was the same as used by wolves circling a moose, or infantrymen attacking an enemy firebase.

Such was the force, originally ten thousand strong, that had protected the Trailheader nest against all enemies. Now the number of able-bodied adults had begun to decline, and the survivors were growing old.

The decline of Trailhead Colony was being closely watched by its closest neighbor, the Streamside Colony. This younger and now more powerful superorganism was prepared to take advantage of its neighbor's misfortune.

Early one morning, an elite Streamsider worker, followed by a squad of her nestmates, left her nest to assess the strength of the Trailhead Colony. Precise monitoring of the enemy strength was not easy. The two nests were separated by about two thousand ant lengths, or a distance of twenty yards. The scout, if allowed to travel in a straight line on a smooth surface, might have covered that distance in under six minutes. But a straight run was not possible, because the terrain was filled with obstacles that were scarcely noticeable to a human being but were daunting to a ten-millimeter-long ant. In the miniature world of antdom, clumps of grass were like groves of trees and bushes, and dead leaves and twigs like fallen timber. A surface of sand smooth to humans was to the ants a jumble of rocks, and pebbles were large boulders. Rain was a deadly threat. One drop striking an ant had the human-equivalent force of a firehose jet. A rivulet of rainwater trickling through a crease in the soil was the equivalent of a flash flood raging down a desert ravine.

As the elite ant left on her journey, she remembered the route more or less precisely. She had been to the Trailhead territory before, and remembered the way. She carried a compass in her head, using the sun as a lodestar. This reliance could have been the source of a huge error for an ant, because the sun travels across the sky and so the correct angle constantly changes. However, each ant also carried in her head a biological clock set on a full day's twenty-four-hour cycle, run with a precision far beyond the capacity of an unaided human brain. Using her clock, the scout continuously changed the angle to the sun needed to keep her on track.

The trajectory of the sun by itself is completely reliable in space and time. At Nokobee it traced a geometrically perfect arc across the sky, rising through the pines on the eastern lakeshore, passing directly above the anthills of Dead Owl Cove, and finally disappearing westward into the forest lying beyond. The azimuth read by the ant, however, unlike the transit of the sun, was less than perfect. So the scout occasionally stopped and gazed at prominent features she had memorized during earlier trips. A pair of pine seedlings were one such signpost, a circular opening in the canopy a second, a dark shadow beneath a holly shrub a third.

Then there was the odor terrain, parts of which the scout memorized from chemical cues she had encountered on earlier trips. In exercising this ability, she was as different from a human being as it is possible to imagine. The scout smelled the ground continuously and precisely as its surface rushed by two millimeters' distance beneath her body. Her nose was the outer segments of her paired antennae—the two feelers on her head. She turned these hypersensitive instruments downward, enough to almost touch the ground, and swung them from side to side. The odors she detected as she ran, specific in their mix, intensity, and gradient, provided detailed information of her location and direction of travel. They were her combined field guide and topographic map.

The nearby pine-leaf litter conveyed its acrid scent to mingle with that from the humus beneath the colony foraging grounds. A surge of one particular blend greeted her here, a countersurge of another kind there. The prevailing background was over-powered now and then by a flashing scent of something radically different—quickly gone but remembered for a while.

The olfactory world of the running Streamsider contained much more than an invisible road map. Bombarding the ant from below and from all sides above were the odors of organisms that inhabited the soil—so densely as to make up a large part of the physical bulk of the soil. There were endless local profusions of fungal hyphae and bacteria. Each gave up its signature smell. There were the rising odors of the animals the size of the ant or smaller, a quarter million packed into every square meter. They were the insects, spiders, pillbugs, nematode roundworms, and other invertebrates that dominate in numbers. One trace within the mix picked up by the sweeping antennae could disclose a potential prey, another a waiting spider or some other ambush predator.

The human mind cannot imagine the tumult of chemical stimuli by which such a traveling ant guides every moment in her life, and thus survives. It cannot conceive of the constant

202 • *The Anthill Chronicles*

enormity of the deadly risks she must skillfully evade, instantaneously at every moment.

The Streamsider scout hurried undistracted through this olfactory cosmos. Her destination was in the direction of the enemy nest but not the nest itself. She was consciously headed for a flat, open area half the distance there. On arriving, the scout mingled with a group of nestmates who had preceded her, and— an extraordinary event for ants—they also mingled freely with scouts from the Trailhead Colony. One of these enemies was the newly arrived elite and former Trailhead Queen attendant.

In a short time the representatives from the two colonies appeared to *dance* with one another. The ants were not performing in any human sense, however. They had come here instead to conduct a tournament between colonies. The scouts were gathering information that allowed them to assess the strength of the opposing Trailhead Colony. They could use this information and simultaneously advertise their own strength to the enemy without risk of death or injury. The dance, in short, was not that, but a highly formalized probe and communication that reinforced the security of the two colonies.

At the time of this day's tournament, the Streamside Colony was at its peak as a superorganism. It was strong enough to challenge any neighboring colony, and especially the declining Trailhead Colony. The Streamside Queen was only six years old, the equivalent of thirty years in a human life-span. She was in her prime, bursting with eggs, and she reeked of sweet-smelling royal pheromone. Her colony's nest was on firm, productive ground at the edge of an undisturbed patch of deciduous scrub woodland. Close by in the woods a small stream gave the nest protection on one side. On the other side a miniature ravine dropped away, too steep to harbor nests of potential rivals. The Streamsiders had not chosen this site for their own protection. They were just lucky that their mother Queen had landed there.

As the Streamsider scouts gathered in the arena, they found their Trailheader counterparts also assembling in almost equal numbers. A few had climbed up on the tops of pebbles to serve as sentinels. The first scouts on both sides to encounter the enemy ran home to recruit reinforcements. They laid odor trails to excite and guide their nestmates, and they carried faint smears of the enemy odor on their own body surface to identify the opposition. Within an hour hundreds of ants from both colonies were milling around one another. The original scouts, all of whom were relatively small and thin, were soon joined by contingents of the more massively built soldiers.

The opposing forces were careful not to start a battle. Their strategy was the opposite: the displays were the equivalent of competing military parades by human armies. They wanted their performance to be viewed by the enemy.

As the tournament unfolded, the individual performers made themselves appear as large as possible. They inflated their abdomens by pumping them up with fluid. They straightened their legs to form stilts and strutted around every foreign worker they encountered—sometimes bumping against them. Still others climbed up and posed on top of pebbles, exaggerating their size still more. They never threatened to attack. The effort they were making was meant to persuade the other side that their colony had a great many soldiers. A few small workers served as counters, not engaged in displays themselves but moving about among the crowds of performing workers in order to gain an estimate of the size of the soldier force. The larger the enemy force, the more intense the effort the counters made to attract others to the tournament. A weakness in their recruiting effort was a signal to the other side of that colony's weakness. It was an unintended encouraging clue for the opposing colony.

Even before the death of the Trailhead Queen, and increasingly now that she was gone, the military pomp of the Trailhead Colony had become noticeably less impressive. Gradually and carefully over a period of a week, led by signals from the elite scout and several of her nestmates, the Trailheaders pulled back from the first territorial boundary. They tried to start tournaments closer to home, where their soldiers together with the make-believe soldiers among the smaller ants who filled out the force could be called to the field more quickly. But this tactic did not fool the elite Streamsider scout and her frontline nestmates on the other side, who pushed even harder and mounted increasingly conspicuous displays. There was nothing the Trailheaders could do but continue to pull back, day after day, thereby ceding some of their foraging territory.

Still, the retreat was not by itself a defeat. There was a chance that the Trailhead Colony might eke out a victory, or at least force a draw. The reason was that as the tournament arena moved closer to their nest, the defenders were able to reach the arena more quickly. They could draw out whatever reinforcements were available on a minute-by-minute basis. The Streamsiders were forced, on the other hand, to accept a comparable disadvantage. They had to travel almost the entire distance between the two nests in order to continue the tournaments. With the lines of communication stretched so far, the adjustments made by the Streamsider force were slow and inaccurate. The weaker Trailheaders, by retreating slowly, were close to striking a balance. If that occurred, they might hold their opponents in place indefinitely, perhaps all the way to the end of the foraging season. The loss of part of their territory would be an acceptable price to a colony with a declining population.

The Trailheaders had now surrendered all their territory to the east of their nest in the direction of the Streamsider nest. There was a possibility that this conquest would be enough for the Streamsiders. They had achieved a great victory without the loss of a single life on either side. If they called off the tournaments now, a long standoff peace—a Pax Formicana, so to speak—might come to the two domains.

Peace with honor was not, however, the way of the Nokobee anthills. After three weeks of advance, culminating finally when the tournaments were held at the edge of the Trailheader nest mound, the Streamsider dancers suddenly switched to an all-out attack on the Trailhead Colony. No more propaganda for them, no more bluffing.

The assault began as an unplanned chain reaction among the Streamsider players. They had grown increasingly excited during each day's event. They seemed to be approaching the threshold that separates hostile display from overt combat. They circled around the Trailheaders more tightly, bumping harder and more frequently.

Finally, near the beginning of one tournament when the Trailheaders had been crowded into a space only several feet wide in front of their nest mound, a Streamsider worker—the elite scout and tournament veteran—crossed the threshold of aggression and single-handedly began the war. She attacked the first Trailheader she encountered, spraying it with a combination of alarm pheromones and poisonous secretions. The odor of these materials galvanized the nestmates closest to her. They crossed the aggression threshold also and launched an attack of their own. Two workers in combat quickly led to three, three to four, and on upward, spreading violence exponentially through the assembled Streamsider ranks. Some of the Trailheaders quickly broke away from the battle and rushed back to their nest to recruit reinforcements. Others responded to the attack by standing their ground and fighting back.

Soon the battle turned into a furious and deadly melee. The Trailheaders were too weak to hold their ground. The Streamsiders drove through the dissolving mass of defenders, attacking each one they could catch. All the ants on both sides now abandoned the tournament mode. They deflated their abdomens to normal size and relaxed the stiltlike stiffness of their legs. Fighters on both sides instead climbed on top of their opponents, seizing legs and antennae with their sawtooth jaws, gnashing and stinging whatever vulnerable body parts they could reach. When two or more Streamsider fighters managed to take hold of a Trailheader at the same time, they spread-eagled her, exposing her body to a fatal bite or sting by others who charged in. Soon dead and dying workers from both sides littered the battlefield. Most of the casualties were Trailheaders. Among them was the elite scout and former nurse, who was stung to death and dismembered.

More of the surviving Trailheaders gave up combat and retreated into the nest entrance. Those who hesitated were run down and killed as though they were insect prey.

They were in fact insect prey. Their bodies were treated the same as those of subdued grasshoppers and caterpillars. After battle the dead and injured would be collected and eaten by their conquerors. Cannibalism was more than just the fruit of conquest. The conquest turned into a foraging expedition.

The defense of the Trailhead Colony completely collapsed within a half hour. A few of the survivors, dodging their pursuers, ran back and forth between their nest and the main battle site, somehow measuring the magnitude of the disaster. The last among them finally pulled back into the nest entirely. As they neared the entrance, a few turned and continued the fight, keeping the area immediately around it clear of the enemy. With the help of others, they dragged in nearby pieces of soil, charcoal, and leaf litter, and piled them up to form a plug in and on top of the nest entrance.

The Trailheader nest was now a sealed and hidden bunker. The victorious Streamsider army poured over its mound surface, and some of their scouts pressed on to explore the newly conquered land beyond.

The siege of the Trailheader nest had begun. During the next day, and for days to follow, Trailheader foragers slipped out for brief periods to search for whatever scraps of food had been overlooked by the Streamsider patrols combing the surrounding area. Some were caught, others killed. The others retreated too quickly to be successful in their foraging.

Within a week the colony began to starve. The nurse ants killed and cannibalized the last of the larvae and pupae, their own baby sisters, and regurgitated their liquid and tissue to other adults. Finally, no reserves were left except dwindling fat in the bodies of the huddled survivors.

The Streamside Colony relentlessly pressed its conquest. Its workers explored the new land to the outer edges of the old Trailheader domain. They tolerated no remaining trace of the Trailhead Colony. If its scouts could find the newly hidden entrance of the nest, they would summon a force to invade the interior. If they then succeeded, the conflict between the two colonies would escalate to a quick and final end.

Under these conditions the Trailhead Colony was unable to conceal itself for long. The surviving population huddled inside the nest was too big and the odor it emitted too strong. The pre-war territorial secretions Trailheader workers had laid over the nest surface, thickest near the entrance, now pointed like traffic signs to the nest entrance. The chemical signals that once guided homecoming workers and warned off intruders were about to become the agent of the Trailheader downfall.

The failed strategy of the Trailheaders was the opposite of another neighbor, the meek little Woodland Colony hidden nearby. These ants were even closer to the Trailhead Colony than was the Streamsider Colony. The Woodlanders had been forced by competition from the Trailheaders to remain in a small, hidden nest. They were unable to increase their population size, and persisted only at constant great risk of discovery and destruction.

As their own population grew, the Trailheaders, in contrast, had invested a large amount of their resources in defense and propaganda. They had built a large soldier force and committed themselves to elaborate tournaments. They used territorial pheromones to advertise the nest. Now in decline, their earlier strength had turned into a fatal liability.

The Woodlanders survived as the Trailheaders perished. They were too few to play in the formicid big league. To survive, they had been forced to rely on the hidden site of their nest and on their timid demeanor when they left to hunt for food. They went unnoticed while war raged next door. Woodlanders fought no battles. They were excused from the necessity either to win or to lose. Their weakness had become a strength—at least for the moment.

Meanwhile, as the Woodlanders held fast, the end approached for the Trailhead Colony. Three weeks following the big victory, Streamsider scouts converged on the shielded entrance of the Trailheader nest and immediately attacked it. Some ran away briefly to recruit more nestmate soldiers to the spot. The assembled force pulled aside the debris the defenders had dragged in to serve as a cover. Trailheader soldiers poured out of the nest in a last desperate effort to protect the entrance. In the tumult that followed, many fighters on both sides were killed or crippled. Finally, the weakened Trailheaders began to pull back. One by one the minors gave up the last of their resistance, turning away and running down the main gallery and into the lateral galleries and chambers deep in the nest.

The Trailheader soldiers, however, did not retreat. They regrouped instead, forming a tight circle around the nest entrance with their heads facing outward, ready to fight to the last ant. Their snapping jaws held off the attackers into the late afternoon hours. At first it appeared that they had succeeded in reversing the battle. As the light faded, the Streamsiders, true to the biological clock of their species in all things including even war, pulled away and returned home.

The withdrawal was not a retreat by the Streamsiders; nor was it a victory for the Trailheaders. In the confusion that reigned through the night, the Trailhead Colony felt—it knew—that it was in extreme difficulty. It had no conception of defeat, but only because it had never suffered one. The nest interior was filled with the odor of alarm and recruitment pheromones released by both sides during the attempted Streamsider break-in at the entrance. The fighters were contaminated by the alien body odor of the invaders. They could see the battle flags of the enemy, so to speak, while listening to the continuous shriek of loudspeaker alarms.

The entire colony was on the edge of panic. Agitated ants ran back and forth through the rooms and galleries of the nest, to no special purpose. The colony was not yet aware of the ultimate meaning of its own mood and actions, but it was instinctively preparing for one last maneuver, a final, almost suicidal response that might yet save some of its members. What remained to them as an option was a burst of flight to the outside, every ant for herself. With luck a few survivors might then reassemble and restart the colony elsewhere. That is, if they had a real queen. But of course they had only their inadequate Soldier-Queen.

During the desperate hours the oldest Trailheader workers remembered another extraordinary event that occurred the previous summer, when they were young and most of their nestmates now present had not yet been born. The sun was shining that day. The Trailhead Queen was strong, and well-fed larvae crowded the floors and walls of the brood chambers. A large number of foragers had taken the field, including workers just old enough to leave their nursing duties and embark on their first exploration outdoors.

As the sun approached its zenith in the cloudless sky, it was suddenly blotted out. Then, as abruptly, it returned, and disappeared again, and so on off and on for a long while. With an ant's dim vision the foragers saw that gigantic elongate objects were casting shadows. They seemed to be trees reaching into the sky. But moving! Then down from somewhere high came strange, loud sounds very different from those made by birds, squirrels, or singing insects. There were hissing and grunting noises, mingled together, and traded back and forth, their volume shifting up and down. Strange odors also came down to blanket the ground. The disturbance was unique in the experience of Trailheader elders. It was as violent as any wind or rainstorm they had ever experienced. Most of the foragers fled into the nest. A few chased the moving trees and tried to climb and attack them.

The visit, by a human family that had spread its picnic lunch carelessly next to the Trailheader nest, continued into the middle of the afternoon, then suddenly ended. The strange sounds faded into the distance. The odors began to fade. When the Trailheader workers ventured out again, they found a scene as odd as the gargantuan apparitions themselves. Some of their nestmates who stayed outside had been crushed flat into the ground. Far more oddly, all around the nest surface and beyond, food particles were scattered. They were a kind never before encountered by the ants. Some were the size of a worker ant, others hundreds of thousands of times larger. None resembled dead insects, parts of plants, or anything else the Trailheaders could remember. Still, they were pure food, rich in protein, fat, and sugar. The ants found the heaven-born gifts more delicious even than aphid feces, and more nourishing than freshly butchered cockroaches. To their good fortune, the humans had thoughtlessly dumped the garbage from their lunch on top of the Trailheader territory.

It was in the memories of the older ants that most of the distributed intelligence of the colony existed, as opposed to mere instinct and emotion. To the mind of a young ant, born just this year, the elders' memories of an event of the previous year, if such could be communicated at all, was a nonexistent formicid antiquity.

But for some elders in the Trailheader superorganism, the moving trees were powers that lived outside the ant cosmos, equivalent to the way gods are viewed in the human mind. The elders thought, and therefore the colony thought in part, as a segment of the human brain might think, that the moving-tree gods cared about them in some inexplicable way. Perhaps they were gigantic nestmates. They might now, in the hour of the Trailheaders' dire peril, spread benevolence again.

Other elders did not think this way. To them the gods were just a less common version of what the colony experienced routinely, such as a powerful wind off the lake or a violent thunderstorm. At least, not a living force concerned with the fate of ants. Still others—a small minority, to be sure—doubted that the gods ever existed. Instead, they thought of the gods as just a strong delusion acquired long ago—human decades ago as measured by ant standards.

Lamentation and hope were mingled among the Trailheader inhabitants. The ants were like a doomed people in a besieged city. Their unity of purpose was gone, and their social machinery halted. No foraging, no cleaning and feeding larvae, no Queen for them to rally around. The pheromones of her substitute, the Soldier-Queen, were too weak to hold them together. The order of the colony was dissolving. Out there, indomitable and waiting, were the hated, filthy, unformicid Streamsiders. Finally, all the Trailheaders knew was terror, and the existence of a choice—they could fight or run from the horror. There was nothing else left in their collective mind.

To deceive and intimidate enemies, to build the sturdiest fortress, to maneuver, to reinforce, to safeguard, to preempt, to emigrate to a better home—such were the actions that might have saved them. But all that had now passed.

22

ARLY THE NEXT DAY, as the rising sun warmed and dried the dew from the grassy ground of Dead Owl Cove and the Nokobee anthills all around it came to life, the Streamsider army resumed its attack. Once again Trailheader soldiers formed a defensive ring around the entrance to their nest. This time no Trailheader minors joined the sally. The buffer previously provided by these smaller workers outside the soldiers' ring was gone. The Streamsider assault was focused, massive, and unrelenting. Within an hour the force had built to maximum field strength. The Trailheader soldiers, weakening, fell one by one. No new fighters crowded in to replace those lost, and the ring broke. Streamsider soldiers and minor workers, with the elite scout in the front rank, rushed past the last of the remaining defenders and poured down the central tunnel.

As they penetrated deep and fanned out into the peripheral galleries and chambers, the Streamsider conquerors met almost no resistance. The growing strength of alarm pheromone and their own alien colony smell, filling the nest interior, drew them forth. In contrast, the Trailhead Colony exploded into pandemonium. Each defending worker was now concerned only with her own survival. The entire surviving worker force was a panicked, helpless mob. It fled upward and out into the open to break through the enemy workers massed there. Many were snared as they rushed past Streamsiders running in the opposite direction. No further communication was attempted. There would be no chance to return as an organized group. Without a queen or nest, the Trailhead Colony no longer existed. All its land, including the underground nest, was now Streamsider territory.

Most of the individual Trailheader refugees found temporary shelters on the surface, hiding beneath fallen leaves and cracks in the soil. A few met by chance and stayed together for a while. One by one, nevertheless, they were picked off by predators and enemy ants. They tried to dodge and run to hide again, but there were no odor trails and visual markers to guide them anywhere, and no nest to serve as a destination. The social organization that had defined their antness had now been stripped away. They lived individually only hours or, at most, a few days longer. One was snatched by a wolf spider, and another fell into a rain puddle. Yet another came too close to a running column of army ants, which seized it and cut it into pieces for food.

As the invaders explored the abandoned nest interior, they gathered a few newly hatched adult workers too weak to run out of the nest with their older nestmates. All these captives the Streamsider raiders carried back unharmed to their own nest, a few to be eaten but most to be kept as slaves. Their captors took advantage of a trait basic to all kinds of ants: the individual slaves learned and thereafter accepted the odor of the colony in which they lived during the first several days following their emergence from pupa into active adult life. In that brief period the Trailheader callows acquired the odor of the Streamside Colony. From that time those who were brought into the Streamsider nest and survived being cannibalized became part of the slave-maker colony. They would thereafter live on equal terms with their captors, attacking any ant with a different odor.

By adopting the young adults at the age they learned the colony odor, the victorious Streamsider Colony added to its labor force with no great effort. The slaves—and that is what they were, because they served the victors entirely—made up for some of the Streamsider workers lost in battle.

Had the Trailhead Queen been alive during the war and captured by the Streamsider raiders, she would have been torn to pieces immediately. No queen of a defeated ant colony is allowed to live one unnecessary minute. The ant mind is remorseless in its insistence upon absolute sovereignty. No colony in power, and especially no alien queen, can be tolerated, because it is a threat to that sovereignty. It follows that any alliance between colonies is also out of the question. The absolute imperative of the nest site is the heart of the superorganism's life. The first law of ant colonial existence is that the territory must be protected at any cost.

There were forces, however, above and outside the colony's frame of reference. Just three weeks before, after their victory over the Trailheaders, the Streamsiders' nest had been visited by the moving trees. The event was similar to that experienced by the defeated Trailhead Colony the previous year. The giants came from nowhere, they departed abruptly without any reason understandable to ants, and they left behind vast quantities of strange food on the ground. The conjunction of all these events, and the magnitude of the gift, made the inexplicable visitors the equivalent of benevolent gods to the Streamsiders. The ants counted the coming of the gods as special to themselves, indeed a great blessing. True to the rules of learning by association, which applies to ants as it does to men, they also saw the gods as part of their extended society: *They think like us (there is no other way to think, or way to conceive of another way to think about thinking), and they are part of our power.*

The Streamsiders had defeated the Trailheaders, and then, as a parallel of some Old Testament tribe wiping out a defeated people, they committed myrmicide, the ant equivalent of genocide. Total destruction ensured, as for the Roman conquerors at Carthage, that their rivals would never rise again. Now the Streamsiders spread throughout the conquered territory, laying their own odor trails and marking the ground everywhere with moist spots of feces, which contained the territorial pheromone with substances particular to them. But they did not occupy the spacious nest interior of their defeated enemy. They were content for the time being to maintain headquarters in the mother nest. They patrolled their new territory to harvest food consisting variously of prey, sugary sap-sucker excrement, and arthropod corpses. The increased supply allowed the Streamside Colony to grow more rapidly in size.

They had been summoned, and they came unknowingly to die as needed. They conquered and enslaved, and occupied the land their tribe coveted. They were obedient to their instincts, and successfully completed the cycle necessary for the survival of their species.

· 23 ·

A T THIS TIME, to the east of the triumphant Streamside Colony, along the shore of Dead Owl Cove farther away from the trailhead, and still unknown to
the Streamsiders, an ominous change had come upon the environment. The sounds of birds and singing insects were no longer heard. Fewer squirrels, voles, and other mammals foraged
across the quitted land. Butterflies and other pollinators of the
ground plants were close to extinction.

The suppressing agent was a population explosion of ants.
They belonged to the same species as the Streamsiders and other
anthill builders living along the shore of Lake Nokobee, but
had undergone a simple hereditary change with profound social
consequences. So great was the mutation that they seemed out-
wardly to be a different species. Colonies that once contained
up to ten thousand workers and a single mother queen had been
replaced by Supercolony, a single gigantic society composed of
millions of workers and thousands of queens. With no territories to defend, no tournaments to hold, no competition for
food across its vast domain, Supercolony packed all the habitable
ground with multiple interconnected nests.

Its foragers continuously patrolled every square foot. They explored tunnels and crevices in the soil. They checked every earthworm and beetle-grub burrow. They ate every spider that could be pulled from its web. They tolerated no other kind of ant in their domain. Unlike the ordinary anthill colonies of the Streamsiders and others of their same species, they ventured far up the trunks of the surrounding longleaf pines and searched through the lower branches. Supercolony patrolled, as no ordinary anthill colony ever had, the sparse understory of shrubs and high perennials. It turned a substantial part of the upland longleaf savanna on Lake Nokobee's shore into an otherwise lifeless carpet of ants.

Ant empires like this one have cropped up from time to time in different parts of the world. A similar transformation, introduced by a mutant colony accidentally introduced from South America, had swept through the fire ants after the species had occupied most of the southern United States. The origin of the Nokobee Supercolony was due to a change in only one gene in the hereditary code of the ants. The mutation did not create new processes in the brain and sensory system. Instead, it shut a couple of them down. Supercolony was much less sensitive to colony odors than others of its species. Although it could still distinguish the odors of other kinds of ants and nonmutated colonies of its own species, it was unable to make territorial divisions within its own borders.

By weakening Supercolony's sense of smell, the mutation also diminished the workers' ability to detect the queen odor. As a result a multitude of queens were now tolerated, in contrast to the single mother queen allowed in nonmutated colonies. These queenlets, as they might be called, were distributed widely through the webwork of galleries and chambers of the vast Supercolony nest. The queenlets were also smaller in size than nonmutant queens. They did not fly away to mate, and they made no effort to start new colonies of their own. Instead, at the mating hour they simply copulated with males they met on the nest surface, including their own brothers as well as cousins of varying degrees of remove, and then returned immediately to the nest interior to take up the production of more eggs for the growth of Supercolony.

A genetic mistake and a physical disability were for Supercolony ironically the key to success. The erasure of internal territories, combined with perpetual refreshment of the supply of queens, made Supercolony both boundless in size and potentially immortal. The mutation also gave it the power to extract far more resources from its environment than was possible for unmutated colonies of the same species. The ants had more space in which to pack their nests. Their dense populations allowed them to subdue more insects and arthropods as prey, and they were able to eliminate other ant species that competed with them for food.

The mutation had changed not only the social structure of its carriers but also the rules of engagement in war. The myrmidons of Supercolony fell upon rival colonies like a Mongol horde. By early spring in the year following the Streamside Colony victory over the Trailhead Colony, the first Supercolony patrols reached the eastern boundary of the newly secured Streamsider territory. The first workers to encounter the patrols had no conception of what they were now facing. It was nothing less than the greatest natural threat imaginable for these ants. Supercolony armies expanded their own domain by the simple process of building nests on newly conquered land and then sending forth scouts to explore the terrain a relatively short distance beyond. When a large enough expeditionary force could be assembled on the border to confront whatever colonies stood in their way, they attacked their neighbors without hesitation.

As Supercolony scouts appeared with increasing frequency, their counterparts from the Streamside Colony offered to hold a tournament. In the ancient ritual of their species, they puffed up their abdomens, straightened their legs into stilts, and tried to strut around the intruders. Supercolony scouts did not respond in kind. If alone, they fled immediately, laying an odor trail homeward to recruit reinforcements. If already present in groups, they attacked at once.

After a few days of such sorties and mismatched responses, the ants of the closest Supercolony nests reached a level of ant power and excitement sufficient for a military expedition. By this time some of the scouts had already pressed forward and discovered the Streamsider nest itself. The odor trails they laid, the alarm pheromones they broadcast, and the scent of enemy on the bodies of the scouts returning home brought even more Supercolony workers to the frontier. The number of Supercolony fighters able to invade grew faster and faster. For a little while longer Streamsider defenders suggested a tournament. They were answered with unhesitating aggression from the Supercolony invaders.

Finally, the Streamsiders dropped the diplomatic response

and began to fight back on contact. It was too late and too little for the unfortunate defenders. By this time the invading horde was unstoppable. In the course of a single day a wave of lethal fighting spread across the approaches to the Streamsider nest entrance. The jaws that serve as the hands of ants in times of peace and prosperity were now the swords of battle wielded with abandon by overwhelming numbers of the Supercolony invaders. The stings through which the ancestor wasps laid eggs were now poison-tipped stilettos of predation and war.

Within a few hours the ground was covered with severed limbs and dead and injured ants from both sides. The supply of fighters was limited for the Streamside Colony, as usual for their species, but not for Supercolony. The Supercolony army on the field increased as that of Streamsider declined. The minor workers among the defenders started to pull back into the nest, while many of the soldiers formed a circle around the nest entrance, heads facing outward, in the characteristic maneuver of their kind. The tactic, which often works for a strong colony facing another strong colony with the same methods of war, utterly failed this time. The Supercolony force grew to a size never seen in ordinary combat practiced by Nokobee mound ants.

The attackers broke through the Streamsider soldier ring and poured into the interior of the nest. They pressed downward into the labyrinth of subterranean chambers and galleries, subduing and killing every inhabitant they found. They located the mother Queen in the lowermost chamber, huddled beneath a mass of her praetorian soldier guards and minor worker nurses. The invaders pulled off the defenders and killed them all. A dozen seized and spread-eagled the Queen. A soldier cut off her head, and others began to drag her body upward on its long journey to the Supercolony nest, to serve as food. Barely an hour after they had launched the final assault on the Streamsider nest entrance, the battle was over.

The conquerors did not take any of the Streamsider pupae and newly emerged workers alive. Because of the prodigious reproductive capacity of their own colony, especially when enjoying the resources of newly conquered terrain, they had no need of slaves. They killed all the young captives on the spot and carried their bodies back to the Supercolony nest for food.

Only a few Streamsiders managed to escape the final battle and hide in nearby vegetation. Like the Trailheader refugees their own colony had driven out, most died within hours.

Other colonies along the Nokobee lakeside suffered the same fate during the remainder of the summer. By midsummer, the species and most of the rest of antdom across a quarter mile of shore at Dead Owl Cove had been replaced by a continuous, gigantic Supercolony. The ant empire had conquered all. Now there settled a strange new calm upon the region.

Peace and the stability of empire had come to this little parcel of the longleaf pine savanna. No more fighting among colonies of their species, no more wars, no more conflict within the colony over who had the right to reproduce. No more colony boundaries of any kind. Forget the old way of depending on a mother queen. There was now an abundance of surplus queenlets to take her place, any one of which could die without noticeable consequence. Peace across the land, perfect equality among all its citizens, and potential immortality for the empire were the rewards from a change in social structure.

In this one stroke, by intervention of a single micromutation, an era had ended and a new one begun. This part of the Nokobee ecosystem had been shifted in its governance and in the quality of its life.

· 24 ·

Yet, even with its triumph, the Supercolony empire was not healthy. It was out of balance with nature. Its huge, dense population was too heavy a burden for the habitat to carry. Many kinds of plants and animals within reach of the worker swarms began to decline, and a few disappeared altogether. Among the first to suffer were other kinds of ants. Those that occupied soil nests similar to that of Supercolony were driven away, or killed and eaten. Those that depended on similar kinds of food found their supplies declining. Their scouts and harvesters were beaten to new food sites by the ubiquitous Supercolony workers. Spiders and ground beetles that once ranked among the chief predators of the Nokobee anthill species were now themselves hunted down as prey.

Supercolony workers were driven by the need for ever more food to supply the unrestrained egg production of the queenlets and the nurseries of hungry grublike larvae located throughout the giant nest. They penetrated parts of the surrounding environment once shunned as dangerous and unproductive by others of their species. They hunted along the waterline, a habitat dangerous for ants. They climbed the trunks of the trees and combed the lower branches, cleaning out caterpillars, sawfly larvae, tree crickets, and any other living thing that could be caught and killed. They captured or unintentionally frightened away pollinators of flowering plants, including the diversity of butterflies, moths, bees, wasps, hoverflies, and flower beetles that once swarmed over the area.

A small number of species were able to stand up to the onslaught of the new myrmidons. Among them were the most heavily armored of the beetles, centipedes, and millipedes. Also relatively safe were mites, springtails, and other arthropods too small to serve as prey. Earthworms were both elusive and shielded by their thick mucus. These survivors were the equivalent of the house sparrows, rock pigeons, and rats that thrive around humans, each either unpalatable or hard to catch.

A very few creatures did love Supercolony and were loved in return. These were the scale insects, aphids, and mealybugs, delicate and sluggish little insects that pierce plants with hollow beaks and suck out the sap. They were protected by the ants in the same manner and for the same reasons that humans cultivate domestic animals. Supercolony nurtured herds of the sap-suckers throughout its domain. The protection the ants provided against sap-sucker enemies, such as ichneumonid wasps that laid eggs in the bodies of the sap-suckers, and ladybird beetles able to kill and eat the little insects outright, allowed the herds to grow abnormally large. The sap-suckers stunted the growth of the infested plants, causing their leaves to turn yellow and drop off.

Unfettered through the absence of all but a few competitors, freed from most ant-eating predators, Supercolony increased not only in total population but also in density. It came to pass that there were simply more ants per square foot than could be supported by the Lake Nokobee shore. What was once a scattering of nests separated by open space was now a nearly continuous ant city. The problem of meeting Supercolony's ravenous needs was basically the same as supporting an overpopulated human city.

By late summer, the growth of Supercolony had already begun to falter. The ecosystem as a whole, their life support system, was suffering. Many of the surviving plants were too weak to set seed. Ground-foraging animals, including brown thrashers, flickers, squirrels, rabbits, voles, lizards, and snakes, avoided the area. They were repelled as much by the scarcity of food as by the bites and stings they were forced to endure when they tried to forage among the aggressive ants.

Supercolony also had become a subject of talk among humans. Picnickers and fishermen who visited Dead Owl Cove steered around the heaped-up soil of its hundreds of nests. The original formicid inhabitants, including the now-vanished Trailheader and Streamsider Colonies, had been scarcely noticed in previous years. Only a few people, usually children, paused to look at the conspicuous but scattered mound nests. Now everyone paid attention to the amazing Supercolony. "It is," they agreed, "a new kind of ant out there, worse than fire ants." Some added, "What's needed is purely and simply an exterminator."

Supercolony had mastered the environment, subdued its rivals and enemies, increased its space, drawn down new sources of energy, and raised the production of ant flesh to record levels.

The truth, nonetheless, was that Supercolony did not have permanent control of Dead Owl Cove. In the long train of eco-logical time it was guaranteed only a few seasons of success. By trading sustainability of the home for wider dominance, its genes had made a terrible mistake. A price had to be paid, first by the ecosystem and then, with its support systems declining, by Supercolony itself. Life for Supercolony was at its maximum that summer, in the season of maximum growth, but the quality of its life was falling. It owed to nature a debt of energy and materials incurred by overconsumption, the payment of which might be postponed for a little while, especially if Supercolony could conquer more territory—but then it must conquer still more, and yet more, to maintain what it had. The debt could also be postponed if its workers discovered new sources of food on the occupied territory. Yet even that unlikely event would merely increase the density of the population, and the debt would only be increased, not retired.

There should be nothing surprising about the looming crisis of Supercolony. Every species walks a tightrope through ecological time. Launched upon it, there is only one way to keep going, and a thousand ways to fall off. That is the way evolution works, and that is how the natural world as a whole runs itself. The instincts driving the anthill are those that succeeded in the past. The genes that programmed them were selected by particular events in the past. Neither the instincts nor the genes, however, had any way to plan for the future. A major change in the immediate environment, or a mutation of the kind that occurred in Supercolony, could quickly lead to disaster. For a species to continue on in a particular environment indefinitely required precision and luck.

Supercolony had fallen off the tightrope. In this vital way it resembled the great human anthill above and around it. When its end came, it would be at the hands of the moving-tree gods.

· 25 ·

ON A CLOUDLESS AFTERNOON in late August the
denizens of Supercolony, blind to any danger facing
them, prepared for the greatest event of their yearly
cycle. They were about to hold a mating swarm. It was to be the
culmination of all their activities, the central purpose of their
existence as a colony. It made possible the immortality of their
kind. The season and the weather were right. Two days previously a thunderstorm moving northeast off the Gulf of Mexico
had dumped a full two inches of rain on the Lake Nokobee tract.
This morning the ground was still moist, and plants wilted by
the midsummer drought had begun to regain a little of their
springtime turgidity and greenness. The sun heated the soil of
the sprawling nest, and humid air weighed heavy and still upon
its surface.

At midmorning a biological clock in the brains of the
Supercolony ants triggered the nuptial event. Workers by the
thousands came pouring out of the entrance holes. They spread
over the nest surface, milling about in excited chaos. Within
minutes they were joined by a horde of virgin winged queens
and males. None flew off. Mating started immediately. Multiple
males piled on top of each virgin queen, jostling one another,
forcing their way closer to the object of their desire, each strug-

gling to be the one who copulated. Even when one succeeded in joining his genitalia solidly to that of a queen, the tumult around the pair continued. The failed males were frantic. To mate, just once, at this precise time and at this place, was the only purpose for which they existed. Locating a queen a few seconds too late or making less than a do-or-die effort spelled defeat and a childless death.

Winners and losers alike among the males flew away, but only to die. That night thousands of the corpses piled up beneath the porch light of a nearby farmhouse on the Lake Nokobee road. At dawn small birds came to feast on them. Later in the morning the owner, an elderly lady, murmuring "What on God's earth is this all about?," swept the remainder off the porch into the front yard.

Queens, in contrast, had no reason to be desperate. Each one was all but certain to be mated. After copulating with one or more males, they broke off their dry, membranous wings and climbed back down into the nest interior. If their luck held, they would soon join the egg-laying reproductive force of Supercolony.

That would not happen this day, however. Wholly by chance, the gods seen as moving trees had chosen the day and hour of mating to fix the environment. The nuptial frenzy was dying down on the Supercolony nest domes when the divine presence arrived. In one instant there was no sign of the moving-tree gods, but in the next instant they were there, bodies towering into the sky, tree-trunk appendages moving swiftly, their shadows and odors sweeping over the Supercolony nest. There were many of them this time. Large objects floated through the air by their sides. The ground trembled where they stepped. Strange noises descended from above, not like thunder, more like a strong wind blowing through the tree branches.

The apparitions moved on, beyond the eastern reaches of the Supercolony nest area, until a few minutes later no sign of them remained.

An hour later the ants still out on the nest sensed that the gods were coming back. But they did not see the giants this time. Instead they detected a strange and unpleasant odor. The ants were alarmed. They responded to the smell as though it were an alarm pheromone of their own, released from some among them in an odorous shout against impending catastrophe. They began to run about in loops and circles, searching for enemies. Nothing was there. Then, in less than a minute, a faint chemical cloud passed silently over them, a fog rolling off a poison sea. Those ants who remained aboveground lifted their heads and waved their antennae in curiosity. Within seconds they collapsed, paralyzed. In minutes they were all dead. As the fog settled closer to the ground, the gods arrived with their accoutrements floating by their sides, and poured streams of deadly liquid down into the nest entrances.

The next morning the great ant conurbation was an environmental dead zone, a killing field, the site of a myrmicide, a cemetery, all of it lifeless and still. Not an ant, not any other kind of small creature, moved within it. No birds or lizards or squirrels, which still abounded beyond the perimeter, visited the ruined land. Clusters of vegetation not trampled by the divine visitors still stood intact, but not a trace of insect life stirred upon or around them. The only sounds were the whispers of wind over the lake through the canopy of the surrounding pines, and the soft lapping of waves at the water's edge.

26

HUDDLED IN A NATURAL HOLE between two roots of a gallberry bush, the tiny Woodland Colony had survived the destruction of its overbearing neighbor. The kill zone in which the Supercolony died, now still and silent, had stopped just short of the Woodlander retreat along the shore of Dead Owl Cove. When first the Trailhead and then the Streamside Colonies ruled this region, their scouts sometimes ventured far enough into the forest to pass close by the Woodlander nest entrance. They never found the little colony. But a few came near, and often enough to frighten the inhabitants. The Woodlanders stayed close to home, forced to survive on a few small scraps of food, mostly dead insects. After Supercolony took over, their situation worsened. Forays by Supercolony scouts were more frequent than those of the earlier colonies, and some approached dangerously near. Woodlander foragers were forced to stay still closer to the entrance of their little nest. Even then, a few were picked off by the Supercolony scouts.

At the time of the destruction of Supercolony, the Woodland Colony was also dying, although in a different way. The number of workers had dropped from close to a hundred in the Trailhead Colony era to the twenty that huddled inside now.

There were no soldiers at all. The Queen was starving. Her ovaries had shriveled and she no longer laid eggs. The death rate of workers was inexorably rising, while the birth rate fell to zero. The little colony, it seemed, could not last the remainder of the warm season as a close neighbor of Supercolony.

Then came the moving tree trunks, the ant gods, who miraculously wiped Supercolony off the face of antdom. Their lethal pressure was lifted instantly from the imperiled Woodlanders. A scattering of Supercolony scouts had still been exploring outside the kill zone when the gods came, but they offered no further threat. All died within hours, as soon as they tried to return home and unknowingly touched the still-toxic soil. Now, within a week, not a trace of their scent remained around the Woodlander nest.

Woodlander workers, timid at first, began to venture farther than ever before from their nest. They found more and better food, mostly in the form of dead or easily captured insects of the kind preempted earlier by their dominant neighbors. Also newly available in generous quantity were droplets of sugary excrement that had fallen from aphids living on nearby understory plants.

By late September, with the weather still warm and the vegetation green, the ovaries of the Woodland Queen revived. She was laying eggs, and healthy young larvae filled the brood chamber of the hidden nest.

By the following April, with the last of the winter's chill lifted from the deeper recesses of the soil and the spring renewal of plant growth well under way, the Woodlander foragers began traveling farther afield. The colony resumed its growth with greater vigor. In only a matter of days, the first Woodlander scouts entered the wasteland that was once the Supercolony territory. The pesticide had entirely dissipated from the kill zone, and insects and other small invertebrates were infiltrating the area to explore it on their own. Many were easy prey for the Woodlanders.

Wasteland it had been, but now it was like a newly planted garden, because ironically, it had flourished from the former occupation by Supercolony. Its soil, having been aerated by the tunnels and chambers of their nests and then enriched by their decomposing bodies, was ideal for plant growth. Grasses and herbs native to the longleaf pine flatland reasserted themselves among the species that had survived the ant Armageddon. By June, a resurgent ground vegetation formed a thick green carpet over the entirety of the old nest surface. The fastest growing of the summer herbs came into full bloom by early June, and a full cast of pollinators visited to serve them—flower beetles, syrphid flies, sweat bees, wood nymph butterflies, sulphurs, whites, blues, skippers, swallowtails swarmed in as though there had never been an episode of violence and death.

By the height of summer, the grassroots jungle teemed with hundreds of insect species, variously adapted to every major niche. A multiplicity of spiders had settled there to feed on them. Individual species snared their prey in orb webs or tangle webs, or sprinted out from silk-spun tunnels to pounce on unsuspecting passersby. A few lay motionless and camouflaged on flower heads, waiting to ambush bees and other pollinators landing there. The arachnids came in many shapes and sizes, from linyphiid dwarf spiderlings less than a pinhead in size to wolf spiders half the span of a human hand.

Spiders, although wingless, were strangely among the first

animals to colonize the regenerating Supercolony tract. A few walked in, but even more oddly, other pioneers arrived by ballooning. The method is widespread and ancient among their kind. When an immature spider possessing this ability wishes to travel a long distance, it crawls to an unrestricted site on a blade of grass or twig of a bush, lifts the rear part of its body to point the spinnerets at the tip upward, and lets out a line of silk. The delicate little thread is the spiderling's kite. The air current lifts and pulls at it until the young spider, feeling the tension, gradually lengthens the thread. When the strength of the pull exceeds its own body weight, it lets go with all eight feet and sets sail. A flying spiderling can reach thousands of feet of altitude and travel miles downwind. When it wishes to descend, it pulls in the silk thread and eats it, millimeter by millimeter, heading for a soft if precarious landing. The risk it takes offers good odds. Sailing aloft under its silk balloon, the spiderling can reach land still uncrowded by competing spiders. Such openness, for a while at least, was the condition of the newly vacated Supercolony territory.

27

THE WOODLANDER ANTS were like human explorers coming ashore on an uninhabited island. The abandoned Supercolony terrain presented the starving colony with a rich and temporarily boundless food supply. The Woodlanders were free for a while of competition from other ant colonies. But their bonanza could not be harvested easily. The moving, nervous prey that ants hunt are not the same as low-hanging fruit on a bush ripe for the picking. They can only be subdued with skill and swiftness. As Woodlander patrols penetrated the ground cover, their target species met them with protective devices of anatomy and behavior perfected by millions of years of evolution. Such defenses are legion in variety, and some are designed specifically to thwart ants. Many are ingenious even by human military standards. The Woodlander huntresses encountered slow-moving oribatid mites, which resembled a cross between a spider and a turtle. They seemed to be convenient morsels, but were protected by hard shells not easily broken even by the powerful jaws of an ant. Millipedes—thousand-leggers—were prize catches, but they too were armored, in a different way. Their elongated bodies were covered, like those of medieval knights, with hinged plates that gave a measure of flexibility. If those proved insufficient, the thousand-leggers unleashed poisons, including cyanide, on their attackers. Pillbugs, which are land-dwelling crustaceans, had similarly jointed armor and could also roll themselves into an almost impenetrable sphere. Springtails had tiny soft bodies ready for the eating, but were intensely alert and nervous in manner. They were equipped with a spring-loaded lever on their undersides that launched them into the air over a distance equivalent in human terms to the length of a football field, thence out of danger. Nematode roundworms, the most abundant animals on earth, were everywhere in the soil but too small for ants to gather efficiently. Ground beetles, the archrivals of ants in the kinds of food and space they require, proved to be all-purpose fighters. They were not only armored, poisonous, and swift on the ground, but also capable of taking flight if stressed—and, finally, as a last resort, they had jaws sharp and powerful enough to chop an ant in two during insect-to-insect combat.

The Woodlander huntresses did best with the few prey available that were soft, slow, and tasty. When a Woodlander came upon a fallen caterpillar or some other invertebrate that met these exacting standards—in other words, not poisonous, did not strike out with slashing jaws or flee with the equivalent speed of a drag racer, and not least was big enough to be worth the effort—her response was enthusiastic. She reported her find to the colony by laying a chemical odor trail back to the nest and tapping her nestmates with rapid strokes of her forelegs. Out came the alerted workers, and if they found the prey attractive themselves, they attacked. If the prey was so big it could fling a single worker away, it could still be overcome by a swarm of workers rushing it simultaneously.

In one episode that occurred during the exploration of their new territory, a Woodlander force was summoned to the nymph of a mole cricket. While immature, it was still the same size compared to a worker as a cow is to a human. The first dozen workers who arrived proved sufficient for the kill. Several of the attackers were able to pin the still-active cricket nymph by seizing and spreading its legs, while others stung it in vulnerable seams between its chitinous armor plates.

Another target discovered by the Woodlander scouts, the prize of the week, was the grown caterpillar of a cecropia moth, the equivalent in size to the ants as a whale is to humans. Hundreds of workers, accompanied by a score of soldiers this time, were needed to subdue the monster and drag it back to the nest.

The Woodland Colony used the same method to claim and retrieve large, already dead animals before rivals could preempt them. The reward in calories for winning such a bonanza could be enormous. On one occasion a worker force was gathering around the newly discovered corpse of a lizard. It had been led there by one of its most enterprising elite scouts. The prize contained enough food to support the colony for days. Suddenly, however, the bonanza was discovered by a squad of fire ants. The enemy, recruited by their own scouts from a distant colony, did what fire ants do best. They quickly gathered in strength and attacked anything that moved. And they were formidable in combat, especially in groups. A battle was joined, and soon the dead and injured piled up on both sides. The Woodlanders managed to prevail, mainly because their nest was close by and their buildup of fighting forces faster. The presence of soldiers also helped: the members of this larger caste not only stung the fire ants fatally but also used their razor-sharp jaws to clip them into pieces. The fighting Woodlanders were able to clear the lizard's body of fire ants and drag it inch by inch to their own nest.

By this time the Woodland Colony had an adequate military force. Each of its hoplite soldiers was a formidable fighting machine, not only in defense of the colony, but as an escort for workers retrieving food. Its body was thick and muscular. Its head was huge in proportion to the body and was heart-shaped. The swollen posterior lobes were filled with adductor muscles that closed the jaws with enough force to cut through the chitinous exoskeleton and muscle of most kinds of insects. The inner margin of each jaw was lined with a row of eight sharp teeth. The tooth at the tip of the mandible was the longest, serving as a dagger to stab opponents and a hook to seize and hold them while others moved in. The pair of spines extending backward from the upper surface of the middle of the body protected the soldier's thin waist, making it difficult for the ant to be cut in half during combat.

The brain of a soldier was wired for battle. In a gland at the base of each jaw, each carried quantities of alarm pheromones ready to be spritzed into the air when the ant met an enemy. When challenged, the soldier not only produced more of these substances than did an ordinary worker, but was also more sensitive to them. On detecting even a faint trace of the chemicals, the soldier rushed about in search of enemies. Soldiers in combat attracted other soldiers. When they entered a high concentration of the alarm signal at the site of the action, they ran in frenzied loops and threw themselves at any alien object that moved. Deadly threats and overwhelming opposition were of no concern to the soldiers. They were the suicide warriors of the colony.

The Woodland Colony could not afford to raise soldiers while it was small. The investment would have increased the defense capability of the colony and lessened the risk of total destruction by a dangerous enemy. But additions to the worker force were more important for colony growth, and rapid growth was crucial. The colony could gamble that no lethal enemy would appear during its infancy, but it could not gamble with its growth. The larger the population of workers specialized to gather food and feed the young, the faster the colony grew. And the faster its growth, the better chance it had to live another day, and yet another day, until it could afford to convert some of its time and energy into the production of virgin queens and males, thus creating new colonies of its own kind. Soldiers were added along the way, but the number of these military specialists was kept under strict control. Too few, and the colony was at higher risk of destruction by enemies—especially during wars with colonies of the same species. Too many, and the colony grew more slowly. It harvested less food from its territory, and, again, failure was imminent. A colony out of kilter in its military investment could not compete for long with colonies of the same species that kept their investment closer to the optimum for both survival and growth. To reach the right balance between defense and productive labor was a matter of life and death.

The Woodland Colony added its first soldier only when the worker population reached approximately two hundred. The colony grew swiftly during the long hot days of the summer.

When the total population reached a thousand, more soldiers were added. The year following the Supercolony disaster, the total Woodlander population approached ten thousand. Of this number, five hundred were soldiers, ready and waiting for any call to action. Their presence made the colony almost invulnerable to invasion by fire ants and other enemies short of armadillos and poison-wielding gods.

This summer the formerly meek Woodlanders were at the height of power for a colony of their species. They found themselves on the edge of an unexplored ant continent left empty by the god-given extinction of Supercolony. As they expanded their territory, in a growing circle foot by foot away from their nest, the colony as a whole grew in overall intelligence. The mental life of the colony was not shared by each worker equally. What any worker knew and thought was only part of what the colony knew and thought. The colony intelligence was distributed among its members, in the same way human intelligence is distributed among the gyri, lobes, and nuclei of the human brain. One cadre of Woodlander workers knew about a particular part of the territory outside the nest, a second cadre knew about another part. Groups of nest-builders remembered their way through various sections of the nest perimeter, and still others were informed about the condition of the brood. Different veteran huntresses had experienced separate conditions of rain, enemy combat, and the nectar-milking of aphids and other sap-suckers. A few scouts knew the way to the expanding frontier of the colony territory.

The Woodland Colony as a whole learned in this manner by calling up pieces of knowledge and putting them together as need demanded, communicated by means of a pheromonal language. Because the superorganism knew much more than any individual ant, it was far smarter.

Enjoying its good fortune, the Woodland Colony also learned the price of prosperity. It was soon cramped in its original hiding place. The workers had been excavating new tunnels and rooms beneath and around the original nest, piece by tiny piece as large as a single ant could carry between her two mandibles. But the meager duff and soil in which the nest was sited was too dry and friable to be ideal for a colony of this species, and the rootlets all around were too thick and tough for the workers to cut. Even worse, the tangled and heavily shaded scrub woodland at the site was poorly suited for foraging.

As scouts explored the Supercolony ghost town, they quickly discovered the large and widely dispersed system of tunnels and chambers left by the former inhabitants. There were many exits, although most were now filled with collapsed earth. Some of the scouts exploring the new terrain began to lay trails from the available exits back to the scrub-woodland mother nest. A few of the nestmates returned along the trails, but their response upon arriving at the Supercolony exits advertised by the scouts was halfhearted. They then either laid weak, fragmented trails of their own, or else returned home without communicating the information to any other nestmate.

Meanwhile, the housing problem at home was becoming severe. The Woodland Colony began a serious search for a better location. By laying and following trails to more and more potential sites and with varying degree of vigor, the colony members voted on the locations presented to them. Some candidate homes received a few votes, others none at all. At first the response failed to build a surge of trail-laying to any of the competing sites, and in time the recruitment died out for most. Then, one mid-August morning, a few scouts hit upon an unusually favorable spot, near the center of what had been the old Trailhead Colony nest. They dug into the plug of soil that closed the original main entrance. As they broke through into the partially empty nestwork below, their enthusiasm grew. At shorter and shorter intervals, some reported back with the good news. Others arriving at the site laid trails of their own. The combined trails grew strong, and some of the more excited scouts began to tap their antennae on the bodies of their nestmates to add emphasis. The message proclaimed urgently, *Follow me! Follow me!* The voting then swung decisively to the newly favored site. The number of workers running back and forth from the mother nest grew exponentially. The more trail substance laid and the more scouts tapping with their antennae, the more nestmates left the mother nest to inspect the new site. The formicid electorate was soon decided. The communal intelligence said, *This is the place!* Excavation of the new nest quickly began in earnest. By noon the cleaned-out vertical shaft was three feet deep, and the construction of new lateral galleries and rooms and reopening of old ones was far advanced. The living space came to resemble a snake skeleton, with the central shaft the spine and the lateral galleries the ribs sticking out in all directions.

All through the nest-changing process, from the most aggressive early recruitment to the excavation, elite workers led the way. A tunnel begun by just one such leader caused others close by to help deepen it, or to start tunnels of their own. Elites inspired followers and work generated more work of the same kind until each task was done. The colony depended on the elites to initiate change, and then to keep nestmates on the job.

As shadows of the longleaf pines began to lengthen across the now-teeming center of the Woodlander territory, the underground construction was mostly complete, and the emigration began. The colony had to hurry. If the moving column was caught between the old and new nests after nightfall, when dangerous nocturnal predators emerged, the Woodlanders could easily be wiped out. First came workers carrying nestmates who had been reluctant to undertake the journey. Slackers were a problem for the colony as a whole. Ant colonies may have elites to lead them, but they also have layabouts who need strong encouragement.

Each transport was performed the same way. The recruiter faced the ant to be carried, and pulled gently on her jaws. Quieted by the touch, the ant grew passive, allowing the recruiter to grasp her more firmly on her jaws or another part of her head. The recruited ant next pulled her legs and antennae close to her body, in the same posture she had as a completely immobile pupa. This allowed her to be lifted up and curled over the body of the recruiter. She became an inert package easily carried to the new nest site.

At the peak of the emigration a large majority of the workers were active in the transfer of all the other colony members. Out came the pupae and grublike larvae, held gently in the jaws of a recruiter. Also carefully moved were clusters of eggs laid recently by the Queen and not yet hatched into larvae.

Then out came the Queen herself, sluggish, careful, timid, dragging her abdomen swollen with eggs. A praetorian guard of nurse workers swarmed over and around her, hiding her body from view. Some guided her by gently pulling at her mandibles. She was too large and heavy to be lifted and carried swiftly like a worker, even by a team of nurses. Her painful progress was the critical step in the entire colony emigration. If a bird or lizard saw her and plucked her out as a tidy morsel, or if a force of enemy ants broke through the guard and killed her, the Woodland Colony would be doomed. This time, as in the case of most such rare attempts by colonies of this species, she made it to her new home.

By the time the longleaf pine oasis darkened into twilight, the Queen and almost all of her colony had settled into the new nest. A few individuals still streamed back and forth over the heavily reinforced odor trails, but to no great effect.

The Woodland Colony, having grown into a giant compared to the dying midget of the previous summer, soon reached a size as large as any superorganism of the species other than a supercolony could hope to be. The land given to it by the gods stretched beyond the capacity of the colony to fill its entirety. Woodlander scouts regularly traveled farther from the home nest than those of any other colony at Dead Owl Cove.

So it was inevitable that by early the next spring the boldest of the explorers, one of the Woodlander elites, encountered a scout from another colony. She had never met an individual that belonged to the same species but carried a different colony odor. The two strangers warily examined each other with repeated sweeps of their odor-testing antennae. Then they broke off and hurried away in the direction of their faraway home nests.

In the days that followed, more Woodlanders ran out along the trail laid by the first scout. They too encountered strangers from the foreign nest. The rising incidence of hostile exchanges resulted in more and longer odor trails. The same increase occurred with the aliens. In time a large number of workers from both colonies were patrolling the disputed area.

As in earlier wars at Dead Owl Cove, the scouts tried to intimidate their opponents by pretending to be soldiers. They puffed up their abdomens, straightened their legs to gain height, and posed on top of small pebbles to give the impression of even greater size. Real soldiers also came out to join in the displays. The instinctive pattern of the tournament, with circling, sniffing, and mutual bumping, had been established in this new place. Neither colony would escalate it into outright physical attack. Each waited for signs of weakness in the display of the opposing players.

A territory boundary was drawn, but that was of no great consequence. The Queen of the Woodland Colony was young, the colony's population larger than average for the species, its land rich and productive, and its strength and durability beyond threat.

That summer the Woodlanders also began to produce virgin queens and males. The royals left the nest to mate on schedule. The fecund young queens then flew far beyond the boundaries of their home to distant, unknown lands. The Woodland Colony was reproducing itself. It had won the Darwin game.

The collective mind of the Woodland Colony could only grasp a part of the reason for its outstanding success. Its oldest members could remember the deadly enemies that suddenly disappeared. They had learned about the resources of the vast terrain so abruptly given their colony. They and their younger nestmates had explored and mastered most of it. They held a map of it in their collective heads. If they grasped the existence of the moving-tree gods, they might have surmised how these mysterious forces, no less than storms and lightning-kindled ground fires, had decreed to them such a great good fortune.

Thus ended the Anthill Chronicles. A chain of cycles had been completed. The miniature civilizations of Dead Owl Cove had come full circle. The territory of the original Trailhead Colony witnessed two wars of total destruction, followed by a catastrophe inflicted by the ant gods. The habitat, this little segment of the Nokobee tract, was returned to what it had been at the start. All that was in the past. Now a new mound nest typical of the species stood at the original site. The occupant was fittingly not the Supercolony but a daughter colony of the Trailheaders, the first of the occupants. The resiliency of the ancient longleaf ecosystem had been tested there, and found to hold.

The chain of cycles continued as it had for thousands of years. But now it might change. The tree-trunk gods had arrived and were present all around. They had the power to take everything away, at a whim, and by a single stroke. For the first time in the history of Nokobee, the entirety of all of it, ant, colony, and ecosystem, was at stake.

That winter hard rains soaked the Nokobee pine flats. Three freezes came and went, coating the nest dome of the Woodland Colony with ice, while the inhabitants crouched in dormant sleeping clusters in the deepest chambers. Directly above, unknown to them, gods walked back and forth, measuring, planning, and speaking to one another with their strange sibilant voices.

V

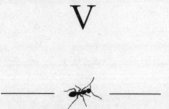

THE
ARMENTARIUM

· 28 ·

THE FATE OF every living thing now depended on one decision by the members of a single family. The Jepsons of Jepson County had owned the Nokobee tract for five generations, keeping it pristine as an outdoors heirloom across 150 years. They were burdened by no more than light county taxes. Wealthy from cotton and outside investments, they chose not to cut even a small part of the valuable longleaf timber. By the end of the twentieth century, however, almost all of the younger family members—by that time a majority in the Jepson Trust—had left the Gulf Coastal Plain. They were settled in the assizes of wealth in Atlanta, Miami, and New York. When the projected market value reached a certain level, they would likely sell to the highest bidder.

"When do you suppose that will happen?" Raff was seated on the sofa in his Uncle Cyrus Semmes's office. Now beginning his third year at Florida State University, and unsure of his own future, he was also growing increasingly anxious about the future of Nokobee.

"Can't say exactly," Cyrus replied.

He had pulled up a chair to face his nephew. He lit a Havana cigar, slipped his eyeglasses down his nose to peer at Raff over the rims, and said, "Why do you ask? You heard something I haven't?"

"Nosir. I just like to keep up with things there."

Cyrus tilted his head back, closed his eyes, and blew a smoke ring. Holding this posture as if in deep contemplation, he said, "Well, I can tell you this much. The word on the street is that the county will be paving the Nokobee Lake road in the next two or three years. That'll bring the value of Nokobee up. My guess is that the Jepsons know that and they're holding off till it happens."

"Well, do you think whoever buys it will develop it? I mean, cut down all the trees and stuff and build houses there?"

"Count on it, Scooter." Cyrus leaned over and laid the cigar on an ashtray close by on the coffee table. "That's the only way they'll be able to break even, much less make any serious money."

"But it's one of the most beautiful places in this part of Alabama. You said that yourself, and you'd think there's got to be some way—"

"Well," Cyrus interrupted, "just because it gets developed doesn't mean it has to be any less beautiful. You've been down to Destin with your parents and seen how nice they're making those resort places and housing developments along the Gulf. They blend in with the landscape just perfectly."

"But they aren't natural. What happens to all the trees and animals and—"

"Scooter!" Cyrus interrupted again. His expression changed from avuncular to annoyed.

"Scooter, I know how much the Nokobee tract means to you, and your mom and dad too, and I admire you for that. If I were a very rich man—and I'm not—I might buy that land myself. It would be a sound financial investment for the family. I don't know where you're going with this, or what you want to do about it. I'm not even sure why you brought it up. You haven't changed your mind about anything, have you?"

"Nosir. I was just—"

"Well, it wouldn't do any good if you did, and just studied biology and planned to stay out at Lake Nokobee. I know you'd be a top-notch wildlife manager or professor, or whatever, but what good would that do for the Nokobee tract, and all those other great places down here you'd like to save?"

"But shouldn't we try to do *something*?"

"Maybe you've forgotten what I told you when we made our deal. If you want to save land, you've got to have power. That means you've got to have a lot of money, or else you have to be in a position to influence land deals and business development. I know it takes a lot of hard work, and for sure you're not going to enjoy all the courses and training you'll have to go through, but if you want real power—and I want you to have it—you've got to succeed inside the system. Now, I'm telling you, just continue what you've been doing. You get on through law school, and do the best you can, and then I'll help you all I can."

Raff felt trapped. He knew, but hadn't yet faced, the solution his uncle had put before him, that maybe the only way to erase such a dilemma of opposing forces was to satisfy both. It takes commitment to a long-term goal and exceptional effort, but there, he thought, you have it.

"You're right, you're right, of course . . . I want to thank—"

"There's one more thing," Cyrus started up again. "You're not going to like this, but the Nokobee tract is going to be developed no matter what *anybody* does. I don't know exactly when, and nobody can say, but it could be as soon as five years and for sure on the outside in ten years."

Raff froze. He held his breath and stared at his uncle. He thought, Here it comes, bad news for sure.

"Raff, I wasn't going to tell you this, but it's something you oughta know. Sunderland Associates has bought the Dead Owl Cove parcel, and at a pretty steep price. Drake Sunderland wouldn't make a move like that unless he intends to acquire the whole west side of the Nokobee tract. When the Jepson family puts the property on the market, and that is surely going to happen as soon as their trust irons out a few wrinkles, like how much and who gets what, Sunderland will move fast. He will be on it like a chicken on a june bug, count on that, Raff. He'll bid high, and as soon as he gets it he'll cut the timber to make up the front money, and he'll do that fast too, and then he'll leverage the funds to develop the whole property."

"I don't understand. Why can't Nokobee be left alone, as it is?" Raff's question was naive, he realized with embarrassment, but now he was grabbing for straws.

"That's elementary. You should know better. The Jepsons want the money."

"Why can't the State of Alabama take it over as a nature reserve?"

"Well, now, that would be nice, wouldn't it? But you're talking twenty million dollars, maybe thirty million with the Nokobee lakeshore included. Then more to fix the road, for a lot of traffic that isn't there now, and still more to put up and maintain park facilities. The state, I'm sorry to say, is broke. It's got a lot of parks already, and it's not going to put up a fortune like that in taxpayer dollars for another one, especially in a remote area with limited access like Nokobee."

"Well, what can be done?"

"Well . . . to tell you the truth, nothing. You have to understand that Sunderland has had a very successful history in just this kind of land acquisition and development. And Nokobee is shaping up as a big deal for them, maybe a make-or-break deal for the company. Scooter, look at me. I know you love the woods there, and it is a beautiful place, and it's your mom and dad's favorite picnic spot, but if I were you I'd find another place to protect."

Cyrus paused for half a minute, which seemed a hundred times longer to Raff. He cleared his throat and rubbed the bald spot on his head with his middle three fingers, as he did in tight business discussions.

"Scooter," he continued, "I'm being frank with you about this matter, and for your own good. I worry about you a lot these days. I think you've gotten a little off the rails here. I was young and idealistic myself, trust me. I nearly got myself killed for it in Vietnam. I think I know how you feel. But you have to realize you've become a bit obsessive. You've lost the big picture. Now, no one wants to hurt you, Scooter, but I just happen to be on Drake Sunderland's side on this one. Nokobee and Jepson Counties are among the poorest places in Alabama, and believe me, that's *really* poor."

"Yessir, that's true enough," Raff agreed.

"The woods up there for the most part are scrub, not much good except for chipping and pulp, and quail and turkey, I guess, and rattlesnakes. A few people, like the Millbrooks of Brewton, made a lot of money a hundred years ago, logging longleaf pine.

Now that's long gone. And the counties are a little far away for Mobile to have much economic input. Your dad would tell you that much, judging from his own hardware business. And I expect you understand it yourself, now that you're taking college courses, that they need better schools in both those counties. Developing Nokobee, if it's done right, and I believe it will be done right, is going to give that area and especially Clayville an economic bump up. A lot of people down here will see real estate around Clayville as a good investment."

"Why would they do that?" Raff asked, perking up a little bit, thinking he'd found a crack in the argument. "It's still a long way from Mobile and Pensacola, and there are all kinds of recreation places around there and on down to the Gulf."

"Your problem, Scooter—and I don't blame you because you're young—is that you don't have vision. Nokobee's isolated now, sure, and its recreational facilities may never compete with the ones we have around Mobile and on over to Pensacola. That'll stay true even after the housing and lakeside docks are built at Nokobee. But this part of the Gulf Coast is filling up with people real fast. And they're not just sharecroppers coming out of the cotton fields either. They're mostly well-educated, hardworking people, with solid incomes."

Raff tried to widen the crack he thought had opened. "But why would just bringing in a lot more people be such a good thing?"

"Look at me, Scooter. You want Nokobee and Jepson Counties to just stay redneck heaven forever? Is that what you want? Please understand, nothing's going to stop progress on the Gulf Coast anyway. We're already a very important part of the Sun

Belt. Mobile and Pensacola are expanding fast even by Sun Belt standards. Am I right?"

Raff hesitated. Then he spoke, almost in a whisper. "Yeah, I guess, yessir." He didn't want to agree with his uncle, but he couldn't think of anything else to say, and he had to be polite.

"Now just compare what used to be with what we have now," Cyrus bore in. "When Granddog was a boy, just about all the land south of Mobile was undeveloped woods and swamps. You could drive all the way from Dog River down to Cedar Point and see only a few houses here and there. The last stretch of the road wasn't even paved. And when you got all the way to Cedar Point, you could look over to Dauphin Island. It was a beautiful place, with beaches and the old Civil War fort at one end, but you had to rent a boat to get there. A lot of that island was simply vacant land. Now most of the area between here and Dauphin Island is developed. It's a thriving part of the economy of Alabama. There's a bridge to Dauphin Island, and you can drive across it in a few minutes. Now, *that* is progress, Scooter. That is real progress. Don't you see that?"

Raff's battle with his uncle was lost. "Yessir," he said, looking down at his knees and then back up.

Then he was surprised to see that his uncle hadn't finished. He was getting excited. Cyrus had stubbed out his cigar on the tray. Now he removed his glasses and waved them at Raff.

"Scooter, America didn't become great by sitting on its ass. We had to be tough and we had to work hard. We thrived on war, to be perfectly frank about it. Just look at American history, and I don't mean the girlie left-wing version they give students in school. We had to push back the Indians to get what God meant us to have. We went to war with Mexico to double the size of this country. That took us to the Pacific. I won't say the way we did it was right and good but that just happens to be the way the world works. Grow or die! We, especially the Semmeses and the Codys and the other old families around here, were the winners, and that means there had to be losers. We didn't win by sitting around writing poetry in nature parks. You're a Semmes, Scooter, and I know you have the stuff of one. I'd hate to see you wander off into some liberal never-never land."

Raff raised his hand like a student in class and said, "But—"

His uncle was not to be interrupted. "I'll tell you where this whole part of the Gulf Coast is headed, Scooter. Pensacola is bound to keep expanding its suburbs and little satellite towns to the west until it meets developments coming out from Fairhope and the rest of Baldwin County. Mobile is going to spread north way past Satsuma and west on across the Mississippi border to include the Gulf Coast there. In fifty years Mobile and Pensacola will be one single urban area surrounded by well-to-do suburbs. I like to think we'll be a metropolis like the Gold Coast on the other side of Florida and the Twin Cities of St. Paul and Minneapolis."

As Cyrus was finishing this oration, his secretary Cindy Sue Lauchaux tapped lightly on the door and entered the room. She was a tall brunette, in her mid-forties, dressed in light tan slacks and a frilled white blouse. Her double first name had been bestowed in Southern accordance with her stature as second daughter in the family. Her last name suggested Cajun or, less likely, Old French Mobile. She spoke slowly in a soft, alto voice.

"Excuse me, Mr. Semmes, but your trainer called. He wants to know if you'll make your four o'clock appointment today?"

Cyrus glanced at his watch and rose from his chair. "Tell him I'm on my way.

"Gotta go, Scooter. I'm getting fit by taking boxing lessons. Best kind of workout there is, boxing. I try to do it like the professionals."

Raff made one last try as he followed his uncle to the door. "Won't there be any room for natural history reserves in the new Twin Cities?"

Cyrus halted, turned to face him. "Well, of course there will be, if we plan all this the right way. There'll be plenty of parks, with easy access, where families can go to relax and see some nature. We can arrange guided tours like the ones at Disney World. There'll be a lot of gardens as beautiful as the one down at Bellingrath. I'm hoping that right here in Mobile we might expand the Azalea Trail, and make it the big deal it once was. The impact on tourism will be just great."

"But won't there be any real wild areas for the native plants and animals?"

Cyrus paused, marinating that concept a bit, and resumed his explanation. "Look, Scooter, I think you're mature enough to understand that what we've got going here is big, and it's wonderful. Drake Sunderland and I, and some other business and political leaders in Mobile and Pensacola, have a nonprofit group we call the Gulf Gateway Coalition. Our aim is to help guide the growth, make it long-term and in the right direction and the right pace, of course. We'll keep the nature lovers happy. Frankly, I've always hoped that you yourself might play an important role in that effort."

With that, he spun around and walked out the door. "I'll be back first thing in the morning," he told Cindy Sue. She waggled her fingers at him but did not look away from her computer screen.

Raff started to follow him. Then he hesitated in order to look up for a moment to the space above the door, as he always did when he visited this office. There hung a stuffed five-foot alligator his uncle had shot during a hunting trip in the swamps of the Mobile-Tensaw Delta. The reptile stared back at him with a yellow glass eye.

Raff thought of Frogman's fourteen-foot-long Old Ben in the Chicobee River. He murmured to the specimen on the wall, "Sorry you got cut down in your childhood."

As he stepped out of the granite-rimmed entrance of the Loding Building, Raff looked down Bledsoe Street for his uncle, and spotted him fifty yards away walking briskly in the direction of the city center. He had no desire to catch up, so he stayed where he was for a short while. Feeling the afternoon sun bearing down through the hot humid air, Raff walked across the narrow street to stand in the shade of a large magnolia tree. When he looked down Bledsoe Street a second time, farther beyond the Loding Building, and from this new angle, he could see a row of small houses built in the mid-1800s and occupied continuously thereafter by Mobile families. Each bore a small medallion next to the front door denoting the house's historical significance. Raff walked on down to them to sit in the shade on a bench next to the first one.

Just as he was settling he heard a chittering sound above his head. He looked up to see a squirrel on the telephone line that crossed the street, balanced like an acrobat on the wire, trying to work its way to a tree canopy on the opposite side. From the thick vegetation there came the same chittering of a second squirrel. Raff focused on the two animals. What was this all about?

He remembered quickly: territory! The two squirrels were engaged in a territorial dispute. Raff knew that sound from the Nokobee tract. The squirrel on the wire was the invader, the one in the canopy the defender. Raff rose from the bench to watch more closely, and his mind connected to the conversation he'd just had with Cyrus. The ownership of land, and the power and security it provided: that was what drove the battles of squirrels. And the cycles of the ant colonies. And that was what Cyrus Semmes was trying to tell him too, in a tragic sense, about what runs the world.

These were no defenders for reserves like Nokobee. No territorial threats emerged from the inhabitants to halt their enemies. The land was falling unopposed to the developers. If the vanishing life within that area was mute, who then would speak for it? Raff started to walk toward the city center again. Now at last he had an idea of where to go and what to do.

29

H E REACHED THE five-story office of the *Mobile News Register* and walked into its green-walled lobby. With the eye of a naturalist entering a new habitat, he looked about to take in the scene before pressing on. Across the room, in a glass-fronted trophy cabinet, were two rows of plaques and statuettes. To the left on the same wall hung a framed front page of a *Mobile News Register*, pale yellowish brown with age, with the banner headline "NAZIS INVADE POLAND." Another next to it, in an identical frame, announced "JAPAN SURRENDERS!"

Between the trophy case and elevator was the reception desk and switchboard. Raff asked the young woman there if he could speak to Mr. Bill Robbins. He was connected at once to the environmental reporter and natural history essayist. Before the journalist could say more than "Robbins here," Raff declared, with the kind of urgent tone used by an accident witness calling the police, that he was from Clayville, and a student at Florida State University, and he had a serious environmental problem he wanted to talk about.

Robbins walked into the lobby five minutes later. He ushered Raff into the elevator and up to the main pressroom floor.

Sitting across from Robbins's desk, Raff took a first close look at the journalist he had read avidly since he was a freshman in high school. Robbins was about what he expected: medium height and average weight, probably in his late thirties, with a short Lincolnesque beard and neatly combed dark blond hair. He was dressed in chinos and a taupe outdoorsman's shirt with two pockets, one of which was stained at the bottom by a leaking pen. He wore no tie. Good. A tie would have had a disorienting impact on the younger man.

Robbins listened intently as Raff poured out the whole story of Nokobee, up to and including the session he'd just had with Uncle Cyrus. He remained impassive, leaning slightly back in his chair, eyes half closed. He slowly rotated a pencil like a parade baton through his moving fingers.

By the time Raff finished his account, he had worked himself into a tone of despair. His tension was close to dissolving in tears. "I just don't know what to do. I thought I could turn to my uncle for help, but that's been a great big disappointment. I'm sorry I didn't know you personally coming here, but I read all your columns, and I thought you might want to know about all this, and help me decide what to do. I don't think Uncle Cyrus understands the issue. Or if he does, he doesn't care. That's even worse. He doesn't have any idea of what natural environments are all about, and he seems so set on what he's doing I don't think he would help even if he did understand."

Raff's anger subsided a bit as he spoke. It was now diluted by a suffusion of guilt. He sure didn't want Cyrus to know about this conversation. So in afterthought he added, "May we keep this confidential?"

Robbins nodded and said quietly, "Of course." Then he put

the pencil down and lifted his hands, fingers spread in a placating gesture.

"Listen, ease up, fella. You've taken this business all on your own shoulders, and it's going to break you down if you keep on going like this. Let me tell you for starters that you're not alone, Raphael. May I call you Raphael?"

"Well, I kind of prefer Raff."

"Okay, Raff. Surely you don't think you're the only conservationist in Alabama. What I need to tell you in particular and right now is that a lot of people care about Nokobee. They're aware that it's one of the last and best stands of old-growth longleaf forest left in this part of the state. And in case you didn't know it, there are a few endangered species living there. In other words, it's a biodiversity hot spot. And Lake Nokobee adds a lot of aquatic biodiversity. We need to protect all that. Everybody who knows the situation agrees." Then he paused.

Raff kept silent, looking down at the floor, waiting for the journalist to say more.

"But in spite of all that," Robbins continued, "your Uncle Cyrus is right on one thing. The whole Nokobee tract could be wiped out in a heartbeat. All it would take would be one of those big circular timber saws and a couple of bulldozers. Put in an experienced crew, and the place could be gone almost before you could get up there. Those of us who've been following the story hoped that the Jepson Trust might donate Nokobee to the State of Alabama as a reserve, and take a big tax deduction. But the members don't live around here anymore, and they don't care enough at a distance to do anything, unfortunately. What's more, I've heard that a couple of the key people are hurting from bad investments. They need as much cash up front as possible, and as quick as they can get it."

Raff's new good feeling was subsiding as quickly as it had risen. "Then who *does* care?" he said.

"A lot of people, a lot of people, Raff. It happens you've come to the right person to get information about this subject. I wrote a pretty detailed article on the tract last fall, and it really had some effect. I'm surprised you didn't see it. But I guess you were over at FSU. It won a prize from the National Association of Environmental Journalists. I also mention Nokobee whenever I give my 'Last Great Places' lecture here in Mobile and elsewhere along the coast. Then you've got several private organizations with a special interest in protecting Nokobee. There's the Alabama Conservancy, the Longleaf Alliance, the Delta Protection Alliance. We need to introduce you to them. There are also a few wealthy individuals in this area and over on the Panhandle who are on top of the situation and might buy in if they thought the whole tract was at risk."

"If everybody helped, could they come up with the price? It seems pretty big to me."

"I'd say all things considered the whole deal is about fifty-fifty at this point. The biggest problem is that there are so many land developers circling around, waiting to pounce. They've got the money, and they can move fast. To be frank, they're like a bunch of buzzards waiting for Nokobee to die. The key player is Drake Sunderland. You mentioned him. He's the worst threat, and what's more, he got a foot solidly in the door a few months ago when he bought the parcel at Dead Owl Cove."

Robbins began tapping the tabletop with an index finger as though pointing to the hard reality of the situation.

"He's also got the support of the Gulf Gateway Coalition, which your uncle told you about. The members of the coalition are all big players in business and politics around here, and they've got something else as important as money going for them. They've got a vision—or at least what they *call* a vision. It's sort of like a religion. In fact, it *is* a kind of religion with them."

"My Uncle Cyrus seems really fired up about it."

"Yeah. They think they have a plan. When people in the future list the great cities of the Deep South, they want it to be Houston, New Orleans, Miami, Atlanta, maybe Birmingham, and—don't laugh—the Mobile-Pensacola Twin Cities. They're even talking to Jet Blue about making it a new airline hub.

"Their philosophy," Robbins went on, frowning and slightly shaking his head, "is that the earth was created for man, and dominion over nature mentioned in the Bible means replacing nature with people. They separate the world into two parts. Here is where we live, and away from us out there is nature, the place where critters, bugs, and wild plants live. Nature is fungible, in their view. I actually had a local banker say to my face what price he thinks will buy Nokobee, 'It'll be twenty million dollars, and a couple of endangered species aren't worth that,' he said."

"Well, what about all the churches? Don't they care about the environment?"

Robbins shook his head again. "Believe it or not, a lot of folks on the Christian hard right around here are dead set against nature reserves. They think saving the wild environment is just an all-around bad idea. Don't get me wrong. Most evangelicals I know are for conservation. They believe God means for us to save the Creation and God's good green earth in general. But a few extremists are absolutely convinced God means us to do the opposite. They're saying, 'Use it all up, the faster the better, because Jesus is coming. The End of Days is almost here. He'll show up as soon as the planet's messed up a little bit more. The devil wants to keep us all here on earth, and Jesus wants to take us on up to heaven, at least He wants to take the true believers up.' They say that's all written in the Book of Revelation."

"Yeah, that's scary. I've heard something like that on the radio. It's pretty bad."

"Yeah. Well, anyway, it's at least a potential complication. This part of Alabama and the Panhandle next door is about as far right in religion and politics as you're going to find anywhere. I think the extremists are a small minority, fortunately—you'll find them mostly in little churches out in the country—but some of those preaching on the radio are powerful way beyond their numbers. And they come close to promoting violence in the name of God. Like, they say Islam is an evil religion. Or the United States ought to kill Castro or somebody else they say is godless and don't like. It's best to stay clear of them. I'd say don't rile them up if you can avoid it. Don't even get in a conversation with any of them."

"Uncle Cyrus said he'd buy Nokobee if he could afford it."

"Yeah, I'm sure he would. But then—and don't get me wrong—what would he do with it? Anyway, buck up. We've probably got three or four years, maybe more, from what I've heard, before all the serious finagling begins. I hear some of the Jepsons want to hold off until they can get a higher price. Public opinion can change a lot in that period of time. If worse comes to worst, and if it looks like Nokobee goes to Sunderland or any other developer who'll bid higher, then the conservationists in this area will form a special coalition to challenge the development in the courts and in public opinion."

Robbins rose and offered his hand. "Meanwhile, the best you can do for Nokobee is to go on to law school. Your uncle is dead right there. Plan on coming back here. We can use you to help represent nature in the courts. Meanwhile, don't worry about this conversation. I'm not going to say anything to anybody about it. I don't want to cause a rift inside your family, and especially with your Uncle Cyrus."

Raff smiled, nodding his head. "Thank you. I really appreciate it. I feel a little better about things, I guess."

"Okay, good," Robbins said. "Anyway, stay in touch, will you, Raff? I promise to let you know of any really serious developments I hear about, and I hope you can get in on the action when you get back."

30

AFTER HIS CONVERSATIONS with Uncle Cyrus, and then Bill Robbins, Raff resolved not only to go to a law school, but if at all possible to one of the most demanding and best. He converted all of his remaining elective courses to those considered most suitable for prelaw students.

"To tell you the truth, Uncle Fred," he said one day, "it's been pretty easy here, once I got into it. I thought FSU would be some kind of boot camp, like MIT and Caltech were rumored to be. There are some hard courses, all right, but the students know all about those, and they only take them if they're really serious about the subject. I tell you one thing, you don't get a very good idea of what a university is like in a little place like Nokobee High. You've got everything here, if you look around a little. You can make it as hard or as easy as you choose. I suppose it depends on how ambitious you are. I've really liked it here. And now I think I'll do well in law school."

To those close to him, familiar with his indifferent record at the permissive Nokobee County Regional High School, Raff's performance at Florida State University had come as a surprise. He qualified for early election to Phi Beta Kappa. For that Uncle Cyrus sent him congratulations and an expensive Omega watch.

His honors thesis on the Anthill Chronicles was widely talked about by those faculty who knew of it to be likely one of the best ever submitted by an undergraduate.

"You could get into any graduate program in the country," Needham told him. "That is, of course, if you decide to stay in biology. It's for sure that if you change your mind about law school, we'll find a place for you here. I don't doubt you'd have enough for your Ph.D. in three, maximum four years.

But Raff's mind could not be diverted now from law school and back into biology. That could be kept for another time. In the fall of his senior year, he applied to a dozen law schools, half in the South and half outside. He had the grades, and he had an unusual science background as an add-on. He'd taken some of the right prelaw courses. He expressed an intention to work on environmental issues, pro bono if need be. He was backed by strong recommendations from faculty members at Florida State University. It did not hurt that as a son of the central Gulf Coast, not known for scholarly achievers, he was a geographical minority.

By April Raff had been accepted by most of the schools. Those rejecting him included, to his surprise, Emory University. The positive responses did include, however, his first choice, Harvard Law School. On hearing the news from Cambridge, his friends and mentors threw a party to cheer him on. Most arrived wearing twin ant antennae made out of wire. Uncle Cyrus sent him a letter of congratulations, as close to ecstatic in tone as the good gray man could manage.

In midsummer, as he was planning to move north, he made one more pilgrimage to Lake Nokobee. He walked its whole perimeter. He halted where he knew one of the resident alligators lived, and caught a glimpse of it, all but eyes and dorsal surface of the head submerged beneath duckweeds. He made a mental note of the ground flora that was in bloom at this time of year, and scanned the big longleaf pines until he saw the flash of a red-cockaded woodpecker traveling from one treetop to another. Before leaving, he silently renewed his pledge to the beloved place.

One week after Labor Day, Ainesley and Marcia drove their son from Clayville to the Mobile Regional Airport for the first air trip of his life. The facility was nowhere close to the international hub envisioned by Cyrus Semmes and the Gulf Gateway Coalition, but busy enough to make the eastern approach to the terminal one of the most congested in the United States.

He flew Delta over to Atlanta, was awestruck by the immensity of the airport, and then almost lost as he puzzled his way through to the departure gate for Boston. In order to travel between terminals there, he took his first train ride.

Emerging from Logan Airport in Boston, Raff confronted in the MBTA the first subway of his life. To his embarrassment, the FSU Phi Beta Kappa and Harvard Law School student had to ask three official looking people in a row, each impatient and surly, to his way of thinking, how to get to Harvard Square. Hauling his heavy suitcase and bent beneath an overladen knapsack, he was humiliated again when he emerged from the exit kiosk and was forced to ask several more people to find his way to the graduate student dormitories on Oxford Street. One of his advisers spoke with a strong East Indian accent. Another, poorly dressed and seemingly frightened by his approach, could respond only in Spanish. Along the way he listened to passersby to see if he could hear the famous Harvard accent.

"There is no such thing as a Harvard accent," his roommate, a black minister's son from Gabon in Africa, said to him when he finally arrived at Richards Hall. "That's not what this place is all about. Welcome to Harvard."

31

Harvard: THE WORLD'S greatest university, they called it up there. Certainly at least a global university, with a culture as different from that of Clayville, Alabama, as it was possible to get and still remain in the United States. The ambience of Harvard University comes not so much from its profusion of museums and libraries, or the rat's maze of its narrow streets, but from its compression of time and space that speak centuries of history.

A cannon shot away from Cambridge Common, where Washington took command of the colonial army, lies Harvard Yard, where students rioted in 1969 against the Vietnam War, "Power to the people!," in the same small space trampled by their predecessors in the Food Riot of 1766, "Behold, our butter doth stink!" The site of the college at its founding in 1636, the Old Yard, is faced by University Hall, where hang the flags of visiting heads of state next to that of Harvard, crimson and emblazoned with the word VE-RI-TAS. Behind University Hall is the open space called the Tercentenary Theatre, which in turn is flanked by Memorial Church to the left and straight ahead by Sever and Emerson Halls, respectively the haunts of great preachers and philosophers, and to the right by massive Widener

Library, given by a wealthy family to memorialize their scion who perished on the *Titanic*. The library, gathering place of all students and some of the world's greatest scholars, is also where a thief was severely injured falling from a window clutching Harvard's Gutenberg Bible. The library's countless front steps seat many of the twenty-four thousand that crowd into the Tercentenary Theatre on each June Commencement Day. The ceremony is marked by the conferring of honorary degrees on up to ten famous people. Their identity is kept secret until the banquet in their honor is celebrated by hundreds the night before in cavernous Memorial Hall, built in 1872 to honor Harvard men who died in the War Between the States—Union dead only, Raff noticed, not Harvard Confederate dead. The Victorian structure, whose clock tower once sheltered a nest of peregrine falcons before the species nearly went extinct from pesticide poisoning, gives way southeastward to several of the greatest art museums in America, and westward to the towering, modern Science Center, neo-ziggurat in design and devoted with imperial grandeur to undergraduate science education. Only a block northeast from Memorial Hall is the even more towering quasi-skyscraper William James Hall, housing the social sciences, and whose vicinity is avoided during winter due to the galelike arctic winds that whip around it, the shape and apartness of the building having been designed inadvertently to make it an inside-out wind tunnel. Thence on northward down Divinity Avenue and Oxford Street are met the buildings and humming bustle of the popularly named Science City, dominated by the glassy palaces of molecular and cellular biology, crowding and dwarfing historic Divinity Hall, home of nineteenth-century great thinkers, and reducing to insignificance other venerable, mostly wooden buildings that house the largest privately owned collection of plants and animals in the world. In the Museum of Comparative Zoology reside a ten-foot moa skeleton from New Zealand, two of the thirty-two specimens of the extinct great auk known to exist, the world's largest fossil turtle, the reference specimen of a new species of bird collected by Lewis and Clark, and over five million carefully curated insect specimens from all over the world. And then finally, beyond to the northeast, on the margin of the university both metaphorically and literally, apart and serene, resembling nothing so much as a squashed-down cathedral, is the Divinity School, with its magnificent book collections, sometimes referred to by skeptics among the nearby scientists as the Library of Revealed Information.

Altogether a human anthill, a kaleidoscope of specialists, whose lives are molded to ensure their own well-being through service to the greater good. The most distracting concern to this son of the Gulf Coast was the length and cruelty of the winter. For as long as four months each year, while early darkness falls upon New England each evening, the region is regularly visited by cyclonic nor'easters. The storms spiral northward up the Atlantic Coast, afflicting New England for three days. Saturated with relatively warm moist air upon arrival, they unload heavy rain, sleet, and snow, whipped along by powerful winds. Boston, it turns out, is one of the three windiest cities in America. The nor'easters next pass on out into the North Atlantic, pulling down masses of arctic air upon the hapless citizens. The first day the streets and sidewalks of Cambridge are filled by rain pools and slush. The next day they are coated with black ice and walls of frozen slush. On through the third day and beyond, high winds, familiarly called the Montreal Express, drive the chill factor down while causing more pedestrians to slip and fall on the slick black ice of the strangled walkways.

There are almost no signs of life during this dreadful season, outside of humans in heavy clothing scurrying through the whistling arctic air amid desperate pigeons and house sparrows, aliens of European origin, their feathers fluffed out to keep warm, hopping about in search of rare scraps of food. Raff was reduced to asking, "Why do people stay here? Don't they know any better?"

The exhilaration Raff felt upon his arrival, in the deceptively cheery fall days, was soon darkly balanced by the hollowing sense of alienation. He would never lose it; he would always feel like an outsider. In time, he was to learn that *everyone* at Harvard is an outsider, or at least feels that way once in a while.

The torrent of Harvard's life spun like a vortex around the new center of Raff's life, the gray stone buildings of the Law School. To step outside his studies and sample it was like trying to sip water from a fire hose. The earnest battalions of smart people and the ideas they promoted were disorienting. Most of the students had achieved intellectual distinction before arriving. Valedictorians and National Merit Scholars were commonplace among the undergraduates. Phi Beta Kappa membership was the rule among the entering graduate students. Ideas were coin of the realm at Harvard, and competition among their champions to express them intimidating.

Before he made the trip north, Raff had comforted himself with the hope that Harvard, while quantitatively different from Florida State University, would prove to be basically the same. Harvard, he thought, might just be FSU on steroids. But he soon learned an important different truth. When any organized system, whether a university, a city, or any assembly of organisms themselves, reaches a large enough size and diverse enough a population, and has enough time to evolve, it also becomes *qualitatively* different. The reason is elementary: the greater the number of parts interacting with one another, the more the new phenomena that emerge within it, therefore the more surprises student and teacher alike encounter each day, and the stranger and more interesting the world as a whole becomes. Exactly the same is true of ant colonies among different species, as Bill Needham had explained to him at Florida State University. Large colonies, like those of the Nokobee anthills, have complicated division of labor, and the queens are much larger than and more physically different from the workers.

One such phenomenon true to the big and venerable principle, Raff soon discovered on campus, was the Gaia Force, a radical student environmental movement. An announcement in the *Crimson* announced its first meeting of the fall term.

GAIA FORCE

There will be a meeting at the Lowell House Common Room, Wednesday, September 25, at 8:00 P.M. The Gaia Force, a democratically organized group of concerned students, will discuss **NATURE FIRST! FOR THE BENEFIT OF HUMANITY!**

The boy from Alabama thought this might be just the group for him. He was after all an environmental radical—well, sort of; at least in Mobile he was.

An added and completely unexpected attraction within Gaia

Force, for Raff upon his arrival at the Lowell House meeting, was one JoLane Simpson, a brilliant undergraduate major in social studies who hailed, of all places, from Fayetteville, Arkansas. JoLane's father was an Assembly of Jesus Christ minister, an evangelical locally famous for leading the crusade against atheism, homosexuality, evolution, abortion, socialism, and godless science. JoLane, brought to Harvard with a scholarship on a perfect-A high school record, had by the end of her freshman year rotated 180 degrees from Dad's beliefs. She had deserted her upbringing as a Fine Young Christian Woman and forged her magnolia steel into a spearpoint of socialist revolution. She settled as far to the political left as possible without seeming to be insane—even by the relaxed clinical standards of Harvard.

Yet while urging revolution against unjust regimes such as those in Fayetteville and Cambridge, JoLane Simpson nevertheless remained her father's daughter in fixity of moral outrage and in rhetorical style. There was no problematic topic about which she did not have a passionate opinion. Her greatest zeal was reserved for destroyers of the environment, whom she had witnessed operating openly in her native state.

JoLane declared that she would never vote. She decreed that no national leader, including her fellow Arkansan Bill Clinton, who had recently finished his presidency, and even the sainted Ralph Nader, was capable of launching the revolution necessary to save humanity. She tried to drop her Southern accent, which to her sounded ignorant and, worse, politically conservative. But she still embarrassed herself occasionally by an accidental "y'all," "much obliged," "fixin' to," and, equally stigmatic, "wont" for "want," "git" for "get," and "ast" for "ask."

When Raff showed up at the Gaia Force reception, JoLane

went straight to him and introduced herself. It was the last thing a proper young lady from Arkansas would do, and the first thing expected of a completely liberated young woman from what was often called the People's Republic of Cambridge.

"Hi, I'm JoLane Simpson, and I'm very glad you've come to our meeting tonight."

"Well, thank you, ma'am," Raff replied, in a still-undiluted Alabama accent, "I'm interested in any organization that's working for the environment."

A Southerner, thought JoLane. She took hold of Raff's arm, got him a drink, led him to a corner of the room, and worked him quickly into a lively conversation. She had to admit to herself that although she was now a global citizen who embraced all peoples, she still suffered twinges of homesickness. And anyway, Raff was in Law School. This guy might be politically useful in future Gaia activities. Most of the other Gaians were majors in English and sociology.

JoLane kept Raff out of reach of the rest of the small crowd gathering, while together they excitedly explored their respective backgrounds and philosophies. JoLane sized up Raff's qualities quickly and favorably. He was not only a fellow environmentalist, but one with a well-defined mission. He was a real down-deep Southerner with a way of talking that, in spite of her un-Southern asseverations, comforted her no end. He was a somewhat older man too, not frivolously excitable, and he wore a *jacket* and *tie*. Raff kept his hair trimmed and, most importantly, openly expressed doubts about his own Episcopalian faith.

Raff, in short, was a sharp contrast to the puerile sweatshirted Californians who regarded themselves as the inner council and fighting vanguard of Gaia Force. He had the look of a leader, and maybe people like him, she thought, were what the group needed most. Being largely the offspring of the 1970s New Left, the other force members considered themselves keepers of the true faith of the new socialist revolution, which they were certain to begin as soon as a few wrinkles from the last time, such as the atrocities of the Khmer Rouge and erection of the Berlin Wall, were ironed out. Meanwhile, no deviation from the articles of faith was permitted. They were committed to an ideology in which the chairpersonship was passed around, alternating gender and minorities to sustain ideological purity. That was of little consequence in practice, as it turned out—all decisions were made by the group at meetings.

The goal of Gaia Force was to tear down the old order to build a correctly engineered new one. What the new order would be was up for discussion, and more discussion, and more on into the future, in order to get everything right this time. The only principles solidly established thus far were two in number: the complete equality of gender and race, and freedom of sex among Gaia members, which in common parlance is called promiscuity.

Inevitably, as things go, Raff was attracted to JoLane. He couldn't help but take an interest in any attractive girl who singled him out so confidently. He assayed her as every heterosexual male does every good-looking young woman who comes into view, however fleetingly. The saccade proceeded in the usual, genetically programmed sequence. The specimen before him was, first, almost as tall as Raff; young, almost adolescent in overall aspect; thin, too much perhaps, but in concert with a quick, excitable demeanor. JoLane had a keen, intelligent face and two of the traits scientifically considered beautiful, small

chin and wide-spaced eyes, but not the third, high cheekbones.
Her dark brown hair was cut too short, whether for revolutionary unisex or a distaste for feminine adornment could not be
divined. Nothing on the ring finger. Finally, from multiple signals in her tone of voice and body language, he presumed she
was not gay.

And, of greater importance to Raff as to most intelligent
men, they were both highly alert and goal-oriented. They were
each anxious to tell the other about their childhood, and they
could comfortably mock and laugh about their upbringing. That
evening their private conversation went on for half an hour, and
then after the meeting another half hour, drawing looks from
other Gaia Force members, until finally the group began to dissolve. Raff was relieved that no male friend of JoLane's intruded
in the conversation, and in the end none came up and said, *Come
on, JoLane, I'll take you home.* Only later did it occur to him that lack
of intervention by a possessive male might be evidence of a taboo
on sexist displays, based in turn on the belief that testosteronic
behavior was a defining trait of environmental evildoers.

Two days later they met for coffee at the student center in
the basement of Memorial Hall. There was more talk, this time
getting into serious matters of environmental activism and
world affairs. Still no sign of Gaian male rivals. The next Saturday, a walk over to the Law School, a tour of the premises by
Raff, more talk. The following weekend, with Raff's roommate
at Richards Hall away at a Gabonese freedom rally, bed and pil-
low talk.

Prior to his arrival at Harvard, Raff had, unlike most of his
fellow students at FSU, no experience with sex. He was too small
physically and immature in physical appearance to attract even

the casual attention of most girls. Further, he was shy in temperament, afraid of impregnating a girl or forming any relationship serious enough to deflect him from his planned career. In any case, he could not drive a car, a prerequisite for romance in most of America.

At Florida State University he nevertheless dated several girls with dinner, conversation, a movie in or as close as possible to the FSU campus. And twice he engaged in moderately heavy petting outside the girl's dormitory when he and his date saw other couples doing it. These encounters he frequently reviewed in his mind, and elaborated them into fantasy. He dreamed of more, but resigned himself to waiting.

Raff was totally unprepared, then, for the physical attentions that JoLane showered upon him. They were a quantum leap from anything he had dreamed he might one day experience. The young ladies of his acquaintance at FSU had been basically very modest, and monogamous. They wished to form sexual relationships with one or a very few partners, leading to a husband or at least what is euphemistically called a boyfriend— in either case, the love of their life. Raff had the same domestic concept.

JoLane, in contrast, aimed to wring from sex every pleasure it had to offer. Hers was an experimental and fearless attitude born of radical feminism. It was less raw physical desire than a political statement. With the certification granted her by ideology, she erased the very idea of limits. She approached sex with the casualness of pouring morning coffee. A wildness consumed her, as she set out to try every position, engage every orifice.

JoLane dragged Raff beyond the limits of his own fantasies. She was Lilith, Aphrodite, a force of nature. He had no way to fold their adventure into his logic-dominated worldview. A normal young male, he released himself and joined JoLane's freeform experiments, wondering where they might ultimately lead.

An affair in a major university like Harvard is like no other, independent of the magnitude of its sexual energy. Raff and JoLane were happily lost in the great brainy anthill, weaving their way through a constantly changing labyrinth of classes, study sessions, meetings with friends separate and mutual, and, whenever they could find an hour or two of privacy, or even semiprivacy, exhausting sessions of lovemaking.

Both discovered a new allure, with deepening satisfaction, in the life of Harvard and the surrounding venues of Cambridge. During a lecture by a Supreme Court justice at the Law School entitled "The Constitution and International Negotiation," she started to giggle and he hushed her. They spent an hour at the Fogg Art Museum peering at Rembrandt sketches and Byzantine iconic art. Raff was thinking about the sex to come later, but he also promised himself he would study art history when he found time—a commitment he knew would be forgotten by the following day.

The couple devoted two hours to a concert of atonal music. Raff didn't understand it at all, but everyone else seemed to, including JoLane, so he kept silent afterward. They held hands through a lecture at Science Center A entitled "Origin and Phylogeny of the Flowering Plants: A Mystery Solved," by a renowned and incomprehensible botany professor from Peking University. They attended a Free Burma rally, and wondered later what the military junta was doing with the rain forest. Both agonized over the Twin Towers attack but also hoped the people of Afghanistan would not suffer unduly. Together, the two sampled Ethiopian cooking in a small restaurant off Harvard Square, both first time, last time.

They laughed over the Harvardian eccentricities all around them. Visiting professors from the University of Oxford speaking with Oxford accents and publishing in the *New York Review of Books*, and American professors also speaking with Oxford accents but publishing in the *London Review of Books*. The forced enthusiasm of the university's official *Harvard Gazette* for Harvard football. The rareness of Harvard students wearing Harvard insignia on their sweatshirts and jackets, instead preferring, in egregious reverse snobbery, Georgia Tech University and Slippery Rock College.

It bothered Raff a little that no one he met, other than JoLane, had ever heard of Admiral Raphael Semmes, and she only vaguely and dismissively. But this minor insult was soon forgotten in the magical ambience of Harvard Law School. By the end of the first semester, with new friends and the rapidly evolving affair with JoLane, his life was as complete and balanced, he thought, as it might ever be. He even sometimes imagined idly what it would be like to give everything up and become a Harvard bum. Audit courses for free, slip into the back rows for big lectures and events. Crash a few receptions for drinks and hors d'oeuvres, maybe even the Faculty Club when a packed room there was partly filled with students. Live on odd jobs. Have a constant lover, maybe JoLane. Pass on into middle age with a speckled beard and ponytail. Be one of the semiprofessional chess players in Harvard Square ("Play chess with an expert, $5"). Learn enough classic chess moves to knock down the amateurs fast, and have dinner that evening in a good restaurant somewhere around the square. But it was just a fantasy. Raphael Semmes Cody soldiered on.

The interests of Raff and JoLane were broadly overlapping, but a difference in their temperament divided them. It emerged disturbingly on the key issue of environmental activism. JoLane wanted a juggernaut, and she thirsted for a revolution. Her preferred strategy was bombardment with propaganda followed by frontal assault by means of public protest and riot. She could not abide Raff's cautious, law-abiding approach.

JoLane tried to avoid the tension between them. In private conversation it diminished the freedom with which they expressed ideas. They softened some opinions and detoured around a few altogether, including race and economics. Raff worried that their conjugal intimacy was putting an edge on some of their intellectual talk, making sex less spontaneous than it had been when they were near-strangers.

Finally, one evening, when he started to talk about the methods of conflict resolution and litigation, she exploded.

"The developers are too powerful, Raff! You *cannot* compromise with these people. They've got the money, they've got the politicians, and not only that, they like to say what they're doing is good for the country. And then if nothing else works, they tell you it's God's will. God the Wildlife Manager, no less. How can you deal with that? You can't compete with them, Raff. You can't reason with them. They'll run over you every time. The only thing to do is to go right at them, believe me. I've learned a few things from my father. Passion and guts, Raff, you gotta have them, and you gotta leave some bodies on the field. We haven't got a lot of time either, Raff."

He did not like being pushed like this, as though his manhood were in question. "I think you want me to be a courthouse lawyer, JoLane, and keep Gaia Force members and other hard chargers out of jail. I have other plans in mind."

"What plans?" she asked, turning suddenly quiet.

"I'll tell you someday, darling." He just didn't want to prolong the argument.

JoLane was stung. She was not used to being cut off in the middle of rhetorical flight. But she too let it pass.

Raff could not offer more. He was not used to aggressive polemics, and the idea of eco-war repelled him. Above all, he could not bear the thought of breaking the law. It wasn't lack of courage. It was an understanding of how the consequences could be severe and counterproductive. He thought that surely JoLane knew that much. Driving nails in Douglas fir trunks to wreck chain saws—no way. Lying down in front of bulldozers, tearing up injunctions, risking prison, and shouting defiance at the television cameras as you're led out of the courtroom—not for him.

Civil disobedience and even occasional violent resistance might be necessary once in a great while. He understood the heroism of Henry David Thoreau and Martin Luther King, Jr., and the Minutemen who died at Lexington and Concord. But this was not his way. He had a deeper philosophical problem with the approach favored by JoLane and the other Gaians. He just could not equate the crusade for the environment with that for civil rights. This was America, not some benighted revolutionary state. Trees and bears were not disenfranchised people. Somehow the prize could be, had to be, won within the law.

Raff began looking for intellectual and emotional support to help close the rift opening between him and JoLane Simpson. He searched about and found it in an interview with Russell Jones, the Joseph Bullard Professor of Environmental Law.

They met in Jones's office, a large rectangular room overlooking the Cambridge Common. One wall was lined with books and in a frieze above them were nineteenth-century prints of West Indian and South American birds. A second wall held award certificates and photographs of Jones with President Óscar Arias of Costa Rica and other pioneers of Latin American environmental reform.

Jones was a tall man of about sixty, still trim, and fit enough to take long bird-watching trips. He had a poet's thatch of tousled medium-length snow-white hair. Before being called to Harvard (as they used to say of professorship offers in the days of Eliot and Lowell), he had served in the Department of State as an expert on Latin American environmental and trade policy. He was fluent in both Spanish and Portuguese.

They took two chairs, each displaying the Harvard seal in gold against a black background and appropriately uncomfortable, and settled them loudly scraping on the bare pinewood floor next to the single window.

"As an environmental lawyer, I don't get a lot of requests from students for interviews," Jones said. "They all seem more interested these days in working at one or the other of two extremes, pro bono for civil liberties, or making a lot of money on Wall Street."

Raff thanked him for agreeing to the meeting, then described the situation at Nokobee. It looked, he said, as though the developers might win, and the priceless heritage would be destroyed. "I'd like to be an environmental lawyer myself someday, but right now I just want to help save Nokobee and as many places like that in the South as I can. We're losing a lot down there. There's just no time left."

"Well," Jones said, "you certainly are a different kind of truth-seeker from the usual law student here. So my answer is, that kind of situation is difficult, all right, and particularly in your part of the country. But you're right, it can be managed within the law."

"*Which* law, though?" Raff asked. "Suppose a company owns a piece of land that ought to be a nature reserve, and it's remote and out of sight—what's to stop that company from clearing it?"

Raff was a bit irritated with himself as he asked the question. He'd noticed lately that he had begun to lose some of his Alabama accent, especially around figures of authority. He was unconsciously speeding up his speech, and clipping short the last syllable of some of the words. He didn't want that to happen. But when he tried to change back, he couldn't help exaggerating the Southern softness. He sounded, he thought, like someone from South Carolina.

"There are laws," Jones said, "and different ways to interpret laws." He paused to let that sink in. "If certain interpretations have a strong moral premise, and pick up public support, they can win in court even if precedents seem to point the other way. That's what you're in law school to learn, I hope. There are a range of legal arguments that can be made to protect the land. And they *can* prevail, even if the case has to go to appellate court, and, at least theoretically, all the way to the Supreme Court. It's a lot like appealing a criminal conviction."

"Lord help us," Raff said. "It's a pretty terrible thing when we have to protect nature in court like it was some kind of a criminal."

"Well, remember you're dealing with common law here, which is always complicated and always based on moral reasoning to some degree. And in the kind of case you're describing, that's particularly true. The reason is that the disputes of your sort come out of the conflict between two sacred precepts of the Republic, private property rights and America's natural heritage. If you own a piece of land, you can do with it what you please—but only up to a point. You can't change it in a way that harms the public good. You can't bury spent uranium fuel there, you can't dam a river there. If the land is important for conservation, that's a public good that could be harmed by development. So you have to make the case on behalf of the Nokobee tract that developing it would be harmful to our natural heritage, to a degree that more than offsets the public good from the increase of jobs and income that might come from developing it."

"That's very subjective."

Jones agreed. "Yeah, I'll grant it's very subjective. And, you know, it's sticky in an area that's been slow on conservation, like Alabama. And it gets harder when you've got an organization like the Gulf Gateway Coalition that pushes development as a primary public good. The bottom line is, I don't envy you."

"I don't envy me either," Raff said.

He rose, thanked his host, and walked to his room in nearby Richards Hall. His Gabonese roommate was out again. He and some of his countrymen seemed to be almost living in the Kennedy School of Government these days. Maybe plotting a revolution, who knew? Raff lay on his bed and stared at the ceiling for a while, musing on the conversation he'd just had. Well, he thought, I'm going to have to study some new subjects.

He decided to search for cases solved by conflict resolution, especially the kinds that had been decided by federal and state law. He devised what he thought would be a powerful methodology. It was to seek influence through challenge and conflict resolution. Achieve conservation while at the same time satisfying—if at all possible—the interests of the property owners and developers. If satisfying them wasn't possible, fall back to an alliance with the green warriors like the Gaians. Be prepared then to use protest and class-action suits to turn up the pressure. But however a particular case unfolded, never, ever willingly give up any of the few precious scraps of wild land still left.

One evening at Lowell House, Raff decided to describe his philosophy to a group of Gaia Force members. He knew he was taking a chance by suggesting negotiation and compromise to the self-described commandos of environmentalism. It was like throwing snowballs at the devil, but he was interested in seeing how they would take it, and, he had to admit, he wanted to impress JoLane.

It was the wrong move, clearly. He could tell that the listeners were restless. Before he could finish his lecture, one chinos-clad Californian, sprawled on a chair in the front row, loudly interrupted him.

"Jesus Christ, man, what is this? Neville Chamberlain time? What the hell do you think you're doing, anyway? Are you working for developers? Or it could be you're just plain gutless. Either way, you're full of shit."

Everyone in the room froze. Raff was speechless. This was not the Harvard way. It was trash talk you'd expect from some gang member on the street.

For a full minute the two young men glowered at each other. Raff's surprise was quickly replaced by anger. Then, oddly, he relaxed. He'd been there before. As a boy in the more primitive world of Clayville he'd had several schoolyard fights, of the kind usually set off when a bully taunts some other kid. His own ended when a teacher or older boy pulled the two scrappers apart. The usual outcome of a confrontation, however, was a standoff, with both talking trash but neither attacking the other. The others crowding around would chant, "One's scared, and the other's damn glad of it."

Raff was back in Clayville. He took a step toward the Californian, who now stood, but did not come forward himself.

It's the way of nature, Raff thought. Animals spend a lot more time displaying and bluffing than they do fighting. Even his ants held tournaments, settling their territorial boundaries without the loss of a drop of hemolymph—ant blood—most of the time.

They stood like that for another half minute. The remainder of the group remained silent. He's preserving status, Raff thought. He's bigger than me, but he may not be in very good shape. All those marijuana tokes, all that beer could have slowed him, and maybe he knows it.

Raff was sure, by the unspoken and primitive dictate of primate emotion, that if he turned and walked away from this, he would lose whatever status he had among the Gaians. More importantly, he would be humiliated in front of JoLane. She might tell him it was all right to walk away and that she was glad he didn't stoop to violence. But she wouldn't mean it.

It was Ainesley who then spoke to Raff, to a ten-year-old boy: *Never back down if you're in the right.* The Gaians to the rear of the room were beginning to stand up, to leave or come forward, he couldn't tell, and Raff could hear whispers. Raff thought he knew his man. It was time to call the bluff. He was ready to pay the price of a bloody nose. He took another step forward. The two were now less than four feet apart. Raff's arms were at his side but with fists clenched.

Then the showdown challenge. "You don't know jackshit about anything, do you, *boy*?" Raff growled. "Let me give you a piece of advice. You keep going where you're headed, *boy*, and you'll end up in jail somewhere. Everybody'd be better off if you did, you ridiculous loudmouth."

It was the Californian's turn to be startled. He stood his ground, but the only response he managed was "Fuck you," the traditional coward's exit line. Raff let him have that last word, making it a draw.

Then both managed to turn away from each other simultaneously, shaking their heads in mock amazement at the perfidy of the other. Testosterone did not win in the confrontation that day, no violence erupted, but it showed Raff in a way mere introspection never could that he was not gutless, and Chinos the Californian was not entirely stupid.

It was then that Raff finally realized the absurdity of the situation. *Nobody*, under *any* circumstance, has a fistfight in the Lowell House Common Room of Harvard University. But Raff felt good about the outcome anyway.

Immediately afterward a greatly relieved and proud Raff walked JoLane home to her room in Leverett House. He decided that the manly thing to do was say nothing to JoLane about the confrontation with the Californian, thus implying, *Oh, that? That was nothing, I can handle that kind of thing easily.* But he was puzzled that she said nothing about it herself, not even enough to signal her loyalty to him. Nothing was said when they met again two days later in the Memorial Hall cafeteria. By that time Raff had begun to put the confrontation out of his mind, but JoLane's silence still troubled him.

Raff dropped by the next Gaia Force meeting, two weeks later, determined to show that he had not been intimidated by the Californian's hostility, and wanting to continue the friendship he had made with several other members. He looked around to locate his enemy, however, determined to plant himself as far away as possible. No point in going through all that again. When he spotted the other man, he was dismayed to see him in an apparent warm conversation with JoLane. When she spotted Raff, she broke away and came over to him.

Raff felt a surge of jealousy as he struggled for the right things to say to JoLane. Why is my girl, he thought, talking with that jerk. As the feeling receded, it was replaced with a sour aftertaste of resentment.

As more days passed, Raff's annoyance grew, and with it came an ebbing away of trust. JoLane continued to offer no support. She then became too busy with a flood of classwork for sex. Raff tried to rationalize her shift in mood. He loved her, he thought, for the fierce free spirit she now was showing. And why should he think he owned her? Still, Raff began to lose some sleep trying to figure out JoLane Simpson. There seemed to be no way to solve the problem and keep his pride too.

JoLane herself brought it all to an end. After coffee in the Leverett House Common Room, she asked him to take a walk with her along the Charles River. She paused midway on the Longfellow Bridge, where lovers sometimes met, and as they gazed down the river, JoLane turned to him, tipped her head up, and kissed him on the lips.

"Raff, I've decided what I'm going to do after graduation. I've joined the American Friends of Haiti. They've got a chapter at Harvard. I'm going to go down there and see what I can do to help the people. I might go into agriculture or reforestation. You know, do something for the environment. God knows, that's what they need. Every little bit helps, doesn't it?"

With that final scrap of inanity, she walked away ahead of him back toward Harvard. It was so very JoLane, he thought. Abrupt, decisive, get on with life. He knew he would never find another woman with the same combination of intellect, fierceness of spirit, and passion as JoLane Simpson.

Wounded more deeply than he wished to fathom, Raff never attended another Gaia Force meeting. He was left to wonder whether JoLane would take the California tough guy with her to Haiti, and whether she would really in the end go herself. It didn't matter; now he had to restore his own balance. He threw himself back into the study of law.

32

WITH EACH PASSING month and as the end of his time at Harvard came in sight, Raff learned better one major advantage of being at an elite law school in a great university. It is the potential power of the network of friends and professional contacts that can be built. Raff did not have to travel around the country in order to meet the right people. They came to Harvard to attend meetings, to give seminars, to consult libraries, to look up others among their peers visiting the university. Raff, in order to get information and help in the future, made contacts now in The Nature Conservancy, the Sierra Club, and the Environmental Defense Fund. While at it, he learned where to go in the federal Departments of Justice and the Interior, and whom best to see there. He made friends with several staff members in Alabama's congressional offices. He began to compile addresses and telephone numbers among environmental leaders and their private supporters in Alabama, the Mississippi coastal counties, and the Florida Panhandle.

He learned how to run down cases of conflict between private rights and public good in domains other than the environment. He became expert in the common law developed all across the breadth of such cases. He was convinced that this knowledge could be applied to even the most difficult problems arising in his homeland of the central Gulf Coast.

Raff increased his command of conflict resolution, building scenarios, arguing them with other students. He became more convinced than ever that the classic nature-versus-jobs could not be solved by outright victory of one side over the other. That would leave the loser bitter and spoiling for a fight the next time around. Much better, and the higher road to take, would be an agreement that satisfies both. But—how best to reach such an agreement? That was much the harder nut to crack. It is always tempting instead to let the courts, America's Solomon on the throne, listen to both sides and settle the matter with a decision.

There was some reason for optimism in taking the middle road. He discovered several promising procedures worked out over the previous several decades by the Department of the Interior and nonprofit Environmental Defense Fund. Suppose, for example, that the owner of a tract of biologically valuable wild land wants to keep it intact but is forced by necessity to sell it to a waiting developer. In some cases the solution is simple: preserve the tract by acquiring it in exchange for biologically less valuable land suitable to the trader, and let the owner sell that for an equal or greater amount. Suppose, in a second situation, an owner wants to preserve the land and pass it on to his heirs but is afraid they would have to sell part or all of it to pay estate taxes. Arrange, if possible, a tax defferal without limit of time, granted so long as the tract is preserved in its natural state.

These kinds of solutions, devised case by case rather than top-down by some abstract application of constitutional law, were the weapon of choice Raff carefully added to his armamentarium for the fight to come.

In starts and reversals, spring comes absentmindedly to New England. April is a month of cold rain and occasional, charitably brief snowstorms. Nor'easters still visit regularly, whipping up winds that drive the chill factor down to the freezing mark. Finally, by the end of April and into early May, the forsythia bushes burst into brilliant yellow and along the narrow residential streets of Boston and Cambridge, and falling white-and-purple petals of deciduous magnolias carpet the ground of the meager gardens. Among them brave crocuses spring up and hurriedly bloom before being smothered by grass and crushed by dog droppings. Until that happy time, however, anyone wishing to see emerging plant growth must drive into the countryside, push his way through brambles into some roadside swamp, and search for clumps of skunk cabbage.

This year, because it was his last at Harvard, Raphael Semmes Cody had cheerfully endured the long postglacial winter. In mid-April letters from law firms began to trickle in: inquiries and even tentative offers from Atlanta, Memphis, Birmingham, Miami, and New York. His specialty had recently become a seller's market. The word among the faculty at the Law School was that the big firms were stocking up on talent able to handle environmental litigation.

Raff made polite, deferential responses, keeping the doors open. But he knew his career would probably never go that way. He was going home to Mobile, with or without a job in hand.

That decision was still firm when he graduated two months later. The Harvard commencement was held, in accordance with custom, on the morning of the first Thursday in June. Raff invited his parents to be his guests for the event. The evening before, he took them to dinner at his favorite Indian restaurant, located on Massachusetts Avenue a block from Harvard Square. Ainesley was clearly uncomfortable with all things Cambridge. He was not feeling well after the long trip up from Mobile, and was irritable. Raff's love surged for him when his father put on spectacles, took a long time studying the menu, and finally asked, "Don't they have anything fried?"

The next day, contrary to custom—and some said in violation of divine providence—a light rain fell on eastern Massachusetts. The commencement ceremony, the grandest and most venerable in the nation, began with bells ringing from all the churches in the neighborhood to bring on happiness, joy, and cheers as President Lawrence Summers, accompanied by members of the Harvard Corporation and Board of Overseers, emerged from the Old Yard and filed into the rain-soaked Tercentenary Theatre. Members of the faculty, draped in flowing pavorine robes from universities all over the world and wielding umbrellas, followed them in.

They passed along a narrow corridor walled in by the massed graduates. Cheers and greetings were exchanged back and forth over the heads of the packed thousands of families and guests assembled on all sides. The noise ended abruptly when, the groups on the platform having been seated, the sheriff of Middlesex County walked to front center with his staff of office, rapped thrice upon the hollow boards, creating a sound like rifle fire, and called the meeting to order.

There followed the singing of "The Star-Spangled Banner" by the whole assembly. Then a prayer, carefully bowdlerized to be ecumenical in tone, the rendering of the anthem "Domine Salvum Fac," followed by student orations in Latin and English, de rigueur since the seventeenth century. There was more choral and instrumental music, and the calling forward of the summa arts and sciences undergraduates.

President Summers now conferred the earned Harvard degrees, school by school. The mood turned from sedate to merry. The M.D.s wore stethoscopes thankfully not yet used on any patient, and of course the Business School graduates threw fistfuls of one-dollar bills into the air. Raff rose with his classmates to receive his degree. He was now certifiably learned, as the president intoned, "in those wise restraints that keep us free." As he stood, Raff looked for his parents in the huge crowd, without success. In a moment of unexpected intense yearning, he also searched for JoLane Simpson among the graduating seniors. It was impossible to find her in the sea of capped heads.

Finally came the awarding of honorary degrees to nine luminaries. Each stood in turn, to applause ranging variously from polite to thunderous. Each heard his encomium read, poetic in tone and short enough to serve as a tombstone epitaph.

After the platform party recessed, filing back through the student-walled corridor, the great anthill of Harvard celebrants dispersed. Marcia and Ainesley went out into Harvard Yard to wait for Raff at the foot of the John Harvard statue.

As he waited, Ainesley went up to the statue and rubbed his hand on the tip of one of the shoes, brightly polished by the ministrations of thousands of tourists before him. He saw an elderly black man standing close by, leaning on a silver-headed cane, and speaking in a courtly Southern voice. Ainesley struck up a conversation and learned he was a professor at Southern Mississippi University, located in Hattiesburg. His granddaughter, who was waiting next to him, turned out to be one of the new graduates of Harvard Law School. She allowed that she had met Raff, but didn't know him well. When Ainesley asked about her plans, she said she was going to enter Mississippi politics. Marcia was startled to hear Ainesley say to the two, "I wish y'all would come over to our neck of the woods. We sure could use you."

The next day was spent touring Cambridge and Boston. At Marcia's insistence, a major part of it was spent at the Museum of Fine Arts. The morning afterward, the Codys returned. At the Mobile Regional Airport, Ainesley retrieved his new plum-colored Toyota pickup, of which he was very proud, and the three returned to Clayville. That evening Raff called some old friends from Nokobee Regional High who were still around, to collect news and gossip. The next day, Sunday, he drove over with his parents to Brewton and attended the Episcopal church service.

Through the rest of the afternoon Raff stretched out on his old bed, next to the unread Sunday *News Register*, and dozed. After supper, as they sat drinking coffee, Raff asked his father if he had any late word on the Nokobee tract.

"It's fine as far as I can see. It's not going away," Ainesley said.

Raff was now set to implement his plan, over a year in the making. It had been constantly on his mind for weeks. Better now than later, he thought. Don't mess around. Just get moving. The next morning he called Cyrus Semmes's office and made an appointment.

Two days later, at seven A.M., he took the bus from Clayville to Mobile. He hoped that it would be one of his last bus trips anywhere. He'd told Ainesley the first thing he was going to buy when he had a job was his own car. From the station near Bienville Square, Raff walked to the Loding Building and rode the elevator up to the top floor.

Cyrus met him at the receptionist's desk, and hugged his nephew.

"By God. I can't tell you how proud I am of you, Scooter. I guess I ought at least to get started by calling you Raff now, or how about *Mr. Cody*? We'll save 'Scooter' for your own son, if you ever have one, and I sure hope you do. I know the Codys, on your father's side, are awfully proud too. I'll tell you one thing: you're going to be the big star in that bunch of peapickers, for sure. Listen, I'm going to take you to lunch at the Cosmopolitan Club. I want you to meet some of our family's friends, and, if you don't mind, let's talk a little bit about your future."

So they strolled together the five blocks to the Bankhead Tower, chatting like father and son. They took the elevator to the gated top floor and entered the sanctum of Mobile's business and professional elite. There followed hearty verbal greetings, handshakes, gripping of arms and shoulders, and good-natured jostling and laughing. The men were mostly middle-aged, white as June wedding gowns, and dressed in coat and tie. But there were also the mayor of Mobile and a sprinkling of other African-American leaders and businessmen. Almost all assembled spoke with Southern accents. Even those from other parts of the country slowed their speech a little, double-syllabled a few names, and dropped *g*'s. "Come Saturday, Fray-yed," he overheard one say, "I think I'll do me some snapper fishin' out of Biloxi."

There were also a scattering of well-dressed women. Several, judging from the ease with which they conversed and laughed with the men, were professionals and executives themselves. The rest, in this proper environment, talked among themselves and were almost certainly all wives. The day you brought a mistress would be your last as a member of the Cosmopolitan Club.

Cyrus, with Raff following, was led to a corner overlooking the Mobile River. Raff went over to the two-sided window to look out. He stared at the traffic twelve stories below, then beyond to Cooper Riverside Park and the new Convention Center. Well away to the south he could see Pinto Island and the northwestern shore of Mobile Bay. He squinted to peer where the river flowed into the bay. Somewhere out there on the water, a great-grandfather on Ainesley's side, working as ship's engineer, had died when the boat caught fire and sank. Raff tried to picture that tragedy. He turned his attention to a freight train moving slowly northward out of the Mobile Yards. Its whistle blew once, the kind of three-o'clock-in-the-night farewell that never fails to stir a wisp of melancholy.

From the Alabama State Docks a bay pilot boat had begun its journey south to the shoals of Dauphin Island, where it would pick up another freighter from the bar pilots and bring it safely down the dredged channels of the Mobile Bay shallow.

Raff had come home. He had perspective now, and seeing its physical whole from this height he thought about Old Mobile when Marybelle was built, when sailing merchantmen crowded close in a forest of spars at the head of the bay. There was still continuous old-growth pine savanna close by to the north and south. People living at the center of the city could take a wagon to the bayfront and harvest crabs and oysters from still-unpolluted waters. The economic engine of Alabama was growing swiftly then, in the plantations and freeholds along the great river that ended here. Bales of cotton and tobacco flowed down onto the docks. Sugar, rum, and tropical hardwood timber flowed in from the West Indies, and every kind of manufactured goods arrived from the Atlantic Seaboard and faraway Europe. Down below, close by the Bankhead Tower, near the foot of Government Street, once stood the open slave market, where African people were bought and sold, families sundered in perpetuity, and sent upriver to work the plantations and docks.

"Beautiful, isn't it?" Cyrus broke Raff's reverie.

Raff sat down, and two waiters brought them water and menus, speaking softly back and forth in a foreign language. It was Spanish. That's something new around here, he thought.

They began lunch. Crab gumbo and lobster Caesar salad. The lobster was the spiny Caribbean species, not the big-clawed kind from up North.

The conversation started up with Raff's career at Harvard Law and his impressions of life there, interspersed with Cyrus's comparing those from his own experience at the University of Alabama Law School.

Coffee and dessert were served, the latter a chocolate-and-brandy concoction Raff did not try to identify. Cyrus pulled out a Havana cigar from an inner coat pocket, unwrapped and lit it. He dragged deeply and blew the smoke upward toward the ceiling in a well-formed ring, as was his custom, then searched for an ashtray. There was no ashtray. Cyrus remembered: these conveniences had grown scarce at the Cosmopolitan Club. Many fewer members used them now, and the younger trustees of the club's board had begun to speak of making the Cosmopolitan Club smoke-free. One had commented, "What's so radical about that? This club used to have spittoons all over the place for tobacco chewers. Would you like to bring those back?"

Diners who still smoked often used coffee-cup saucers as ashtrays. Cyrus would have nothing to do with such an impropriety. He signaled a waiter by pointing to his cigar, and an ashtray was brought to him.

"I may have to bring my own in my pocket one of these days," he said.

Then he turned to Raff and came to the point.

"Well, have you made any plans yet? What do you want to do? All I can say is, I and a lot of our friends around here hope that whatever it is, you won't be straying too far away from Mobile."

Raff tensed. He'd rehearsed his response several times, and he had no idea what kind of reaction he was going to get.

"Well, sir, I know this might surprise you a bit. I've had some wonderful offers, more than you might imagine, from out of town. But what I really want to do is work here in Mobile as a legal counsel for Sunderland Associates. In fact, I was hoping that, unless you see some problem in that, you might speak to Mr. Sunderland on my behalf."

The two men, he knew, were not just allies in business and politics, but also connected in a manner that still mattered a great deal in the Old South. The Mobile Semmeses had been close to the Sunderlands socially for four generations. Promises, deals, and handshakes were binding as a matter of honor—and especially when family histories were intertwined somewhere back in history by marriage.

Cyrus stiffened, bent his head forward, and stared at Raff. When he spoke, he struggled to keep his voice down, to avoid others hearing in the crowded room.

"Are you serious? Is this some kind of Harvard humor?"

"Yes, I'm very serious."

"Do you realize what you're saying, then? You know as well as I do—we talked about it all a couple of years ago—that Drake Sunderland is absolutely determined to buy and develop the Nokobee tract when it comes on the market. He already owns the key parcel at Dead Owl Cove. Are you telling me you want to *help* him?"

"I'm telling you I want to work for him."

"But why? How can you do that honorably?"

"I'm telling you I can do that honorably and to everybody's satisfaction *and* save the Nokobee tract."

Raff then fell silent. He took a sip of coffee. He meant to keep this close to his chest, and say no more.

Cyrus turned and looked out the window and was silent himself for a while, struggling to construct a scenario that would make sense of what Raff had just said. He failed, and chose not to go that way for the time being. He also sensed from Raff's terse answers that his nephew would not disclose more even if he were asked.

Well, either trust your own blood, Cyrus thought, or simply send him away. He chose trust. But first, he wanted something more.

"Okay," he continued. "All right. Actually, I'm very pleased about how things appear to be working out. And it would be wonderful for me and Anne, and your parents, of course, to have you working right here in Mobile. But before I do anything, before I even *think* about approaching Drake Sunderland, I want your solemn promise—I want your *oath*—that you will be working exclusively in the interests of Sunderland Associates, and that you will never, ever undermine Sunderland in any way. Can you do that? Keep in mind here, Raff, that it's the honor of your family, not just your own, that's at stake."

Raff closed his eyes and inhaled deeply. He was now on ethically dangerous ground, but that was inevitable. That was the challenge.

He let ten seconds pass, let out his breath and opened his eyes.

"Yessir." Then he corrected himself. "Yes, Cyrus. I promise. You have my word."

Cyrus picked up his cigar and took another drag. He pursed his lips and this time let the smoke curl out slowly. For one of the few times in his life, he couldn't estimate the consequences of a big decision he had to make. He couldn't calculate the odds. But he had no choice. And it would not look good if he hesitated.

He passed his anxiety on to the cigar, leaned over and with annoyed abruptness, crushed it out, muttering to himself, "Damn things.

"All right, Raff, I'll speak to Drake Sunderland tomorrow if he's around. He knows all about you. Lord knows we've bragged enough about you while you were at Harvard."

Then, nodding his head gravely, rubbing the bald spot on his head with the three middle fingers, he regained a little of the old Cyrus Semmes balance.

"Be warned, though. You might not get the job even with my help. Sunderland's a company that's always used a separate law firm. It would be setting a precedent to use an in-house counsel. On the other hand, to have on board a graduate of Harvard Law School, and a young local lawyer of good family to boot—not to mention one with a strong science background—that surely sounds like something they might want to try. But if they do take you on, you understand it will have to be on a probationary basis. Of course, that's true everywhere, including any law firm you might join."

VI

THE
NOKOBEE
WARS

· 33 ·

THUS IT CAME to pass that against all odds, against all outward reason, Raphael Semmes Cody became the legal arm of one of the most rapacious land developers in South Alabama. As he walked toward his first day at work, he was in a dangerously ambiguous position, balanced on a knife edge between two opposing loyalties. A slight tip in either direction, he knew, could brand him a turncoat—a saboteur to Sunderland or a traitor to the conservationists. Either way, no one would trust him again, and his carefully constructed game plan would come apart. So he would always have to stay focused and think through his every step.

He arrived at the office building at nine o'clock sharp. He paused outside and glanced up at the large steel, squared letters announcing SUNDERLAND ASSOCIATES over the entrance. Then he wiped his hands down the sides of his new J. Press linen jacket to flatten any newly acquired wrinkles. He touched the knot of his maroon Harvard tie to be sure it was perfectly aligned with the buttoned-down tabs of his pale blue Pinpoint Oxford shirt. Satisfied that nothing of Clayville, Alabama, was in sight, he took a deep breath, squared his shoulders, and walked through the revolving doors into the main lobby.

Waiting for him there was the woman who identified herself as his personal secretary.

"Well, good morning, Mr. Cody, and it's so good to see you. Everyone upstairs at Sunderland Associates is so looking forward to meeting you. My name is Sarah Beth Jackson, and I'm the one who's going to be helping you."

"Well, I'm real glad to meet you," Raff responded. "We've got a lot of important work to do together."

Sarah Beth, he thought. How perfectly Alabamian. He recalled again that it was a Southern habit to give a double first name to the second daughter.

Sarah Beth was a talker, who disliked even a brief interval of silence. "I hope you had as nice a weekend as I did," she went on as they entered the elevator. "My family and I went fishing over at Pascagoula. We caught two big wahoos. They're real delicious if you grill them fresh. Have you ever tried wahoo?"

Raff frowned and shook his head slowly as though sad that this experience had been denied him. In fact, he had a hard time even picturing a wahoo. He remembered that it was a large game fish that occasionally showed up in restaurants, and in general was considered a novelty in port towns along the Gulf like Mobile.

They reached the fourth floor and went through a door with an opaque glass window gold-labeled SUNDERLAND ASSOCIATES and into the main administrative office. A large hand-painted sign on the reception desk read WELCOME, MR. CODY.

Sarah Beth led him to his office, located at the far end of the floor. He entered, looked around, then walked over to peer out the window. The view was of tar-papered rooftops with narrow congested streets down below. He figured, correctly, that the offices at the opposite side of the floor had the view of Mobile Bay. The room was bare of books and paperwork, for the last day, he knew, even the last hour. Sarah Beth handed him a handwritten note. He was due for a luncheon meeting in three hours with Drake Sunderland and Richard Sturtevant, vice president and chief financial officer. It would be in Sunderland's suite, on the opposite side of the floor.

Members of the staff began to break away from what they were doing, mostly getting settled in with morning coffee and small talk. They came to meet the new legal counsel, singly or in small groups, and add their welcome. They chatted for a while about this or that, and all left with the mandatory parting, or something close to it: "Now, if there's anything I can do to help you, you just let me know."

He listened carefully to what each said, no matter how perfunctory. He tried hard to memorize their names and read the undertones in their words. He noticed that several spoke with a slight edge, taking overlong to explain the roles of the executive staff members and stressing their own availability to give him advice anytime he felt a need for it.

Raff could understand the implied resentment toward a twenty-five-year-old entering the firm at a level they viewed as above their own. He wanted to remind them, but could not right then, that the legal counsel was a new niche at Sunderland and outside the hierarchy, and that he was not going to be a supervisor or a director of anybody except Sarah Beth Jackson. He made a mental note of those who showed what appeared to be some degree of anxiety. It would be wise, he thought, to draw close to them and gain their trust in the future.

At the luncheon meeting Raff encountered another, more

serious risk. After lunch had been served and pleasantries wound down to the point that serious talk could begin, Sturtevant came quickly to the point.

"Raff, Mr. Sunderland and I just want to clear the air on a certain matter for once and all, and keep it that way. We want to be a hundred percent sure that we don't get any conflict of interest within the firm or even the appearance of one. I'm sure you don't want that either."

"Nosir, absolutely not," Raff said. "Something like that could undermine the operation of this company and even in some cases might open us to litigation. But so I can be perfectly clear, what exactly are we talking about here?"

Raff was pretty sure he knew where Sturtevant was headed. He had arrived on dangerous ground, and more quickly than he had expected.

"Well, we know you're quite a naturalist," Sturtevant replied, steepling his hands, "and you put a lot of effort into environmental law while you were at Harvard. Now, that's all to the good. Don't get me wrong about any of this. Environmental issues are getting more and more important these days, and in the business world too, and we need your kind of expertise in what might turn out to be pretty rough waters. But we'd really like to hear your feelings about where you stand. I mean, suppose push comes to shove on some environment issue. Suppose Sunderland Associates runs into heavy opposition from some environmental group or other on one of our projects. It might even become a big media issue, with reporters interviewing you and all. How are you going to handle that?"

There it was. Sturtevant could not be plainer. Raff knew that how he answered now, right this minute, could set the tone of his relationship with Sturtevant and Sunderland, and his future effectiveness in his new job.

"Mr. Sturtevant," he said, raising and opening his hands, "I'm glad you asked me."

"Rick, call me Rick, let's not stay formal around here, Raff."

"Okay, Rick, I'm glad you asked that question. I've given this matter a lot of thought myself, believe me, and I want to reassure you and Mr. Sunderland right now to your complete satisfaction."

In fact, he had all but memorized the answer he would now make.

"I promise you there will be no conflict of interest, or any appearance of conflict of interest, on any case on which I work. Let me put this as strongly as I can. I do intend to work with environmental groups around here and promote conservation. I hope you'll approve of that. This region needs it badly. But I will also work toward solutions and so forth that are to your complete satisfaction. I think you'll find that my connections with environmental organizations will work out to the benefit of the company."

The group fell silent for the good part of a minute. Then Sturtevant said quietly, "Well, now, I think I can speak for Drake Sunderland also when I say I'm satisfied with that answer."

"Yes," Sunderland quickly added, "thank you. Now, if we're all happy, let's get organized here. If you're ready, we'll move on to the next item on the agenda."

By the end of the week, Raff was deep in legal work of the kind previously sent to independent consultants. He found to his relief that for the most part he could manage his new tasks easily. He also projected that he could do so at an overall saving for Sunderland Associates. Most of the work concerned acquisition and sale of plots in the city and suburbs, and reviews of contracts for construction on them. So far, it was all at the level of Contract Law 101 at Harvard.

After several months, when Raff felt comfortable enough with his new position, he joined the Alabama Nature Conservancy and the state organization of the Audubon Society. At the first opportunity thereafter he offered their local representatives free legal advice, and received enthusiastic responses. That was not difficult work either, nor of great importance. So far, it had not as yet yielded decisions in conflict with the commercial interests of Sunderland Associates. He seldom encountered problems in conservation that could not be settled by standard methods of negotiation.

On the side he began to study the essential players in government, business, and land management at the local and state level. He went out of his way to meet the most important among them. Raff was consciously preparing for the small fraction of future conflicts that would demand exceptional skill and effort. He was bound to honor the promise he had made to Sunderland and Sturtevant. There would be victories for the company and there would be defeats. Then, he expected, there would be a very few with major long-term consequences. The most agonizing of these was the fate of the Nokobee tract. That, Raff knew, would be the game-breaker.

In the meantime, outside of business luncheons and receptions, Raff's social life was not with his professional colleagues at Sunderland Associates. Instead, Raff used his leisure hours to quietly build a circle of friends in the environmental movement.

Raff's key contact was inevitably Bill Robbins, whose office at the *Mobile News Register* was only five blocks from the Sunderland Office Building. Robbins's relationship with Raff soon changed from that as mentor and adviser to close friend and partner. They made it a habit to have lunch together in the Rebel Cafe and Deli, located on Bledsoe Street halfway between their two places of work, and famous for its fried mullet, hushpuppies, and crab gumbo. Occasionally, Bill's wife, Anna Jeanne Longstreet Robbins, joined them when she could break away from her job as a manager at the downtown Sears.

Their conversations ranged widely, usually including the more savory political gossip from around the state: a governor indicted for embezzlement, a famous football coach about to be fired for a dalliance with a member of his staff, a state senator photographed leaving a Biloxi casino with a male prostitute.

But invariably, they settled on the latest events at the South Alabama conservation front. Robbins always brought along a folded map of the surviving pockets of old-growth floodplain cypress and longleaf pine. "Those little parcels are the key to everything," he said.

At their second meeting, Raff decided to disclose his full plan to save Nokobee, so the two men could discuss it at length. The confidence was exclusive. Only Robbins would know. Not even Anna Jeanne would be told, and most certainly not Cyrus Semmes. Raff was desperate to share the subject with someone else who really cared about Alabama conservation, and he needed practical advice from the knowledgeable newsman. He was familiar with the oft-quoted definition of investigative journalism: seduction followed by betrayal. But he trusted Robbins completely. They were full partners, bound together by the same goals.

After a year at Sunderland Associates with nothing decided, Raff began to suffer a growing anxiety over Nokobee. He realized that many would judge his obsession unhealthy. But he had committed too much time and energy, and invested too much of his own self-regard, to let it go. He wanted the Jepsons to move Nokobee into the market. He would put his plan into action and help to settle the issue one way or the other. He felt, he said to Robbins, like a soldier waiting for the whistle ordering him to go over the top of the trench, or, perhaps more appropriately, a prisoner in a courtroom waiting for the verdict. He wanted to be fatalistic, to know what the gods had decided, to have made the issue final, live or die, with maybe some kind of peace at the end.

"There are times," he said one day to Bill Robbins at the Rebel over boiled crayfish, gumbo, and cheese grits, "when I'm almost ready to settle for a flip of the coin. Just to stop worrying about it."

"Listen, my friend, I know how it's been eating you, believe me, but look at it this way. The longer the Jepsons hold off, the more public opinion on the Gulf Coast will turn in favor of preserving the last pieces of the longleaf ecosystem. If the Jepsons wait long enough, it might be difficult for Sunderland or any other developer to tear up Nokobee, and the more so because Nokobee is fast becoming the last really good piece surviving in South Alabama. People in Mobile and the southern tier of counties, and the next counties over in the Panhandle, might be thinking of it as *their* longleaf reserve."

Raff said, "You're thinking the developers might just hold off buying Nokobee and instead put their money somewhere else. In other words, save themselves a lot of trouble."

"That's right," Robbins answered. "If major players like Sunderland pull out, the asking price, or more accurately the preset baseline bid, will probably drop. And, who knows, Nokobee then might get picked up by the State of Alabama or a conservation organization like The Nature Conservancy."

"Oh, yeah. Actually, I've thought about that a lot. It could happen." Raff broke a crayfish in two and sucked out the meat, then followed it with a slug of beer. "But that could also allow some pirate group to grab it and do God knows what to it. Maybe turn it into a pig farm."

"I think that's way too pessimistic," Robbins returned. "Too much money involved. Anyway, I do think that we might have more time. I've been wanting to tell you, it looks like the Jepsons are set to keep arguing over what to do for a while yet."

"That's news to me. How do you know that?"

"I've got a couple of friends at the *Atlanta Constitution* with an ear on the door whenever the Jepson Trust members meet. The trust has a lot more property tied up, around here and over in Georgia. They've been arguing a lot lately over sales and development, and one of the properties they're seriously hung up over is Nokobee."

Raff asked, "Why is that, do you suppose? Some of the Jepsons want to develop it themselves? Or they want to raise the opening bid?"

"No, no. Not either. Nothing like that. It's simply that a couple of the Jepsons want to cash out now, while the others want to milk the best deal out of the tract by picking the optimum

320 • *E. O. Wilson*

time and payout schedule. Fussing around like that could tie up the whole thing for a long time, maybe a couple more years."

"Well, damn it and be gone!" Raff reached over to another plate, lifted out a hushpuppy, chopped at it with a spoon, and mixed the pieces with cheese grits. "I ask you, why didn't God," he said, chewing, "make me the son of a billionaire so I could just buy the whole thing with pocket change and be done with it?"

"Bottom line," Bill Robbins said, brushing oyster cracker crumbs off his lap, "we just wait."

34

WAIT WAS ALL they could do. Finally, two years, four months, and a day after that conversation at the Rebel Cafe and Deli, the news finally came from Atlanta. The Nokobee tract, all of it except for the land around Dead Owl Cove already owned by Sunderland Associates, had been put on the market.

The time leading up to this moment had not been wasted for Raff. In balance, the years spent at Sunderland had been good ones for him. He had expanded his circle of friends dramatically. The grind of Harvard Law School was well behind him, and the more painful part of it mercifully forgotten. He sometimes thought about JoLane Simpson and wondered where she was—but not keenly enough to call the Harvard Alumni Office to find out. His work continued to prove mostly routine, and he began to squeeze out longer stretches of leisure time.

At twenty-eight years, Raphael Semmes Cody had adapted to a very different world from that of his boyhood. Clayville was culturally farther from Mobile than Mobile was from Cleveland or Albany. And unlike his existence at Harvard, Raff now ate regularly at the best restaurants and attended first-run movies and both classical and rock concerts. To these he added Gulf and river fishing. He joined other naturalists in the area on field trips. He dated regularly, but never with serious intent. He dodged relationships with younger women that might, he feared, lead to marriage before he wished. He never dated Sarah Beth, despite the lilt he perceived in her laugh whenever he said anything even remotely funny, or anyone else in the Sunderland offices. Within a year, in any case, his secretary married a divorced bank manager in nearby Lucedale, Mississippi, and the giggles became slightly less pronounced. She still commuted in to Sunderland, however, and continued to fill Raff's office with nonstop sunshine chatter.

Within a year of his arrival at Mobile, Raff had become a respected figure in the local conservation community. He attended meetings of several organizations regularly and continued to give pro bono legal advice in those large majority of cases that had no possible connection with his obligation to Sunderland Associates. A few of his environmentalist associates wondered if his employment at Sunderland represented a conflict of interest, but his advice was consistently good and true, and no public mention was ever made of a possible inconsistency.

Raff no longer attended church, but as a secular substitute he accepted a leadership position in the Boy Scouts of America. He remained faithful to the organization to which he owed so much in his own education and character development. He became scoutmaster of Mobile's Troop 43, holding meetings every two weeks in an annex of the First Methodist Church at Broad and Dauphin Streets. He counseled boys when they needed it. He approved merit badge awards, and individual advancements in rank. Not least, he took groups with him on occasional field trips to the Nokobee tract, and held the boys spellbound with accounts of its natural history.

Raff stayed fit by working out two or three times a week at the Mobile Executive Center Gym. Occasionally, at noon on long days in his office, he went over to Henry's Guns and Shooting Gallery on Oak Street for target practice. His favorite weapon was a .22 single-shot rifle.

It puzzled some of his friends in the environmental movement that a rising star among them enjoyed gun practice. The explanation he gave Bill Robbins was simple and he hoped convincing.

"Look, I sure wish people would understand that I grew up in a gun culture. I've been a pretty good marksman since I was a kid. Trust me, slaughtering helpless birds and animals makes no sense to me. On the other hand, let's be frank about it. Once in a while you've got to kill wild deer, for example. We've wiped out all their natural predators, and so now we have deer populations exploding. People in the suburbs will put up with hunters, but they're not going to tolerate wolves and cougars. Not yet anyway."

"Okay, but what about quail and ducks and turkeys?" Robbins said.

"That's just rhetoric, Bill. You and I wouldn't go out and use quail for target practice, but you know as well as I do that legitimate hunters are the best friends we've got outside the conservation movement. They want habitats preserved as much as we do. So face it, they're conservationists of another kind, with a mission just like ours. I don't think there's a lot of difference between, say, a Cooper's hawk taking a quail out or a hunter shooting it out, so long as we save the woods the hawk and quail live in."

But there was another reason Raff went to Henry's Guns and Shooting Gallery that he never tried to explain to Robbins or anyone else. For him target practice, and especially with a rifle, the most physically compatible and precise weapon ever invented since the bow and arrow, was a form of Zen. He relaxed completely when he put on ear guards and began to fire at a fixed target. It brought him into a little world consisting solely of gun and target, with a meaning all unto itself and private to Raff. The line of sight, the black dead center of the bull's-eye, the stopping of one's breath, the gentle pull of the trigger, these became the whole world and the only reality when he lay prone to shoot. Every other thought was banished, and every other movement ceased except the microscopic involuntary tremble of arm and hand and the trigger pull. The only variable was the distance, twenty yards or fifty yards. The discharge of the .22 was barely detectable. The mental purpose was to travel with the projectile to the dead center of the bull's-eye and touch it, perfectly. Although that happened rarely, the cognitive purpose was different and the more important. It was to bring all the senses together to focus on an object of extreme simplicity, and to shut out the chaotic remainder of ordinary existence.

From that out-of-mind experience and to show his appreciation of the environmental role of hunters, Raff joined the National Rifle Association.

Bill Robbins was alarmed. "You're sending the wrong signal, Raff. Would you please at least take that NRA sticker off your rear bumper?"

"You don't understand, Bill. It's a matter of honesty and

keeping a clear conscience. The only things I know that come anywhere close to target practice with a .22 rifle are a deep massage and sex."

One day, as he stood up, lay the rifle down, and took off his ear guards, a voice behind him said, "That's pretty good shooting. Were you in the army?"

Raff turned to find a man standing there, arms akimbo. He was about forty years old, thin, dressed in an ill-fitting dark blue business suit with an American-flag-design tie that forced his collar flaps slightly up and out. He wore a plain gold cross on his left lapel. He was well groomed and clean-shaven. His smile was broad and welcoming, yet was contradicted by the narrowing of his eyes and incongruous tilt of his head to one side, as though he were sizing Raff up.

Just to his rear stood a second man, about Raff's age, wearing blue jeans and a white sports shirt with three broad red vertical stripes running down the front. He had a three-day-old stubble and a bandito mustache. His long hair was combed straight back over his head and dangled loosely to touch his shirt collar behind. There was a teardrop tattoo below his right eye. He wore blue flame tattoos running up each side of his neck, looking as though they might be ready to grow out further and consume his face. He was chewing something continuously and slowly like a cow's cud—maybe tobacco, but more likely, Raff figured because he couldn't see any stain around the mouth, a large wad of gum.

"No, no, I've never been in the service," Raff said. "I've just enjoyed shooting since I was a kid."

"My name is Wayne LeBow," the first man said, "and this here's Bo Rainey."

Raff shook hands with both.

"He's Reverend Wayne LeBow," Rainey said.

"Yes, Reverend LeBow," the first man said. "But that's no big deal. I have a little congregation up near Monroeville, the Church of the Eternal Redeemer. Most likely you never heard of it." He chuckled and pulled down his coat to straighten it a bit, then added, "Only about fifty members or so. My day job is working at the Monroeville Correctional Facility."

He paused, and Raff said, "Well, Reverend LeBow, my name is Raphael Cody and I'm very pleased to meet you. What can I do for you?"

LeBow smiled and tilted his head again. "We're wondering if you might have a beer with us. There's something we were hoping to get your opinion on."

Raff smiled back. "Sure. I've only got a few minutes, though. I have an appointment back in my office in half an hour."

LeBow led the way to the bar, located in the rear of Henry's Guns and Shooting Gallery. Budweiser, Coors, Miller, and a few other real American, ordinary people's choices were available. No boutique or foreign brews were offered at Henry's patriotic establishment. Inside, a large, slow-turning ceiling fan stirred the thick warm air. An odor of turpentine and cigarette smoke enveloped them.

They sat on benches across from each other at a table beneath the flags of the United States and the State of Alabama hung side by side on the wall. A postcard photograph of the Confederate battle flag was stuck on the side of the cash register. It had been there a long time, and its edges had begun to peel.

LeBow said, "You learn a lot at Harvard?"

Raff hesitated, then replied, "You obviously know more

about me than I do about you, Reverend. Sure, I learned some things at Harvard. It's no big deal. We have good universities down here too. I wouldn't want to make any invidious comparisons with Harvard. But—why do you ask?"

"You're getting to be an important figure around Mobile, is the reason, and some of our religious folk just wanted to know more about you."

Raff thought, All the way up in Monroeville?

Before he could respond, Bo Rainey cleared his throat and asked, "They teach evolution at Harvard?"

Raff thought, okay, I see where this is going. "Sure," he said, "they teach about evolution at Harvard. It's solid science. It's got a lot of evidence to support it. Of course, I know that a lot of good people around here and the rest of America don't believe in it." Principle Number One in Raff's Conflict Resolution Rule Book: Don't antagonize your opponent unnecessarily.

Reverend LeBow ignored the answer and asked, "They teach the Bible too?"

"Of course," Raff replied, relaxing a bit, beginning to get the drift. Do we have here a couple of the hard-right people Bill Robbins said stay away from? "They have a whole School of Divinity, Harvard's been turning out preachers for three hundred and seventy years."

He instantly regretted patronizing LeBow with this little expression of Harvard venerableness. Principle Number Two: Don't brag, don't in any way seem to look down on your adversary. Stay humble. And if that's not possible, at least stay noncommittal.

Before the interrogation could continue, they were interrupted by loud gunfire that reverberated all the way to the bar.

Someone was touching off bursts from an automatic rifle. Raff flinched at the sound. He hated the weapon. It had the same function as the sawed-off shotguns infantry sometimes used in close combat. There wasn't a lot of finesse in either weapon. Or accuracy either. You just sprayed a lot of rounds with the hope that one or more would take the target down. As he waited, Raff thought, No time to aim, so shoot first, kill fast. Are these things legal? I thought not. Must be, though, or else Henry wouldn't allow them on the premises. If I'd been in the army, I'd prefer to be a sniper—use a telescopic sight and silencer, shoot, and slip away.

The firing ceased after a minute or so, and LeBow picked up again. "Do you believe what you read in the Bible?"

Raff was beginning to get annoyed, and he thought about excusing himself and leaving. But that would certainly offend his hosts, and anyway it would be better to find out what LeBow wanted.

"Well, some things in the Bible are surely true," Raff said. "And some are just ways of saying things that might be true. It's certainly worth knowing about what's in the Bible."

"Let's talk about this in another way," LeBow continued, "and don't worry, I've got a point I'm going to come to. I think it's important for you personally, and that's why Bo and I are paying you this visit. Just be patient."

"Okay, go ahead."

"Thank you. First of all, let's you and me stop calling it the Bible. Let's call it what it is, the Word of our Lord God, and through him His Son Jesus Christ."

"Well, I don't object if you want to put it that way. How to interpret the Bible differs a lot among Jews and different Christian denominations. That's why we have freedom of religion, isn't it? Why should it matter a lot in a democracy?"

LeBow bore in: "I'll tell you why it matters a lot. Either you believe the Word of God is truth, or you think you can interpret it any old way you choose, any way that makes you feel better."

Raff didn't like theology and he didn't like LeBow's tone, but he stayed with it. "Okay, that's putting it in a pretty extreme form, but I suppose what you say is basically right. But, again, so what? Where does that get us?"

"Raphael—may I call you that?—may I ask you a personal question?"

"Well—" Raff started to say yes, he indeed minded, but LeBow went on too quickly.

"Raphael, have you been saved by Jesus Christ?"

"Well, I'm an Episcopalian, part-time anyway. Does that count?" Raff looked at his watch and frowned.

LeBow paid no attention to the gesture. "You may belong to that church, Raphael, but that does not mean that you have committed your soul to Jesus Christ, and it does not mean you will enter the Kingdom of Heaven when you die. Is that important to you?"

"I don't agree with you," Raff responded. "Or rather, I don't know what you're talking about. And I'm frankly not sure I care. With all due respect, are you going to tell me why we are having this conversation?"

"What I mean is you belong to a nice club, and you believe in God and maybe His Son Jesus, and you go to church, and pray, and all that, but you haven't been saved, my friend, you haven't given yourself to Jesus Christ."

Raff looked at his watch again, pointedly. "So what's that

supposed to mean? And why are you telling *me* this? Why are we sitting here?"

"I'll explain this to you," LeBow said. "The world is divided into two kinds of people. There are those who believe the Word of God as it was given to us, and they have given their bodies and souls to Jesus Christ, His Son. And on the other side there are those who don't believe the Word, not entirely anyway. They haven't been saved, no matter what else they think or do. Do you want to appear before God on Judgment Day and say, *Well, I only believed half of what you said*? Real Christians are waiting for the Second Coming, and they believe every paragraph, every sentence, every word God has given us. They make it their business to get others to commit. They want as many people as possible to go with them and enter the Kingdom of Heaven."

"I guess you're saying we don't have a lot of time to do that either," Raff said. He knew LeBow was getting to the standard End-of-Time message but he still couldn't understand why he'd been singled out.

"You know we don't have a lot of time, Raphael. If you'd read your Bible, instead of that trash they fed you up at Harvard, you'd know we don't. All the signs that foretell the Second Coming of Jesus are now here. The Jews have come back home, chaos is spreading around the world, the environment is going down the toilet—get that, Raphael, the environment is just another sign. All that means one thing. Jesus is coming, boy. Not in a hundred years either. Real soon. Anytime now. Maybe tomorrow. And when Our Lord comes, those saved in His name will ascend bodily to heaven, and the rest are going to be left behind, and they are going to suffer terribly because of that. It will be so bad for them it'll be hell on earth. And when they die they will all go on down to the real hell, and they'll stay down there for eternity."

"With all due respect, Reverend, I can't see it that way. If the Second Coming is so obvious, why don't other people, and especially the large majority of Christians you say aren't truly saved, see it that way?"

"I am glad you asked me that question, Raphael. That's why I came personally to warn you, 'cause Satan is already here. The Antichrist, he's here. He's preparing in his own way for the battle to come with Jesus and God's holy angels too. He's assembling his forces. You don't know who he is, because he's one of those we least suspect, and he already has a huge army among us. And maybe you *do* know who he is. Most people haven't met him, but they're doing his cause. Satan, he doesn't think he's going to lose the Final Battle. He thinks he's going to win that battle, and take over God's throne. A lot of people are going to perish in the war between God and Satan."

"Pastor, I know a good many people believe what you're saying. And I haven't met the Antichrist, thank you, whatever that means. But tell me this: if God is all-powerful and if Jesus is God incarnate, and part of the Trinity, and Jesus is such a great force of love and mercy in our lives, why would God and Jesus allow war and misery?"

"I suggest, Harvard man, that you go right home and read the book of the Revelation to Saint John the Divine. It's the last book of the Bible, put there for all to read, and it contains the prophesy in Jesus's own words. *His own words.* You've probably been brainwashed to think the Lord is always kind and forgiving. Now, that's a lot of crap! Jesus came to John holding a sword. He said he *hates* those who deceive others and those who refuse to accept His rule. He said He will *kill* them. Yes, He will *kill* people in order to protect God's people, those who choose to believe His Word. That's the kind of war we're in, Raphael, and Satan can't be beaten any other way except by people giving their souls to Jesus Christ, and right now!"

At last Raff began to worry about what this strange man and his tattooed companion might do.

"Well, Pastor, I guess I understand what you're saying. Do you go around making this case to everyone who believes another way? For the last time, why me? What's this all about? Do you think I'm working for the devil and the Antichrist, who-ever *he* is?"

"You listen to me, boy, in your heart, you know who you're working for. You're too smart and too educated not to know what's going on. Why'd you come back down here anyway?"

"How could I be on the devil's side? You know who I am? You seem to know I'm one of the ones around here working to save God's Creation!"

"I see you miss the point. Maybe you intended to do that. Maybe that's what you're up to. God didn't send His only Son to save bugs and snakes. He sent him to save *souls*. God doesn't give *shit* about the land and the creatures on them except how His people can use them. This is just a place on the way to heaven or hell. Anything that's against His will is the devil's work."

Raff stood up to leave, but LeBow couldn't be stopped. "You want an answer? You came from around here, but then you went on up to Harvard and now you're some kind of fuckin' atheist. You're a big-time science lover, bragging on it all the time, they tell me. You're getting to be a big influence around here. And you are not a friend of God and His people."

Raff squeezed silently past LeBow and Rainey and walked toward the exit. The automatic rifle fire started up again.

LeBow shouted after him, "You're one of the deceivers! You're working for the Antichrist and maybe you're too stupid to know it. You're pulling people away from God's Will and God's Word!"

Raff reached the door to the outside, but LeBow caught up with him, and now said in a normal voice close to his ear, "You better listen to me, Raphael. You better change your ways while you still have time!"

35

R AFF EXITED HENRY'S Guns and Shooting Gallery and walked on down Oak Street as fast as he could without breaking into a run. He turned onto Bledsoe Street and continued until he reached the entrance to the Sunderland Office Building. He squeezed into the elevator, which was crowded with employees returning from their lunch hour. Arriving at the executive office floor, he waved away a staffer trying to hand him a file folder, went into his office, closed the door, fell into a swivel chair, and speed-dialed Bill Robbins.

The answering machine announced that the journalist was in the field on assignment and would be back the next day. He didn't like cell phones: "It scares the birds." Raff then remembered that Robbins was with a small group of ecologists visiting the Red Hills, just north of the Mobile-Tensaw Delta. They were going to explore a backcountry tract containing remnant old-growth pine savanna and hardwood-clad ravines.

Raff left a message, "Hey, Bill, must talk. Please call. Urgent."

There was nothing left for him to do for the while except try to calm down. He walked back out of his office, collected the file folder, walked back in, and put it on top of papers already stacked on his desk. He stared at the pile several minutes, keeping his hands folded in his lap. Then he got up and walked over to the window. Looking out at nothing in particular, he mentally rehearsed his bizarre encounter with Reverend Wayne LeBow. That resulted in no new insights. After a while he sat down again at his desk. This time he buried himself in paperwork.

Late that night, while Raff was getting ready for bed and distracting himself with a WBC welterweight championship fight on television, Robbins finally called. He said he was dead tired, begged off, and offered to come over first thing the next day.

Early the next morning they met for breakfast in the first-floor cafeteria of the Sunderland Office Building. As soon as they were settled, Raff said, "I think I just got a death threat." He then gave as verbatim as possible an account of his conversation with Wayne LeBow.

"Well, congratulations. You just met the Sword of Gideon," Robbins said. "I remember I warned you about those people before. Now it looks like they think you're a pretty important guy around here and want to do some pushing around. I know that outfit a little. Rob Davis, on Channel Eight News, talks about them once in a while. LeBow is your classical egomaniac rabble-rouser of the kind that spring up like mushrooms around here. He's actually pretty well educated. He spent a couple of years at Auburn University, can you believe that? With a major in religion studies. He's not a real minister, at least not ordained by any place I ever heard of. He's actually a guard captain at the Monroeville Prison. I hear he's always jabbering at the inmates about finding Jesus. He just took over a little church near there. What's its name?"

"Church of the Eternal Redeemer, I think he said."

"Yeah. Well, anyway, LeBow's a piece of work. But you know, he's not that far out down here in South Alabama. A lot of the country people, not to mention working folks in and around Mobile too, have more or less the same ideas. Jesus is coming in our lifetime, and we better be ready. It's called the Rapture. The ones who've been saved will go right up bodily, Jesus leading the way. LeBow's just taken the prophecy to the extreme. What's worrisome is he's getting aggressive and he's pulling in a lot of followers. That little church is packed every Sunday. He's building a cult, is what he's doing. Shall we call them the LeBowites? They're itching to go to war with the devil. Heaven knows what happened to the original pastor. Rob Davis probably knows the story. I'll try to remember and ask him, or maybe you can go talk to him yourself, if you want."

Raff was breathing hard and sucking air through his teeth. This discourse was not helping him relax at all. He pushed back his chair to get more leg room and squeezed his eyes shut.

"Anyway," Robbins pressed on, "it's an old evangelical tradition with a military twist. Ever heard of Billy Sunday, the big-time evangelist back in the twenties? He'd say—I actually heard him on an old record—'I'll fight sin till I can't use my arms no more, and then I'll bite it, and when I got no teeth left, I'll gum it.' Great stuff! There's a difference here, though, and I don't want to make too much light of it. The radical fringe folks like the Sword of Gideon are always dangerous. A few of them can turn violent on a dime. Either that or they're violent nutcases from the start. There have been quite a few murders and even mass suicides in this country and elsewhere. The Sword of Gideon fits the pattern another way, at least for down here. Like a lot of religious fringe groups, it recruits mostly from poor whites who feel that they've been cheated some way or other. They're the most alienated group in the South right now. Basically, it's the same old same old. They'll get justice any way they can, even if that means getting violent. Social justice anyway, if you can't get economic justice."

"Now that you mention it," Raff said, opening his eyes and pulling himself up in the chair, "the guy with LeBow looked like a real thug. I just assumed he was a bodyguard, or a muscleman of some sort. I wondered why he was there. He sure wasn't any altar boy."

"Yeah, let's make a distinction here if you haven't already thought of it yourself. The way I see it, there are rednecks and then there are redneck white trash. The large part of the population who call themselves rednecks, and laugh about it, are good people—really solid, mostly working-class citizens. But the white trash, they're the underclass. They're the ones with the abandoned automobiles in the front yard and mongrel dogs living off kitchen scraps and running around all over the place—the kind you accidentally squash on the highway and nobody cares. The men like to hang out at strip joints, drink a lot of beer and whiskey—anything they can afford for the night. They'll pull out a knife and cut you if you insult them—which, by the way, you can do just looking at them or their girlfriends too long. They're racists, of course. But mostly they're just proud, and broke, and mad all the time."

"Yeah, I guess the best way to get in big trouble with one is either to kick his motorcycle or come on to his girlfriend. It's part of our tradition down here."

"But, you know," Robbins went on, "and maybe this is your point. They're proud but they're not monsters. Make friends with one of them, he'll give you the shirt off his back—maybe. My point is that they got no education, and they're easily led by anyone who says he speaks for God. If you want to see a big concentration of them, go to the Monroeville Prison. They've all been saved by Jesus up there."

Raff added, "The Klan comes to my mind—you know, these people from the same breed that made up the foot soldiers of the old Klan. The difference, I think, is that the Klan preached raw racism, and groups like the Sword of Gideon are more into religious bigotry."

Robbins affirmed his agreement by pointing both index fingers at Raff. He said, "Except the Klan and the fighting Born Agains you're dealing with are racial and religious bigots *both*, just in different proportions."

"Anyway," Raff said, "the question I need to put to you right now is, should I worry? Are LeBow and his gang going to be dangerous for me personally, with all that 'Jesus kills' stuff? What do you think, should I do anything, go to the police? I've been guessing maybe not. LeBow didn't actually threaten me with anything. He just gave me a hellfire sermon."

"Rob Davis tells me that LeBow's given that little spiel to a few others—academics, high school principals, local politicians. So you're not alone. The fact that it *was* a sermon of a sort, with a 'Come to Jesus' tag line, makes me think he may not be talking to you at all. He's trying to impress his followers. You know, the crusader, tough guy for Jesus. He's saying to his people, *See how I can push those big-shot liberal atheists around*."

"That makes sense," Raff said. "But are they dangerous? Have they actually attacked anybody?"

"Well, you know, yes, they're dangerous. I say that because

there have been a number of beatings and unsolved murders and disappearances. LeBow and his church members haven't been charged with any of it, not yet anyway. And the victims have been, so far as I've heard, just apostates—you know, rivals or defectors. Not outsiders like you."

Raff said, "Sounds like a power struggle. Maybe that's why LeBow is getting so aggressive. That would explain that tattooed guy he brought along. He's desperate."

"Could be. In any case, I'd be careful. I'd talk to Rob Davis about the whole thing, if I were you. You might also want to file a report with the police and let LeBow know about it if you ever run into him again. Who knows? Maybe somebody's trying to kill *him*."

36

THE DAY OF DECISION for Nokobee arrived in the morning of one of those late September days on the Gulf Coastal Plain so hot it seemed that fall as a season had been banished. At eight o'clock three linen-clad executives entered the boardroom on the top floor of the Sunderland Office Building. Drake Sunderland, president and chief executive officer of the company named after his father, moved on past the conference table to the continental breakfast laid at the end of the room, drew a cup of coffee, added skim milk, no sugar, picked up a glazed donut, unglued his fingers with a paper napkin, and slumped into the nearest chair at the table. He was fifty-five years old, thirty pounds overweight, and had an as-yet-undiscovered partly blocked right carotid artery.

Raphael Semmes Cody, chief counsel, a short, slim man of twenty-eight years, dressed in a J. Press summer suit, shirt, and tie, selected croissants, butter substitute, and fruit. Richard Sturtevant, vice president and chief financial officer, sixty-plus, rumply white-haired, and with more than ample girth to advertise the good life he had enjoyed, hesitated, then chose the same. Both took seats opposite the president.

Drake Sunderland crinkled his face into an alpha good-old-boy smile. "Well, Raff, I'm so glad you made it. I'm really happy to see you. What you got?" He pulled himself up straight in his chair as he spoke. Tense this morning, no mistake about that. No feigned humor in his eyes now. All three knew this was going to be a crucial meeting for Sunderland Associates.

Raff urged himself silently, *Stay calm, stay focused.* He breathed deeply but quietly as he spoke. "Well, sir, I've got some good news and, well, a little bit of semi-bad news, or at least a problem or two we'll need to fix."

Sunderland looked up, slid his spectacles down his nose to look over them, and studied Raff's face.

"The good news," Raff said, "is that we won the blind bid on Nokobee Westside. The Jepson lawyers in Atlanta just called me thirty minutes ago, as promised, to give us the word. Furthermore, we came in only five percent over the next-highest bid. So we ended up shaving it close; we did really well."

Sunderland leaned forward, brightened again. He balled and lifted his fists with thumbs up the way he did at Auburn University football games, but this morning a little less emphatically.

"That's good, that's real good. What's the bad news?" Then he frowned, working his mouth from side to side.

"Well, sir, it's the enviros again, as you might guess. They are not going to be happy campers on this one. I think we underestimated how serious they are. Nokobee Westside is what they call 'biologically rich.' "

Vice President Sturtevant said, "What the hell is that supposed to mean?"

Raff continued, ignoring the question. "They've designated it a local biodiversity 'hot spot.' I've checked with the state

Department of Environmental Management, and here's what they've got. The area immediately to the west of Lake Noko-bee has two species of salamanders, a bird, and a turtle listed as vulnerable under the Endangered Species Act. And there's worse. In that pitcher-plant bog that lies on the boundary with the national forest? There are two endemic plant species. That's *endemic*. I mean, found no other place on earth."

Vice President Sturtevant interrupted with mocking exas-peration, "Well, guys, the fucking salamanders and pitcher plants. There goes the golf course."

"I'm afraid there's more," Raff continued. "The longleaf pine stand can't be cut. Just can't be cut at all. We assumed that since longleaf pine is found all over the South, taking it out at Nokobee would be no problem. But that westside stand is origi-nal old growth, and there's only about two percent of real old growth like that left in the entire United States. I know the tim-ber at Nokobee is worth over a million dollars, but we can't har-vest it."

Sturtevant broke in again. Time to talk sense to this fel-low. He's gone over the line, giving everybody a hard time. He slammed his hands on the table, but not too hard, since he was only four feet from Sunderland facing him. "What are you say-ing? That we gotta pull out? This is the best deal the company ever had. People are starting to move into that area big-time. Property prices are going up. Nokobee Westside is going to give us the biggest profit we ever had."

He paused, let it sink in, continued quietly, "Now, look here. That whole region may be piney woods now, but in a few years it's going to be built over as much as the suburbs around Mobile and Pensacola. It's going to be a real nice place to live.

New South and all that, you know. You're going to have your housing developments, your schools, your strip malls. Lots of paved roads. Nobody is going to stop any of that. So endangered species or whatever the hell you're talking about don't have a chance anyway, do they? Why can't we just leave the bog maybe and a couple of acres of piney woods alone, a little nature center maybe, that ought to be enough for any judge or jury, and just present the enviros with a done deal. Let 'em suck it up. Fat accomplee, as they say up at Emory."

Richard Sturtevant was a good man, a moral man, a former Southern Baptist pastor who had never cheated on his wife. His faith had empowered him with an inner calm: whatever happens, good or bad, whether manifest to the human mind or beyond our understanding, is God's will. But he also had an M.B.A. from Emory University, and a soul where dwelleth the eleventh commandment of the bottom line. People counted with him, jobs counted, and economic growth measured in annual per capita net yield was, well, America's bottom line. The fate of a few rare species had to be kept a few notches down on the priority list.

Sturtevant thought he saw Sunderland nodding, so he decided to escalate and bring out the ecclesiastical nuclear weapon. "That's what God intends," he said through tight lips. "You can read it right there in scripture: He gave us dominion over earth—not to sit around and gawk at, but to use, to prosper with it, and to multiply."

Raff was ready for this. He'd known for some time that God would push His way into the discussion. "I understand what you're saying, Rick. But consider this. People care about quality of life, and Nokobee Westside has quality of life written all over it. I'm telling you, this whole business can blow up in our face if we get reckless. I don't know if you ever read him, but that environment reporter at the *News Register*, Bill Robbins, is a killer on things like this. That guy knows the name of every kind of plant in this part of the state, and most of the animals too, and he's got a special thing for bogs and old-growth longleaf pine. If we make a wrong move, he's going to be on us like a hawk on a one-legged chicken. And the big conservation organizations will come in too—Sierra Club, Nature Conservancy, Longleaf Alliance—and a lot of people around here you never heard of."

Sturtevant, throwing up his hands, came back hard at Raff. "Now, that's a one-sided picture of things if I ever heard one. You're forgetting that there are a lot of people around here who don't love piney woods. Most of the population, if truth be told. We're living in one of the most conservative and religious places in America. You've got a lot of folks who like to go out in the woods and hunt and fish and all that, but they believe people should come first if there's any kind of conflict. They don't want a bunch of nature parks with guards all over the place. They don't want government interfering with their lives. They don't want a bunch of liberal bureaucrats up in Montgomery and Washington regulating this and regulating that, and telling them what to do. They believe Jesus came to save souls, not bugs and snakes."

Raff's eyes popped open at this last expression. It was what LeBow had said, nearly word for word.

Sturtevant went on. "They're sure that He's coming again, the End of Time, real soon. Right or wrong, I wouldn't laugh at them, if I were you. There are a lot of people around the country feel that way, and most especially down here. We go ahead and tie up a high-quality property like Nokobee, and they're going to raise hell. There could be a *war*, I'm telling you."

Drake Sunderland turned to look at Raff again over the top rim of his eyeglasses. He was getting twitchy. This was not like poker at the Cosmopolitan Club, where the elite meet and talk up cozy big deals; this wasn't the kind of business news reported in the financial section of the *News Register*. He thought, Maybe we'd have been a lot better off if I didn't take this boy genius into the firm in the first place. But then it came to him, No, no, that can't be. He knows the ropes. He knows which way the trees are gonna fall.

He said to the two men facing him, "Do we really have to worry about a bunch of Bible shouters and peckerwoods?"

"Drake—" Sturtevant protested.

Sunderland silenced him with a rise of his hand. "Just a minute, Rick."

Sunderland was thinking worst-case scenario now. His name and the family's shares might not be enough to save him if he steered Sunderland Associates into both a financial and a public-relations disaster. Who the hell is this Bill Robbins anyway? he wondered. He and his buddies could be big-time trouble, that's who, sorry to say.

Sunderland murmured, almost a whisper, "All right, Raff. What do you suggest? I'm sure you've been giving this a lot of thought."

Sturtevant started to speak again: "Drake, for God's sake—" But Sunderland silenced him a second time by raising his hand.

Raff nodded, reached for an attaché case he'd carried in with him, and laid it on the table. Almost there, he thought, almost there. Focus, focus, focus . . .

"Mr. Sunderland, Drake . . . and Rick, I'm certain we can solve this problem with a shift in strategy. We can do it, and I hope to everybody's satisfaction, just by the way we figure the budget, and with all due respect to you, Rick, as our financial officer. Suppose we didn't make those habitats and species into obstacles that we put on the cost side of the ledger. Suppose we added them to the profit side."

He opened the attaché case and took out copies of a three-page memorandum he'd prepared. He handed one to each of the two men.

"I've been checking. It's getting routine around the country for high-end retirement communities and second-home resorts to make an asset out of nature if they possibly can. As you can see on the first page, the trend started back in the sixties and it really began to climb in the nineties. It's now a national trend, and it's more or less recession-proof. I've broken out the southern tier of states to show it's well on the way here as well.

"I haven't gotten exact data on this point, but it also seems clear that two factors weigh in high on profitability. The closer the development to a major center of population, and the larger the natural area around it, the larger the per-acre profit, especially for homes at the high end. I've checked directly with a number of land management experts and large real estate developers around the country, and they're virtually unanimous on that point. They're listed there on the second page. On page three I've summarized very briefly what I think we should do."

Raff paused to let Sunderland and Sturtevant scan the pages.

"So, bottom line. I think we're in a situation here where it would pay to build a smaller number of estates than we planned.

Maybe have a row of relatively small lots lining most of Lake Nokobee Westside, with a private gated road. Each house would have its own access to the lake, but there would be a community landing and boathouse about in the middle. With that we add some nature trails but leave the rest of the Nokobee tract just as it is. We won't need any developed lots, because each house would have the lake on one side and the reserve on the other. The beauty of it is, we get the amenities of the natural world, at the lake and inland, scott free. And the initial construction payout and asking price can be actually smaller than for most high quality homes. And that's a good thing, now that the real estate market is in a slump. So it's the prudent strategy for this company to follow short-term *or* long-term. Rich people can always buy houses, but the middle class maybe not."

Drake Sunderland was listening carefully, poker-faced. Raff was ready to lay down what he considered his trump card. He took a sip of water and cleared his throat.

"Now, here's something else. The public relations potential would be absolutely tremendous. We could headline the endangered habitats and species we saved. Advertise the concept. Make Nokobee famous. How many developments, especially in this state, can take credit for protecting endangered species? And what's more, in how many places can you just walk out of your home and see them? We can set up tours for residents on the nature trails, provide brochures about the beauty and value of the Nokobee environment. Get the governor here to help celebrate opening day. That would be a super photo op for him and for us. Maybe even get the best part of it declared a state botanical site, with a big tax deduction and management provided by the state."

Raff noticed, as he spoke, that Rick Sturtevant was growing more agitated. His face had begun to redden. Pushing the
memorandum away from him with the back of his hand, he
exploded.

"Oh, for God's sake, what is this? Fucking Earth Day?
Haven't you heard a word I've been saying? South Alabama and
on out to the Panhandle are not the rest of America. They don't
fit anywhere on your charts. I keep telling you this is the most
conservative and religious part of the United States. People
around here believe what they read in the Good Book, every
word, and I might as well tell you, so do I. They're angry. They
don't like government control in the first place, and they sure
don't like some rich tree-huggers coming here and gobbling up
the best land, taking away their jobs."

Sunderland's mouth had fallen slightly open, as though he
were stunned and struggling to find a response. Raff moved in
quickly, relieved at the outburst. Rick Sturtevant was unraveling.
He was confused and starting to whine. He had obviously not
been prepared for anything like Raff's proposal. His response
had been emotional.

Raff lived by three maxims. Fortune favors the prepared
mind. People follow someone who knows where he's going. And
control the middle, because that's where the extremes eventually
have to meet.

"Rick, like I say, I understand where you're coming from,"
Raff continued, "but hear me out, please. I grant you that
twenty or thirty years ago what I've suggested might have stirred
up trouble, you're right about that. But you've got to admit
that things are changing fast. A lot of people coming into the
upscale housing market are native to the coast, not just out-

siders, and a lot of them are religious and conservative just as you are, and we have to respect that political position for sure and put a lot of weight on it. But a lot of others—and especially among the retirees—more and more are going green, and that's true regardless of their origin."

Sturtevant was regaining his composure, and he felt encouraged by Raff's courteous response. "That might be true of a bunch of granola-crunching left-wingers, but what makes you think it's going to be true of the conservative majority in South Alabama and the Panhandle? These people get their conservatism from their mother's milk."

That was a hardball, but Raff caught it. "You're right. That's true. But think about the two words conservatism and conservation; they both come from the same Latin stem, *conservare*." Smiling, he added, "Now, don't tell me that's something I picked up at Harvard. In fact, I learned it down there at Florida State University from a Southern professor who's an expert in both subjects. He asked his class, what is conservatism without conservation? And how are we ever going to be energy independent and save our natural resources without conservation? Here's something to consider. A recent author put it this way: green is the new red, white, and blue."

Raff now lifted his hands in supplication. "And you gotta admit, not everybody wants to play golf. A lot of people want to live close to nature. And down here, you know as well as I do, you can go out and enjoy nature in shorts and a T-shirt almost all year-round, if you want to."

Richard Sturtevant had stopped listening. He was scribbling something on the back of the memorandum Raff had given him.

Sunderland cleared his throat loudly, halting talk from the other two, then he stood up and walked over to the wall-length window on the sunrise side. The morning sky was still unbroken blue. The sun had risen to fade the Mobile River from black into a light brown. The buildings of the city had changed from the bronze of dawn to a brilliant polychrome in the full sunlight. A flock of herring gulls caught Sunderland's eye as they took flight from a parking lot, roused by an approaching automobile. They circled out over Mobile Bay.

Sunderland turned to look at Bankhead Tower a half mile south, still the highest building in the city, its upper floors prominent over the roofs of other midtown buildings. It housed the premier luxury apartments of the city. The large American flag on top caught an errant breeze, unfurled a bit, and fell back. There's the company's greatest achievement, he mused. My father's achievement.

He'd already made up his mind while Raff was talking. Now he tried to put the words together.

"We might do something like that," he said, still looking out.

Then he turned, walked over, and, looking down at Raff said, "But would the enviros trust us? After all, this company is the big bad wolf as far as they are concerned. We've already got a black mark at Nokobee. The fiasco at Dead Owl Cove is the only environmental decision we ever made there. They probably won't understand that we didn't have any other choice. Those ants were eating the place alive—so much for leaving nature alone. Even people couldn't stay there for more than a few minutes. So we had to spray, or do something. Sure, it turned out to be the wrong way, I'll admit that. Half the junk washed on down into the lake, and Good Lord help us, it killed everything along the shore at Dead Owl Cove. There were dead fish floating halfway up the lake. There were dead birds lying all around the trailhead. The enviros and the locals both gave us hell. People thought we were going to give them cancer. Why we weren't fined or sued, big-time, I'll never know.

"So I ask you, what if the ants come back, and we can't spray them?"

"I don't think that's likely, sir," Raff said. "You know, I studied those ants for years while I was at Florida State. It's just something I happen to know a lot about. What happened was a rare genetic mutation. I'm not positive—who can ever be positive about something like that?—but it's never happened before that I know of, and I'm pretty sure it won't happen again." He wasn't pretty sure, but he had to say so now.

Sunderland turned to his chief financial officer. "Well, Rick? Give it a try?"

Sturtevant said sarcastically, "Maybe you can persuade Mr. Cody to put the boathouse and ramp there. Then the whole place'll be under concrete and lawn grass. That'll stop the ants."

Then, grimacing, he threw up his hands. "Hell, Drake, it's your call. But I'm not going to change my mind. I don't want to sound melodramatic, but I even think it's a little dangerous, with some of the kind of people we have around here. Anyway, that's the last I'm going to say on the subject. I'm not going to throw myself on the barbed wire for you guys to charge over. I'll just handle the books for you on this one and hope for the best."

He turned then and stared deadpan at Raff for a moment,

thinking, Well, I guess I'm looking at the future power around here. I don't want the company to fail, but I'd sure like to see that little shithead fall on his face.

"Thank you, Rick," Drake Sunderland said. "I guess we have a decision."

The meeting was ended. Outside, clouds had formed across the western horizon. There would be some rain in the evening, as another front rolled onto the Gulf. Weather here in the beautiful country was always an intrusion from Kansas, or Illinois, or some other far-off part of America.

They started walking out of the room together, Sturtevant leading. At the door, Drake Sunderland asked Raff to hold back for a minute. His eyes were half closed, his expression somber.

"Look, Raff, I'm going to go with you on this one. It's a gamble, sure, let's not kid ourselves, but I think it's the one that's likely to succeed with a minimum of headaches. I pray to God it does so. And to tell you the truth, if it does succeed, we'll have something to be proud of. I really never did want to cover the Nokobee tract with a bunch of tacky houses if we could manage something better. Especially if we might go bankrupt by investing in too big a project."

Raff gave an emphatic nod. "Yessir, thank you. Thank you for saying that."

"But I also have to warn you, Raff, I'm really upset by what Rick Sturtevant was saying. There may be some truth in it. Development and religion are all mixed up down here. Some say God wants all the land He gave us to be used, meaning developed; some say God wants us to save all His Creation. If we let fanatics on either side take over, we could be in deep shit. I

don't want Nokobee turned into some kind of a courtroom battleground. The media would make us look like fools.

"So I'll say one thing to you. Don't let us run into any kind
of public relations trouble. Not from your environment friends,
not from any Bible-thumping wackos, and especially I want you
to keep that goddamn *Mobile News Register* off our backs. Do I
make myself perfectly clear? And here's another thing. If I see
this thing is going to tank, I'm going to pull back faster than a
frog off a hot stove. I'll leverage the property for a loan, and I'll
develop the whole thing in small plots."

Raff nodded gravely. "Yessir, that is perfectly clear."

37

SIX MONTHS LATER, Raff was at the verdant shore of Lake Nokobee, kneeling as though in prayer, photographing a small lavender wildflower. All around him rose the evidences of the Nokobee spring. Wild azaleas bloomed in scarlet explosions along the lakeshore. The last chill had departed the soil, and the ground flora was renewing itself in a blanket of light green shoots and leaves.

His victory on behalf of the reserve was as complete as he could have hoped. Back at Sunderland Associates everyone agreed that the Nokobee plan could now be initiated. Architectural plans were spread on executive desks at Sunderland Associates. Conferences were under way with contractors in several locations around the city and one in Fort Walton Beach. Advanced marketing was under way, and inquiries had begun to arrive. All of the Nokobee tract beyond the lakeside lots, nearly ninety percent of the whole, would be left untouched. Water filtration would protect the lake itself from pollution. The two alligators resident on the west shore would be invited to move, with assistance, to the east shore.

Raff had proved correct in one important respect. The Sunderland plan had attracted a lot of publicity, all of it favorable so far. A three-part series by Bill Robbins of the *Mobile News Register* was entitled "The Best of Two Worlds." An *Atlanta Constitution* editorial proclaimed the Nokobee compromise "a para digm for Southern development and wildland conservation." Bets were laid that Robbins's series would make the following year's short list for the Pulitzer Prize for investigative reporting. Sunderland Associates itself was rumored to be in line for a Green Leaf Award from The Nature Conservancy. Raff had been invited to speak to civic groups and churches around Mobile and Pensacola.

Still, when he could find time while visiting his parents, Raff came to Nokobee alone, to putter around the lakeside strip before it was developed. He walked back and forth along the already existing trail that led from Dead Owl Cove through to the marsh around the outflow creek. Inch by inch he studied the spaces marked out with the surveyors' red-tipped stakes. He took photographs of the vegetation, wrote notes, and collected snippets of vegetation for identification. By the time the chain saws and bulldozers arrived he would have a detailed biodiversity map of the original lakeshore habitat. It would be entered in the University of South Alabama archives, in the city of Mobile, for study by future generations of naturalists. If he could not have this part of Nokobee preserved, at least he would have it remembered.

In late afternoon, as the shadows of the pines lengthened and the tangled lakeside vegetation grew dark, Raff walked from the trailhead back to his car. As he came close he was surprised to see three men waiting there for him. He recognized the Reverend Wayne LeBow, and his assistant Bo Rainey. Ohhh, boy, he thought. They were accompanied by a younger man, in his late teens, fashionably stubble-cheeked and wearing dark glasses and a broad-brimmed hat. LeBow was in his business clothes, but this time tieless. Rainey and the cowboy wore chinos and white, short-sleeved shirts pulled outside over their belts. The three stood between him and his car, looking at him without speaking.

Raff was alarmed at the sight of them, then slid close to panic. He thought of turning back and simply losing himself in the woods. But that will look foolish, he thought. Who knows? Maybe they're here to declare peace, or raise some legitimate issue. Or just argue some more. But why three? Who's the kid with the cowboy hat?

As he came up to them, he said to LeBow, "Hello, it's Reverend LeBow, isn't it? Can I help you?"

"We need to have a talk with you," LeBow replied.

Raff didn't like the abruptness in the other man's voice. "I'd like to," he said, "but I'm late for an appointment. We can get together later, if you'd like. Just give me a call." He started to pass on around them.

"No, we want to talk to you right now," LeBow said.

"Look, I can't do that right now. By all means we can get together soon, at some future time convenient to you, Reverend. I'll take you to lunch. I owe you a beer anyhow."

"No, right now," LeBow replied.

Rainey casually pulled back the loose fold in his shirt, giving Raff a glimpse of a snub-nosed pistol stuck in his waistband.

Jesus Christ, Raff thought, I've got to play along with this, buy time, work out their grievance. "Okay, go ahead, if it's that urgent."

"We want to show you something first," LeBow said with a jerk of his head in the direction of the trailhead.

Show me what? Raff thought. They're going to threaten me, try to force me to do something about the plans for Nokobee. I wish I'd made that report to the police.

Bunched together, they all walked silently to the trailhead, then on to the westside trail, LeBow and Raff leading, with Rainey and Cowboy Hat close behind. LeBow showed no sign of slowing down.

"Where are we going? What do you want to show me?" Raff asked.

"You'll see," LeBow said.

"Okay, where are we going?" Raff repeated.

"To the river," LeBow answered.

Oh, my God, it's worse, Raff thought. They're not even afraid to let me know what they want. They're going to kill me and throw me in the river. Make me just disappear. They're crazy.

Raff's mind was flooded with possible escape plans. He had to act now. Rainey and probably Cowboy Hat too have guns, he decided, but LeBow's unarmed. Got to find some way to break away and get into cover before they can pull the guns and shoot. That's the only possible way. Do it fast, do it before we get much further.

Raff, with his intimate knowledge of Nokobee, immediately pictured where an escape might be possible. They were still close to the lake, in shaded woodland. As they approached the out-flow creek there would come into view off the west side of the trail a dome—a dense hardwood copse growing around a vernal pool. Behind it, on the other side, as Raff pictured it, there was a small clearing, and behind that lay dense but navigable mixed hardwood-pine forest. If he could just dodge behind the dome and make it on into thick woods without getting shot, he had a chance.

When they reached the right place on the trail, Raff stopped abruptly and said, "Listen, I've got to take a leak real bad. It'll just take a second." He kept his voice as level as possible, trying to pretend he was unaware of his predicament.

LeBow, playing the humanitarian to a condemned man, said, "Okay, but just take a few steps and don't try anything. Sunky," he said to Cowboy Hat, "you stay right behind him, and if he tries to run, shoot him."

At that Raff walked off the trail, one careful stiff-legged step at a time, pulling close to the dome. Sunky walked behind him in near-lockstep. Raff kept moving until he was in low under-growth of the dome perimeter and about twenty feet off the trail. In his mind, he plotted each step of his coming sprint around the dome.

Sunky pushed him in the back roughly. "That's far enough," he said.

Raff stood still for a moment, with his back to Sunky, and then moved his arms as though unzipping his pants. After a few seconds, he turned his upper body partly around to glance at Sunky, who was only arm's length away, and saw that the young man had not yet pulled his gun. On the trail, Rainey was talking softly to LeBow and he also still had his gun under his shirt.

Raff started to turn all the way around and began to speak.

"Stop, Sunky, there's a snake—"

At that instant, having turned enough to gain purchase, he

pushed Sunky as hard as he could. The young gunman fell backward, landing hard on the ground, yelling, his arms flung out,
his hat sailing off to the side. As Sunky hit the ground, Raff was
already at the edge of the dome and sprinting around it. Rainey's
response was immediate. Within five seconds he had his gun out
and up and started firing. Raff had just passed out of sight before
the first shot. Rainey tried to calculate Raff's progress through
the vegetation and fired several more shots through the densely
shaded foliage. It works only rarely, hunting for deer running
through forest cover, and this time also the tactic failed.

Raff continued on his way across the little clearing and into
the brush ahead. He disappeared just as his pursuers rounded
the dome. Rainey and Sunky, who was now recovered and in
pursuit, held their fire for a clear shot, didn't get it, and, with
LeBow following, plunged in after him.

At this point Raff had less than a fifty-yard lead. Only the
thick leafy vegetation saved him from being gunned down in the
first minute or two. He knew he could lengthen the distance,
however, because he was familiar with the wild terrain of Nokobee and they were not. He knew the location of openings in the
undergrowth in this part of the tract and paths around the tangled ruins of fallen trees. By the time he broke out of the hardwood undergrowth and into the more open spaces of the pine
savanna, he was nearly a hundred yards ahead, widening the gap
and still on a nearly straight course. When his pursuers broke
out into the open themselves, they could catch only glimpses
of him.

Soon afterward Raff noticed that the men were beginning to
fan out while shouting back and forth to one another. At first he
thought they had lost him and were trying to locate him. Then

he realized the awful truth. The trio knew where he was, at least approximately. They, not he, had the upper hand. LeBow and his men were almost certainly experienced hunters. They were not yelling just to communicate. They were quartering the terrain, while driving their prey forward in a confined space of their choosing. They were forcing him toward the riverbank as if they were hunting down a wild pig. If he continued on a straight course to the bank, they would then converge toward each other, closing the net.

Raff, running hard, desperately sought a way to break out of the trap. He thought about reaching the river first and diving in, but he was a poor swimmer and if he didn't drown, his head would be an easy target for pistol fire from the bank.

Then a plan came to him. From the voices of his pursuers, Raff knew that LeBow was on his left. He was fairly sure LeBow was unarmed, and the minister was older than the others and hadn't looked in very good shape to Raff. If Raff cut diagonally to the left and sprinted even just a little bit faster, he might beat LeBow to the Chicobee and then cut to the left along the riverbank ahead of the whole lot of them. If he didn't make it in time, he might still fight his way past LeBow and continue down the river before the others arrived on the scene.

He angled left and within three minutes, zigzagging through the last of the savanna and into the second-growth cypress of the floodplain, arrived, sooner than he had guessed, at the riverbank. He had made his decision just in time. LeBow was almost there himself, only thirty yards away and coming on hard. Raff passed in front, and the pastor fell in closely behind him, shouting to the others to come his way.

Raff was now hemmed in by the river to his right and unfamiliar mud flats to his left. He thought of turning back into the floodplain forest and trying to lose the pursuers there, but he knew they would track him and start hemming him in again. He would also risk being blocked by one of the many sloughs running parallel to the river. If that happened he would end up within easy pistol fire, and it would be over.

Raff's one hope lay in staying next to the riverbank. If only he could find some other people, there or out on the water, LeBow and his fellow assassins might turn back for fear their chase would be witnessed. But this reprieve was only a slim possibility. This stretch of riverbank, far from the nearest road or landing, was one of the least visited on all the Chicobee.

What was the first house along this stretch of the Chicobee, other than a fisherman's shack? All he could think of was Frogman, the ogre of Chicobee. His house was perhaps three miles away. If Raff could run fast enough that far, he had a chance to survive. It might be small. Frogman was ferociously paranoid, and maybe clinically insane. But now Raff put all such thoughts out of his mind—and ran.

Somewhere along the way he realized that he had heard nothing from the three pursuers since the chase along the riverbank began. Had they given up? Fallen too far behind to catch him? They had to run the same obstacle course. Maybe he could stop just a moment to catch his breath. So he paused, partly concealed behind a cypress stump. And quickly realized that was a mistake. Two pistol shots—close!—rang out, and Raff stumbled onward.

The run was far from straight; it was a zigzagging steeplechase. Raff frequently had to slosh through backwater sloughs or work around them, struggling to pull his feet free from the gluelike mud. He was forced to crawl over cypress buttresses and fallen logs; he no longer had the strength to vault these obstacles and increase his lead.

But at last he made it to Frogman's house. Thinking that to pause even a moment meant a bullet in the back, he simply rushed up the path from the rustic landing and through the front door. Frogman must have heard Raff's approach and was standing in the entrance to the back room. He was about the same as Raff remembered him, except that now his beard was long and grizzled. He wore denim cotton pants cut off at the knee, and a soiled white T-shirt emblazoned with the five interlacing rings of the Olympic games and the faded words ATLANTA 1996. Now he waited for Raff, stock-still.

"Please," gasped Raff, "can you help me? Some men are right behind me, chasing me, and they have guns and they're going to kill me."

Frogman studied him with calm detachment. He pointed to a closet to one side of the short hallway. Through the open closet door Raff could see it was half filled with tools, rags, and fishing gear.

"Git in there, close the door, and keep quiet."

In less than two minutes, Rainey and Sunky walked through the door, breathing hard, and Rainey said to Frogman, "We're police officers. We're chasing a fugitive that just ran in here. Our chief'll be along in just a minute."

Frogman made no reply.

They all stood there quietly, and three minutes later Wayne LeBow entered, soaked in sweat and gasping for breath.

"Chief," Rainey said to the minister, "I just explained to the gentleman here that we are police in pursuit of a fugitive."

"That's right," LeBow wheezed without missing a beat. "State police. The man we're after robbed a filling station and shot the attendant. He ran this way. You seen him? Can you help us?"

"You got credentials?" Frogman asked.

"Left them in the car upriver. We were in a big hurry. Can you help us?" LeBow saw Rainey nodding to him. They knew Raff was in the house.

"Sure can," Frogman said. He walked back to the hallway and picked a pump-action shotgun off a rack there. Then he turned in the direction of the closet and said in a loud voice, "Come on out here, you little pissant."

Raff didn't respond, and Frogman commanded, this time bellowing, "Come on out now, or I'll put a load of shot through that door you're hiding behind."

Raff emerged, his hands raised partly in surrender. He was terrified, and only half conscious from exhaustion. He was in shock and so tired he could scarcely grasp the scene before him.

Frogman was facing him, the pump-action shotgun leveled at his chest. LeBow and the two others stood close behind him. Rainey and Sunky had pushed their revolvers back under their belts and smoothed their shirts. Their clothes, like Raff's, were mud-splattered and torn in places.

Frogman turned his head slightly and said, "One of you git on down and see if anybody's on the river, and call up and let us know."

Rainey looked at Sunky and hooked his thumb in the direction of the river. The younger man, now hatless, headed out the door.

A minute later, Sunky called up, "All's clear."

At that, Frogman turned his shotgun and shot Bo Rainey in

the chest. The gunman's body jackknifed and he landed backward, with his legs straight and his arms flung outward. The explosion deafened Raff. Rainey's body bucked once on the floor as a mist of blood and bone fragments settled around him.

Wayne LeBow started to turn away, but Frogman pumped the gun and fired again, hitting him in midbody on the left side, spinning him around. A ruptured loop of intestine, torn free, landed in a splash of blood at his side. LeBow fell on his face.

Sunky started running up the trail to the house at the first shot, with his pistol pulled out. "Hey! Hey! Hey! What's happenin'? What's happenin'?"

These were the last words of his life. He flew through the front door and instantly flew out again, backward, as a load of double-ought shot caught him full in the chest. His pistol was thrown into the air and clattered to the floor of the little porch.

Raff was frozen in place, his hands still partly raised in surrender. Was he next? Frogman turned and looked at him.

"Sons of bitches, come in here carrying guns and lying to me. Wantin' to kill me, take my land, and trash it and all."

He paused to look over the carnage he had wrought, and said, "I'm not going to kill *you*, boy, but if I ever see you again, I'll kill you. You think I don't remember you from when you came a long time ago? And if you ever say anything to anybody about what just happened here, and I mean *anybody*, I'm gonna hunt you down and kill you and kill your family too. You understand me?"

Raff could think of nothing to say. So he just murmured, "Yessir, Yes, *sir!*"

His hands were trembling. Sweat soaked his shirt and dripped off the tip of his nose. He was desperately thirsty. He noticed that Frogman had begun to calmly pick his front teeth with a fingernail. Time for Raff to leave. *Now.* But he felt such a relief flooding through him, and such gratitude, that he had to say more. He had to do more. Perversely, he wanted to be some sort of a friend to this savage man who had saved his life.

He glanced briefly down at the bodies of Rainey and LeBow, blown open, ribs exposed, blood pooling from torn arteries and veins, the ripped intestine from LeBow trailing out like a grotesque appendage. He said tremulously, "What are you going to do if somebody comes looking for these guys?"

"Nobody's goin' to come lookin' 'round here," Frogman said quietly. "It weren't in their mind to come here, was it, so nobody but you and me knows. But even if they got friends who do know, they ain't gonna tell, 'cause they'll git taken in for bein' part of the whole thing." He walked back and remounted the shotgun.

"But the bodies could turn up if you just put them in the river."

"Oh, these boys are goin' in the river, all right, but there ain't goin' to be any bodies to find. I'm gonna cut them in little pieces and feed them to Old Ben. He's a thousand pounds if he's an ounce, and he'll handle most of it, bones and all, no trouble at all. The guts and what's left over of the meat'll make a fine meal for the big catfish down there on the riverbottom. The only thing anybody's going to pick up downriver is gator shit.

"Now git the hell out of here and jes' remember what I told you. I can kill you as quick as I did these shitheads, now or anytime and anywhere, and I will truly never lose a minute's sleep over it."

Raff immediately turned, picked his way around the

remains of Wayne, Bo, and Sunky, aware of the odor of fresh blood, coming up at him like wet rusted iron, and of newly voided feces—the smell of a slaughterhouse. Tottering down to the river's edge, he knew he could get a shotgun blast in the back at any moment. But he thought at least his life would end suddenly and without lingering pain. It didn't matter, just didn't matter anymore. He was too tired and dulled by shock to care. For the first time, though, some feeling returned to his body.

At the edge of the Chicobee River, Raff turned and plodded back the way he had run just minutes before. His mind, beginning to revive, churned into an insane mix of fear, relief, and horrific images of the three butchered men. And he couldn't escape the image of Old Ben feeding the way alligators do, lying there in shallow water, head up, gulping down chunks of meat and bone thrown to him piece by piece from the bank by Frogman.

Stumbling often, he finally reached the creek flowing out from Lake Nokobee. The glossy dark foliage of the waterside shrubs welcomed him back to the world of the living. He knelt to its clear water, splashing some on his face, and drank heavily from his cupped hands.

He then headed upstream through familiar terrain. In the waning sunlight, a zebra swallowtail flew in front of him, black-striped wings flashing, its long tails streaming behind. To his surprise he saw it with perfect clarity, every detail of its body and wings growing in size and intensifying in pattern. They forced their way into his consciousness, like the images of a twilight dream, just before merciful sleep descends.

He walked on, and as he did, he could think only about

butterflies. He began to search for more individuals, more species. Everything else was pushed from his mind. Butterflies were all that remained in the Nokobee woodland. Their beauty shut out the horror. Butterflies were the only thing that mattered to him now.

Obsessed with the beautiful insects, he walked the Nokobee trail and passed from a descent toward death back into life. He saw a dogface sulphur settle on a twig. He stopped and watched two little blues fluttering around each other over flowers in a clearing. He went on, and soon came to the woodland dome that had saved his life. A wood nymph flew with jerky wing flaps into the deepening shade. He stood there awhile, his head beginning to clear.

He noticed Sunky's cowboy hat still sitting atop the bush where it had fallen. He picked it off and carried it with him. He would dispose of it later, and wipe out the trail of his would-be killers. He had to protect Frogman.

Close to the trailhead a giant swallowtail soared overhead in brown and yellow magnificence and on down the path, then turned into a grove of trees at the lake's edge. It was going home to spend the night on some high arboreal perch.

Hey, hello, *Papilio cresphontes*, he murmured, addressing it by its scientific name to show proper respect. Hey, hello, hello, he continued, growing light-headed and feeling a tickle of silliness. I'm going home too. We're both alive, we're well and safe. He settled into his car, took a deep breath, and turned the key. He drove out and onto the road toward Clayville.

He arrived at his parents' house as the last light was fading, stopping short at the near corner of the front yard, and sat quietly for a while. He asked himself, Why have I come here? Then he remembered. He had to see them with his own eyes, to be sure they were safe.

Raff stayed rooted to the car seat, and his mind began to clear some more. He looked about him as the darkness closed in. A bat skittered over the top of the house and out of sight among the tree canopies beyond. A lantern fly, flashing its mating call in points of light, flew across the backyard: dot-dot-dot-dash-dot-dot . . . He focused on its semaphore code and asked himself, Did I get that right, dot-dot-dot-dash-dot-dot-dash? How comforting it would be to return this way to the safe and predictable world of nature. He recognized the coming of delusion again, and with effort he pulled himself together.

He could just go up to the front door, walk into the living room, and embrace his parents. He felt an intense desire to do that. But he could not chance it. He knew that he looked like someone who had just crawled away from an automobile accident. That would demand an explanation, and he dared not give it. There was no need to burden Ainesley and Marcia with the horror he had just experienced. And worse: he feared that Frogman might somehow learn he had told someone and come raging out of the swamp to commit another mass murder. Raff would be an evil spirit spreading a fatal curse.

So he sat there quietly, trying to catch a glimpse of his parents through the front windshield. After a few more minutes a light began to flicker in the living room window. It meant that his father had settled in his favorite chair to watch the early evening news. Ainesley, he reflected, wasn't running around much these days. He'd suffered a mild heart attack the previous winter and was now on medication for hypertension and angina. He still went in mornings to run the hardware store, but hunting and fishing trips and evenings in the usual honky-tonk saloons had been severely curtailed. So had his consumption of cigarettes. Marcia had tried everything short of divorce proceedings to stop him from smoking altogether, but so far without success.

Raff especially yearned to see his mother now, alive and healthy. Ever since Cyrus had bestowed his gift of a college education on Raff a decade earlier, Marcia had become more content with her own existence. She had joined social activities at the local First Methodist Church, and she looked forward more than ever, with growing self-confidence, to family gatherings at Marybelle. The identity she had craved had been granted. She was more than Mrs. Cody now. She was also the Mobile Semmes who lived up in Clayville to be with her husband.

Tonight the light was on in the kitchen. She could be fixing supper about now. And once, then a second time, Raff caught a glimpse of her head in the window as she came up to the sink.

Then he turned the key and drove on through Clayville, down the main street, which was already emptied of traffic for the evening, and took the alternate, less-traveled two-lane highway to Mobile. Even on the road he wanted to be alone and hidden. Frogman and the LeBowites must not know where he was. Stopping at a liquor store just south of Atmore, he bought a quart of Johnnie Walker Gold Label, the most expensive whiskey on the shelves. Down the road he pulled into the Southern Hospitality Motel, which he remembered having passed on earlier trips. It looked quiet and cheap this evening, and its orange neon sign flashed VACANCY.

Clutching his bottle of Johnnie Walker, Raff signed in for a room. The clerk thought, He's drunk and lucky to get off the road. In his room Raff double-locked the door, stripped off his clothes, showered, and threw himself naked onto the queen-sized bed. He turned on the television and adjusted the sound to barely audible. He paid no attention to it. He just wanted the feel of normal people around him. The first thing that came on was news of suicide bombers in Pakistan. Medics were carrying broken bodies through the streets of Islamabad. He winced, and surfed through other channels until he picked up a talk show with people smiling and laughing. He uncapped the whiskey and began to drink from the bottle. He stared at the wall, trying to think about nothing at all. His physical exhaustion made that easy. Soon he was sinking into a stupor. He managed to screw the cap back on the bottle and drop it on the bed before he fell asleep.

Raff awoke the next morning just after eleven. He had a cannonading headache, nausea, and a desperate thirst. He rubbed water on his face, downed a glass of water, dressed, and walked over to the motel office. He got aspirin from the morning clerk, walked across the room to a machine advertising FREE COFFEE, and washed the aspirin down.

Three cups later, still hurting, Raff checked out of the Southern Hospitality and drove on to Mobile. Arriving there, fear-stricken to near paralysis, he didn't go to his apartment. Instead, he parked his car at the Bledsoe Street lot. From there he walked to the Sunderland Office Building and took the elevator to the company headquarters. He went straight to his office, waving away Sarah Beth as she tried to ask him a question, ignoring nearby employees staring at his disheveled appearance.

Raff shut the door and sat at his desk with his eyes closed, listening to the beat of his heart as it was translated into thumps of pain in his head. He focused on the phenomenon. Thump,

thump, thump . . . *Alive, alive, alive* . . . He wondered why he was there in his office. Then he remembered it was to have people around him. Frogman and the LeBowites would have to go through all of them first if either came here to get him.

At last anger came to him, forcing aside some of his fear and despair, and he began to think more rationally. What about his nemesis at Sunderland Associates, Rick Sturtevant? He had said the same thing as Wayne LeBow: Jesus came to save people, not bugs and snakes. Was Sturtevant in collusion with the LeBow-ites, and would he betray Raff? Probably not. More likely the remark was just a common piece of evangelical bombast.

Raff struggled for release from the unpleasant emotions. Finally, he took an oath. I'm twenty-eight now. And I say, let it happen, whatever comes. I'm going to find somebody and get married, stop catting around. Have a family. Be normal. Let somebody else go to war. I just don't fucking care anymore.

Just then the phone rang. It was Bill Robbins.

"How you doing, buddy?"

"Well, I'm alive," Raff croaked.

"Where you been? I tried to reach you all day yesterday. I just wanted to congratulate you on the good news that the Noko-bee plan is now finalized. It's thanks to you, of course, that Sun-derland came through all the way. We're going to run another special on it this Sunday. I'm not exaggerating, Raff. There are a lot of people grateful for all you've done."

"Thank you," Raff said. The effort triggered another bom-bardment in his head, and his nausea began to return. He didn't want to talk anymore, but he couldn't just hang up on his best friend. "I really appreciate it. We'll talk about it all later."

"Raff?" Robbins said. "You okay? You sound half dead. I

know it's been hard. You've been through a lot. Maybe you ought to take a good long rest. You deserve it."

"It's been rough, all right, Bill, *very* rough. Rougher than you'll ever know."

Raff in fact would never tell Bill Robbins what had happened. That, he felt keenly, would be a terrible thing to do to his best friend. The dilemma would be an especially painful burden for a journalist and public figure. If Robbins had the story but remained silent, he would be more than just holding on to a story. He would be denying justice and likely risking prosecution if the truth finally came out. But if he shared the information with anyone else, he would risk the lives of Raff and his family. Frogman or the vengeful LeBowites were out there waiting. Who would come looking first? It didn't matter. Bill Robbins would never know.

In time, however, he knew he would tell his Uncle Fred Norville, his lifelong companion at Nokobee and adviser at college. In so many ways the two shared the same pleasures and dreams. Uncle Fred was closer to the inner thoughts of Raphael Semmes Cody than were his parents. He needed such a confidant, and in a few months, perhaps years, he would tell the story. Who could say when?

· 38 ·

ON A FALL morning at Dead Owl Cove six months later, rays of the sun first touched the longleaf pine canopy, then climbed silently down the branches and trunks until, filtered by the understory, they cast a kaleidoscope of light and shadow, of warmth and chill, onto the forest floor. A breeze lifted off the water and worked its way across the bluff forming the lake margin. It passed over the anthills and into the surrounding woods, where it raised a fresh, life-affirming scent of fallen pine needles accented by holly and clethra.

In the forest, beads of dew still clung to drooping webs spun by orb-weaving spiders the night before. Wolf spiders, deadly hunters of nocturnal insects but tasty prey for ground-foraging birds in the day, retreated into their silk-lined burrows to await another night. Midges danced in a mating flight above a nearby stream. Their tiny bodies formed a ghostly cloud that dissipated and reformed and dissipated again, then vanished for good. Their brief performance was instinctively timed for safety—the little flies came and left too late for hungry bats and too early for dragonflies.

A biological clock also turned on in the anthill nearby, once the home of the Trailhead Colony, now owned by its lineal descendant, the Woodland Colony. A wave of activity spread down the vertical nest channels to deep nursery chambers filled with pupae and hungry grublike larvae.

Life was at its best this day, following a summer's growth, for the Woodlanders and their many allies and predators. All around the nest, caterpillar prey still fell to the ground from the pine canopy like ripened fruit, and mealybug herds grew thick on succulent vegetation in the understory. The skies had cleared during the night after a brief shower. Workers old enough to forage were poised to take the field.

As the sun warmed the upper chambers of the nest mound, some of the clustered workers made their way through them and out of the central exit. A few stayed close to rearrange bits of straw and charcoal, the heat-retaining debris used to thatch the mound surface. Others drifted farther away and began to patrol the nest perimeter, then pressed on into the surrounding terrain to search for bounty accumulated during the night— new prey, fresh arthropod corpses, and the sugary excrement dropped by mealybugs and other sap-sucking insects.

Within an hour human visitors arrived at Dead Owl Cove. They were the Panther and Hawk Patrols of Troop 43 of the Boy Scouts of America out of Mobile, prepared for a day-long nature hike around Lake Nokobee. They were led by their scoutmaster, Raphael Semmes Cody. They could not know how desperately he wanted to return to Nokobee, yet was unable to come alone. He had to have a crowd of people around him. The boys, turning to him often, served the purpose splendidly.

Shouting back and forth in the distinctive too-loud and honking voices of adolescent boys, they spilled out of the vans that brought them. They passed the anthill without notice and walked on to the trailhead. In their backpacks they carried waterproof notebooks to record their observations. Around their necks were slung cameras ready to capture all things visual. Their discoveries at Lake Nokobee would be gathered together later as a dispatch to Troop 43 headquarters.

As the day unfolded, Raff and the scouts saw a great blue heron spear a catfish. Found the shed skin of a diamondback rattlesnake wrapped partly around the stump of a longleaf pine. Watched a large cottonmouth moccasin slide off the bank into the water and undulate with insolent slow deliberation toward the shelter of a cattail thicket. Recorded mud turtles in the lake shallows, desmognath salamanders under wet mats of vegetation at the shoreline, bronze frogs calling, three kinds of lizards scurrying for cover, dozens of species of flowering plants, legions of flying and crawling insects none could identify. They saw twenty-three species of birds, including the main goal of the trip, the rare red-cockaded woodpecker.

The high point of the expedition was not, however, the endangered woodpecker. It was the discovery of a snake, eighteen inches in length, brilliantly colored from its nose to the tip of its tail with red, black, and yellow rings. This beautiful prize was uncovered by a scout when he turned over a dead tree limb lying at the edge of the trail.

"Coral snake!" shouted Raff. "Stay away from that. It's deadly poisonous!"

The boys, of course, moved close to get a look at the snake. But at least they kept well out of range, and one said, "Yeah, you get bit by that sucker and you die in an hour."

The colorful serpent started to push its way into the duff beneath the tree limb. Raff leaned over and looked more closely.

"Wait a minute. Hold everything. That's not a coral snake. It's a scarlet king snake! It just looks like a coral snake. Hey, it's not poisonous at all! It fools everybody and nobody messes with it because they're fooled. Look at the bands: red, black, yellow, black, red, black, yellow, black, and so on. Coral snakes have red, yellow, black. Y'all know how to tell a king snake and a coral snake apart? Just remember the little ditty: Red next to black, you're all right, Jack; Red next to yellow can kill a fellow."

No one stepped forward to touch the reputedly harmless king snake. The protective mimicry used by the species for countless millennia worked its magic once again, and the scarlet king snake left the scene unharmed.

In late afternoon the sixteen members of the Panther and Hawk Patrols arrived back with Raff at the clearing between the trailhead and the road leading from Dead Owl Cove. They sat and sprawled on the ground to await the vans that would take them home, chattering about snake folklore they had heard and some half believed—of giant snakes, snakes that spit poison, snakes that roll in hoops, snakes that chase you on sight. And the Chicobee Serpent. Then they turned to football at Nokobee County Regional High School, the next big nature hike, and, for the few who could boast of it, travel to other states and abroad. Because an adult was within earshot, girls and sex, among the usual favorite topics, were not mentioned.

"Jesus, look at that!" a scout interrupted, standing up. He pointed to hundreds of large ants dragging a small lizard in the direction of the Woodlander anthill. A few yards away, a stream of their formicid nestmates passed in and out of the nest entrance, running in a ragged line to the forager group. Some turned around soon after reaching the lizard and sped homeward, apparently to report news of the bonanza to the rest of the colony. The lizard was mangled, its tail gone and its head nearly severed from the body.

Most likely caught and then dropped by a sparrow hawk or loggerhead shrike, thought Raff.

"Hey, there must be a million of them in that nest." The scouts now began to talk about ants.

Ten thousand, actually, Raff said to himself. He had settled apart from the scouts, on a knoll clothed in bunchgrass and low herbaceous plants in bloom. He could just make out a sliver of Lake Nokobee through the longleaf pines that fringed its shore. The late afternoon sunlight, having fled the ground around him, still lit the canopy of the pines and open water of the lake.

A faint roll of thunder came from the south beyond the wall of trees behind him, although the sky directly above and as far as he could see remained cloudless. Here, on the Gulf Coastal Plain, at the fringe of the North American subtropics, the weather was always changing. In the far distance, a thousand feet up, Raff watched a kettle of hawks and vultures leisurely tracing circles in the air. They rose on the last thermal drafts of the day, gliding stiff-winged in a spiral to gain height, then down and out to gain distance. Then they caught another current, rode it up and down and forward yet again. Together they resembled leaves in a boiling kettle of water. They were headed south, in their fall migration. They flew together, but were otherwise indifferent to one another. They were neither friends nor enemies.

The birds seldom flapped their wings. The moving air that carried them up and down like magic could not be seen. Watching the kettle had a hypnotic effect on Raff. He thought how powerfully liberating it would be to travel on tireless wings south with them, across the tranquil Gulf waters into some unimagined new land, and stay for a while.

Raff was very tired at this day's end, and his thoughts drew inward to become reverie. The voices of the boys, jumbling together, faded into white noise. Only an occasional loud laugh or whoop broke through their collective monotone. He had returned to Nokobee to see this small world that managed to hold together perfectly while human forces raged around it. This time it was a crowd of boys who made a visit possible, albeit unknowingly.

No matter, it was done. Nokobee was here, now and forever, living and whole and serene as he had first found it in his childhood. This was his sacred place, just as his immemorial ancestors had their sacred places. Nokobee was a habitat of infinite knowledge and mystery, beyond the reach of the meager human brain, as were the habitats of his ancestors. It was his island in a meaningless sea. Because Nokobee survived, he survived. Because it preserved its meaning, he preserved his meaning. Nokobee had granted him these precious gifts. Now it would heal him. In return, he had restored its immortality, and eternal youth, and the continuity of its deep history.

· ACKNOWLEDGMENTS ·

FOR SUGGESTING I write this book and for his wise counsel throughout its writing, I am extremely grateful to my editor, Robert Weil. For additional advice and help, I fervently thank William Finch, Kathleen M. Horton, D. Bruce Means, Anne Semmes, James Stone, Walter Tschinkel, and Irene K. Wilson. I owe much to Dave Cole for his close and expert editing of the final text. David Cain drew the map, placing Nokobee County with pleasing exactitude within the preexisting geography of South Alabama. And not least, I thank my literary agent, John Taylor (Ike) Williams, who with expertise, friendship, and refreshing good humor has aided me through the development of this and much of my earlier published work.

"The Anthill Chronicles," a section of the present narrative, is derived from scientific information about several real ant species compounded into one, documented individually, for example, by Bert Hölldobler and Edward O. Wilson in *The Ants* (1990) and *The Superorganism* (2009). It is written in a manner that presents the lives of these insects, as exactly as possible, from the ants' point of view.

· ABOUT THE AUTHOR ·

EDWARD O. WILSON is regarded as one of the world's leading biologists and naturalists. He grew up in South Alabama and the Florida Panhandle, where as a boy he spent much of his time exploring the region's forests and swamps, collecting snakes, butterflies, and ants—the latter to become his lifelong specialty. Descended on both sides from families that came to Alabama before the Civil War, Wilson developed a deep love of the history and natural environment of his native state, and especially of the region that made the setting for the present story. After graduating from the University of Alabama, he traveled to Harvard University to earn a doctorate in biology. As a professor there (now emeritus) he became a pioneering researcher on the environment, animal behavior, communication, and biodiversity. His many awards in science include the U.S. National Medal of Science and the Crafoord Prize of the Royal Swedish Academy of Sciences—the latter the most prestigious award given in ecology. In letters he won two Pulitzer Prizes in nonfiction, for *On Human Nature* (1978) and, with Bert Hölldobler, *The Ants* (1990). In recent years he has spent much of his time on issues of global conservation, while returning often to the South of his childhood and to the wildlands that nurtured his spirit.